The Blue Key Chronicles

Oliver Grant

Contents

1. Prologue — 1
2. Chapter 1 — 8
3. Chapter 2 — 14
4. Chapter 3 — 19
5. Chapter 4 — 24
6. Chapter 5 — 32
7. Chapter 6 — 38
8. Chapter 7 — 46
9. Chapter 8 — 57
10. Chapter 9 — 71
11. Chapter 10 — 77
12. Chapter 11 — 87
13. Chapter 12 — 97
14. Chapter 13 — 110
15. Chapter 14 — 121
16. Chapter 15 — 132
17. Chapter 16 — 143

18. Chapter 17   157

19. Chapter 18   170

20. Chapter 19   194

21. Chapter 20   210

22. Chapter 21   227

23. Chapter 22   237

24. Epilogue   247

Prologue

A loud ringing could be heard when the school bell rang. Winter break has ended and school has started again, overwhelming the students with a lot of homework. The thing every student hated the most about school was homework.

Mrs. Cockney: "Damn it, Michael! Why didn't you do your homework!"

Her wrinkled face expressed pure anger and hatred toward him. Michael was one of the students she hated the most. He was the kind of student who never did his homework.

Michael: "I forgot."

Truth be told, he hadn't forgotten it. He had just burned it with his lighter just before winter break came.

Mrs. Cockney: "What a lame excuse! Detention for you! And if you don't show up like last time, I'll call your parents and tell them what a pathetic student you are! You got that!?"

Michael: "Uh-huh."

She trudged back to the lectern and began teaching the class.

Mrs. Cockney: "Okay kids, today we are going to learn about parables."

Mrs. Cockney began to draw a parable on the board and explained the basic outline of it.

Man, it's really boring here....

Michael is seventeen years old and is not happy with his life. The last time he really smiled was years ago. He has no friends to spend time with. His parents are rarely home because they both have important jobs. Most of the time he felt lonely, and he hated school above everything else.

School was like a prison for him. He spends six to seven hours a day in those lousy classrooms, breathing in the toxic school air. The classrooms looked depressing, the only colors were white and gray. The chairs creaked and were uncomfortable to sit on. And worst of all was his math teacher, Mrs. Cockney. Michael hated her guts. To him, she was the worst teacher in the school. Not only was her math class boring as hell, but she blamed him for a lot of things Michael didn't even do. She got mad about even the simplest things. Like when he threw a paper airplane at another student.

Michael remembered the one time he threw a paper airplane because another student threw a paper airplane at him. Michael got the famous response "If your classmate jumped out the window, would you do the same thing". Of course he wouldn't fucking do that! What kind of logic is that?

Oh, screw the boredom!

To relieve his boredom, he listens to music in class most of the time. That's also why he always sits in the back corner. It was pretty relaxing for him back here. The teacher would pay less attention to him. He covers his headphones with a hood and selects his own music playlist on his smartphone under the table.

Ahhh, much better!

Michael loved fast, energetic and aggressive music, like dubstep and metal. Most of the students laughed at the fact that he didn't listen to real music, but they also didn't listen to anything better, like modern raps and overrated radio music. Music and video games were one of the only motivations that kept him going in this miserable life. They acted like drugs that got him addicted and temporarily suppressed his problems and inner demons.

Oh man, I love this soundtrack! One of my all time favorite tracks! Holy shit! This beat just hit harder than.... Uhh... Nah man, I got nothing.

Mrs. Cockney: "Michael!"

So much for less attention. Shit!

Michael: "Oh a-ah, y-yes Mrs. Cockney?"

Mrs. Cockney: "Could you solve this problem I wrote on the board?"

Michael's heart began to race as he looked at the board. It was completely covered with confusing numbers and letters.

Stupid cunt! Out of thirty other students in this classroom, it has to be me! There are more than ten people here raising their hands, and you fucking picked me! I don't even know how to solve this because I wasn't paying attention! Only three more minutes and the math lesson will be over. I've got to come up with something fast.

Michael: "I'm sorry, Mrs. Cockney, but I can't read the numbers from back here."

Mrs. Cockney: "And why is that, Michael?"

Your face made me want to use bleach on my eyes. If I had a face like yours, I'd sue my parents!

Michael: "Because I forgot my glasses.... At home... In my room."

Mrs. Cockney: "Ha! Another pathetic excuse from you! That's all I could have expected from you! Get real, Michael! I've never seen you with glasses on!"

And she rants again.... great.

Mrs. Cockney: "Well, why don't you come up front and solve the problem in front of the whole class if that's what you asked for?"

Come on! How long does this class last! Ring already, you damn bell!

The bell finally began to ring. The whole class cheered with joy and rushed out of the classroom toward the school cafeteria because it was lunch time.

Mrs. Cockney: "Hey! Come back here right now! I still have to give you all homework!"

Yes! Finally a break from her!

Mrs. Cockney: "I'll see you again later today, Michael. And I'll be sure to talk some sense into you then!"

Yeah, and I hope you die by choking on your next breakfast, you wrinkled whore.

Michael: "Whatever..."

He grabbed his backpack and left the classroom. The hallways were full of students hurrying toward the school cafeteria. Some were together in groups, talking, joking and laughing with each other. Others were bullying the shit out of other students. Some were even romantically involved. Michael kind of wanted a relationship. The thing is, no one wanted to be with a worthless person like Michael. No one even wanted to be his friend.

As Michael followed the corridor, a double door greeted him. He pushed it open and entered the school's cafeteria. The school's cafeteria was a huge hall filled with many tables. There were also a few vending machines where one could buy snacks and drinks.

Holy hell!

More than hundreds of students were waiting in the front row for their food. That's one heck of a long line for a simple school cafeteria.

Well, shit! Ugh, I'm not hungry anyway. The school cafeteria food tastes like crap. I bet the prison food is way better.

Michael would have bought some snacks from the vending machines. But since his parents knew about his "homework problem," they stopped giving him pocket money.

He walked to an empty table in the corner of the hall, secluded from everyone else, and sat down. Scrawled on the table and chairs were words like "loser," "worthless," and "pathetic.' He propped his head on his right hand and thought about how he had become like this. His thoughts were soon interrupted by a female voice.

???: "Hey, Why the long face?"

Michael: "Huh?"

Michael turned around and standing in frort of him was a beautiful girl. She looked two to three years older than him. She had a curvy and fit body. Her hair was blonde and long. She had hazel green eyes that you could get lost in if you stared at them too long. And her damn smile was really cute!

???: "You're Michael, right?"

Michael: "Y-yes... How do you know that?"

???: "I heard about you. And I thought, why not befriend someone as handsome as you?"

Did she just call me handsome?

Michael blushed a little at her statement and looked away. He couldn't believe it. Someone actually wanted to be his friend. And it was a girl! And this girl just called him pretty!

Michael: "You really want to be my friend?"

???: "Well, only if that's what you want. We could be more than friends too.... If that's what you like."

Her grin grew even wider as she placed her tray of food on the table right in front of Michael.

???: "My name is Jennie, by the way. You look hungry. You can have some of my food if you want."

Michael: "R-really?"

Jennie: "Mhm."

Michael: "Th-thank you."

Michael did something he thought he would never do again in his life. He smiled. Just as he was about to take something from the tray, he felt a sudden blow to the back of his head, causing his face to collide with the tray full of hot food. The whole cafeteria pointed at Michael and laughed as if they had just seen the funniest shit in their entire lives.

Michael didn't dare lift his head again. Tears leaked from his eyes as his hope of getting a friend died within seconds. Even though the students' laughter was louder than anything else, he could only hear her voice.

Jenny: "Hahahaha!!! What a loser!!! Did you really think anyone would want to be your friend!!! You're a pathetic excuse for a human!!! A worthless piece of shit!!! Not even an alien would want to lay hands on you!!!"

Her words managed to cut the last string in him. The last string that prevented him from feeling suicidal. Everything became silent for him as he ignored everything. Without any emotion, he stood up and left the school.

He didn't care that his whole face was covered with food. He didn't care that school wasn't over yet. He didn't care that he had to show up for detention. He didn't care if he was going to be expelled from this shit hole called school. He just wanted one thing, to go home and lock himself in his room for a few days.

Chapter 1

The streets were empty. No one was to be seen outside, except for a walking Michael. He felt as if he was wandering through a ghost town. But it was better that way. Michael didn't need people reminding him how pathetic he really was. As an outcast, he already knew it. It was quiet, just as it should be.

The only sound heard was the raindrops splashing on the ground. It was raining lightly. The temperature was not cold, but not warm either. Michael liked cloudy and rainy weather.

The rainy atmosphere gave him a pleasant chill. It also gave him a feeling of hope, but that quickly faded as he crossed a long wooden bridge.

He stopped in the middle of the wooden bridge and stared down at the overfilled river. The flow of the river was certainly strong and swift, it was impossible to swim through. It also led to a small waterfall. Through the loud rush of water, he heard her words again. Words that he could not forget. Words that kept running through his head.

Jenny: "What a loser!!! You're a pathetic excuse for a human!!! A worthless piece of shit!!! Not even an alien would want to lay hands on you!!!"

She was right... I am worthless, capable of nothing but wasting oxygen.... I'm just a waste of space.... Maybe I should give up this pathetic life and end it once and for all. It's not like anyone would care.... No one would even notice!

Michael climbed up the wooden fence and stared at the dark gray water as if his eyes were fixed on it. The rain became heavier and lightning struck the water, followed by a loud bang and crackling sounds. He closed his eyes as tears escaped. Just as he was about to jump, an unknown female voice sounded in his head.

???: "There's still some hope for you, Michael. Just... don't give up yet."

Michael: "And what do you expect me to do, huh? Go home and have a big wank off session!?"

He roared in anger, but that strange voice didn't respond.

Michael: "Answer me, damn it!!!"

This time he got a response from a screeching crow that was struck by lightning. Its feathers formed a plume of smoke as it dropped down and landed behind him. Michael opened his eyes and looked back at the wooden bridge floor where the burned bird had landed. He spotted a string wrapped around one of the bird's legs with a mysterious blue key with a letter attached.

What the heck? This crow was carrying a key? There is also a letter attached to it.... Interesting...

Michael grabbed the key and ripped it off the string from the dead bird. He first examined the key before he began to read the letter. The letter said:

"The key to open any door with a lock. The key that leads to something else, to another gate. The key to escape the sad and depressing reality."

So... This letter tells me that this key would lead to another world. Yeah, yeah... Right, like I'm so damaged that I would believe this poorly written story that is probably just a silly prank.

Michael decided to take it anyway and continued on his way home instead of leaping to his death. As he walked, he thought about the strange voice that told him not to give up.

Maybe it had something to do with the key? I mean, this couldn't be coincidence.... Or could it?

After what felt like twenty minutes of walking, Michael arrived at his home. His parents were thankfully not home and he had the whole house to himself. Because of their "business" they wouldn't be back for a few weeks.

Good riddance....

Michael was not in the mood for his parents to be upset about how depressed he was acting. His parents tried so hard to make him happy by buying him a lot of things. They thought they could easily buy happiness for Michael. Even if he got great things, like a couch that could be turned into a bed, a nice big TV, a powerful gaming PC, or even a damn refrigerator, he still couldn't be happy because he didn't really want those things. The only thing Michael wanted was a real friend to talk to and spend time with.

Michael walked up the stairs and entered his messy room. He walked past his desk and saw some of the drawings he had done a year ago to relieve his boredom and depression. They all showed a white fox and a forest as a background. He used to watch videos on how to draw realistic foxes with a forest in the background. His pictures weren't as good as the ones in those videos, but they still looked good. Foxes had been his favorite animals since kindergarten. He would have continued to draw these kinds of pictures if only they had continued to act as medicine.

Michael walked over to his bed and sat on it. He took the blue, mysterious key out of his pocket and looked at it a little closer. He read the letter a few more times until an idea popped into his head. A silly idea, he thought. Michael locked himself in his room and tried to unlock it with his new key he had found today.

Why am I even trying. Surely this isn't going to work... Holy shit...

Michael was stunned and shocked. He couldn't say a single word. He couldn't move for five minutes. Words could not describe the beautiful sight he saw on the other side of the door. Instead of a hallway, there was a completely different world. A world with a big forest, but not a normal one.

The trees were really wide and tall. There were completely different kinds of plants than in his world. Everything was so green that the color burned in his eyes. The sky was clear and bright. The fresh air and breeze felt so good and clean. The sun was really bright and the weather was hot. Michael could feel the warmth emanating from this portal.

It's like a paradise...

Michael could not believe his own eyes. He closed the door and opened it again, only to see a hallway again.

What!? But, h-how!? There was no way this was real. I'm probably on drugs or something. I'm probably dreaming right now. This can't be my imagination, or.... Could it be, because it looked and felt so... real?

Michael had never been so excited. For several years he had felt miserable, and now he had a chance to change that. He wanted to explore this strange and beautiful world he had just found.

Michael had never had a real adventure before, but he would like to, and he knew that this would be one of the greatest adventures he could have. Michael was not stupid. He knew it could be very dangerous. Who knows, maybe death was waiting right under his nose. But in the end, he didn't care. He had nothing to lose, so why shouldn't he risk it?

No risk, no fun... Right?

But before he set out to explore this new, strange world, he had to pack a few things into his backpack. Things he needed to survive in the wilderness, like a survival tutorial book, some medikits in case he got hurt, a flashlight with spare batteries, his favorite pocket knife, a lighter, his own bow with some arrows, some snacks and drinks, powerbanks to charge his smartphone and his earphones to listen to music.

Back when Michael was in third grade at school, his father didn't work that much. They both spent several hours a day in the woods and his father taught him the basics of wilderness survival. His father taught him how to make fire, he taught him how to make spears with a pocket knife, and he taught him how to skin small animals like squirrels and rabbits. In fifth grade, Michael also learned how to properly use a bow. Those were the good times Michael would love to return to, but life kept forcing him further and further away.

I don't know if I'll ever be able to come home again, but screw it! I've finally found meaning in my depressed life, and I'm going to take the chance I've been given. Goodbye old world.... I hope I never have to come back to you again.

Then he unlocked the door with the blue key again and stepped through the portal, a portal to another world and a new, different life.

Chapter 2

Michael was shot out of the portal and landed hard on the ground, but wait, there's more! He slid down a high hill and was about to crash into a thorn bush.

Michael: "No! No!!! NO!!! NOOO!!!"

He crashed all the way through the thorn bush and slid further down until a large tree blocked his path.

Michael: "ARGH!!!"

He crashed face first into the tree. His nose was bleeding like hell, probably broken too. His face was covered with bloody scratches. It hurt him so much that he cursed in every language he could think of to quell the pain. Michael took a few deep breaths and looked back at the top of the hill. The portal was no longer there.

Well… Now there will definitely be no way back, unless I can find a door to open with that blue key. Anyway, any place is better than where I was born.

Before Michael set out to explore this new world, he opened his backpack and took out a medikit. He began to clean his face to prevent infection. After he finished, his face looked better. He got up from the mossy ground and looked around a little. There were wide and tall trees all around him. The atmosphere was really relaxing. The birds were chirping happily and the trees were rustling in the rhythm of the wind. Michael felt a sensation that he had not felt for a long time. It was a feeling of peace and serenity. He was glad that he had made the right choice.

Alright... Step one. Find a place to set up a small shelter. A shelter near a water source would be an excellent place to start! Not only would I find water there, but perhaps food as wel..

Michael randomly picked a direction and began his adventure.

This kind of reminds me of a video game called 'The Forest". Just like in that game, I'm somewhere in the middle of nowhere and I have to survive. Hopefully there are no naked cannibals with huge tits running around. That would be the last thing I need right now.

As Michael wandered through the woods, he began to sweat dramatically and paused for a moment to catch his breath. The temperature was hot and nothing like the temperature back at home. The sun was so bright that Michael even felt a slight burning sensation on his skin, but that wouldn't stop h m. He wouldn't give up yet, even if it meant being roasted alive out there. Michael wanted to explore more and more until he found the right place to settle down. He didn't really care if he got sunstroke.

Michael wanted to listen to music to lift his spirits a little, but he decided against it. He needed to focus on the world around him, because it was a matter of life and death. Who knows what's out there. There could be dangerous animals and creatures roaming this forest. It would be a great coincidence if cannibals were running naked through the forest, but Michael hoped for the best that it wouldn't happen.

After all, he knew how to fight. Earlier, when he was still bullied, he had taken several fighting classes just to beat his bullies bloody. He never regretted a single punch.

After walking for about an hour, Michael heard water noise from his right. He turned his head and was amazed at what he saw. It was a small cave entrance on the side of a mountain. Next to it was a small waterfall that led to a small, clean pond. The pond was so clean that he could see his own reflection pretty well. It was like a perfect mirror. Best of all, it was filled with lots of fish. He couldn't have been any luckier than that.

Still, he wasn't quite sure about the cave. It might offer him good protection from wind and rainy weather. But what if something lived there? If it was empty, that could mean that something was not at home. Whatever lived there could return at any time, and that thought scared the hell out of Michael.

I have a really bad feeling about this cave, and I don't like the way the pitch black darkness stares back at me.

Michael grabbed a smaller rock nearby and threw it inside the cave. Immediately, several thudding sounds echoed through the cave as the small rock hit the cave walls, which meant it was a small cave. Fortunately, nothing leaked out of the cave, which also meant it was empty and no one was home.

Thank God... That could have ended really badly. I had actually expected a bear to jump out at me.

Still, Michael wanted to be one hundred percent sure. He took out his flashlight and shined it into the cave. Now that he had a good picture of the cave, he could see that it was actually quite small. There was enough room for just under three people.

Great, now that I have a nice place to sleep, it's time for step two. I need to gather some sticks, rocks, and leaves so I can build a fire pit.

Michael didn't go too far from the cave, so he could easily return without getting lost. He looked for sticks and stones on the ground. He easily got the leaves by tearing them off a bush. After gathering enough materials, Michael began to build a small fireplace outside the cave. After that, he set about making a spear.

It was a good thing he had his sharp pocket knife with him. It was much easier with that than with a damn rock. He also cut himself a few times with his knife, but he didn't care. He wanted his spear to be very sharp so he could pierce skulls with ease. One spear probably wasn't enough either. What if he threw his one spear into nowhere while he was looking for it somewhere? He will also be able to throw several spears in one fight. Michael came to this conclusion and made two more spears. A torch wouldn't hurt either. Who knows, maybe one day his flashlight will go out and he'll have to wander in the night. As silly as it sounds, it would be suicide.

The temperature dropped from hot to a comfortable warmth as the sun slowly set. Michael was just sitting in the cave enjoying his meal. He ate two energy bars and drank a can of soda. It wasn't really much, but he didn't want to eat it all in a single day. The next day he would have to go hunting for food.

Suddenly, Michael heard a loud roar not far away. He immediately jumped up and dropped his can of soda. His heart was beating a million times a minute. The trees were no longer rustling. The birds were no longer chirping. There was no wind at all. Everything was quiet, far too quiet for his liking. The only thing he could hear was his own heartbeat.

Woah, what the fuck was that!?

It was followed shortly by a scream that sounded like a woman.

Okey, what the hell is happening in this forest!? That was most likely a woman screaming for help. Maybe there are some people I can team up with. I need to find her and help her right now!

Michael left his things in the cave, except for his knife, spears and bow with arrows. He ran in the direction of the scream while thinking about what was waiting for him. He didn't know if he should be involved in what was happening over there. Maybe it's something that attacked that person? Michael felt fear. Many questions rushed through his mind.

What if it wasn't a human scream? What if it is a trap? What if I have to fight something? What will I be fighting? Will it even be a fair fight? Will it be painful? Will my death be quick and painless?

Michael's questions were interrupted by a pool of blood. On the dirt ground he saw something lying unconscious.

Chapter 3

Michael was speechless at what he saw before him. On the ground laid an unconscious fox, but it was not just a normal fox. It appeared to be much larger than a full grown fox and was also wearing some sort of tribal clothing. It was just lying on the ground, slowly bleeding to death. Then he heard that strange voice in his head again. That voice that stopped him from committing suicide.

???: "Please... Somebody... help me..."

Poor thing...

Watching this poor animal bleed to death hurt Michael inside. He wanted to help it get back on its feet and give it another chance at life. Foxes were his favorite animals because they have fluffy tails and make cute noises. When he was younger, he always wanted a fox as a pet, but his parents didn't agree and always told him that this kind of animal belonged in the wild and not in a house.

It's losing a lot of blood. I left my backpack in the cave with a medikit in it! What a bummer! I have to help it, take it back to my cave and take care of its injuries! I hope I have enough time to do that....

Michael picked up the fox and carried it over his right shoulder.

Whew, you're pretty heavy, aren't you?

Michael made his way back to his shelter. He wanted to take the fox to his cave so he could tend to its injuries. While he was on his way, it also began to rain lightly and the sun was getting a little lower with each passing minute. The temperature dropped to a pleasant coolness and the sky changed its blue color to a beautiful purple. Some stars were already appearing in the sky and crickets started chirping. On the way back, he questioned himself.

How could the fox even end up like this? Normally, a predator would not leave its prey alive and behind. And what was that roaring and screaming sound I heard a little while ago?

Michael arrived back at his new home and placed the sleeping fox on the ground. He wasted no further time and immediately retrieved a medikit from his backpack. He first cleaned up the fox's injuries before beginning to stitch up the deep scratch marks. After bandaging the fox to prevent blood loss, he took a closer look. It appeared to be a somewhat human-like fox, and judging by the fact that it had one of the female assets, tits, it was a female! She also wore a tribal style bra, loincloth and sandals. Her fur was beautiful snow white with green front paws and black back paws. Her tail looked really fluffy and big.

Wow... She looks... really beautiful....I feel like I'm in a Disney world where anthropomorphic animals live in a huge magical forest. I wonder if she can walk on two legs and talk like a human.

A loud thunder sounded and caught Michael's attention. He looked out of the small cave and saw that the rain was increasing heavily.

What a fucking thunderstorm! I hope it doesn't rain for so long. I don't want my cave to be flooded with water. It's getting a little cold, too. I should have brought some blankets.

???: "Mmhhh, mh..."

Michael heard her stirring and looked back at her.

She is waking up...

She opened her beautiful green colored eyes and saw only blurry. She felt pain in her head and held a paw to her forehead. After a minute, her vision cleared and she sat up. She looked around and saw that she was in a small cave. She was also covered with some bandages and her bleeding had stopped. The confused vixen noticed Michael sitting next to her and turned to him.

Michael: "Ehm, h-hello, fellow friend."

She had never seen a living creature like him before, as Michael was a alien to her. She got scared and jumped up.

???: "Who are you and what have you done to me, you furless pervert?"

Michael's tension grew as she walked toward h m with her fists clenched.

Michael: "H-hey w-wait! I-I didn't do anything, I swear! I- Ack!!!"

For an anthropomorphic vixen a head shorter than Michael, she was really strong. With one paw she pulled him up by his shirt and with the other paw she punched him out of the cave.Michael flew out of the cave and landed on the wet, dirty ground.

Shit! My leg!

He held his leg in pain and looked back into the cave. The crazy vixen came out of it and towards Michael. Her green eyes glowed and expressed pure hatred. She opened both of her clenched fists and green fire appeared around them.

Mother of God, have mercy!!!

Without thinking further, Michael got up and ran as fast as he could through the dark forest. His leg hurt like hell, but being roasted by that furry chick would probably be worse. Michael took a quick look back and saw her chasing him as she threw green fireballs.

Holy shit!!!

Michael felt a hot, burning pain on his right cheek as a green fireball flew way too close to him, leaving a burn mark on his back.

Crap! That hurts like hell! If I had my pocket knife right now, I'd cut her tail off, strangle her with her own tail, and then I'd rip all her fur off and make a damn fur coat out of it!

She growled in rage, as if she could hear his thoughts, and fired more fireballs at Michael until one hit him in the left arm. Michael felt a hot, burning sensation and stumbled to the ground, screaming to quell the pain a bit.

Michael: "ARGH!!!"

???: "What a pathetic weakling you are!"

Her words ran through his head and his depressed mood took over. Michael just laid motionless on the muddy ground, staring up at the cloudy night sky.

Is this the thanks I get for living miserably for so long, without any friends? Is this how she repays me, by calling me a pathetic weakling and killing me after I saved her life?

Tears came out of his eyes and mixed with the raindrops running down his face. He heard her hurtful words, once again.

Jenny: "What a loser!!! You're a pathetic excuse for a human!!! A worthless piece of shit!!! Not even an alien would want to lay hands on you!!!"

She was right... Not even an alien would want to be my friend.... No one wants that. It doesn't matter what world I'm in, I'm going to end up miserable and alone either way, like it's my destiny. Maybe it's better if she just kills me. I have nothing to live for anyway....

The anthropomorphic vixen looked guiltily at Michael. Michael sobbed and clawed at his left arm, biting his lip to fght the burning pain he still felt. In this state, he had no chance to fight back. He didn't even want to fight. He had escaped his old, miserable life just to relax and be happy again. He had come this far. And now he was finally done for good. The anthropomorphic vixen calmed down and the green fire around her paws disappeared. She walked up to him and crouched down. She placed her paw on his burnt flesh, and suddenly Michael felt no more pain.

???: "I'm sorry..."

They stared at each other calmly. Her emerald eyes were glowing and Michael couldn't take his eyes off them. He had the feeling of being hypnotized. He felt like something was invading his mind. It felt like time was standing still. Michael closed his eyes and took a few deep breaths until he felt tired and fell asleep. For the first time in many years, he dreamed again. In his dream, he was greeted by a black void. The only thing he could see in the pitch darkness was her green glowing eyes looking at him warmly. Once again, he heard this strange voice.

???: "Please... Forgive me..."

Chapter 4

What the hell happened? Where am I anyway? All I see is darkness and I can't move at all.... I can't even feel my body.... Is this what it feels like to be dead...? Without anything but the pitch black darkness and my own lonely mind...? It's definitely better this way. I'm going to be alone for the rest of my miserable life no matter what, so why shouldn't I get used to it? This is the perfect moment! Now I won't be a burden to other people.

???: "You can't think like that, Michael. You're not all alone. You still have..."

What do I have, huh?!? I have nothing left!!! Nothing!!! I managed to do something that no one else managed to do!!! And that was to enter another world, a new and different life!!!! I got my hopes up, only to have them crumbled by this white furried bastard!!!! Not even another world welcomes me!!! And now I'm surrounded by darkness, probably dead too!

???: "You are not dead, Michael. You're just sleeping. And... I'm really sorry that I hurt you..."

You're sorry that you hurt me? I don't understand... Who are you anyway?

???: "My name is Zoe."

Okay, Zoe. What do you want from me?

Zoe: "I want you to wake up."

Michael's eyes shot open and he immediately sat up, his vision spinning.

???: "Good morning."

Michael waited until his vision cleared. Right in front of him sat this anthropomorphic vixen with white fur, smiling up at him.

Oh, no! Not her again!

Michael: "Shit!"

Michael wanted to jump up and run away, but the human-like vixen lunged at him to keep him in his place.

???: "Wait!"

Her face was now only a few inches away from Michael's. They stared at each other for a long time. Her beautiful emerald eyes bored into his brown, lifeless eyes. Her fur, pressed against him, felt as soft as a cloud and warmer than summer days.

She really is beautiful... And her fur looks so fluffy. I wish I could pet her head and feel the fur on my hands....

The humanoid vixen blushed at this thought, but it was not visible through her thick fur. Still, she enjoyed hearing that thought from him and smiled.

???: "R-really? You think I'm beautiful? Well, if that's the case, then I'm fine with you giving me pettings!"

Now it was Michael's turn to blush.

Michael: "W-wait, did I say it out loud!? Y-you weren't supposed to hear that!"

She giggled at his outburst, a sound that sounded so adorable to Michael that he wished he could hear it for hours.

???: "Sorry, sometimes I can't help but intrude on other people's thoughts. By the way, I'm Zoe."

Michael: "Oh, so you were the voice in my head…? Wait, does that mean you can read and hear my thoughts?"

Zoe: "Mhm, right!"

She's a fucking mind reader!? A telepath!? And she heard my thoughts before, great! She's probably hearing this too! Shit!

She giggled again at his thoughts and got off of him. As she did, Michael felt the temperature change from warm to cool. He already missed her warm fur.

Zoe: "Don't worry about it! I'll try not to read your mind so much anymore, but I can't promise you anything."

Michael: "Uh-huh."

Michael stared outside the cave. It was already daytime and the birds were chirping happily. The mist from last night's rain combined with the sunlight created beautiful rays of light scattering through the leaves and the cave.

I hope it rains more often….

Zoe: "So, are you going to forgive me? You know, about yesterday."

Michael snapped out of his thoughts and looked back at Zoe while doing something he almost never does: he smiled.

Michael: "Yes, apology accepted."

Zoe: "Great! So, friends?"

She stretched out her paw and waited for Michael to take it. He examined it a little, it looked like a normal hand, but covered with fur and instead of fingernails it had claws. He took her paw and shook it.

Michael: "Friends."

Zoe: "Sweet! I also want to thank you for saving me from losing blood. It was really a close call yesterday and without you I wouldn't be alive."

Michael: "No problem. And please, call me Michi, it's my favorite nick name."

Zoe: "Sure, now come here."

She pounced on him and licked his left cheek. Michael was speechless. He touched the spot where she had licked his cheek and noticed that all the scratches from yesterday's fall were no longer there. His other injuries were also completely gone.

They all disappeared? But how?

Zoe: "Oh yeah, I almost forgot to tell you. Besides mind-reading and firepower, my species also has healing powers."

Hearing that she had three different superpowers made him envious. Ever since Michael was a little kid, he always wanted superpowers. Superpowers like running super fast or turning invisible.

Zoe: "Oh, don't make such a sad face. I'm sure you have a secret power too that you have to figure out first."

Michael: "Yeah, whatever. Can I ask you a few questions? You know, now that we're friends, I was thinking of getting to know each other better."

Zoe: "Only if we play a little game on the side."

Michael: "Uh, okey. What kind of game?"

Zoe: "You ask a question and I'll answer it. Then it's my turn to ask you a question, and it's your turn to answer it. And then we'll switch roles again and again until all our questions are answered."

Michael: "Well, all right. Why not?"

Zoe: "You go first. Fire away."

Michael: "Well, since you have healing powers, why don't you heal yourself? Even though I did my best to bandage you up, you still look hurt."

Zoe looked down at her stomach, which was covered with bandages.

Zoe: "Well, these powers of my species are resistant to ourselves. For example, I can't set my own species on fire, I can't read their minds, and I can't heal them, and I can't do that to myself either. Now it's my turn. What exactly are you? I've never seen a creature like you before. You don't have any fur or scales."

Michael: "My species is called human, and I don't think we're that different. I mean, we can both talk and understand each other, we both walk on two legs, and…. I… I don't know. In my world, people would call you a human vixen, a mix of human and animal or something. Okay, now it's my turn. Where exactly am I?"

Zoe: "You're on the planet Xenanon. It's a magical place covered mostly in trees and plants. But where exactly you are right now, I don't really know. I'm a little lost, too. My turn. How did you get here in the first place?"

Michael: "One day I found a blue, mysterious key. Wait, no. A crow had it and was struck by lightning. It fell down and died right in front of me. Anyway, this key somehow managed to open a portal, and it led me here."

Michael took the blue, mysterious key out of his pocket and gave it to Zoe. Zoe noticed a letter attached to it and read it aloud.

Zoe: "The key to open any door with a lock. The key that leads to something else, to another gate. The key to escape the sad and depressing reality."

Michael: "Well, Zoe. You mentioned that there are more of your species. If that's the case, why did I find you all alone, wounded, like someone was trying to cut you to death?"

Zoe: "Well..."

Zoe's expression quickly changed from happy to sad. Her ears folded down, her head drooped, and her tail went limp.

Zoe: "It's a long story.... It all started in my village. Everyone lived happily until those redclaws showed up. They killed most of us and destroyed everything. This caused my father to choose a husband for me, since he was the king of my species and I am the princess. He wanted me to marry the strongest man of my people so that I could be well protected.

The thing is that I did not love the chosen one. I hated him with all my heart. He always tried to get into my loincloth and almost raped me twice. He did not really love me. I told my father that many times, but he just didn't believe me and always listened to that asshole, the so-called hero.

One day before the arranged marriage, I just ran away because I couldn't take it anymore. I ran away from my home, my family and my friends. That was almost two years ago... And since then I was all alone, without anyone to talk to. One day, a group of three redclaws found me while I was looking for food. They attacked me and left me bleeding on the ground. And then... you showed up and saved my life."

Michael: "That was... really hard for you."

Zoe: "Anyway, do you want to tell me your story?"

Zoe felt a lot of anger, sadness and depression come out of Michael's mind. Michael just sat there staring at the floor, not moving. Zoe put a paw on his shoulder and sat closer to him.

Zoe: "Michi, you don't have to answer this if you don't want to. You can skip this question."

Michael: "No... That's all right. At some point you have to know anyway. I hated it at home.... To be honest, it didn't feel like home at all. Most things were boring and I had no friends to spend time with. My parents cared more about their professional careers than their own son.

They were rarely home and I was all alone. At school, everyone considered me an outsider. Everyone else was happy, had friends, or was even in a romantic relationship. But me... I was just there to be made fun of. One day at school, I completely lost it.

I was sitting alone in the corner of the school cafeteria and a really beautiful girl came up to me. She got my hopes up after telling me she wanted to be my friend, only to have my hopes and feelings crumbled. She told me that I was a loser, that no one wanted to be my friend, that I was a worthless piece of shit and that not even an alien would want to lay hands on me.

That was the moment I completely gave up on my pathetic life. I was on the verge of putting an end to it all. Then a voice sounded in my head telling me not to give up yet. That voice was you, Zoe."

Zoe burst into tears when she heard Michael's story. She couldn't take it anymore and wrapped her arms around him tightly.

Zoe: "You tried to commit suicide, didn't you?"

Michael was at a loss for words to answer. He was ashamed of himself and a few tears escaped from his eyes.

Zoe: "You are not worthless, Michi, and you are not alone anymore. I'll be there for you no matter what."

Michael smiled and hugged her back. He felt a warm feeling inside him that made him feel happy and important. There was finally someone who cared deeply about him.

Michael: "And I'll be there for you. Now we have each other."

Zoe: "Yeah..."

Michael: "Uh, Zoe?"

Zoe: "Huh?"

Michael: "Can you explain what a redclaw is?"

Zoe let go of him and stood up.

Zoe: "Well, a redclaw is another species that lives on Xenonan. Instead of fur, they have red scales and really sharp claws that they can use to cut anything to pieces. They know no mercy and kill everything that crosses their path. They are mainly active at night, but that doesn't mean they can't show up during the day as well. Their large, fearsome yellow eyes glow in the dark and express murderous intent."

Just her description of the redclaws gave Michael the creeps.

Michael: "Okey, I think I've heard enough. If they really are as scary as you described, then we should prepare for them immediately, starting today."

Zoe: "Yes, but first let me show you the way to my shelter. It's much bigger than yours and has enough room for both of us."

Michael: "All right, lead the way, Zoe."

The two left the small cave and walked through the lumpy forest.

Chapter 5

Zoe and Michael hiked for hours through the forest. While walking, Michael decided to listen to some music. It was now noon and they were both hungry since they hadn't even had breakfast yet.

Man, am I hungry!

Michael: "Zoe, can't we take a break for a few minutes? I'm starving here!"

Zoe: "Well, to get a good meal, we have to find something to eat first. We're almost there and I have plenty of food in my shelter.... Uh, Michi? Where did you go?"

Michael: "I'm over here!"

Zoe turned around and spotted Michael sitting on a fallen tree eating some snacks he had brought from his home world.

Zoe: "Are you kidding me!? You had food all along!? Why didn't you tell me that!?"

Zoe stomped up to Michael and sat down next to him. She grabbed his backpack, which was already open, and stuck her whole head inside while sniffing for something edible.

Michael: "Zoe, stop it! There are a lot of important things in there and I don't want you to break them. Give me back my backpack and I'll give you something to eat."

Zoe: "Hmph!"

She threw Michael's backpack back at him and he was just able to catch it. Michael took out two candy bars and handed them to Zoe. She sniffed them for a few seconds and a delicious smell she had never smelled in her life hit her nose.

Zoe: "I've never seen anything like this before, but it smells appetizing. What is that anyway?"

Michael: "It's chocolate, a very common candy in my home world."

Zoe: "Ohhhh, candy! I love candy!"

She opened her mouth and threw the two candy bars in as she devoured them like a hungry animal.

Damn! What an animal!

Zoe: "Heyw, Iw hearth thath!"

She spoke back to him with her mouth full. With one gulp, the two chocolate snack bars landed in her stomach.

Zoe: "Ahh, so yummy! Say, you have more, don't you?"

Michael: "No, those were the last ones. Uh, Zoe?"

Zoe: "Yes?"

Michael: "Actually, you should unwrap the wrappers first before you eat them."

Zoe: "Oh!"

Michael pulled a can of soda out of his backpack and opened it. He was about to take a sip, but Zoe caught his attention because she was curious.

Zoe: "What's that?"

Michael: "You mean that?"

Michael pointed to his can of soda and Zoe nodded in response.

Michael: "That's a drink called soda. I think you'll like it. Do you want to try it?"

Zoe: "Yes, please."

Michael pulled another can of soda out of his backpack and tossed it to Zoe. She caught it with one of her paws and looked at it more closely. She sniffed at it before considering how to open the can.

Zoe: "Michi? How did you open yours?"

Michael: "It's actually quite simple. You just have to- Wait Zoe! Don't shake it like that!"

Zoe: "I think I got it!"

Zoe managed to open the can with her sharp teeth, but then a lot of soda splashed in her face.

Zoe: "Ah! My eyes!"

Michael: "I warned you."

Zoe wiped her face with her furried arms and took a sip from her soda can. Her ears perked up and she took another sip.

Zoe: "This tastes amazing! It's really-"

A small, loud burp escaped her, interrupting her mid-sentence. Zoe blushed and covered her mouth with her paws.

Zoe: "I'm sorry, really, I'm so sorry! That was unexpected!"

Michael: "Don't worry about it. There's nothing to be ashamed of. In fact, I do it all the time. Let me show you what a real burp sounds like."

Michael finished his can of soda in one go and waited for the right moment while Zoe watched him curiously.

Michael: "I think it's coming up-"

Michael belched louder than a roaring bear. The birds stopped chirping and the nearby animals ran away scared. The whole forest went silent because he burped so uncontrollably loud.

Holy shit! That's a new record!

Zoe: "Ew! You just silenced the whole forest! You were even louder than a roaring redclaw! I bet you could scare them away like that!"

Michael stood up and grabbed his backpack.

Michael: "Now I'm ready to continue on our way. Are you, Zoe?"

Zoe: "You bet!"

Michael: "Alright then, lead the way, my friend."

The two continued on their way, walking for a couple of hours until a cliff blocked their path. The view was truly breathtaking. The whole forest could be seen from above and the setting sun made the view even more beautiful. Michael sat down on the edge of the cliff and enjoyed the view. Zoe smiled and sat down next to him.

Zoe: "It looks really beautiful, doesn't it?"

Michael: "Yes..."

But nothing can beat your beauty....

Zoe heard his thought and blushed madly. She didn't expect such a thought from him. The thing is, Michael completely forgot that she was able to hear thoughts. She shouldn't have heard that at all. Still, it made her happy and her smile widened. She moved closer to him and leaned her head against his shoulder.

Michael: "Oh, so you do want to be petted?"

Michael stroked her ears and head. His hand felt so good on her fur and she melted into him. Her fluffy tail wrapped around him as she relaxed and thought about how she could repay him for his kindness. He had saved her life, was now her friend, kept her company and was now petting her. For her, it was one of the best days of her life and she hoped it would stay that way.

Michael: "Z-zoe?"

Zoe: "Huh?"

Michael: "Uh-uh, can you excuse me for a minute?"

Zoe: "Five more minutes, please..."

Michael: "But it's important!"

Zoe: "Alright."

Zoe let go of him and Michael got up off the floor and unzipped his jeans so he could play firefighter.

Zoe: "Michi, what are you- oh..."

Zoe blushed and turned around when she saw his yellow stream of piss running down the cliff.

Ah, man... What a relief! I haven't pissed all day. I feel like I'm being revived.

Zoe: "Did you really have to ruin our moment just to pee?"

Michael: "Do you want me to piss myself next time we have another moment?"

Zoe: "Wha!? No! That's not what I meant! I mean, you could have held it a little longer. Anyway, are you done now?"

Michael: "No! I'm just having fun hitting passing birds down there with my piss stream. Give me a few more seconds."

After Michael finished, he zipped up his jeans and they both made their way to Zoe's shelter. As they walked, Zoe looked at Michael often and caught something strange in his ear with her eyes.

Zoe: "Michi, what is that thing in your ear?"

Michael took both of his earphones out of his ears and showed them to Zoe.

Michael: "You mean these? They're called earphones and they're for listening to music."

Zoe: "Ugh, music! I can't stand it! I hated the music in the village. It was always the same thing, and it bored me to death. It was just a bunch of guys hammering away on bongos."

Michael: "Well, you're in luck, Zoe! Because later today, I'm going to show you what real music sounds like."

Zoe: "I hope it's worth it. What does your music sound like anyway?"

Michael: "It's hard to explain. There are many different kinds and each song has its own charm."

Zoe: "Sounds really interesting."

They both wandered through the big forest as Michael continued to explain what music is really like in his world and how it plays a big part in his life. Finally, they reached Zoe's shelter, and Michael was amazed at how big it was.

Chapter 6

Damn, what a shelter!

Michael's jaw dropped when he looked at Zoe's so-called shelter. It was huge! A large cavernous room on the side of a mountain. The walls of the cave were covered with green crystals that lit up the dark areas. Roots hung from the ceiling, making the cave room look a bit like a natural plant life. In the center of the cave room was a large fireplace with stones surounding it to sit on. Nearby were several large bowls made of wooden sticks.

One of them was completely filled with some kind of round, yellow fruit that Michael had never seen before. He also spotted leaves and cloths covering the ground on a small section. Michael guessed that this must be her sleeping place.

Zoe: "Ah, finally! Home sweet home! Welcome to my cozy lair, Michi. You can enter and leave this place anytime you like."

Zoe entered her lair and walked toward the fire pit. She summoned a green flame on her paw and lit the fire pit. She sat down on one of the stones as the small flame in the fire pit began to burn. She looked back at Michael, who was still standing in front of the cave, speechless, motionless, and open-mouthed.

This is her shelter? Look how massive it is! And she called it a shelter, as if it was something simple!? Enough room for both of us, yeah right! It's even bigger than my classroom, probably twice as big! This looks so stunning!

Zoe: "Are you coming or are you planning on sleeping right outside my cave?"

Michael looked back at Zoe, who smiled and gestured with her paw to enter her shelter. Michael walked up to Zoe and sat down next to her.

Zoe: "Nice, isn't it?"

Michael: "Yes… It really is. I've never seen anything like it! I wonder what else this world has to offer!"

Michael and Zoe looked out of the cave. The sun had already set and the sky was pitch black.

Zoe: "Well, if you want, tomorrow we could go to one of the biggest lakes nearby. It wouldn't hurt to clean ourselves up a bit either."

Michael smelled himself under his armpits and an unpleasant smell rose to his nose.

Michael: "Yeah, you're right."

Zoe: "Are you hungry?"

Just as Michael was about to answer, his stomach answered her with a growl.

Zoe: "I'll take that as a yes! Let me show you my great cooking skills!"

She grabbed a nearby stick and a yellow round fruit from the fully loaded wooden bowl. She attached the strange fruit to the stick and roasted it over the fire. After a while, the fruit changed its color from yellow to brown.

Zoe: "Here, try this! This was a local delicacy in my home village!"

She held the stick with the fruit in front of his mouth. Michael looked at the fruit with a disgusted look. Not only was it brown and wrinkled, but it was also moist and sticky. It also kind of reminded him of the food in the school cafeteria, which tasted like crap.

It looks like- Okey, better not think about that, Michael! You don't want to piss her off, do you, mate?

Zoe: "Say ahhhh."

Well, at least it smells good. I hope it tastes like it smells....

Michael opened his mouth and took a bite. Zoe's eyes widened and her smile grew as she waited patiently for her food critique.

Hey, this isn't so bad after all....

No sooner had he thought about it his tongue detected hairs and a moving something in his mouth. It tasted awful and he immediately spit it out into the fire pit in front of him.

What the hell kind of disgusting abomination is this? How the fuck can this be a local delicacy!!!?

Zoe: "Hey! I worked hard to find those! Do you have any idea how rare they are!"

Michael: "Do you have any idea how shitty this tastes!!!? Are you trying to poison me or something!"

Zoe: "Y-you didn't like it?"

She lowered her ears and looked at the floor.

Michael: "Uh, Zoe? Are you-"

Zoe: "Don't worry Michi! I have something else you might like!"

Michael: "Really?"

Zoe: "Yes! Just wait here."

Zoe walked out of the cave into the darkness and came back with a bowl full of insects and worms. She set the bowl down next to Michael and sat back down.

Zoe: "Here!"

Michael: "Uhh..."

Michael had never seen this kind of small crawling insects before. Most of them had five or seven legs, some even more! The worst part was that their legs were really long and thin and their bodies were small for that. Some were even still alive in the bowl and crawling around.

Michael: "Zoe, I don't think I would like it any better than what I tasted a minute ago."

Zoe: "Suit yourself."

She took the bowl of those creepy looking crawlies and devoured them all in seconds. When Michael saw how sharp her teeth were and how aggressively she ate, he made a mertal note: Do not piss her off!

A small belch escaped her as she emptied the bowl. She covered her muzzle with her paws.

Zoe: "I'm sorry."

Michael: "Zoe, isn't there anything else for me to eat?"

Zoe: "Well, there is one thing left."

Michael: "And that would be?"

Zoe: "You can have some of my breast milk if you want."

Michael: "Wait, what!?"

Zoe was about to take off her bra, but Michael stopped her in time. He was redder than a tomato by this time.

Michael: "Zoe! You can't just do that in front of me!"

Zoe: "Why not? Aren't you hungry?"

Michael: "Fuck that! I'm going to skip dinner! I'm not hungry anymore anyway because you've ruined my appetite!"

Zoe covered her snout with her paws as she giggled.

Michael: "What's so funny now!"

Zoe: "Sorry, that was just a silly joke I made. But if you're really that hungry, we could make an exception."

Michael: "NO!"

Zoe: "Relax, I was just messing with you."

They both sat at the fire pit and looked out the cave at the night sky. The night sky looked breathtaking! It was covered with many colorful stars, some bigger, some smaller. Zoe pressed closer to Michael and wrapped her fluffy tail around him.

Zoe: "Michi?"

Michael: "Huh?"

Zoe: "You know... You said you wanted to show me what music sounds like where you come from."

Michael: "Oh, that's right. I forgot all about that. Well, it's pretty hard to show you everything because there are many different kinds of music styles. I can only show you the kind of music I always listen to."

Zoe: "That's perfectly fine."

Michael: "I mostly listen to metal and dubstep. Those two genres of music always sound fast, aggressive, energetic and deep. I don't expect you to like them at first, because it took me some time to get used to them too."

Michael handed Zoe his earphones and connected them to his phone. He put the earphones in her ears and selected one of his favorite metal songs on his phone. When the song played, Zoe couldn't believe her ears. Her jaw dropped open. She heard things and sounds she had never heard before. It was impossible to describe it with her limited vocabulary. It sounded like madness, it was fast and energetic, but she loved it.

Her fur straightened and she danced a little to the rhythm as she smiled broadly and closed her eyes. She felt her adraline level shoot up. Her fluffy tail began to swing happily from right to left and back. She opened her eyes again as an idea formed in her mind.

Zoe: "Come on, Michi! Dance with me!"

Michael: "Wait! First of all, you don't dance to that kind of music, and second of all, I can't dance at all-"

Michael was interrupted as Zoe pulled him closer, forcing him to follow her steps. It was hard enough for him to dance since he couldn't, but then there was the fact that he couldn't hear the song at all.

Michael: "Zoe, stop, please!"

Zoe couldn't hear him because the music was too loud. She danced faster and faster the longer the song went on, which made it even harder for Michael. Right after the song ended, Michael tripped over a rock and fell on his back, pulling Zoe down to him as well. They both blushed as Zoe lay on top of Michael. They both stared at each other and Michael felt his cheeks heat up. He felt that warm feeling again.

Zoe: "Wow, that sounded so cool! I've never felt so happy in my life! Thank you so much for showing me that!"

Michael: "Ha, no problem."

Zoe wrapped her arms around him and licked his face with her warm and wet tongue.

Eww! She ate all those bugs a few minutes ago! Gross!!!

Michael: "Z-zoe, w-what was that for?"

Zoe: "A thank you kiss for making me happy again."

Michael: "But that was more of a lick than a kiss."

Zoe: "And how does a kiss work then, Mr. Expert?"

Michael: "It's more like a smack with the lips than a lick across the face."

Zoe: "So, like that?"

Michael felt her warm lips on his skin as she kissed him several times on his face.

Michael: "Zoe, please stop! My whole face is covered in your spit!"

Zoe: "Okey okey, I'll stop for now..."

Zoe yawned and laid her head on his chest.

Zoe: "I think we should go to sleep now. Being happy really makes me tired."

Michael: "Yeah, me too. Uh, could you get off me?"

Zoe: "Why should I? Don't you love my soft and warm fur? Even though the days here are sometimes very hot, the nights are always cold. Besides, I could use some company while I sleep."

Michael: "O-okey, good night Zoe."

Zoe: "Good night, Michi."

It wasn't long before she fell asleep, snoring like a speeding tractor. For some reason, Michael couldn't fall asleep. He just laid under Zoe and stared at her awkwardly. All he could think about was Zoe, her emerald green eyes, her beautiful warm white fur, and her fluffy tail.

The more time I spend with her, the more I like her.... I can't believe I'm actually falling for her.

His eyelids were getting heavier by the second and he closed his eyes. He fell asleep and dreamed again. In his dream, he was again greeted by Zoe's emerald green eyes. They stared at him warmly, and he heard her soothing voice again.

Zoe: "From now on, you will never be alone again, Michi. I love you."

Chapter 7

The sun was slowly rising and the light was scattering through the leaves, creating beautiful rays of light that shone on Michael and Zoe inside the cave. Suddenly, Michael's smartphone rang with the ringtone "Get up, you lazy bastard".

Michael: "Uhhh..."

Michael groaned and tried to find his phone next to him with his hands while his eyes were still closed. He missed it many times and almost got it twice.

God damn it! Where is it?

Finally, he opened his eyes and reached for his phone. He turned off the morning alarm clock and deactivated it completely so it wouldn't bother him in the future. He didn't need the morning alarm clock anymore anyway.

Oh man.... That was the most fucked up dream I've ever had in my life. Me and Zoe were... Don't even think about it, Michael. You don't want her to set you on fire, do you, mate? So, what now? I don't know what to do now. I've managed to tame a friendly furry animal, and she even shares her home with me. Zoe is still asleep, and I wish I was too. Damn alarm clock, you damn phone! Now can't get up because she's sleeping on me! I hope she didn't catch my dream. She'd cook me if she did.

Michael looked at the sleeping Zoe. She was lying on top of him with her arms wrapped around him as if she had just caught her prey. Her grip was tight and didn't allow Michael to move much. Still, it felt very comfortable, because her fur was very soft and warm.... And smelly. Moreover, she blushed and smiled in her sleep, which Michael found really adorable. Michael decided to think about his homeworld for a while, while stroking Zoe's head.

I wonder what my world is like right now. Did my parents even realize I was gone? Probably, because today is... Wednesday, I think. I'm supposed to be at this shithole called school. I'm sure Mrs. Cockney has already called my parents. Even though I hated it there... I kind of miss home. I hope my parents haven't found out I'm gone. I don't want them to worry about me.

Even though they both worked a lot and were rarely home, they still loved me and took care of me. But now I can't go back anyway.... Or can I? If there was a door with a lock somewhere, then maybe I could. I don't know for sure. Anyway, I'm staying here in this world. Any place is better than home. Besides, I don't want to leave Zoe alone. She is in the same situation as I am.

She escaped her home and her inner demons to be free. She's all alone, with no one by her side but me. And even if I took her with me to my world, I would have to hide her from everyone.

If furries found out there was a half-naked anthropomorphic vixen running around their neighborhood, they'd go nuts! And even worse is the government! What if the government found out about her existence? They would immediately capture her and perform experiments on her because she is basically an alien, a sentient and intelligent being from another world that has powers! I can't let that happen and I won't let that happen.

I will stay here on this world no matter what! I finally got a second chance! A chance at a new and happy life with Zoe by my side! We could both explore new territories and fight for our survival. We could both have an exciting adventure! We could both build our own paradise where we could make our own rules. This time, no stupid law will stop us from enjoying life! I'm just glad I met a kind and caring friend like Zoe, and I don't care that she's not human! That's all I need in my life, and that's all I wished for. Now I can finally be happy again.

Michael smiled and wrapped his arms around her. In his vision, Zoe shone so brightly, as if she were some kind of angel. An angel who healed his depression and made him feel important in life.

I can't believe that I am actually in love with her. She is more than perfect.

Zoe: "Really? Is that so, Michi?"

She heard that all along?!! Shit!!!

Now Michael knew that he had screwed up. He forgot once again that she could hear his thoughts. He shouldn't have thought about it at all. His eyes were wide, expressing only shock, and his cheeks glowed redder than the red light of the traffic light. Zoe's tear-soaked eyes were wide open, staring into his shocked brown eyes. She moved even closer to his face and smiled happily as Michael backed away a bit.

Michael: "U-uhh, Z-zo Zoe, I-I can explain!"

Zoe: "You don't have to explain anything to me, because you explained it to me in your head. Now don't be shy and kiss me already!"

She bent closer to his face, because she wanted to give him a kiss full of love and passion. Just as their lips were about to meet, they heard a loud and deep roar coming from outside the cave, which was not far away, but not that close either. They both froze and stared out of the cave.

What the hell was that!? Am I in some kind of "Jurassic Park" world!?

Zoe: "That was a redclaw! We should stay down and be quiet for a moment!"

Michael could hear Zoe speaking, but her mouth and lips were not moving at all, as if she were speaking in his mind. Michael decided to talk to her in his mind.

Zoe, get off me now! We must prepare before it finds us!

Zoe got off Michael without making a sound. Michael stood up and sneaked to his backpack. He grabbed his bow and a couple of arrows that were attached to his backpack. They both heard growling, sniffing, and rustling as the bush in front of the cave moved.

Zoe: "I think it found us! Redclaw is looking at us from that bush over there! He's mostly out to attack me, but he's also curious about you Michi! What should we do now!?

Hey! I thought you would know, since you live here on this world! I am an alien on this world! Okey, I think I have a plan! Throw a fireball at the bush the redclaw is hiding in. It will surely jump out and I can shoot an arrow through its skull!

Zoe: "Are you sure? Maybe we should wait until it runs away. As long as it doesn't attack us, we shouldn't attack the redclaw."

Trust me, Zoe! I am a good archer! The second it jumps out, it will be pierced by an arrow and die!

Zoe nodded and her paws glowed green as green flames appeared around them. Michael aimed his bow loaded with an arrow at the bush Zoe was pointing at.

I'm ready!

Zoe created a green fireball with her paws and hurled it at one of the bushes. Not even a second later, a red-scaled, human-like dinosaur jumped out of the bushes and toward Michael. It fit Zoe s description perfectly because it looked terrifying. Its sharp claws reached for Michael as it lunged, but Michael remained patient, waiting for the right moment to fire. Time slowed down as the yellow-eyed beast approached Michael by the second.

Just a little longer...

The red-scaled beast opened its mouth, which was filled with thousands of razor-sharp teeth, when it was only a meter away from Michael.

Now!!!

The arrow flew at high speed into the creature's mouth and pierced its skull. It immediately fell to the ground and died after making a few growling and gurgling sounds. A pool of blood formed under the now dead Redclaw. Michael stomped on the redclaw's body to make sure it was really dead. Michael was proud of himself because the redclaw was no longer responding. He turned back to Zoe and walked toward her, smiling.

Michael: "See, that wasn't hard, was it? Now we can-"

Zoe: "Watch out Michi!!!"

Michael turned around and saw another redclaw armed with a club ready to strike at him. Just as the redclaw swung its club, Michael ducked and narrowly dodged the attack, only to get kicked in the balls afterwards.

Ouch, I think my ballsack fell off!!!

Michael went to his knees and dropped his bow. He gritted his teeth to fight back the nerve-wracking pain. The redclaw answered with an ugly laugh mixed with a roar. Two more redclaws entered the cave and approached Zoe.

Michael: "Leave her alone you red scaled fuckers!!!! I'm not done yet!!!"

Michael tried to get up, but the redclaw that had knocked him down smiled and pushed him back to the ground with its clawed foot. Michael was held in place and could only watch as Zoe struggled with two redclaws. Zoe created a fireball with her paws and was about to throw it at the two redclaws approaching her, but one of them was faster and knocked her down with a club.

Michael: "Noo!!!"

The two redclaws were laughing at Zoe, who was holding her head in pain. They were about to undress her. Michael already suspected what they were up to. They were about to rape her while Michael had to watch.

No, option declined!

His adnerdraline levels soared. The rage he had built up over the many years finally became unstable as it took control of him.

Michael: "I said leave her alone!!!"

He managed to get his pocket knife out of his pocket and sliced the leg of the redclaw that was holding him down. The redclaw roared in pain as it stumbled back. Michael took the opportunity to get up and lunged at the redclaw. He took out a carrot peeler from his pocket and scaled the scales of the redclaw, which shrieked in pain and agony. The other two redclaws stood there in shock and watched as Michael scaled one of their comrades alive.

One of the two redclaws mustered up the courage to attack Michael, but Michael saw it coming. He took out his lighter and a hairspray. Just as the redclaw was about to strike at him with a club, he ignited it. The red-scaled beast hadn't seen it coming and roared loudly to fight the burning pain. Michael laughed like a madman as if his school was on fire right in front of him. The flaming redclaw fell lifeless to the ground as its body continued to burn.

Michael quickly turned his head to the remaining redclaw, which was running toward him while it swung its axe like a drunken lumberjack. Michael also flamed this redclaw, but it didn't care at all that it was on fire, instead continuing to swing its axe furiously at Michael. Michael jumped out of the way just as the redclaw managed to give him a cut on the cheek.

Son of a...

Michael gave the redclaw a roadhouse kick. His hard boots hit the redclaw's jaw. A crack was heard and the third redclaw fell to its death.

Good riddance...And where is the last one? I still have to remove his scales, because I was interrupted!

Michael looked around Zoe's cave room, but couldn't find the last remaining redclaw anywhere. Michael assumed the worst, that it escaped.

Yeah, just run away and tell off your cousins, you little coward!

Michael went to the fireplace and lit it. He dragged the three dead redclaws to the fire pit and threw them on top. He poured out the remains of the hairspray to make the fire even bigger. The smell of burnt flesh and blood hit his nose.

Now they will completely disappear, decay into atoms! That's what you get for messing with me and Zoe!

Michael heard a whimper from Zoe and glanced at her. Her fur stood on end and she trembled with fear as she stared at Michael.

Michael: "Are you okay, Zoe? Are you hurt?"

When he approached Zoe, she began to cry and backed away.

Michael: "Hey, why are you crying, Zoe? I took care of them. You don't have to be afraid anymore. You're safe... safe..."

Michael now really realized what had happened. He was not only a raging beast, but also a killing machine. He looked at his bloody hands and at the burning corpses of the redclaws. No wonder she was scared shitless of him now. He managed to fight four redclaws by himself and killed three of them.

Great, now she is afraid of me. She probably hates me now.... Another friendship ruined.

Zoe: "I-I don't hate you Michi. I... it's just... Are all humans like you?"

Michael: "I... I don't know. Probably not, because I was considered an outsider. Listen Zoe, I will never hurt you, I promise. You don't have to be afraid of me."

Zoe: "I've never felt so much anger in a person's head. And the look you had when you were fighting them was..."

Michael: "Demonic? Listen, a few minutes ago I wasn't myself. The rage got the best of me. I guess those two redclaws who tried to 'lay a hand on you' set it off."

Zoe threw herself at Michael and wrapped her arms around him. She began to sob and rubbed her head against his chest.

Zoe: "Looks like you saved me again. I thank you for that. Now we can pick up where we left off!"

Michael: "Where we left of... Wait, where were we left off?"

Zoe: "Uh, don't tell me you've already forgotten!"

Michael just shrugged his shoulders, because he had no idea.

Zoe: "Then I'll show you.... Close your eyes."

Michael had a lot of questions, but decided to oblige her, not wanting to upset her. After he closed his eyes, Zoe grabbed his head and kissed him passionately. Michael blushed madly and his eyes were wide open. All he could think about was Zoe and all he could feel were her soft, warm and moist lips on his. Michael couldn't believe it. Zoe was actually kissing him!

(In Michael's head)

Michael-AI: "Warning! System failure! Faulty cable detected in sector three! Fire detected in lab three!"

Michael-253: "OH MY GOD!!! We are all about to die!!!! AH-Hhhh!!!"

Michael-547: "Holy crap! Did he just jump out the window!!!"

Michael-AI: "Warning! Minus one brain cell! Lockdown initiated!"

Michael-173: "Great! How are we even supposed to escape now!!! What caused the fire in the first place!?"

Michael-891: "I don't know! I heard rumors that he got kissed by a furry girl."

Michael-9011: "He got.... What?!"

Michael-2156: "Oh no!!! The fire is on its way to us!!! What should we do, guys!?"

Michael-891: "There's no way to survive this, guys.... I think we should sit down and enjoy the remaining seconds. It was nice working with you lads."

Michael-AI: "Warning! Explosion detected in lab forty! Minus five brain cells!"

(Outside Michael's head)

Zoe giggled slightly at his thoughts. She had never seen Michael's head as red as a tomato. She thought it was really funny. She waved her paw in front of Michael's face to wake him up from the trance she had put him in.

Zoe: "Hello, Michael? Knock, knock. Are you still there?"

Michael shook his head and finally awoke from his trance. Zoe giggled even more.

Zoe: "You look so cute when you're like this. Maybe I need to do this more often."

She stroked his face with her muzzle and licked the wound on his cheek. A few licks later, the cut was completely gone.

Michael: "Thanks."

Zoe: "You know, about that kick…. Your baby maker isn't hurt, is he?"

Michael choked on his own spit and coughed several times.

Michael: "Okey, I think it's time for me to go."

Zoe laughed and got off him.

Zoe: "No, but seriously. Are you hurt down there?"

Michael: "No, I'm fine."

Zoe: "Let's go to the lake I was talking about yesterday. You definitely need a bath now."

Michael: "And you need a bath too, Zoe! I was forced to smell your dirty fur all night!"

Michael got up from the ground and gathered his belongings. He also took the redclaw's club and axe, as they might still be of great use. He gave the three burning corpses one last glare before leaving their home with Zoe.

Chapter 8

Michael and Zoe walked through the forest and made their way to the lake where they were going to clean up. It was lunchtime and not a single cloud was visible in the sky. The weather was hot and the birds were chirping happily.

Michael: "Zoe, when will we be there?"

Michael was all sweaty and Zoe was panting because she had thick fur.

Zoe: "We shouldn't be that far away. It's probably going to take us ten minutes to get there."

Michael: "Ahh, man."

Zoe giggled as a joke popped into her head. She wanted to tease Michael a little.

Zoe: "Oh, you really want to take a bath with me that bad?"

Michael blushed as an image of Zoe splashing naked in the water came to his mind. He immediately threw that thought away so as not to expose it to Zoe.

Zoe: "Well, how about we play a little game to pass the time, huh?"

Michael: "Alright, what game?"

I wonder what game she wants to play. Hunt down the human? Burn Michael, burn? Zoe's fun in the bush?

Zoe giggled again and blushed.

Zoe: "No, although I really liked your last idea."

Michael gave her a "what the hell" look and raised one of h¡s eyebrows.

Zoe: "I didn't say anything! Forget it. I was thinking of a little game like "I spy with my little eye."

Pretty boring, but at least a game to pass the time with.

Michael: "Alright."

Zoe: "You go first."

Michael: "I spy with my little eye and it has the color white."

Zoe: "Is that me? That's my fur, isn't it?"

Michael: "Congratulations, that was the one million dollar question."

Zoe: "Oh, come on Michael! Make it more creative and exciting like me. I spy with my little eye and it has the color brown."

Michael looked around but couldn't see anything brown except for the trees and dirt on the ground. Surely she wouldn't pick something out so easily, but Michael wanted to try anyway.

Michael: "Hmm, the trees?"

Zoe shook her head in response.

Michael: "The dirt and mud?"

Zoe: "Nopedie nope."

Michael: "That stick over there on the ground."

Zoe: "Wrong."

Michael looked around again, but couldn't spot anything else that was brown.

Michael: "I haven't got a clue! Maybe my whole bathroom after an explosive diarrhea?"

Zoe giggled at his answer.

Zoe: "Well, it's something else. Guess again."

Michael: "I don't know. I can't detect anything else that's the color brown. Just tell me."

She stood in front of him, blocking his way. Michael just stood there staring at her curiously.

Zoe: "Okey, I'll tell you…. Your beautiful eyes. I could stare at them forever."

This was the first time anyone complimented him on his eyes. Everyone at school called his eyes ugly, disgusting and lifeless, even Michael told himself that while looking at himself in the mirror. But Zoe called his eyes the exact opposite, and that made him smile.

Zoe: "You know, you should smile more often. I've only seen you smile a few times."

Michael's smile widened even more and his cheeks flushed red.

Michael: "Th-thank you. It really means a lot to me, especially if these words are coming from you."

Zoe smiled and hugged him tightly while resting her head on Michael's shoulder.

Zoe: "Anything for you, Michi."

Michael wrapped his arms around her as well and they both closed their eyes as they paused for a moment.

Such soft fur…

Zoe let go of him and gave him a quick kiss on the lips. Michael jumped a little at the sudden kiss.

Zoe: "Come on, we want to spend the day at the lake, not standing around here all day."

Michael: "Y-yes…"

The two continued to wander through the endless forest until a large spider web blocked their path. Michael had never seen such a huge spider web before.

That must be one hell of a big spider! I hope it's not around here somewhere. Ugh, how I hate those eight-legged fuckers!

Michael hated spiders because he was scared shitless of them, especially if they were big. He didn't mind if some of them were friendly and only ate small insects. He still hated them though.

Zoe: "Why are you staying here? Are you afraid of spiders?"

Michael: "Wh-what? No! Of course not!"

Zoe laughed.

Zoe: "Oh, come on. It's impossible to hide anything from me. I can sense your fear, can't I?"

Michael: "Then I guess your telepathy is broken. I'll show you that I'm not afraid of those friendly little eight-legged freaks!"

Michael grabbed his spear and swung it at the massive spider web. It made ugly noises as the sticky threads separated from each other, as if someone was tearing flesh. The spider web was also much thicker and harder to cut than the spider webs in his home world.

That shit is fucking disgusting, man! I wish I still had my hair-spray! I would have burned it down completely, including some nearby trees and plants, to make sure whatever built it was one hundred percent dead!

He rolled up all the spider web on his spear and lit it with his lighter.

Ta da! Now I have a torch!

Michael: "See? Not scared at all!"

Zoe: "Impressive! Now we can keep moving forward! We should actually be close by now."

Suddenly, Michael heard a loud and deep buzzing to his right. He turned and waved his burning torch to the right, but there was nothing there. Now he heard this strange low buzzing to his left and looked to Zoe, who just smiled innocently at him. Nothing else was there that could have caused that buzzing sound until Michael looked up and spotted something he wished he never had to experience in his life. It was a spider as big as his whole face, and the worst part was that it had wings on its back.

Holy shit...

Suddenly, the flying spider lunged at him and landed on Michael's face.

Michael: "AHH!!! Get it off of me! Get it off of me! Get it off me before it lays eggs!!! Kill it with fire Zoe before it spreads like the corona virus!!!"

Zoe burst out laughing as she watched the struggling Michael swing his torch around while screaming "Bloody Spider".

Zoe: "You know, you've got some pretty sick dance moves. Too bad you didn't use them yesterday when we danced together."

Zoe carefully grabbed the spider out of his face and held it on her paw while the spider crawled around flapping its wings to make a peace sign.

Zoe: "That's it, my little friend."

She held her paw on the ground and the spider crawled away.

Zoe: "Oh, no! Don't!

Michael pierced his spear through the spider. He then stomped and jumped on it until there was nothing left of the spider.

Zoe: "Michael! Why do you have to be so cruel to other small animals!"

Michael: "That filthy creature jumped on my face and bit me! Son of a bitch got what he deserved!"

Zoe: "Really? Where did it bite you?"

Michael: "Left cheek..."

Zoe: "Let me see.... Looks clean to me."

Michael: "Other left, Zoe."

Zoe: "Oops, sorry."

As Zoe examined Michael's left cheek, she saw that it was completely swollen. She grabbed his head and kissed his left cheek several times.

Zoe: "That's it! All healed!"

Michael touched the spot where she had kissed him and blushed a little.

Michael: "Th-thank you."

Zoe: "Anything for you, dear. And Michael, I've been thinking of some sort of favor in return from you, too."

Michael's eyes widened.

She wants a quid pro quo from me!?

Michael: "Wha!?"

Zoe: "Well, I've healed you a few times, and I'm sharing my shelter with you, too."

Michael: "And I saved your life twice! What else do you want in return?"

Zoe: "Well, don't worry, it's just a small request."

Michael: "Well, what's your little request? Do you want to be petted, or maybe a little treat?"

Zoe smiled at Michael, which made him feel uncomfortable.

Zoe: "I wouldn't mind either, but I was thinking of something else."

(Time skip)

Uh, why did I agree with her? She's so freaking heavy! No comparison to what she weighed when I carried her into my cave two days ago! What a fat little vixen!

Zoe: "Ey! I heard that!"

Zoe sat on Michael's shoulders, enjoying the view from above as he gasped from her weight and the hot weather.

Michael: "Zoe, I thought you told me it would only take ten minutes to get there. I carried you for about fifteen minutes!"

Zoe: "Well, if you walked a little faster, we would have been there in five minutes! Look! There's the lake!"

Thank goodness!

Zoe jumped down from Michael's shoulders and took off her loincloth and tribal bra.

Dayuuum!!!

Michael immediately turned away, blushing more than the color red could ever be.

Zoe: "Ass cannon!!!"

Michael heard her scream as she ran to the water and jumped in. She giggled with delight as she splashed around and noticed that Michael had his back to her.

Zoe: "Ohh Michael! Don't be shy and come in! You need to be clean if you're going to re-enter my shelter."

Michael slowly turned around and covered his eyes with his hands. He had never felt so uncomfortable. He took a quick glance and saw only Zoe's head above the water.

Zoe: "Michael, what are you waiting for? Take your clothes off and get in here!"

Okey, don't panic Michael! You've already been through so much shit today and it can't hurt to take a relaxing bath to cool down your overheated processor. Just take off everything but your boxers and stay as far away from her as possible.

Michael dropped his backpack on the floor and undressed. He got into the water with his boxers on and immediately shivered as the water was freezing cold.

Great, now I miss the heat.

Since the lake was huge, Michael decided to keep swimming to the middle until Zoe spoke to him from behind.

Zoe: "You're finally here! Took you long enough!"

Her sudden outburst, coming from behind, startled him. He turned around and spotted Zoe swimming toward him with her paws reaching up to him.

Zoe: "I'm going to get you!"

Oh no...

Michael didn't need to be told twice to swim away as fast as he could.

Zoe: "Ah, I see. You want to play cat and mouse in the water."

Michael swam away from her as fast as he could while Zoe followed. He turned his head briefly to see Zoe catch up to him. Michael immediately dove into the water and swam underwater a couple of metres away from her. He heard his head scream for air and swam to the top. He took a deep breath, his eyes searching for Zoe.

Where the hell is she? Did I lose her?

He looked around a few times and was satisfied that he couldn't spot her anywhere.

Thank God I got rid of her! Now I can bathe alone in peace.

Zoe: "I don't think so!

His mind went crazy as he heard her voice in his head, but couldn't see her anywhere. Suddenly, a pair of paws grabbed Michael and pulled him under the water and toward Zoe.

Oh-oh!

Zoe: "I got you!"

Michael couldn't see her as she hugged him from behind, but he could feel her furried chest and bare nipples pressing against his back.

Zoe! Let go of me!

Zoe: "Oh, why are you so shy? After all we are all by ourselfs!"

She let go of him and turned him around. Michael's eyes widened when he saw her completely naked. Her fur swung in all directions. His mind stopped working properly as he didn't know what to do except stare at both of her fur balls.

Zoe: "Oh my! Looks like your friend is getting pretty exciting down there!"

Michael looked down at himself and spotted a tent on his boxers.

Don't mind him. Fucker got a mind of his own!

He blushed even more and covered his boner with both hands. Once again his lungs were screaming for air as he was still under-water. Zoe sensed his distress, grabbed him and swam with him on her arms to the top. When they were above the water, they both took a deep breath.

Michael: "Z-zoe? C-can we g-g-go out now? I'm freezing t-t-to d-death right now."

Michael's teeth chattered from the cold.

Zoe: "Fine, there's a big rock where we can both take a long sunbath to dry off. Want to make a bet?"

Michael: "What kind of bet? A race?"

Zoe: "Yeah, if you lose, you will be at the bottom. If I lose, I will be at the bottom."

Michael: "Wait, what do you mean by at the bottom?"

Zoe: "Okey, go!!!"

Michael: "Hey, what the hell!!?"

Zoe swam as fast as she could toward the rock at the edge of the lake.

Unfair! I've got to get a move on!

Michael swam quickly after Zoe, but she was already halfway there. It would be very difficult for Michael to catch up with her, but he tried his best anyway. He was about to reach his goal with Zoe at the same time, but she splashed water in his eyes with her paws and made it first.

Zoe: "Yes! I won!"

Michael didn't really care that he had lost the bet. What mattered most to him was that he was having fun with her.

Michael: "Congratulations, I guess."

They both left the lake and walked to the rock. Zoe shook her fur in all directions to remove the remaining drops of water. Her fur puffed out and covered her private parts. She looked like a big ball of fur.

Zoe: "Let's climb up on the rock and have a nice sunbath."

She grabbed his hand and pulled him all the way up. Michael almost tripped three times.

Michael: "Hey, not so fast, furball!"

Michael sat down on the large rock. His skin felt like it was on fire because the rock was hot and the sun was shining on him. Zoe immediately pounced on him and wrapped her puffy arms around him. He could feel her soft breasts again as they pressed against his chest.

Michael: "Z-zoe! What a-are you doing!?"

Zoe: "I won the bet, didn't I?"

Michael: "But you're naked and lying on top of me!"

Zoe: "Yeah, so? What's wrong with me being naked? Don't you think I look so much prettier? Don't you want to feel my fur on your smooth skin? After all, I'm your lover!"

Michael: "My l-lover!?"

Zoe: "Yes, don't you love me?"

Michael: "I-I, uh, me and a, uh, me and, I'm..."

Zoe giggled and held her paw in front of his mouth to shut him up.

Zoe: "I know you love me too, Michi. My telepathy never betrays me. Now kiss me."

She aggressively pressed her lips against his and pushed her tongue into his mouth. Michael's eyes widened as he felt her warm and wet tongue exploring every inch of him. A few seconds passed and Michael finally gave in as they both wrestled with their tongues for a few minutes. They both wished that this moment would last forever, but they had to part soon because they needed air. A trace of salvia remained as their lips parted.

(Once again, in Michael's mind.)

Michael-AI: "Warning! Core meltdown detected! Explosion detected in sector five, sector twelve, and sector eighteen! Fire detected in lab three and lab seven! Warning! Minus one thousand seven hundred eighty-nine brain cells! Take shelter in the evacuation zone immediately!"

Michael-9399: "Fuck!!! Not again!!! How did it get that way this time!!!?"

Michael-8254: "He's doing it again, dude! He's really kissing her now!"

Michael-9399: "WHAT!?"

Michael-3765: "Yep, we're fucking done forever! You two were my best friends! I hope we meet again in another head, in another life!"

Michael-AI: "Warning! Gas leak detected in lab fifteen! Minus three brain cells!"

Zoe: "Michi?"

Michael-AI: "Warning! Cause of core meltdown detected! Initiate safety protocols!"

Zoe: "Michi!"

(Outside of Michi's head.)

Zoe: "Michi!!!"

Michael was completely out of it. Salvia drooled from his open mouth and he looked like he was brain dead. Zoe giggled and licked his neck a few times to wake him from his trance.

Michael: "Wait, Zoe! S-stop! That tickles!"

Michael couldn't help but laugh as she continued to lick his neck.

Zoe: "I finally heard you laugh! What a suprise!"

She rested her head on his chest and continued to lick him. Her tail was happily swinging from right to left and back again.

I can't believe me and Zoe met two days ago and we are already that close! I feel like I've known her for years!

They just laid on the rock until they were completely dried out. Zoe's fur was now normal and not fluffed up anymore.

Zoe: "I think we should go home now. It's past lunchtime and we haven't eaten anything yet today."

Both their stomachs growled at each other, argumenting who was hungrier.

Michael: "Yeah, now that I think about it, I'm actually starving. If only there was something else to eat that tastes really good."

Zoe: "Then let's get our clothes on and find something you like."

Zoe got off Michael and stood up. Now he could get a much better look at the naked Zoe in front of him. Her furried chest had a green heart pattern. Her private parts were still covered by her beautiful white fur and she had the hips! He felt the urge to wipe under his nose, only to see that his hand was full of blood. His nose was bleeding.

Zoe: "Hey! My eyes are up there!"

She licked his bloody hand and face clean and kissed him on the cheek, leaving a red, bloody stain from her lips onto his cheek.

I'll never wash my cheek again....

They both got dressed and made their way back to Zoe's shelter.

Zoe: "So Michi, now that you've seen me all naked, I expect you to be all naked the next time we bathe together!"

Michael: "Uh-hu..."

Michael wasn't listening to her at all, as he was dreaming about her. Zoe giggled and hugged him.

Zoe: "Great!"

Suddenly, Michael felt a sharp pain in his leg. He took a look and discovered some kind of dart.

Michael: "What the...? Who did...?"

Michael felt very tired and collapsed on the floor.

Zoe: "Michi? Michi! Wake up!"

He could no longer move, but he could hear her pleading and crying. Before Michael fell into a deep sleep, he felt himself being lifted up and thrown onto someone's shoulder.

Chapter 9

Argh, my head hurts like I rammed it full force through a door! What the hell happened anyway!? The only thing I can remember is that Zoe and I went home after taking a bath at the lake. And once again I'm just surrounded by darkness, great....

Michael heard some people yelling, but couldn't understand a word they were saying because they sounded pretty far away. They were clearly ranting about something and Michael had a feeling it had something to do with him. He also heard a lot of other people whispering around him, which made him very uncomfortable. Michael could hear someone approaching him as he heard footsteps and soon a deep, aggressive male voice spoke to him.

???: "Wake up!"

Michael slowly opened his eyes only to see that he was trapped in a large wooden cage. A huge crowd of human-like foxes surrounded the cage.

Damn! Is this some kind of furry convention!? Uh, um... Okey Michael, don't think of anything weird!

They all stared at Michael curiously, for they had never seen a creature like him before. Just like Zoe, they all had white fur, black back paws, green front paws, and wore these tribal-like clothes.

Next to the cage, he spotted a larger human-like fox. Instead of tribal clothing, he wore royal clothing with a crown on his head. He gave Michael an angry look.

This must be the king of this species, I think.

The king circled the cage Michael was sitting in, staring at him from all directions as he growled in anger.

???: "What have you done to my daughter!?"

Michael: "D-daughter? What daughter?"

???: "My daughter Zoe! What have you done to her!?"

Michael: "I- uh, n-nothing serious! I s-swear!"

Oh shit!!! That's her dad and he's the king too! I forgot Zoe told me that once!

???: "What are you and where are you from!?"

Michael: "I-I am a human being and I come in peace. I am not from here. I-I come from another world."

The crowd gasped and whispered to each other as they heard another intelligent and sentient being came from another world.

???: "What is your name and why are you here!?"

Michael: "M-my name is Michael, but everyone calls me Michi. I-I'm not here to cause any trouble, I swear! I just wanted to escape my old life and start over somewhere else!"

Michael felt someone's presence enter his mind. He looked into the king's eyes, which were glowing green. Michael's eyes widened as he realised something. Zoe's father was trying to figure out the truth all by himself. If Zoe's father found out that Michael had fallen in love with his daughter and even bathed with her, her father would surely set his willy boy on fire. Michael did his best to block out the king by thinking of everything else that came to mind. Michael thought about his old life, music, school, and any other random bullshit he could think of. The King couldn't process Michael's thoughts because they were too many and caused confusion in his mind. The king held his head in pa n and growled angrily at Michael.

???: "You are definitely hiding something from me! Zoe!!! Zak!!! Both of you come here right now!!!"

A few seconds later, another human-like fox pushed the crowd aside and dragged Zoe towards the king while she tried to escape his grip.

Zoe: "Zak! Let me the fuck go!"

Zak: "Shut up!"

Right after Zak arrived, he stared at Michael with murderous intent, which scared Michael. Not only was he as tall as the king, but he was powerfully built and his hands looked like they could crush anything into juice.

Jesus! This guy is built as strong as a goddamn tank!

???: "Zak, you found these two while patrolling the woods. Can you explain what you saw?"

Zoe: "That's none of your business, father!"

This guy is going to rat me and Zoe out!

Zak: "Of course, your highness! I happened to be wandering through the forest until I heard splashing sounds! I decided to follow those sounds, and they led me to a lake! Turned out Zoe and this furless prick were bathing in a lake together, both naked!!!"

The crowd around them groaned in disbelief as they heard Zak's outburst. Everyone stared at Michael and Zoe who were both blushing madly. More and more foxes appeared around them and the crowd grew larger by the second. Now Michael was about to shit his pants full. All the time he had been bathing with Zoe was apparently being watched by Zak.

I'll probably end up as a chew toy for all of them!!! FUCK!!!

Zak: "I decided to spy on them a little more and found out they were even in love!"

Some people in the crowd lost consciousness and fell to the ground while the rest yelled at Michael.

??? 1: "Kill him!!!"

??? 2: "He deserves the death penalty!!!"

??? 3: "Pervert scumbag!!!"

???: 4: "You rapist!!!"

??? 5: "Furless monster!!!"

Zoe looked down at the ground in shame, tears forming in her eyes. Not only had their relationship been exposed, but now all her people were after Michael.

???: "Zoe, first you leave us for two years and now this!?!? Explain yourself!!!"

Zoe: "F-father! It's not what it looks like!"

Michael held his head in pain as the words of the crowd shot through his head like bullets. His inner demons awoke as he could no longer hold them back. Depressive thoughts overcame him as this was probably his last moment. He was on the verge of losing his tears.

N-no! I can't show them my weakness! I am not weak, not anymore!!! And I'm not sad... I am... I'M ANGRY!!!

The voices of the crowd slowly faded away as Michael could no longer hear them. He could only hear what the king was saying.

???: "I, King Zalkan, have decided that this filthy human will be sentenced to death! And now that my daughter is finally back after being missing for two years, the wedding between her and Zak will go on tomorrow night!"

A high-pitched noise rang in Michael's head and his anger grew with each passing second. Finally, his anger became unstable and his head turned all red.

Michael: "ALRIGHT, SHUT YOUR HOLES!!!"

The whole crowd was startled by his sudden outburst and became silent. That was the loudest Michael could ever be as roared in anger. His throat burned with pain. Now everyone was watching him curiously.

Michael: "Didn't you maybe think about why she left in the first place!? Are you so stupid not to realize that she was not happy with your decision and Zak's behavior!? Did you take the devil's deal to be a king among these people just to have a smooth little brain upstairs in return!!!?"

Zalkan: "..."

Michael: "No wonder she fled this hellhole!!! I would have done the same thing if I had to marry someone who tried to rape me twice!!!! Looks like your delusional idea of protecting her didn't end well, because she ran away and almost died twice!!!"

Zalkan: "She... W-what!!!"

Michael: "You heard me, twat! Luckily I was able to save her ass! I gained her trust faster than you ever could have! I was there for her the whole time and made her smile, which didn't take that much effort at all! You weren't even able to do a single fucking thing out of these, and yet you did your best, calling yourself her father, calling yourself the king of these people!!!? Shame on you!!!"

Zalkan: "ENOUGH!!!"

Michael: "What!!! can't you face the truth!!!? Is that why your wife isn't here ruling by your side, because you probably weren't able to protect her properly aswell!!!?"

The crowd roared at Michael again as they threw dirt and spit at him. Zalkan, however, had heard enough from Michael's words.

Zalkan: "Zak! Escort this human to his jail cell where he awaits further instructions!"

Zak: "You can count on me, your highness!"

Zoe: "No!!!"

At this, the king simply walked away.

Zalkan: "Get out of my way!"

He commanded as he forcefully pushed the crowd aside and walked away.

Zoe: "Father, wait!"

Zoe gave Michael a worried look before running off and chasing after her father.

Zoe...

Zak: "You will pay for insulting King Zalkan and for stealing my precious little Zoe!"

Before Michael could reply, a fist hit his face and he fell into a deep slumber. He was once again unconscious.

Chapter 10

Zoe: "Father, wait!!!"

Zoe ran after her father, who entered a cemetery near the village, the village where Michael was held captive. King Zalkan went further inside the cemetery and stopped in front of a particular grave. There was something scrawled on the tombstone:

"You will always be in our hearts. May you never be forgotten for what you did for all your people. God bless this queen. Rest in peace."

Zoe: "Father..."

Her father took a deep breath and let out a long sigh. He turned to her and gave her a facial expression that expressed betrayal, sadness, anger and concern all at once.

Zalkan: "Why? Why did you run away from me, from all of us? Two years have passed since then! I thought you didn't make it..."

Zoe was silent and looked to the ground. She felt guilty for leaving her father and her people so suddenly, without leaving a single trace.

Zalkan: "The thought of losing my own daughter sucked the life out of me.... Everyone was so deathly worried about you!"

Zoe: "I...am sorry...I didn't mean to cause any pain...I just wanted to be as far away from him as possible!"

Zalkan: "You still haven't changed your mind about Zak?"

Zoe: "No... Not after what he tried to do to me!"

Zalkan: "Zak would never do something like that, Zoe! We've discussed this many times. He loves you and cares about your well-being!"

Zoe: "I doubt that... He only cared about my body and nothing else! He treated me like I was his toy!"

Zalkan: "Look Zoe, I'm really sorry that I forced you to do this.... I knew you weren't happy with him. I wanted you to marry the strongest of our people so he could protect you from those damn Redclaws! I don't want you to end up like your dear mother.... I couldn't protect her from them..."

A tear ran down his cheek as he continued to stare at the grave in front of him.

Zalkan: "If you really feel that way about him, and if he really tried to rape you, then I will call off the wedding today and send him to prison."

Zoe's ears perk up.

Zoe: "Really!"

Zalkan: "I will do everything I can to win you back as my daughter."

Zoe: "Thank you father!"

They both hugged each other.

Zalkan: "I missed you, Zoe."

Zoe: "I missed you too."

The two let go of each other and walked to the exit of the cemetery.

Zalkan: "Was what Zak told me about you and that strange creature true? What was it called again, Hooman?"

Zoe: "I... uh, um..."

Zoe blushed and looked away from her father.

Zoe: "Y-yes, we both have feelings for each other. But we didn't do anything dirty, I swear!"

Zalkan: "Hmm, may I ask where he's from? I've never seen a creature like him before."

Zoe: "He's human and his name is Michael, but he prefers to be called Michi. He told me that he comes from a cruel world where he was considered an outcast. He was not happy with himself and almost committed suicide."

Zalkan: "How tragic... And how did you meet him?"

Zoe: "I was patrolling in the forest to find something to eat, and I was attacked by two redclaws. They left me here in the dirt to bleed to death, and then he came and saved me."

Zalkan: "He saved your life?"

Zoe: "Yes, twice. He was always there for me, taking care of me, showing me things from his world that I've never seen, and he made me laugh a lot."

Zalkan: "He seems like a really nice guy. Now I feel bad about sending him to prison. When we come back, I will thank him properly and release him. If he really did those things, then I guess I don't have a problem with you guys being a couple."

Zoe's eyes widened in shock. Her ears perked up and a wide smile appeared on her muzzle.

Zoe: "Really!? You would let that happen!?"

Zalkan: "I'll do anything to make you happy, Zoe."

Zoe: "B-But what about the village? Don't I have to marry a prince?"

Zalkan: "Don't worry about that, Zoe. I think your brother should take your place and marry a princess from another village."

Zoe: "Thanks, Dad!"

Zalkan: "Anything for you, my darling."

They both left the cemetery and walked back toward the village. Meanwhile, Michael sat in his prison cell trying to open the lock with his pocket knife.

Stupid! Stupid!!! STUPID!!! Why did they have to take everything away from me, except for my pocket knife!!? If only I'd had that darn blue key, I could have escaped from this godforsaken prison!

Michael played with his knife and the lock for another minute, but nothing seemed to work.

Come on! Open sesame! Open up already! The king will be back any minute!

As he continued his prison break, Michael was stared at by the other prisoners in the other cells around him. They were all redclaws chained to the walls. Michael paused for a moment and looked around.

Michael: "Da fuck are you all staring at me!? Mind your own business!"

They all looked away and Michael tried to pick the lock again. A few seconds later, Michael heard footsteps that grew louder with each step.

Shit!

He immediately hid his pocket knife in his pocket and whistled innocently. A humanoid fox walked up to his cell, geared all up from head to paw. He pushed a tray with something inside and just walked away. Michael waited a few minutes until he could no longer hear the guard's footsteps.

Finally, some good fucking food! It's been a whole day since I've eaten anything serious! I wonder what it is....

Michael looked at the bowl filled with those creepy looking crawlies and those brown, roasted fruits that he never wanted to put his tongue on again.

No, I don't think I will eat this crap! Might as well starve to death here.

Michael walked toward the corner of the cell and sat down.

I wonder what Zoe is doing right now. I hope she's all right. All she wanted was to never come back here. She escaped her nightmare, only to be caught up in it.... I failed miserably....

Michael actually fell into a deep hole that he couldn't get out of. All he wanted was to live his new life with Zoe happily, but now he was waiting to die in a rotten prison cell.

Maybe she is happy to be back home and her family welcomes her with open arms. She has probably already forgotten about me. I'm worthless, after all...

Michael took his pocket knife out of his pocket and examined it closely. Even though it was covered with dirt and blood, it showed him the reflection of his lifeless face.

Maybe I should just end it all. I lost Zoe to her "future husband" and her brainless father. I can't live without her...

Michael heard someone clear his throat and looked up. Standing in front of his cell was the king. The king opened Michael's cell door and beckoned him to follow him.

Zalkan: "Stand up and come out."

Michael was now confused. He thought death awaited him, but instead the king wanted him to come out. Michael obeyed anyway so as not to anger the king. Maybe there is still a chance for him.

Zalkan: "Now follow me. I have an important speech soon and you will accompany me."

The king led the way through the prison and Michael followed him. The walls and floor were made of mossy bricks mixed with earth. Michael assumed that the prison was underground. Soon a staircase greeted them, leading upward into the orange sky as the sun slowly set. Once at the top, Michael could see many small houses made of logs and bricks. There were bars, blacksmith stores, restaurants, saunas and much, much more! It looked like he had traveled back in time many years.

At home, Michael was never very interested in history. At school, he usually skipped history classes because he hated them. Not only were they more boring than watching a retarded fly fly against the window to escape, but his history teacher turned out to be a Hitler fan girl.

When Michael heard the word "history," he thought only of war and the colors white, gray, and black. But in front of him was the complete opposite. It was colorful! Lanterns everywhere glowed with yellow and orange light. There were human-like fox children running around, laughing and playing happily with each other. When Michael saw this, he couldn't help but smile. He missed the days when he was a toddler in kindergarten and played with his old friends non-stop.

Why did they have to abandon me...? Why did they have to turn on me.... Even though they turned into horrible, unloving friends, they still shared their childhood with me. If only I could see them again.... I miss them...

The children circled Michael and ran off laughing to play some-where else. Michael looked around some more and noticed that there were no other villagers. He was in the middle of a village, a big one at that, and no one was around.

Zalkan: "Concentrate on following me, Michael. We don't want to be late, do we?"

Michael: "I- uh, sorry."

How did he know my name!?

The king continued to walk ahead and Michael followed him until they reached a large opening in the middle of the village. In the center were two large thrones and a smaller one. A huge crowd of villagers surrounded the thrones.

Oh my gawd!!! No wonder the village is so empty! They're all sitting up there chilling! Wonder what kind of gathering that is? Wait, is that...

Michael spotted Zoe sitting on the smaller throne, peering over one of her paws as she rested her head on the other paw.

That's Zoe!

Michael's thought was loud enough to reach Zoe's ears, which perked up in response. She looked ahead and smiled as she saw her father walking toward her with Michael. Michael couldn't help but smile, even though he didn't know what was about to happen to him. His smile quickly disappeared when a familiar person stood in front of Zoe and broke their eye contact. It was Zak.

Zak: "There he is!!! The human scum!!!"

Motherfu-

The whole crowd stared at Michael transfixed as their paws produced green flames.

Zalkan: "Don't worry about it. They will all behave as intended soon."

Michael heard the king's voice in his head, which calmed him down a bit. The crowd roared at Michael, spitting every insult they could think of at him.

Zalkan: "SILENCE!!!"

The crowd quieted down very quickly. Even Michael jumped at his sudden outburst. The king stomped over to his throne next to Zoe's and sat down. Then he signaled Michael with his paw to come to him.

Zalkan: "Come to me, Michael!"

Michael walked toward the king's throne. Zak's eyes were on Michael and he growled in anger. Everyone looked at the king, curious as to what he had to say.

Zalkan: "Today we have all gathered to for an important speech that I must share with you. There will be some changes in plans. First of all, this human will not be punished because he is not a threat to Zoe and us."

The crowd roared in anger and disbelief and threw every insult they could at Michael.

Zalkan: "SILENCE!!! That person there didn't deserve such disrespect after what he did for Zoe. If it wasn't for him, Zoe wouldn't be alive right now!"

Wait, why the sudden change? I thought he was going to kick my ass!

Zak growled even louder and clenched his fists in anger. He bared his sharp teeth as he faked a throat puncture with his thumb at Michael.

Zak: "I know you can hear me, Michael, as I speak through your mind! Remember this, when this is all over, I will kill you!!!"

Michael responded with a simple smile and a middle finger towards Zak. Zak's fist glowed green and flames appeared around it.

Zalkan: "This person named Michael not only saved my little princess, but also took good care of her. He made her smile and laugh every day like a true friend should."

Zak stopped giving Michael murderous looks and focused more on the King's words.

Zak: "Huh?"

The crowd immediately changed their minds about Michael and cheered for him.

Zalkan: "Due to rumors from my daughter that Zak has treated her abominably, I, King Zalkan, have decided to cancel the wedding between them and send Zak to prison!"

Zak: "Ha!!! Wait, WHAT!!!?"

The crowd now began to insult Zak instead of Michael and threw stones at him. Two guards pushed an opening into the crowd and dragged Zak all the way to the jail while he screamed in rage and squirmed like a worm.

Zak: "Mark my words!!! I will get my revenge Zalkan!!! I will kill you and this furless asshole!!!! I will achieve my goal and have Zoe by my side!!!! MARK MY WORDS!!!"

Zalkan: "Hmph! Anyway, Michael will be treated like a civilian in this village from now on, just like any of you. Since Zoe has fallen in love with this person, her brother, Prince Conror, will take her place and marry a princess from another village."

Uh... Did I... Did I win?

Zalkan: "Since Connor is not here at the moment, he will share us his speech after his patrol. Later that night, we will celebrate this wonderful moment of my daughter's comeback!"

The crowd of people cheered enthusiastically. They were happy that Zoe was finally back home. They were also very interested in Michael, because they had never seen such a white-paled, flat-faced, top head-haired, side-eared, square-toothed creature.

Hey!

Zalkan: "I, King Zalkan, will show Michael our proud homeland. Until then, see you all at the celebration tonight!"

The crowd cheered Michael again. Zoe blew Michael a kiss and waved at him. Michael waved back at her and smiled as if this was his best day. Who knows, maybe it was. After all, Zoe is saved from Zak and the village welcomes Michael with open arms.

Maybe I've found my new true home.

Zalkan cleared his throat to get Michael's attention.

Zalkan: "Well Michael, let me show you the village."

Michael: "But of course! I'd love to."

Chapter 11

The sun had already set and the beautiful lights of the village replaced the sun's task by illuminating every path. The night sky was filled with bright yellow and light blue stars. The moon showed itself in full glory and shone. While following King Zalkan through the village, Michael often looked up at the night sky and lost concentration on listening to the king. A crowd of these anthropomorphic foxes passed them by.

Some bowed to their king, some stared at Michael, some even cheered him, and some simply ignored them and went on about their daily tasks.

Zalkan: "And here we are in the best bar in the world, where you can order beer, wine, alcohol and much, much more!"

Michael: "Uh-huh."

Zalkan glanced back at Michael and found that he was staring upward into the dark abyss.

Zalkan: "Hmm, I see. No matter how long you live here, everyone still finds the night sky the most beautiful thing in this universe."

King Zalkan cleared his throat to get Michael's attention.

Zalkan: "Michael, why don't we go to the bar and order some drinks so we can talk about some things."

I wonder what he wants to talk about. Probably about me and Zoe.

Michael: "Uh, yeah sure."

Michael followed the King inside the bar. The air inside smelled of beer and alcohol. The atmosphere was filled with clinking glasses and loud burps. Many humanoid foxes sat inside talking and laughing with each other. When the king cleared his throat, everyone in the bar fell silent and stared at them. The bartender walked up to the king and bowed to him.

Bartender: "Your Highness, your private bar room is prepared and waiting for you."

Zalkan nodded and thanked the bartender. The king beckoned Michael with his paw to follow him. They walked up to a wooden door guarded by a knight.

Knight: "Your Highness!"

The knight bowed to the king before opening the door and letting the king in. Suddenly, Michael felt a burning pain on his nose as he also tried to enter the room. The knight held his sword, sheathed in green flames, out to him. The tip of the sword touched Michael's nose.

Zalkan: "Leave him be. He is my guest."

The knight nodded and lowered his sword to give Michael a passage.

Knight: "I beg your pardon, your highness!"

Michael touched the tip of his nose and felt something wet. His nose clearly had a small cut and was bleeding slightly.

Tin-shelled prick...

Michael entered the room and slammed the door behind him. He discovered a table with two chairs in the middle of the room. Two bottles filled with an unknown green liquid stood on the nobly dressed table, fresh and cold, ready to be drunk. The king already sat down on his chair and waited for Michael to do the same.

Zalkan: "Why don't you take a seat, Michael?"

Michael agreed and sat down across from him.

Zalkan: "I hope you don't mind taking a few sips of Xenonan's best beer while we talk."

Michael knew he wasn't allowed to drink beer because he wasn't allowed to consume alcohol until he was twenty-one. He had drunk beer a few times behind his parents' backs to conquer his inner demons. Once he even poured beer into an empty apple spritzer bottle and took it to school. What a little criminal bastard Michael is.

Yeah, fuck the law!

Michael: "No, I really don't mind."

Zalkan: "Great!"

They both reached for their bottles and held them in the air.

Zalkan: "Cheers."

Michael: "Cheers."

Both bottles clinked together once before they started sipping them.

Zalkan: "Zoe told me a little bit about you. But I have a feeling there's a lot more to you, and I hope you don't mind if I ask you a few personal questions."

Michael: "Well, not really. It depends on the question."

Zalkan: "All right. I'd like to know a little more about you and the world you come from."

Michael: "Uh-huh."

Zalkan: "So Michael, what species are you actually from? My people and I have never seen anything like you in our lives."

Michael: "I am a human. A dominant species living on planet Earth. Actually, we humans are not that different from your people. The only difference is that your people have superpowers and have an animal appearance. In my world, we would call you an anthropomorphic fox, a human version of a fox or something like that."

Zalkan: "Interesting... And what exactly is your homeworld like?"

Michael: "Not so great."

Zalkan leaned forward and raised an eyebrow. He silently looked Michael in the eye and waited for him to continue.

Michael: "I hated it there. Every day was the same for me. Waking up, depressing thoughts, going to school, teachers yelling and screaming at me, being mocked by others, coming home, locking myself in my room, suicidal thoughts, mental breakdowns, repetition."

Zalkan: "I'm really sorry to hear that, Michael."

A small smile spread across Michael's face.

Michael: "Don't be sorry. Besides, I'm happy now, happy that I managed to escape my old life."

Zalkan: "I see... Was it bad all along or...?"

Michael: "No... When I was younger, things were much better. I enjoyed my life and was happy with it. I wish I could go back there."

Zalkan: "And how exactly did it get out of hand?"

Michael held his head with both arms as he stared at the table. His eyes widened and he got goosebumps. A horrible flashback played in his head like an uninterrupted recording.

Zalkan: "Michael? Are you still here? Are you okay?"

Zalkan waved his paw in front of Michael's face to bring him back to reality. Michael snapped out of his thoughts and looked around disdainfully. Sweat trickled down his face and dripped from his chin. His beer bottle had been accidentally knocked over, creating a puddle on the table and floor.

Michael: "Yeah, I don't think I'm ready to tell anyone the reason yet."

Zalkan: "I see... Maybe some other time."

Zalkan knew exactly what was bothering Michael, seeing Michael's flashback in his mind, yet he decided to keep it quiet and sighed sadly. Michael looked at the mess he had made and reached for a tissue.

Michael: "I'm sorry about the beer. I'll clean it up in a minute!"

Zalkan: "Don't worry about it. My personal servant should come as soon as we leave my private bar room and w ll clean up this mess. I wanted to give you something before we leave."

Michael: "Really? What is it?"

Zalkan: "Open your- uh... your..."

The confused king stared at Michael's hands. He had only seen paws and claws before, but Michael's were somehow different.

Michael: "My hand?"

Michael extended his hand to Zalkan, who chuckled.

Zalkan: "Yeah, hand, right."

A strange energy surrounded Michael's hand as the king touched it, giving him a hard, cold, round object. After the king took his paw away, Michael looked closer and discovered a small, red glowing, transparent pearl in his hand.

Zalkan: "It was once owned by the Red Claw tribe. A few hundred years ago, our kind took it from them. It was passed from family member to family member until it came to me. I want to give it to you."

Michael: "Me? I... uh..."

Zalkan: "It's a really long story that involves many wars. A story that will take too long to tell."

Michael: "Why are you giving me this? What is this anyway?"

Zalkan: "It's the eye of Kaltraff! Everyone who possesses it will receive a different kind of hidden power. You have to seek it out for yourself, as it can be triggered by any situation."

Woah, it looks so stunning. It looks like there's a whole other universe in it.

Zalkan: "I want you to protect my precious little daughter at all costs. From the redclaws, from people like Zak, and from anything else that could be dangerous to her. I can't risk losing her again. That's why I chose you, Michael. You're the only one who managed to win her feelings, you saved her life and made her happy."

Michael's cheeks turned a little red as he imagined Zoe's happy smiling face.

Zalkan: "Can I trust you, Michael?"

Michael clasped his hand with the red pearl in it. His grip tightened as he looked at the king with a serious expression.

Michael: "Your Highness, I swear on my life that I will protect her from anything that might be a threat to her. Not a single hair shall she ever lose again."

King Zalkan smiled pricelessly when he heard this.

Zalkan: "I'm glad to hear that, my boy! Welcome to the Xenonan royal family!"

Michael: "Wait, am I really welcome to your family!? Just like that!? Does that mean I get to live in a castle!?"

Zalkan: "Absolutely! Ah! I almost forgot something."

King Zalkan grabbed Michael's backpack from under the table and placed it on the tabletop, causing a loud bang as it was almost packed full.

Michael: "My belongings!"

Zalkan: "Hm mh, I also took a peek and looked at some things a little closer as curiosity got the better of me, I apologize."

Michael: "No problem! As long as everything is still in order, that's perfectly fine."

Zalkan: "I also found some things that I found very interesting and have never seen before in my life, for example this hard and cold barrel-shaped thing. What is it?"

King held this strange object up in the air.

Michael: "This is a flashlight."

Zalkan: "What purpose does it serve?"

Michael: "When you press the button on the back, it lights up brightly so you can see better in the dark."

Zalkan: "What button? I can't find one, but-"

After a click was heard, a bright light shone directly on Zalkan's face, blinding him completely.

Zalkan: "MY EYES!!!"

Michael: "That's a powerful flashlight! Don't shine it on your eyes! Turn it off!"

Suddenly the door flew open and the knight ran in, his sword ready to slash the threat.

Knight: "Your Highness, what's the prob- WOAH!!!"

The knight stepped into the puddle of beer and slipped. Since his armor weighs more than a ton, he couldn't keep his balance and crashed into the table, breaking it completely. His metal armor made a loud noise as it hit the table and the floor, startling the bar user.

Bartender: "What's going on in there!?"

When the bartender entered the room, he was shocked at the sight that confronted him. A broken table, spilled beer, and many small, sharp pieces of glass lay on the floor.

Bartender: "Oi oi oi!!! Look at the fucking mess you made Gabriel!!! You're not even capable of protecting your own king!!!"

Knight: "It wasn't my fault, I swear! I heard our king screaming in there and I was worried!"

Bartender: "Get out!!! Out of my bar!!!"

The bartender dragged the still prone knight out of the room while Zalkan and Michael chuckled. After their laughter died away, King Zalkan looked up at Michael and rose from his chair.

Zalkan: "Well Michael, I think it is time to show you my castle, since you will be getting a room there."

I can't believe it! I'm going to be able to live in a real castle!

Zalkan was waiting at the door for Michael, who was strapping his backpack to his back. After the two left the king's private bar room, they noticed that all the other guests had already left for the upcoming celebration. The bartender was busily cleaning glasses after the events with the knight that had taken place a few minutes ago. As they approached the door to leave the bar, Michael stopped for a moment and looked at the bartender. Behind the bartender were many shelves with all kinds of drinks. A plan was forming in Michael's mind. Zalkan noticed that Michael was no longer following him and turned to him.

Zalkan: "What's the matter, boy?"

Michael: "I... uh, I think I'll stay here for a bit. Maybe I'll have a drink or two."

The King gave him a cold look for a few seconds, but then left the bar after shrugging and nodding in agreement. Michael cleared his throat to get the bartender's attention. The bartender stopped cleaning the glasses and looked up. When he met Michael's gaze, the bartender's eyes widened in astonishment.

Bartender: "Oi, you must be the young man everyone's talking about so much! Sorry about that thing with Gabriel earlier."

Michael: "No need to apologize, and yes, I'm brand new here."

Bartender: "Well, since you're still here, I assume you'd like to order something."

Michael: "Uh, yes. I'd like to order three bottles of your strongest vodka."

The bartender grabbed three bottles of vodka and placed them on the table in front of Michael.

Bartender: "All right, newbie! That'll be fifteen xeno coins."

What the fuck are xeno coins???

Michael searched his pockets for similar items, but found only a paper clip and the crumbs of a cookie.

Michael: "Uh, sir, is there any way to pay you back anything else? I don't even know what a xeno coin is, nor do I have any."

A concentrated expression appeared on the bartender's face as he thoughtfully rubbed his paw over his muzzle.

Bartender: "Hmmmm..."

Michael: "I'll even give you something from my world, something that doesn't exist in yours."

Bartender's ears pricked up with interest.

Bartender: "Really!? What have you got there?"

Michael pulled his flashlight out of his backpack.

Bartender: "What's that?"

Michael: "This is a flashlight. You can use it to light up the dark."

Bartender: "Ooo, deal!"

The bartender grabbed the now his flashlight from Michael and Michael packed the three vodka bottles into his backpack. Now you might wonder why a seventeen year old boy would buy vodka. Not to drink it, of course. Michael had a far greater use for it.

Michael: "All right, thanks. I have to go now."

Bartender: "W-wait! How does this flashlight thing work?"

Michael headed for the door to leave the bar.

Michael: "Push the button, duh."

Bartender: "What button!?"

Michael left the bar and chose a random direction to walk through the village. As he walked away, he heard the bartender screaming in agony in the distance. The bartender blinded himself when he finally found the button.

Bartender: "BRIGHT!!! MY EYES!!!"

Chapter 12

Hm, strange. The whole village seems to be empty. Not even a single soul is outside. Maybe everyone is asleep, it is the middle of the night after all.

Michael roamed through the silent village looking for the one person he cared about, the white-furred vixen named Zoe.

I wonder what she was up to.

As he walked through the empty paths, Michael had an uncomfortable feeling, a feeling of being watched. He stopped in the middle of the path and turned in all directions to find whoever was spying on him, but couldn't spot anyone.

Hm...

An idea formed in his mind and he took out a red glowing transparent pearl from his pocket, the eye of Kaltraff that the king had given him in the bar two hours ago.

The eye of Kaltraff, eh?

He looked through the pearl and was surprised. Not only was the whole sight completely red and upside down, but this strange object also functioned as a small night vision device. Michael could see what was lurking in every dark corner of the village.

Now, where are you, you spying cunt!?

He held the pearl in front of his right eye and closed the left to get an even better look. He whirled around, looking for whoever was responsible for this uneasy feeling, like a pirate with his binoculars looking for an incoming enemy ship or island. But Michael still could not make out anyone.

Nothing suspicious...

He put the pearl back in his pocket and wandered on to find Zoe. The sound of his boots hitting the gravel was the only thing he could hear. There was no howling wind, no rustling, and no chirping crickets. Michael was confused because the village was in the middle of an endless forest, and yet it was quiet, too quiet.

The feeling of being watched and followed was much stronger now, as if something was behind him. Michael stopped, but the sounds of footsteps did not stop. Someone was definitely behind him. He felt a warm breath on his neck and the frightened boy got goosebumps all over his body.

Michael: "Oooouuuuuuhhhhh HYAA!!!"

Michael spun on his left foot while the other swept high through the air, ready to hit the pursuer behind him in the head, but his right foot hit no target. There was nothing but the cold night air.

FUCK!!!

Michael lost his balance and his back was about to hit the sharp gravel below him. He closed his eyes and clenched his teeth to ward off the oncoming pain. But instead of pain, he felt two warm, fluffy arms wrap around him and hold him in place to prevent him from hitting the deadly ground. The next thing he felt was his body pressed against someone else's. It felt fluffy, soft and warm like the summer weather.

Michael: "What the..."

Zoe: "Shh, it's just me."

Michael opened his eyes and saw only her emerald green eyes. They sparkled and Michael could see his shocked face in her reflection. He sighed in relief and hugged her back.

Michael: "Man, you scared the shit out of me, Zoe!"

When Zoe heard that, she couldn't help but g ggle. Her little prank had worked pricelessly!

Michael: "For a moment I thought a bounty hunter was after me! I felt like I was being watched and followed, but-"

Zoe: "Shh!"

The snow-white vixen held her paw over his mouth to silence his ramblings.

Zoe: "There's a big festival going on over there and everyone's here. I've been looking all over the village for you so we can go over there.... And, you know, maybe do a little dancing together and get something to eat."

Michael was never the type to go to big events to party. He hated being surrounded by crowded people and loud noise. If Michael was at a disco party, he wouldn't dance, drink, or socialize like most people did. Instead, he would isolated himself from the others by sitting in a corner and watching them have a good time. He was a shy introvert, and a big one at that.

Still, Michael didn't want to turn the happiest smile he'd ever seen from Zoe upside down, and simply agreed with her while using his special skill he'd always used to fool his parents on his homeworld: faking a smile.

Zoe knew exactly what was bothering him. Not only is she able to read and hear minds, but she can feel what others are feeling.

Her smile faded for a few seconds as she thought of something. Her delighted smile returned as she had an even better idea.

Zoe: "Forget about the party. I have an even better idea!"

Michael: "Huh? What is it?"

Zoe grabbed him by the hand and pulled him all the way out of the village and into the woods.

Michael: "Hey, hold still for a minute! Where are we going?"

Zoe: "There is a special place not far from this village that I want to show you. When I was a kid, I used to love spending time there."

Michael: "What is that place?"

Zoe: "It's a big surprise for you!"

(Time skip)

Zoe and Michi were walking through the dark forest. Zoe had no real problem seeing in the dark, but for Michael it was pitch black except for the night sky. Michael thought it was a good idea to trust Zoe, following her every move while holding her paw. He traded his flashlight for a couple of vodka bottles, and he didn't want to waste his smartphone battery on lighting his way for a few feet. On the other hand, he could use the eye of Kaltraff, but that would look pretty stupid in his opinion. He didn't want Zoe to make fun of him any more, because her teasing was already enough.

Zoe: "Careful, darling."

Michael: "What should I be careful of?"

Suddenly, a few leaves slapped his face and scratched his cheeks.

Michael: "Ouch…"

But wait, that wasn't all. Zoe dragged him through a thorny bush and down a rocky path.

Michael: "Ow! Ah! Ouch! What the fuck, Zoe!!?"

One of his feet got stuck between two rocks and he lost his balance by flying right onto Zoe's back. Fortunately, she managed to keep her balance as Michael lunged for her back, digging his fingers into her soft fur to keep him up.

Zoe: "Oh dear, Michi. If you really wanted to do it here and now, why didn't you say so?"

Michael: "Shut it hairball!"

Zoe: "Aw, are you mad at me?"

She turned around and licked his face to heal any wounds.

Michael: "Ugh, your breath stinks!"

Then Michael felt it again. That strange feeling of being watched. He felt very uncomfortable and worried.

Michael: "Zoe, shouldn't we go back? We've been walking for over twenty minutes and I can't see shit! What if there's an entire redclaw army watching us, waiting for us to walk right into their booty trap?"

Her green eyes glowed in the darkness as she looked deep into his eyes.

Zoe: "Don't worry about that. They don't even know this place exists. Besides, my telepathy doesn't pick up any one around us. I want to show you my favorite place in this forest. We're almost there."

Michael: "Why do we have to do this right now? Wouldn't it be safer if we did this in the morning at daytime?"

Zoe: "Trust me, Michi. This place only has its appeal at night. It will be worth it."

Michael sighed softly.

Michael: "Alright, you've convinced me."

They both continued walking through the night forest. Crickets chirped and the leaves of the trees rustled in the soothing wind. It was a relaxing and peaceful atmosphere until a low growl gave Zoe a good scare. She stopped halfway and whimpered in fear.

Zoe: "Michi, what was t-that?!"

Michael couldn't hold it in anymore and smiled. His smile turned into a giggle, and his giggle turned into a laugh. He sank to his knees and laughed his tears away as he pounded his fist on the ground.

Zoe: "What are you laughing at!? You made that noise, didn't you!?"

Michael: "You're damn right I did! I was farting! I never thought that would scare you to death!"

Michael laughed even harder and louder.

Zoe: "Shut up now! That was beyond disgusting! Didn't your parents teach you how to act around a girl!"

Michael: "Oh man, I bet it reached the village!"

Zoe: "Ugh, boys..."

After walking for another five minutes, the two finally arrived at the spot Zoe had been talking about. It was one of the most beautiful things Michael had seen in his life. In the middle of the forest, there was a small field with lots of fireflies flying around, but instead of glowing yellow and green, they glowed bright blue and purple.

Zoe: "Beautiful, isn't it?"

Whoa...

Michael grinned and pulled out his smartphone. He took a few photos of the amazing scene that was before him. Normally, he wouldn't do something like this because it bored him to death.

Most of the pictures and videos he saved on his smartphone were either school fights or road rages.

This picture definitely looks qualified enough to become my new wallpaper!

Zoe: "What are you doing, Michi?"

She giggled as she looked at Michael doing strange poses with his weird little device. She had no idea what the boy was doing, but she thought it was funny.

Michael: "I'm taking pictures!"

Zoe: "Pictures? How does that work?"

Michael smiled even more.

Michael: "Here, let me show you!"

He handed her his smartphone, the screen showed one of the pictures he had recently taken. Zoe's eyes widened in amazement and wonder.

Zoe: "B-but how? What a strange function this thing has. I've never seen anything like it!"

Michael: "Yeah, it has a lot of neat features. You can even record videos!"

Michael carefully took the smartphone from her paw and tapped the screen once. He held it in front of his face, the camera pointed at his face as he began talking to the device.

Michael: "Hello you! It's Michael here, and today I thought it wouldn't be a bad idea if I took a nice little recording of showing you a little bit of the most beautiful place in all of existence that I stumbled upon today!"

Zoe stood quietly, watching Michael curiously as she tried to stifle her laughter. Her tail swished with excitement. Michael switched camera mode, showing every little detail of this place as he told random things.

Michael: "And holy shit! Look at that view! Outstanding! But nothing beats the beauty of a certain beautiful vixen I'm about to show you now!"

Michael pointed his cell phone at Zoe.

Michael: "Her name is Zoe. She's a human-like vixen from another world and one of the best friends you could ask for! The best cure for a miserable life! She means more to me than anything. I love her more than anything. And end of video."

Zoe: "Aww, how sweet of you!"

Zoe pushed Michael to the ground and pounced on him, kissing and licking his face several times. Her soft and warm fur brushed over his skin. Michael was redder than a tomato at this point.

Michael: "Now come on, Zoe! My whole face is covered in your spit now!"

Zoe giggled and got off of Michael. She sat down next to him and leaned her head against his shoulder.

Zoe: "So, can you show me the video?"

Michael: "Yes."

Zoe was surprised to see herself in the video Michael had taken. In her world, there were no mirrors and she could only see herself unclearly on the reflection of the water. But on the video, it was very different. She could see herself very clearly because the video had a high resolution.

Zoe: "Woah! I don't even know how to react to that! This is actually the first time I've seen myself in detail! It's so clear..."

Michael: "Yeah..."

They both sat there staring up at the beautiful night sky. Zoe rested her head on his shoulder, her arms and tail wrapped around him for warmth and comfort. A nice cold breeze passed them by, swirling Zoe's fur and Michael's hair.

Zoe: "Michael?"

Michael: "Yes?"

She nervously rubbed her paws together and looked at the ground.

Zoe: "C-could we maybe take a picture of the two of us?"

Michael smiled.

Michael: "Of course! Why didn't I think of that before?"

He held his smartphone in front of Zoe and himself and activated the camera.

Michael: "Ready?"

Zoe: "Wait!"

Zoe moved much closer to him and hugged him tightly, making him blush.

Zoe: "Now I'm ready!"

Michael: "Alright."

Michael hugged her with his free hand and they both stared at the front camera of the smartphone, smiling happily. Michael tapped the screen a few times and took a few pictures.

Michael: "And... Done!"

Michael pulled up the photo app where all his pictures were stored and selected the recent picture he had taken.

Zoe: "Oh, just look at the two of us! So cute!"

Yes... That's going to be a great memory. From now on, this picture will always remind me of that special night.

Zoe: "You have no idea how lucky I am to have someone like you by my side. You are just full of suprises!"

She gently grabbed his face with both paws and forced him to turn towards her.

Michael: "I'm happy aswell.... I came here hoping to find a true friend and a point to continue my life. Now I have got a sweet girlfriend, the love of my life. That's a bonus!"

A small tear ran down her fur covered cheek.

Zoe: "Oh Michi!"

She closed her eyes as the wall could no longer hold the flow of her tears and collapsed. Their warm lips met and their tongues fought for dominance. Her wet nose touched his. After a few minutes of constant smooching, they pulled away, leaving a trail of salvia that Michael wiped away. They both lay on their backs and continued to watch the stars.

Michael: "So, how long are we going to stay here?"

Zoe: "I don't know. Maybe all night?"

Michael: "Oh man, I'm so damn tired."

Zoe snuggled up to Michael so he wouldn't freeze out there. Her fur did a good job of that.

Zoe: "Michi?"

Michael: "Huh?"

Zoe: "Have you ever thought about starting a family of your own?"

Michael: "Zoe, I don't like where this is going. Can't we talk about something else?"

Zoe: "Pleaseee."

Michael: "..."

Zoe: "Come on, Michael. Think about our future."

Michael: "Zoe, I really love you, but I'll probably never be ready for a family. I don't even know if it would work out with you. I mean, you're something very different from me."

Zoe: "We may be different on the outside, but on the inside I'm-"

Michael: "Shalalalala!!! I can't hear you and I don't want to!!! Next topic!!!"

Zoe: "Hush! If you yell like that, I'm sure a group of redclaws will find us!"

Suddenly, Michael's eyes glowed red as they saw something sharp flying towards him. His heart began to race at full speed. Without thinking and not knowing what to do, he pushed Zoe off of him and rolled away as if he was being controlled. The sharp object turned out to be a spear that could have pierced his skull if he had not dodged it. His once smiling and happy face was now replaced by a hateful and angry expression.

Zoe: "Ouch! What's wrong with you Michael!!?"

Several green fireballs rushed at Michael from the dark forest, but his red glowing eyes caught them all. Within millie-seconds, he managed to calculate the exact flying path of the fireballs and dodged them with inhuman speed. Zoe remained speechless on the ground, staring at Michael, who had suddenly changed.

His vision turned red as he could see in the darkness like a predator searching for its prey. Michael spotted a figure up a tree with eyes glowing green. Its hand, which looked more like a paw, held a green flame, ready to throw it at Michael. He heard a familiar voice in his head, threatening him.

???: "You will pay for stealing my precious little Zoe! Just you wait!"

Just as he heard these words, the mysterious person vanished into thin air. Sensing no more danger, Michael's eyes became normal and he held his head in pain. He took a deep breath to calm his heart, which was still racing.

Ow, my head... What the hell happened?

Zoe: "Michi, are you okay!"

She stood up and ran towards him, hugging him tightly. Her bright green eyes expressed only fear and worry.

Zoe: "Geez Michi! Your eyes were bloodshot and you dodged those fireballs with incredible speed! Who attacked you anyway!?"

Michael: "I-I don't know what happened! My vision suddenly changed and my eyes showed me how to handle the situation without getting hurt! My body moved on its own, as if I was being controlled..."

A realization flashed through his mind.

It must have something to do with the red pearl Zalkan gave me! It just has to be!

Zoe: "What pearl? What are you thinking about?"

Michael took out the red glowing transparent pearl from his pocket and showed it to Zoe.

Michael: "I'm pretty sure it is its doing. I forgot what the name of it was."

Zoe gasped in surprise.

Zoe: "That's the eye of Kaltraff! That is a very dangerous object and not a toy to play with! How did you even get your hands on it!?"

Michael: "Your father gave it to me to protect you."

Zoe's ears pricked up as she picked up something Michael couldn't.

Michael: "What is it? Did you hear something?"

Zoe: "Redclaws! I heard a roar coming from that direction!"

Michael: "Um, Zoe? We came from there, didn't we?"

Both eyes widened in shock as they realised something.

Zoe: "My home!!!"

Zoe grabbed Michael's hand and they both ran as fast as they could towards the village.

Zoe: "We need to get here as soon as possible!.! My father and brother might still be in there!!!"

Chapter 13

Total madness reigned in the village. The buildings that had been set on fire by the redclaws spread the flames and collapsed. The once fresh air was replaced by thick black smoke and the ground was littered with corpses. The redclaws stormed the buildings, stealing everything their sharp eyes could see, and fighting the villagers in the process.

The poor villagers, mostly mothers with their young children, ran for their lives. The men, determined as best their strength would allow, fought the red-scaled beasts. The burning village glowed in the darkness of the night.

My fucking god!

Michael sat on a branch of the tallest tree he could find, watching the scene with his binoculars from a distance.

Zoe: "Can you see anything from up here!?"

Zoe stood down there next to the tree, waiting for Michael. Ever since she heard the redclaws roaring from a distance, she was getting quite anxious and worried about her home and family.

Michael: "Yes, I think I've seen enough...."

He packed his binoculars back into his backpack and stared at the view below. Zoe was down there looking at him.

Wait a minute, how did I get up there so easily!?

Michael just realized that he was actually afraid of heights. Besides, it was still dark outside.

Bummer.

Zoe: "Stop looking at me so stupidly and come down right now!"

Michael: "Uh... Zoe!?"

Zoe: "What!?"

Michael took a deep breath and swallowed.

Michael: "I'm kind of stuck up there!"

Zoe: "Ah yes, climbing a tall tree without thinking about how to get back down safely, you genius!"

Michael: "Shut it, hairball! It was your idea after all!"

Zoe: "Wait, I have an even greater idea! How about you jump down, barely survive the fall, and I'll heal your crushed knees afterwards!"

Michael: "What!? Oh hell no!!!"

At least the moon showed itself in its full glory, shining down on him and dimly illuminating the branches below. However, the moonlight did not manage to reach the ground. When Michael looked down, he saw only a void of darkness and Zoe's green glowing eyes staring at him back. He would have used the built-in flashlight on his smartphone, but its battery was dead.

Michael: "Alright, I'm coming!"

Step by step, Michael carefully climbed from branch to branch. The further down he got, the harder it became for him to see. On the last branch he could make out, he stopped, seeing no other way to get further down.

Uhh...

Zoe: "What are you waiting for Michael!? You're really close now!"

Michael: "I-I... uh..."

Zoe: "Now jump already!"

Michael crouched down, shaking with fear. Never in his life had he felt so cold. He was scared out of his wits.

Michael: "Whaa!!!"

Zoe grabbed him by the ankle and dragged him down to her.

Zoe: "Come on Michael! We don't have much time!"

She grabbed his hand and ran as fast as she could towards her village. Michael struggled behind her, since he couldn't see anything.

Michael: "Slow down, will ya-"

Michael couldn't see what was in front of him, but he somehow knew that if he didn't duck, he would die. His eyes glowed red and his vision turned so he could see in the darkness. He spotted a thick branch that he was about to run into and dodged it with inhuman speed. After that, his eyes returned to their normal color. All this happened in just a single second.

Michael: "A little warning would have been nice, Zoe!"

Zoe: "Sorry! We're almost there!"

They both kept running through the dark forest until they finally reached the village. It looked much worse. Most of the buildings had already turned into pile of ashes mixed with rubble, while the rest continued to burn. The ground was covered with the bloody corpses of the Redclaws and Xenonians who had fought for their lives. Not a single soul was to be seen, not even a redclaw.

Zoe: "Damn it!!! We're too late!"

The thought that her father and brother were buried under the collapsed buildings broke her. She sank to her knees and sobbed as she could no longer hold back her tears. The sight before her was a true nightmare from which she could not wake up.

Michael: "Come on Zoe! We don't have time for this! Let's just get out of here before-"

Growling noises caught their attention. Michael spotted a group of redclaws staring at them, five in total. Three were pointing their razor-sharp spears at them, and the other two held their clubs tightly in their hands, ready to beat anything to a pulp.

Ohh, shit!

The group of redclaws continued to stare curiously at Michael, for they had never seen a creature like him before, except for one of them. With its sharp yellow eyes, it showed nothing but anger, as if it hated Michael for something very personal. Most of his scales were gone and he had scratches everywhere. When Michael examined this redclaw a little closer, he realized that this was the one that had gotten away from him.

So, we finally meet again, don't we? This time I'm going to make sure I can finish scaling you!

The redclaw roared out all of his rage and was about to charge towards Michael, but he was already prepared. Michael was already holding one of his vodka bottles tightly in his hand. A piece of cloth was wrapped around the top of the bottle, which was already on fire, ready to be thrown.

Michael: "Eat this, you red scaled fuckers!!!"

He threw the burning bottle at the group of the redclaws. They just stood there confused, looking ignorantly at the incoming bomb. The vodka bottle landed right in the middle of the five redclaws and exploded instantly, giving them no time to react. All five were now on fire and roaring in pain and agony.

Michael could only smile at his perfect throw, as if he were the villain in this story. The redclaws fell to the ground after trying for minutes to carry out the fire. Their bodies were now lifeless and continued to burn, the fire having encrusted their scales. Unfortunately, Michael had no marshmallows with him.

Bull's eye!

Unnoticed by them, a humanoid fox in knight's armor poked its head out of a ruined building and spied on Zoe and Michael. His breathing was deep and shaky. He had just witnessed Michael kill five Redclaws with a single bottle.

???: "My God! This must be the hooman Zalkan talked so much about!"

Michael turned to the building where the knight was hiding and saw something moving.

???: "Fuck! He probably saw me!"

Michael: "Hey! Stop hiding and get your ass over here!"

The knight left his hiding place and exposed himself. His armor was covered in dents, scratches, and blood, and his sword was bent. Zoe peeked out from behind Michael's shoulder.

Zoe: "Brother, is that you!?"

With his remaining strength, the knight took one last step before falling to his knees in front of Michael. He groaned in pain and dropped his sword. Zoe walked up to his brother and knelt down.

Zoe: "Connor, are you okay!? What happened!?"

Connor: "Son of a bitch betrayed everyone!!! He managed to escape from prison and freed all the redclaws!!!! You need to get out while you still can and stop him, sister! Forget about me!"

Zoe: "No way! We are not leaving without you!"

Michael: "Stop who?"

Suddenly the ground began to shake as something very heavy took a step. With each step it got louder and worse. The vibration of the floor startled all three of them and Zoe began to whimper in fear.

Connor: "Oh, shit!!!"

What the actual fuck is happening!?

Suddenly, a loud roar was heard! The three of them turned around to face a redclaw three times the size of a normal redclaw!

Connor: "We're all going to die!!! AHHHH!!!"

It pointed his claw at the three of them and roared uncontrollably loud. Without hesitation, Michael took out his second Molotov and lit it.

Michael: "H-hey, you! How about we play a nice game of bottle catch!?"

Michael readied his arm for that one throw and tossed the bottle with the burning cloth on it with all his might at the massive redclaw. It was a perfect throw, and the burning bottle crashed against the giant redclaw's head and exploded. It roared in pain as it tried to put out the fire on his face with his bare claws. After a few tries, it succeeded. Its face didn't even have a single scratch or burn mark. Michael's Molotovs were nothing compared to the triple-sized redclaw.

Holy shit! He's immune to fire!!!

Connor: "Yeah, I think it's best if you run now!"

The big monster took out a huge skull club from his back and slammed it on the ground with all its might, roaring as loud as it could. Michael's head began to hurt. The only thing he could hear now was a ringing sound. He held his nose to keep that horrible stench from entering his nose.

Holy shit! This guy's breath is the most horrible thing a human nose can catch in its entire life. I could actually throw up right now!

Michael: "Uhh, Zoe? Connor? Anyone? I could use some help here!"

Connor: "Nah, fam, you can handle it on your own."

I think I'm totally fucked....

The giant redhead roared loudly again before charging at Michael and swinging its heavy club at him. Michael's eyes glowed ruby red and his vision turned blood red as the scene in front of him slowed down as if a slow motion effect was added. The blood inside him boiled and he felt his adderdraline level rise to its maximum. His eyes were fixed on his enemy, expressing nothing but merciless rage. He had never felt such a strong desire to strangle someone alive with his bare hands. Michael's transformation was now finally complete.

The oversized redclaw smiled as it saw his opponent not move an inch. It let out another loud roar as it swung his club with all its might against Michael, who still stood motionless. A loud woosh was heard as the club was hurled through the air, picking up all the dust from the ground.

Connor: "Get down Zoe!!!"

The dirt flying through the air left Zoe and her brother on the ground. Their vision was now blocked and they were coughing like crazy as the dust entered their lungs. After the dust cleared, the triple-sized redclaw smiled even more as it no longer saw its opponent in front of him, assuming that it had hit Michael and sent him to another planet. The giant redclaw now walked toward Zoe and Connor, who were still on the ground, whimpering in fear.

The huge redclaw chuckled and lunged at the two with its club. But before it could lay a hit on the two, it felt someone poke his leg from behind. The big redclaw grunted in surprise and turned its head. Its eyes widened when it saw Michael standing behind him, still with that damn creepy killer look.

The oversized Redclaw gave the human an angry look before turning and slamming its club down on the ground where Michael was standing. Rocks and dirt flew in all directions. Dust was every-where in the air. Once again, the oversized redhead waited for the dust to clear as it took a deep breath, unaware that Michael was standing right behind him, smiling wickedly.

Michael: "Hey, dumbass! Behind you!"

Hearing the human mocking him, the giant redhead roared loudly in anger, turned around and struck with its club with full force at the dust where the human was standing, but Michael's red glowing eyes and reflexes were much faster now and he managed to catch the club and prevented it from crushing his head. The oversized redhead grunted again in surprise as the human took the club from his grasp and snapped it in two.

Michael: "Your kind is nothing more than a ridiculous excuse for being a sentient life form on this world, and so I will obliterate it, moving on with you!"

Michael's words sounded cold and serious. His sadistic smile widened even more and before the now fearsome redclaw could do anything to him, Michael jumped up, used the sharp edge of the snapped club and stabbed it through one of the eye of the oversized redclaw.

A loud and deafening screech filled the air as the huge monster held its head in pain. After a few seconds, it regained its strength and fought the pain. It grabbed the piece of wood with both of its claws and ripped it out of its eye socket while grunting in pain. In place of its eye was now a black hole from which blood oozed out.

Redclaw: "You will pay for this!"

His voice sounded deep and rough, as if he was possessed by a demon, or maybe he was a demon himself.

Michael: "Hmm, I didn't know your pathetic kind could actually speak!"

The redclaw, three times its size, lunged at the human with fury. Its claw, sharper than any razor blade, swung through the air at Michael several times, but he simply dodged it with inhuman speed before disappearing completely. The red-scaled beast grunted in surprise and shook its head in disbelief.

Meanwhile, Michael hid behind a nearby tree, grinning pricelessly as he reached into his pocket. A weak, metallic slide sounded as he pulled out his pocket knife.

Let's see if this tree is a match for you!

Without a single pause, Michael sliced with his pocket knife against the tree several times with incredible speed.

Michael: "Radadadadadadadada..."

With each strike, splinters of wood flew in all directions and the tree was closer to falling over.

Michael: "YAH!!!"

With one final blow, the tree had no more grip under it and lost its balance. It flew straight into the big, wide-eyed redclaw who just stood there with his maw wide open. The ground shook as the tree crashed into the oversized redclaw. The massive monster roared and shrieked in pain and anger as it lay under the fallen tree, unable to get to his feet because of the heavy load. Michael took out an axe he had gotten from a redclaw he had killed a few days ago and lunged at the helpless red-scaled creature under the tree.

Redclaw: "You won't get away with this! You have no chance of winning against this war! No one can defeat our great leader Bi-"

Before the triple-sized redclaw could finish h s sentence, his head was split in two by the berserk Michael. Blood flowed in streams and the inner parts slid out, hitting the ground with a slapping and gurgling sound. The red-scaled beast now lay dead under the fallen tree, and may it never rise up again.

Michael's eyes twitched as he smiled at his well-deserved victory. He let out a maniacal laugh and looked back at Zoe, who was staring at him with wide teary eyes, and at Conncr, who was now scared shitless of Michael and curled up into a ball, sucking on both of his paws in turns.

Suddenly Michael felt a strong urge to pull out the red pearl hidden in his pocket, the eye of Kaltraff. As he reached for it and took it out, a bright red light blinded him. At that moment Michael had to cover his eyes, because the red transparent pearl was brighter than the sun. His head began to hurt massively and he felt a strange sensation that he had never felt before. It felt like something was taking away his borrowed powers. He closed his eyes and mumbled something in another language that he couldn't even understand himself.

Before Michael lost his will to stay conscious from the pain, it suddenly stopped. He felt a warm paw resting on his right shoulder.

Zoe: "M-Michael? A-are you all right?"

Zoe...

Her voice sounded like she was about to cry. Michael turned to her and opened his eyes, which returned to their normal brown color. He dropped the bloodied axe. For some reason he couldn't talk back to her. He could no longer think clearly. All he could do was stare at her sad face.

Why does she look so sad?

When she didn't get an answer from Michael, Zoe became even more worried. Her breathing was getting shakier and tears were running down her cheeks.

Why is she crying?

Zoe: "Michael? Please answer me, please!"

I'm so tired…

Michael: "Uhh… I…"

Before Michael could say anything, he lost consciousness and fell into her arms. Blackness filled his vision. He could only hear her calling him and sobbing for a few more minutes until it faded away.

Chapter 14

Blackness. An endless emptiness, filled with darkness, surrounded Michael. There was nothing he could do about it. He could not move or see. The only thing he felt was a slight breeze.

Where the hell am I and what happened?

His inner voice echoed through the void, but no one answered him. He was really alone in this dimension, at least that's what he thought.

The only thing I can remember is entering a village with a paranoid Zoe after it was devastated by a war! I can't remember anything that happened after that!

???: "Actually, there are many more things you don't remember, Michael."

A deep female voice spoke back to him.

W-what do you mean? Wait a minute... Who are you and what do you want from me?

???: "Don't be afraid. I'm not here to hurt you, not that I could. You will soon find out what is happening around you."

I'm not dead, am I?

The deep female voice replied with a soft giggle.

???: "No Michael, you are not dead. You are currently in a liminal world between life and death."

WHAT!!!?

???: "But don't worry, you will wake up very soon."

A bright white light appeared in front of Michael. With every second it became bigger and brighter. He could feel the power emanating from it, and he was about to wake up. But before that happened, Michael wanted to know more about this strange voice.

Wait! You still haven't told me who you are!

Zahra: "My name is Zahra. There is no more time to tell you more about me. Farewell."

Suddenly, Michael's eyes opened. The sun slowly rose and tickled Michael's nose. The light fell through the leaves of the trees and the birds began to chirp happily. It was going to be a sunny day.

Zoe: "Good morning!"

Michael: "Wha...?"

Michael turned his head to the side and discovered Zoe's face very close to his. Her moist and warm nose touched his as they stared at each other. Her sparkling emerald eyes put him in a hypnotic state. She clasped his face with both paws and licked it, waking him up from his hypnotic state.

Michael: "Zoe, stop it!"

Her licking turned to kisses as she moved much closer to him. She was on top of him now and had her arms wrapped around him to hold him tight. At this point Michael's face was redder than the color red itself.

Michael: "Okey Zoe, that's enough!"

Zoe: "I was so worried I was going to lose you! But you're still here with me, alive."

Tears leaked from her eyes as she couldn't hold them back. She buried her face in his chest as she sobbed.

Michael: "Come on, Zoe, don't cry. I'm fine, see?"

Zoe: "You weren't then!"

Her crying intensified and Michael was lost in thought. He had never put himself in a situation like this before. He didn't know how to comfort anyone. Michael did what he thought Zoe would do to him if she were to comfort him. He hugged her back and stroked her head.

Michael: "It's all right. Let it all out."

It took a few minutes for Zoe to calm down, and when she finally did, a smile settled on her muzzle as she snuggled against him. Even though Michael's expression showed that he didn't really enjoy this moment, deep down he did.

Connor: "Hey you, you're finally awake."

Michael turned to his right and spotted Zoe's brother Connor leaning against a tree. His knight's armor, covered in dents and scratches, lay beside him. Michael blushed even more as Zoe still cuddled with him.

Michael: "Uh… Hi?"

I remember Zoe calling him her brother back when we both met him in the village. I think his name was Connor.

Connor smiled proudly, showing off his bombastic muscles.

Connor: "That's right, lad! My name is Connor and I am the knight in shining armor! And you must be the hooman everyone's talking about!"

Michael: "Uh, yeah."

Both Zoe and Michael sat up.

Why do I have a feeling this guy is going to be annoying as hell?

Connor: "Man, now that I can examine you a little more closely, I see that you don't have any fur or scales at all. And what happened to your ears? Why are they on the side? And look at your nose! Why do you have two big holes under it? Are you using them to slurp something up? And what are those paws, lad!? They look like ..."

Spit flew from Connor's mouth as he continued to ask a lot of nonsense. His teeth were a mixture of yellow and brown. Most of them were even crooked.

Dude's having British teeth.

Connor: "Man, I'm telling you! You whipped that big guy up in no time like it was a piece of cake! You split that monster's head in bloody half, lad!"

What the fuck is he talking about?

Connor: "Oh! You can't remember? Then let me tell you. You went completely nuts and your eyes were blood red and glowed in the dark like a predator's! I even pissed myself looking at you!"

Michael held his head and tried to concentrate as best he could to remember everything that happened after he turned into a merciless killing machine. Unfortunately, all the memories he had during the fight were gone.

Michael: "I can't remember what happened earlier, no matter how hard I try."

Connor: "Mmm, there has to be an explanation for that at some point."

Zoe: "It just has to do with the eye of Kaltraff! I don't know why my father gave you that dangerous object. Like I said, it's not a toy to play with! There will be a big talk once we find him."

A mixture of shock and horror showed on Connor's face.

Connor: "He has the eye of KALTRAFF!!?"

Michael: "Why are you all going so crazy over this? It saved my ass a couple of times."

Zoe: "Michael, now listen to me. Did my dad ever tell you about the consequences you're going to get if you own this pearl?"

Michael: "No? What consequences?"

Zoe: "Well, the eye of Kaltraff will give you certain powers at certain times. The thing is, it drains life force from you in the process. The more you use its powers, the longer you fall asleep. That's the reason you passed out in the village and can't remember."

Realisation struck Michael's mind.

Michael: "Ohh..."

Zoe: "The reason I was so worried about you was because I was afraid of losing you. To make a long story short: My mother once used the eye of Kaltraff to protect our home from those red-clawed abominations. That was more than ten years ago and she has not woken up to this day. Five years ago we lost hope in her and decided to bury her."

A single tear trickled down Zoe's fur-covered cheek. Connor's expression was not pleasant either and he looked to the ground.

Michael: "I'm really sorry to hear that. I didn't know anything about it."

Zoe: "Don't be. There was nothing you could do about it."

Michael took the red transperent pearl out of his pocket and stared at it. Even if it took his life force to protect Zoe, it would be worth it. Besides, it would be stupid to leave such a powerful item behind.

Michael: "When Zalkan gave me this pearl, he told me that it was once owned by the redclaws. We can't just throw it away. What if they find it? That would make things harder anyway."

Zoe: "But-"

Connor: "He's right. We have to keep it. The reason the redclaws are still on our tail is because we still have their eye of Kaltraff. We can't afford to lose it to them, not again."

Zoe: "So what should we do now?"

Michael: "I think the best thing to do would be to split their leader into atoms, if they even have one, you know? Let's wipe him out."

Connor: "Excellent idea!"

Zoe: "And how are you going to do that? We don't even know where the Redclaw kingdom is."

Michael: "That's up to you guys. I mean, you both live in this world. I came here a couple of days ago."

Connor: "Couple of days!!!? You've only been here in this world for a few days and you and Zoe are already acting like a married couple!?"

Michael's cheeks turned a deep red.

Michael: "Problem? Are you jealous that I took your hot sister away from you?"

Connor: "Well... um, no... I was just..."

Oh my god! I can't believe I said something cringe like this!

Michael turned to Zoe, who was also blushing under her fur and giggling.

Michael: "You know what? Let's change the subject. What are we supposed to do now, guys?"

Conner scratched his ears for a while as he thought about the things that needed to be done.

Connor: "We still need to find my father Zalkan. He disappeared without a trace after the village went down. And then there's that buffoon Zak, who's responsible for this whole fucking mess!"

Michael: "Oh, him? What did that fucker do?"

Connor: "He somehow escaped from prison and freed all the hostages that were redclaws!"

Michael: "Yeah, and Zoe and I were attacked that night by a 'mystery' person sitting in a tree above us firing fireballs at us. I bet that was him too."

Zoe: "To me, he was always kind of suspicious. Like he was working for the Redclaw Kingdom. I also have a feeling that his attack last night wasn't his last. I bet he'll strike again tonight."

Michael: "All right then! Let's find this bastarc and show him what happens when someone messes with us! Maybe he's working for the Redclaw kingdom as some kind of spy and has some clues as to where the Redclaw Kingdom might be."

Connor: "Agreed!"

Zoe: "And how are we supposed to do that? Have you forgotten that our species' powers are immune to each other. Plus, he's one of the strongest in our tribe. We don't stand a chance against him at all!"

Michael smiled as an idea popped into his head.

Michael: "Don't worry, I have a plan for how we're going to do this."

Michael picked up a random stick from the ground and began drawing his plan being in a beta phase, while explaining every little detail to them. First, Michael drew something that looked like a cage surrounded by trees.

Michael: "First, we will find a suitable place to build a trap. The trap should be surrounded by trees to give it cover."

Conner: "You want to trap Zak in a wooden cage that he can burn down? Are you kidding me!?"

Michael: "That's step one of five, so shut up and listen!"

Zoe: "And what's step two?"

Michael continued to draw his plan on the floor, which was a fcx head in a cage emitting sound waves.

Michael: "Zoe, for step two, I need you to be the voice actor. Since Zak is a complete idiot who is completely obsessed with you, I firmly believe that your voice will lead him to the sound source.'

Zoe was now frustrated and angry as she realized what Michael was up to.

Zoe: "Are you telling me that I am the bait in this cage?"

Michael: "Well, yes but actually no."

Zoe: "And what do you mean by that!?"

Her paw was already extended in the air, ready to deliver a painful ass-wooping. When Michael saw her claws, he winced in fear.

Michael: "H-hey c-calm down, all right? By that I meant I'm going to record your voice with my smartphone. Problem solved."

Zoe: "Oh."

Connor: "What is a smartphone?"

Michael: "No time to answer your question. I need to tell you my plan before I forget it myself. Anyway, Zoe's recorded voice will be the bait in the cage. To Zak, it will look like Zoe is trapped in the cage, which he will then rush toward."

Connor and Zoe nodded in agreement.

Michael: "For the third step, I need my survival book, hold on a second."

Michael opened his backpack and searched inside for his survival book.

Michael: "Got it!"

Michael took out his survival book and searched for a specific section of the book.

Oh crap. What page was it again. Ah, here it is the section on traps. Now which trap would be the best? Mm, the happy birthday trap? Nah, too much work. Maybe the snare trap or the deadfall trap. I think I'll go with the deadfall trap.

Michael: "The third step will be the trap itself. We're going to build a deadfall trap on each side of the cage."

Both Connor and Zoe were confused and also interested, not knowing what kind of trap Michael was talking about.

Connor: "Uh, what kind of trap is that?"

Michael showed them both the page and explained it to them.

Michael: "Well, it's a trap that works quite simply, but is also quite hard to build. It consists of a couple of sticks that support a log on one side. When you walk through the trap, you trip over a certain stick, which brings down the other sticks. Since there are no more sticks to support the heavy weight, the log will come crashing down on whoever set it off."

Connor: "Wow..."

Zoe: "Michi, I don't want to judge you, but as stupid as Zak is, I don't think Zak is that stupid. I mean, he'll know those are traps just by looking at them."

Michael: "Don't worry, I've got that covered. Step four will be to make the traps look innocent. We will need to collect tree sap from the trees. With the tree sap we collected, we can glue leaves, flowers, and other plants to our traps. In the end, it will look like it was built by Mother Nature herself."

Connor: "Genius!"

Zoe: "And what will be the final step in your plan?"

Michael drew a bush on the ground next to his drawn trap, from which all three poked their heads out.

Michael: "The final step will either be a win or a fuck-up. We need to hide near the trap where we can safely watch it without getting caught and-"

Connor interrupts Michael.

Connor: "What do you mean by either win or fuck up?"

Michael: "Well, if Zak somehow survives the trap, then we have to take him down before he gets on his feet, which shouldn't be that hard. If Zak has no clues as to where the Redclaw Kingdom might be, then all that work was for nothing. And finally, if Zak somehow finds us before he sets foot in the trap, then we have no choice but to fight him. The best outcome would be that Zak is killed by the trap and we get clues that help us."

Zoe: "That means we can either win, tie, or lose. So the odds of us winning are one in three?"

Connor: "Hmm, I guess so..."

Something's not right here. I feel like I'm forgetting something very important in our plan. Fuck! What was it again!!! Uh, sometimes I hate my Alzheimer's brain for doing things like that!

Have you ever felt like you forgot something very important just a second before you wanted to talk about it? That's the kind of bullshit Michael has to put up with every week and Michael knew that trying to remember as best he could the things he had so suddenly forgotten recently would not help him one bit.

Zoe: "I can sense that something is bothering you, Michi. Is everything okay?"

Zoe's face showed a worried expression.

Michael: "Oh, it doesn't matter. Just a thought that's been going through my head and won't come back on command. I'll remember it soon enough either way."

Zoe: "Well, if you say so."

Michael rose from the floor, stretched his body, and cracked his knuckles.

Michael: "All right, guys! Who's ready to put our plan into action?"

Connor: "Me!"

Zoe: "I'm in!"

Michael held out his hand. Zoe and Connor placed their paws on top afterwards and a friend group was created.

Chapter 15

Michael, Connor and Zoe wandered through the mighty woods looking for the best place to put Michael's plan into action. In this case, building a trap for Zak. Even though the sun was still rising and they had the whole day ahead of them, they still had a lot of work to do and needed to finish before the sun set again.

Connor walked behind Michael and Zoe, whistling the whole time and minding his own business. Michael, on the other hand, was deep in thought. He was afraid that his plan would not work as he had imagined and that all the work would be for nothing. He still had the feeling that he had forgotten something very important.

Connor: "Ay, hooman!"

Michael heard Connor from beside him on the left and turned to him with an annoyed expression on his face.

Michael: "You know my name, use it."

Connor: "Ay, I'm sorry, boy. Michael, right? Anyway, I was wondering why you're here on this strange world and how you managed to get here in the first place. Mind explaining it to me?"

Uh, how many times do I have to tell this damn story!? When will be the end of this!?

Michael: "Sorry, but I don't think I have enough nerves to tell it once again. Why don't you ask Zoe, I told her all about why I'm here."

Much to Michael's annoyance, Zoe explained everything to Connor about his story.

Zoe: "Well, from what I heard from Michi, his world was cruel to him. No one wanted to be friends with him and he was really alone and miserable, and after he had a bad day at school, he-"

Michael: "After I had the worst day at school."

Michael corrected Zoe.

Zoe: "Sorry, after the worst day at school he got fed up and decided it was best for him to-"

Michael: "To bungee jump off a bridge without a rope."

Zoe: "...Yeah.... But before he did that, he found a blue mystery key and it somehow brought him here."

Connor: "With a key to open a door? How did that work?"

Zoe: "He tried to open a locked door with it, and it worked, but instead of his room, there was another world on the other side. I still don't know how something like that works."

Michael: "Neither do I. But I'm glad it worked out that way. I like it here a lot better, and I even have friends, right?"

Connor: "Yeah, you can count on us!"

All three smiled as they walked a few more minutes until they found the perfect place to put Michael's plan into action. It was a small field in the middle of the forest that even had tall grass.

Zoe: "How about this place?"

Michael: "I say it's a jackpot! Even covered with tall grass, which makes it even harder to see the trap. And it's still early in the morning, so we have the whole day ahead of us."

Connor: "Splendid! So, who needs to do what?"

Michael: "Well, a little camp for the three of us would be important. It shouldn't be near the trap, but it should also be somewhere we can keep an eye on it."

Zoe: "I can do that."

Michael: "Good, then we also need someone to gather the resources to build the trap."

Connor: "Will do!"

Michael: "In the meantime, I'll go find some food for us. And when we're all done with our tasks, we'll set the traps and catch that mofo!"

Connor: "Yes! Let's do this!"

Michael opened his backpack and pulled out his survival book.

Michael: "Zoe, you might need this book for building our little camp. It shows you step by step how to build something and tells you everything you need to know about it. But be careful with it. I don't want any pages to get damaged."

Michael handed Zoe the survival book, which she happily accepted.

Zoe: "Thank you."

Michael took out an axe he had gotten a few days ago when he killed a previous redclaw.

Michael: "Oh, and Connor. This axe might be useful for you since you'll be gathering resources."

Connor gripped the axe tightly as he took it from Michael's hands.

Connor: "Alright, I'm going to cut down some trees and gather some logs and sticks. And Michael, since you're going to find some food for us, you have to be very careful. Any fruit that grows on a tree is edible, and also try to find some purple berries. Don't touch the orange ones! They are poisonous!"

Michael: "Got it! And what about meat?"

Connor: "Meat?"

Zoe: "What's meat?"

Don't tell me they're actually vegan!

Michael: "Oh, just forget about it. I'm going to go and look for what I can find."

Zoe grabbed Michael by his shirt and gave him a kiss on the cheek, followed by a big hug.

Zoe: "Please be careful."

Michael: "S-sure."

Zoe grabbed Michael's cheek and playfully pulled on it while speaking in a seductive voice, making Michael very uncomfortable.

Zoe: "And if you come back with lots of food, there's a big reward waiting for you here."

Connor: "Uh, the fuck?"

Uh, well, this is awkward.

Michael: "Okey bye!"

Connor: "And don't you dare take that long! I'm starving already!"

Michael took a random direction and went deeper into the forest. As he did so, he marked every two or three trees with his pocket knife so he could find his way back home safely. He stared up at the sky and spotted some thick gray clouds.

It looks like some shit weather is about to happen. Even though I like the rainy atmosphere, I don't like getting my clothes wet. I also can't believe Connor and Zoe don't know what meat is, haven't they ever tried hunting? Have they only ever eaten fruit and those nasty little creepy crawlies?

Michael walked through the woods for countless minutes without finding anything edible. All he could discover were those poisonous berries Connor had warned him about earlier.

You know what?! I don't give a shit about those fruits! It's time to kill something and do my job! It's already noon and I haven't accomplished anything yet.

Suddenly, Michael heard a rustling sound next to him and looked to his right. He saw a bush moving and heard the rustling again. Slowly and quietly, he drew his bow and crept closer to the bush. On the other side, he spotted a deer eating berries that had not yet noticed the human.

Here we go! Food at last!

Michael slowly aimed his bow at the deer's head and took a deep breath.

All right, here we go.

Suddenly, Michael's nose began to itch badly and he couldn't suppress the urge to sneeze.

Michael: "ACHOOO!!!"

The arrow flew away at high speed, somewhere into nowhere. The birds nearby were scared to death and flew away with loud chirping. The frightened deer, of course, noticed Michael's presence near it and ran away.

Fuck my pollen allergy!

(Time skip)

An exhausted Michael was hiding behind a tree. For twenty minutes he had been running after the deer all the time and now he was hiding from it. Michael peeked out of his hiding place and spotted the deer on the edge of a cliff, where it was unsuspectingly eating berries from a bush.

Now there is no way to run away from me. Oh no, you won't, bitch.

He aimed his bow at the deer's head and shot his arrow without hesitation. The arrow flew over the deer's head at high speed, as the deer decided to sniff the ground a bit.

What the...?

Now Michael has a problem, a big problem. The arrow he had used was his last. The only weapon he had now was his pocket knife. It was going to be very difficult to kill the deer now. He looked around and spotted a rock on the ground. He had an idea, but it wasn't going to be easy. He aimed at the deer's head and threw the stone with all his might. Of course, he missed and the deer continued to eat the berries unnoticed.

Shit!!! Okey, calm down Michael. You still have your pocket knife. The deer is cornered and has no way to escape. Just get the hell out of your hiding spot and stab it in the head!

Michael took out his pocket knife and rushed at the deer as fast as he could. The deer stopped eating and just stared at the attacking human.

Michael: "RAAARGH!!!"

Michael tried to attack the deer, but it dodged him and fled away through Michael's legs. Michael's eyes were wide open as he realised he lost his balance. He rolled all the way down the cliff, hitting bushes and rocks on the way.

Michael: "Oh Noo!!! Ouch!!! Fuck!!! Shit!!! God damn!!! My ass!!! Ouch!!! Ouch!!! Augh!!! Uhh..."

Michael opened his eyes, only to close them immediately as the bright sun shone down on him, blinding him.

Damn sun! Oh man, I can't believe I survived that!

Michael stood up, his ribs hurting like hell and his back cracking.

Ouch! Shit, I think I broke some ribs!

He examined himself some more and found bloody wounds and scratches everywhere.

I need to find my way back right now. Connor and Zoe are able to make me whole again.

Michael looked up at the cliff he had fallen down.

That's pretty far up. How did I even survive that? And why is there a dead deer on the ground? Wait, did I land on it? Did it save my landing? No wonder I'm still alive. What a coincidence! Well, mission accomplished. Now I have to find my way back, great.

Meanwhile, Connor began chopping down a tree. The weather was hot and after a few swings he was exhausted.

Connor: "TIMBER!!!"

He yelled as the tree threatened to fall. With a loud cracking sound, the tree landed on the ground.

Connor: "Ughf, this is hard! Man, it's so freaking hot out here!"

Zoe: "Yeah, I know. Just take a break and relax. You've already done enough and we still have half a day."

Connor: "I'm so hungry. Where is the hooman with our food! Shouldn't he be back?"

Zoe: "I don't know?"

Shock is written all over Zoe's face.

Zoe: "Maybe he got lost or the redclaws ambushed him?!"

Connor: "Oh please, Zoe. Didn't you see how that boy treated the big one? He's probably still looking for food, or he got lost."

Zoe: "I hope he's okay..."

By the time Zoe and Connor were done with their tasks, it was evening and there were only a few hours left before the sun set completely. The two even managed to build the trap completely. The two anthropomorphic foxes sat by a fire pit they had built themselves and waited patiently for Michael to return to them.

Connor: "We even managed to build the whole trap without him and he's still not there. The lazy bastard is probably playing hide and seek with us."

Zoe nodded in agreement, her face wearing a tired expression. She was pretty exhausted from all the work she had done today.

Zoe: "Mhm..."

Connor: "So, have you two already...? You know?"

When Zoe heard that, her ears perked up and she blushed madly. Connor could only smile at her reaction.

Zoe: "What?! N-no!"

Connor: "But you want it, don't you?"

Connor smiled even more.

Zoe: "J-just shut up!"

Connor: "You know, I would be glad to be uncle Connor."

Zoe's anger grew as she summoned a green ball of flame on her paw and threw it at Connor's head. The green fire disappeared after it touched Connor's fur. He just chuckled at the effects of the fire on his fur.

Connor: "Heheh. That tickled!"

Zoe: "Shut up, will you?"

Meanwhile, it took Michael an hour to find a way back upwards, and another hour to get to Connor and Zoe while dragging the heavy deer behind him. He looked really tired. He had wounds and scratches all over him. Some of his clothes were torn and had holes in them. He looked like a hobo or a dead man who had been woken up. Zoe noticed Michael and was scared out of her wits.

Zoe: "Michi!? Oh my! W-what happened to you!!! You look aw-ful!"

Connor: "There you are! Where have you been for so long!!! Holy shit! What happened to you and why are you dragging around a dead deer!!!? Did you kill it?!"

Michael: "Y-yes..."

Connor: "Why would you kill a deer!!!"

Michael: "F-foodd..."

Connor: "You call that food?! Where are my ordered berries with extra-"

Zoe: "Now is not the time! We need to get him fixed up right away. He's lost a lot of blood."

Michael: "Y-yes..."

Michael was about to collapse on the floor, but Zoe was quick enough and caught him. Michael was tired as hell and needed his rest. Running after a deer and almost dying by rolling down an entire cliff had taken a lot out of him. Zoe's paw began to glow slightly yellow as she healed all of his injuries. After she was done, Michael felt more energized and better.

Michael: "Thank you so much, Zoe."

Zoe smiled.

Zoe: "No problem."

Connor: "What took you so long? Did you run into some red scaled abominations?"

Michael: "No, I had a really crazy trip. I was looking for food and of course found nothing until I spotted a deer that I had a hard time tracking down! The damn animal made me trip and roll down a whole cliff!"

Connor: "Heheh."

Connor started giggling at Michael's story. Michael continued telling his adventurous story after Connor's laughter died down.

Michael: "Well, I fell down and landed on another deer. It broke my fall and was dead on the spot and I luckily survived."

Connor: "No way!"

Now Connor was wheezing. Tears were running from his eyes due to the constant laughter. This annoyed Michael quite a bit. Something snapped in his head and his anger came up.

Michael: "Yeah, yeah, keep laughing and I'll throw you off that damn cliff and there won't be a deer down there to save you! I almost died if it wasn't for the deer!"

Connor: "Okey okey, I'll get it together."

Michael: "And in the meantime, what were you guys doing while I was rolling through the woods?"

Zoe: "Our secret camp for sleeping and spying out the trap is ready."

Connor: "I gathered all the materials we needed and even managed to finish building the trap, which was actually your job. Me and Zoe did most of the work while you patrolled the woods playing cat and mouse with a deer that tricked you into falling down an entire cliff!"

Michael: "Oh yeah!? Maybe you should have gone looking for food because you've been living in this cursed forest since you crawled out of your mom's cave! How about that!?"

Connor: "Don't you dare mention her!!!"

Michael: "Then don't blame me for taking forever to find food!!!! At least I found something to eat!"

Connor: "A deer!? You want us to eat a freaking deer!!!? I don't know much about your skin-dwelling kind, but if that's your average meal, then-"

Michael: "Shut up!!! Of course we're not just going to eat it like this! First we have to skin it and take out its organs before we throw it on the fire!"

Zoe: "I think I'm about to puke."

Michael: "Yeah, I'm about to puke too, knowing your kind eats fruit that tastes like oil mixed with piss. You know what, fuck both of you! You can either look for food for yourselves or starve to death! I'm outta here!"

Zoe's ears and tail lowered as she heard Michael's choice of words directed at her and her brother.

Zoe: "W-wait! Where are you going?"

Michael ignored her and angrily stomped away from the two of them, dragging the deer all the way behind him. He decided to find a place where he could prepare his well-deserved meal. After all, he was starving himself.

How dare they insult mankind's taste in food! I will show them what real food is! It's time to build a big fire and put my Gordon Ramsay skills to work. I'm going to prove them wrong and show them how delicious God's works can be!

And with that, Michael went off to find the perfect spot for a fire pit, the deer sliding behind him as he dragged it.

Chapter 16

The fire crackled and spat sparks of fire without ceasing. The many pieces of meat hanging above it on a homemade drying rack sizzled as the fire cooked them. They looked juicy and crispy brown, in other words, well cooked. While the fire was doing its work, Michael decided to make some more useful things that he needed to survive in the wilderness, such as a small pouch made from the deer skin that he had obtained after skinning the deer.

It will be useful to store small things, for example berries. He also made a few more arrows, ten in total. It wasn't really much, but it was better than nothing. Michael didn't want to hunt another deer without having any arrows left. He learned pretty quickly from his last mistake.

Michael just sat in front of a tree, leaning against it, watching the fire roast the meat. He was listening to music, but without his smartphone. Now you may be wondering how such a thing is even possible. Well, Michael listened to his playlist a dozen times, which caused his mind to play it back in his head. It was like a recorder. His musical paradise had to be interrupted, however, when he felt someone grab him by the shoulder. He jumped at the sudden touch and turned around, where he spotted Zoe.

Michael: "My God, Zoe! Don't scare me like that!"

Zoe laughed at his jump, finding it funny and cute how he reacted to such things.

Zoe: "Sorry about that. I was just looking for you. I also wanted to apologize to you because my brother and I made fun of your food."

Michael: "Don't worry about it. You're already forgiven. Besides, I wasn't that nice either. I'm also sorry for making fun of your food and for cussing. Sometimes we have to remind ourselves in our minds that we are still a different species, from a different world and home."

Zoe sat down next to him and stroked him with her muzzle, her warm and soft fur brushing him. Michael blushed at her way of caring for him. It made his blood boil and his heart race. It was still a strange feeling for him, but he clearly enjoyed it. When Zoe was by his side, all his problems, fears and worries instantly disappeared. Her beautiful emerald green eyes, sparkling with excitement and love, looked into his brown ones. She took his hand and their fingers overlapped.

Connor: "Am I interrupting something?"

Hearing Connor next to them, both Michael and Zoe jumped up and immediately separated from each other.

Michael: "My God! What is wrong with you guys scaring the shit out of me!? First Zoe and now you too!?"

Zoe: "Connor, why do you always have to ruin the moment for us!? At least show us some privacy!"

Connor: "Well, let's just say I detected an unknown delicious smell in the air that led me right here."

Connor and Zoe looked to the fire and spotted the meat hanging and sizzling over the fire. They had never seen food like this before, but it smelled damn tasty. They sniffed the air again and their mouths began to water.

Zoe: "What are you cooking? My sensitive nose has never been so pleased?"

Connor: "FOOD!!!"

Michael: "You guessed it. I got it from the deer after I ripped its fur off."

Connor and Zoe looked past Michael and saw a bloodied deer lying on the ground with its fur completely torn off and its belly wide open with some bones sticking out. Some of its limbs were even missing. They turned to Michael and looked at his hands, which were covered in blood. A brief red gleam appeared in his eyes and he smiled wickedly. For a second he looked evil, which scared the hell out of Connor and Zoe.

Zoe: "M-Michael? Y-your hands..."

Michael took one look at his hands and just shrugged.

Michael: "Yeah, don't worry about them. It's not my blood."

The sound of a microwave oven finishing its work sounded in Michael's head to let him know that the food was ready to be eaten. Michael also had the ability to judge time very well. On his homeworld, he had never used the alarm function on his smartphone. After waking up on command, he simply estimated the time, only to be correct after glancing at his smartphone.

Michael: "So, who's ready for some real food?"

Their stomachs growled hungrily at each other

Zoe: "Me!"

Connor: "Well, it smells pretty good, so I'm in. I guess it can't taste that bad."

(Time skip.)

Connor: "Ohhh maaaaan..."

Zoe: "So... full... My stomach... It hurts..."

The two of them lay down on the floor with their stomachs facing up towards the sky. Never in their lives had Zoe and Connor eaten anything so hearty. After Michael was also finished with his well-deserved meal, he began to gather his things and put out the campfire. It would be best to do so, as he didn't want any redlaws or a certain bastard named Zak to find proof that they were here. Michael looked up at the yellow-orange sky. The sun was about to set, and they still had about an hour before it would get dark.

Oh no!

Michael: "Uh, guys? We need to head back now. Our plan isn't done yet, and I still need to record your voice, Zoe, for the decoy."

Zoe: "Alright, can you record my voice now?"

Michael: "Sure."

Michael took his smartphone out of his pocket and examined it a bit. There were several scratches and cracks on the screen, probably from having rolled down an entire cliff earlier.

Oh, now I know why all my classmates have smartphones with cracked screens. Rolling down a flight of stairs after being full on crack. I'm a little glad I was considered an outsider.

He chuckled and pressed the side button to turn it on, only to be greeted back by a black screen.

Connor: "Woah! What is that weird shiny tablet!? Is that some kind of weapon!"

Michael thought nothing of it at first and tried several more times to turn it on, but it still didn't respond.

What the hell is going on with this thing now!!!? Why won't it turn on!!!?

A frightening realization spread through Michael's mind. One that had his heart sucking from the inside out. Either his smartphone was beyond saving or it simply had no battery left. If it really was broken, then his plan would fall apart and they would have to come up with something new within the hour.

Bullshit!!! Please don't tell me it's broken!

Zoe: "Is there something wrong, Michi?"

Michael: "Yes, as a matter of fact, there is. I think it's broken! Great, every time we accomplish something, there must be more problems!"

Connor: "Wait, does that mean we can't record Zoe's voice and get on with our plan that way? Are you saying that all the hard work we did today was for nothing?"

Zoe: "I'm afraid so."

Steam came out of Connor's nose and ears as he let out all his pent-up anger. He grabbed Michael by his shirt with one paw and held him up. With the other paw, he conjured up a green hot flame, ready to roast Michael alive.

Zoe: "Connor, stop it!!! Put him back down!!!"

Michael yelped as he felt the hot flame in Connor's paw. He began to sweat dramatically from panic and heat.

Michael: "U-unless the b-battery is dead. I can try to charge it. With a little luck, it might still work."

Connor: "It better work, or I'll make you pay for all the hard work we basically did for free!"

Connor released Michael from his grip, who then fell to the ground. Without wasting any more time, Michael opened his backpack and searched for his charging cable and powerbank. After finding them, he immediately connected his smartphone to the powerbank and waited patiently for his smartphone to turn on.

Michael: "Now we wait."

The longer he waited, the longer the seconds felt. Michael took a deep breath to calm himself. It wouldn't be long before his patience would run out. The state of his smartphone was now the fate of this plan. Without its functions, all was lost. The sun was coming closer and closer to settle with each passing minute. It wouldn't be long before nightfall and Zak would surely take this opportunity to strike again.

Come on!!! Turn on already!!!

Still nothing. Only a black screen stared back at him. His hands shook at this realization. In the screen's reflection, he saw Zoe approaching from behind. She put her paw on his shoulder and he felt her reassuring presence in his mind. That calmed him a little.

Zoe: "Don't beat yourself up about it, Michi. Calm down first and be patient. Maybe it will still work."

Michael: "Unlikely... I think it's definitely fucked..."

Not only did his plan crumble, but he lost all of his personal pictures and videos where he had captured the best moments of his life he had so far, until it all went down the drain. The good times with his old friends before they turned on him. The good moments with his parents before they stopped giving shit about him, and the good moments with Zoe. It hurt a lot to think about it. That data was gone forever now, unless he went back to his home and had it restored.

Damn...

Suddenly, a ringing sounded and the display of Michael's smartphone lit up.

Michael: "Oh my God!!! Yes!!! YES!!! It's still working!!! We're saved!!!"

Zoe: "Yay!!!"

Connor: "Woo hoo."

Michael did a back flip for joy. Now they could finally finish their plan. Now Michael had to record Zoe's voice as a decoy and play that recording on a loop.

Michael: "It's only running at one percent power. The battery might be damaged since it takes much longer to charge it, but as long as it's plugged into the power bank, it should last at least a full night, which is hopefully enough time to lure Zak into our trap."

Michael selected the app displayed on the screen for his voice recorder and waited for it to charge.

Michael: "All right, Zoe. I'm going to count down from three to one, and then I'm going to start recording."

Zoe: "Wait! I don't even know what to say!"

Connor: "Just yell 'I'm in heat' or something like that. I bet that'll drive Zak crazy and he'll sprint straight to the trap."

Michael: "Uhh, yeah.... Or a simple cry for help. That would work too."

Zoe: "All right. I think I can get it to work somehow."

Michael: "Ready?"

Seeing Zoe nod in response, Michael counted down from three to one.

Michael: "Three... Two... One... And action!"

Michael pressed the red circular button on his screen that made him start the audio recording. He waited patiently for her to say something, but nothing came out of her mouth as she was at a loss for words.

Come on Zoe. Say something.

Michael looked at Connor, who shrugged at him. Connor walked up to Zoe and decided the best thing to do was to force her to speak, which he did by elbowing her in the side. In response, Zoe let out a loud, pained moan that sounded very, well, off topic. Satisfied with the result, Michael tapped the red round button again to stop recording.

Michael: "Good job, guys!"

Zoe: "Ow!!! Why did you hit me, you idiot!"

Connor: "To finally get a peep out of you! Look behind you and you'll see why!"

They all looked at what Connor was pointing at behind Zoe. It was the sun, which was already halfway down. It would be dark soon and the three of them had to be quick now.

Connor: "Quick, what else do we have to do!"

Michael: "Not much. I'll set Zoe's recording as my alarm clock, and set it to ring at the beginning of the night and then on and on. All we have to do is put the bait in the cage and call it a day.'

Connor: "Then let's go! We don't have much time!"

Connor immediately began sprinting back to the location of the trap. Without any warning, Zoe grabbed Michael's hand and pulled him along with her as she ran full speed after Connor.

Michael: "Zoe! Don't be so fast! I can barely keep up with you!"

He yelled at her to slow down, but it didn't help as she continued to run after Connor, pulling Michael along with her, who struggled to keep up and stumbled several times.

(One stumbling race later.)

It was night now and the beautiful stars were showing in all their glory, but Connor, Zoe and Michael didn't care. They had more important things to do than watch the wonderful light show in the night sky, such as keeping an eye on their trap. The three were currently sitting in a small cave, which for the moment was also their temporary shelter. In the center of the cave was an empty fireplace and two logs for them to sit on.

Connor: "So, when does the alarm go off? You know, the bait."

Connor whispered to Michael. They had to be as quiet as possible so as not to give away their position to the enemy, who could just stand nearby and listen. Even though the crickets were chirping happily and drowning out most of the other sounds in nature, the group of friends didn't want to risk it.

Michael: "It shouldn't take that much longer."

Just as Michael answered Connor with a whisper, the alarm on his smartphone turned to maximum volume, startling the three. The alarm played Zoe's recorded moans on a loop. It wouldn't stop until Michael turned it off himself or the battery died. It took a few seconds for the three to register what had actually happened, but then Connor laughed.

Connor: "Oh my god! Hahahaha! That scared the crap out of me for a moment. What other functions does this device have besides capturing voices? That's just insane! Hahaha!"

Michael: "Ha! I know, right?"

Connor: "It sounds just like her during heat!"

Zoe bared her teeth in anger and growled at Connor. Not only was she embarrassed, but she felt anger.

Zoe: "Connor! I'm going to take my anger out on you if you don't shut up right now!"

Connor: "What, a man can't make a little joke? Come on, man."

Zoe: "This is no time for jokes!"

Michael: "She's right. We're dealing with a mentally deranged guy who set fire to an innocent village. He could be here watching us where we can't see him and can't hear him. We should stay quiet now and wait for more signs. Let's just hope he falls for the bait trap."

Zoe: "We should also take turns monitoring the trap. One person needs to be awake while the other two are resting. If something happens, the one who is awake has to alert the others."

Michael: "Good idea, Zoe. So, who's going to…"

Michael broke off in mid-sentence when he heard the two of them snoring softly. Both were already in a deep sleep.

Michael: "Yeah, really funny, guys."

Now that their conversation had fallen silent, Michael could hear much better what was happening outside the cave. He could hear the rustling of leaves swaying in the wind. The crickets were chirping louder. And then there was the recorded moaning of Zoe, which kind of turned him on. If he could punish his brain for thinking about a naked Zoe taking lewd positions in front of him, he already would have.

Thank god she is asleep. If she were awake, this would not end well.

He stared out of the cave and could only see the stunning night sky. The rest was pitch black darkness. It wouldn't be a problem if his eyes were like his furry friends', because they could see in the dark better than Michael could.

Great! Now how can I keep an eye on the trap? I gave away my flashlight to catch some vodka bottles. My smartphone is inside the cage, which is the bait. And even if I had these devices with me now, it would only alert the enemy and give away our position. This sucks!

Michael noticed a glowing red spot on his pants, right where his pocket is. He reached in and pulled out a glowing red pearl, the Eye of Kaltraff.

Yeah, I could use this thing to see in the dark.

Michael held the pearl in front of his eye while he closed the other and looked out of the cave toward the trap. The vision that presented itself to him was red and upside down. There was no sign that anyone was around. The trap was still intact and no one had triggered it.

Man, this is going to be a boring, long night.

A yawn escaped him. He was tired as hell and his body was begging for a rest, but he just couldn't agree to it. He had to stay awake and keep an eye out for the trap and his friends. At least he could wake up Zoe or Connor in about two hours so one of them could continue his work.

Suddenly, that strange feeling of having forgotten something important came over him again. Earlier in the day, the same strange feeling had plagued him.

(Start of flashback.)

Zoe: "I can sense that something is bothering you, Michi. Is everything okay?"

Zoe's face showed a worried expression.

Michael: "Oh, it doesn't matter. Just a thought that's been going through my head and won't come back on command. I'll remember it soon enough either way."

Zoe: "Well, if you say so."

(End of flashback.)

Suddenly, something clicked in his head. He remembered now and he didn't like that at all. The possible, horrific consequences of his plan were now playing out in his mind. The Xenonans couldn't read or sense the minds of eachother, but they could do that to other living beings, including Michael, which meant that Zak could sense his presence. The worst part was that Zak probably already knew about this trap and would most certainly take advantage of it. Now Michael was scared to death. He was shaking with fear and didn't know what to do except to imagine a "no tresspassing" sign in his mind, hoping that would help him at least a little.

Meanwhile, deep in the night forest, a dark silhouette walked around. Its green glowing, hateful eyes darted in all directions, searching for its prey. With each step, it crushed plants and sticks, driving away other resting animals with its noise. At the end of a cliff, it stopped before speaking to itself.

Zak: "Your scent is here, still fresh. I can feel your presence now. You are not far from here. You can't run from me, nor can you hide. I already have your exact position."

Zak looked up at the night sky and closed his eyes. He fully concentrated on entering Michael's personal space, that is, his mind. He could feel that he was awake, and he wanted to find out what the human was up to. However, he found something in the human's mind that he had not expected. A simple wooden sign with red letters that said "no tresspassing". He dropped to the ground and pounded his fists on the ground while he couldn't stop laughing.

Zak: "Haha! Hahaha!!! HAHAHA!!!"

Suddenly he heard a familiar voice. Immediately he stopped laughing and stood up again. There, he heard it again. It sounded just like Zoe. But it didn't sound like she was talking, crying, laughing, or screaming. It was something else. Zak's ears pricked up to listen more closely. He heard some kind of moaning, but couldn't classify it as pain or sexual.

Zak: "I-Is she moaning!?"

Now it all made sense to him. The human who had thought of a "no trespassing" sign, and a Zoe who moaned loudly in the night. Zoe, who was his, and his alone, was having sex with a furless, pathetic creature. Anger built in his head. His long-lived dream was gone. The urge to do violence rose even higher. With all his strength, he screamed through the forest.

Zak: "I'M GOING TO FUCKING KILL YOU BOTH!!!"

Not even a second later, he sprinted as fast as he could toward Zoe's voice. His paws were clenched into fists, green fire surrounding them, ready to set everything on fire. The moaning grew louder and louder, which meant he had gotten closer. In front of him, he spotted a wooden cage that undoubtedly contained Zoe with that furless monster. He yelled a war cry and immediately charged towards the cage, only to trip over something.

Zak: "Argh!!! What the hell!!!?"

Just as Zak was about to get back on his feet, a heavy log crashed into his back, crushing every single bone inside into a million pieces. Zak could feel some of his bone shards piercing through his organs as he just lay there gasping for air and coughing up blood. The anthromorph spent his last moments looking toward a nearby cave entrance, where the human stood still and watched with a satisfied smile. Only now did Zak realize that this was all a trap, a set-up. The human had defeated him, and so he was ashamed of himself. His eyelids became so heavy that he could no longer hold them, and the pain was unbearable. He closed his eyes and waited for his end, which fortunately did not last long.

Chapter 17

A yawn escaped him and his nose began to itch badly, making him sneeze loudly. Michael groaned and opened his eyes, only to close them again.

Damn sun!

The sun was shining directly on him, heating up his skin. He sat up and scratched his butt before deciding to open his eyes again. He reached out and prevented the sunlight from shining on his face.

Sunglasses or a cap would be nice. Too bad I didn't bring them with me.

Michael looked around and realized he was sleeping outside the cave next to a tree.

Wait a minute... How did I get here? Didn't I fall asleep in the cave?

He glanced in the direction of the trap and noticed that something was wrong with one of the four deadfall traps. One had been triggered and under the fallen log lay a fur-covered body. Now Michael remembered what had happened. Hearing from outside the cave that someone had triggered the trap, he came out to check and saw Zak lying there bleeding. After that, Michael just fell asleep outside, not caring about the risk of the redclaws finding him.

Holy fuck! It actually worked! I have to tell Zoe and Connor about that!

Michael smiled pricelessly as he rushed into the cave to wake them from their deep slumber.

Michael: "Hey guys! GUYS!!! Wake up!!!"

He walked up to Zoe and gently wiggled her, causing her to moan softly.

Michael: "Come on Zoe! We don't have time for this! Get your ass up! We have got him!"

He wiggled her more roughly, but it still didn't help. He changed his decision and was about to stomp towards Connor to wake him up, who was sleeping on the other side of the cave, but something stopped him. He felt something soft wrap around his leg and looked down to see it was Zoe's fluffy tail.

Michael: "What are you doing-"

Suddenly her tail swung the other way with a force Michael couldn't anticipate. He lost his balance and stumbled, but before he hit the ground he was pulled into a thick embrace by his lover. Now he was lying on top of her, her arms and legs wrapped around him, preventing him from escaping.

Still, he decided not to do anything about it and just sighed. He glanced outside and saw that it hadn't been long since the sun had risen. It was still pretty early in the morning, and now that Zak was gone, they had one less problem. So he decided to give in and rest with Zoe for a few more hours. He hugged her back, buried his head in her thick fur, and closed his eyes. A pleasant warmth flowed from all directions, warming his body. Her fur was so soft that he felt like he was sleeping on a cloud. It was not long before he fell into a deep slumber.

Wow, where am I?

A black and empty void greeted him. But it was different from the others he had experienced. He could actually move, feel and see himself.

Zoe: "Michi!"

He heard her call his name from some distance behind him. He turned and spotted her running toward him. Arriving at his side, she jumped up and clung to Michael.

Zoe: "Hey."

Michael: "Woah!"

Michael struggled to regain his balance as Zoe's jump was uncalled for. Just as he was about to fall with her in his arms into the endless darkness, the scene turned into a bedroom of sorts.

Zoe: "Ah!"

Zoe shrieked as they fell, and Michael closed his eyes and waited for the impact. They both landed on something soft and comfortable. Michael opened his eyes and saw that they both landed on a bed, his bed, in his room, at home.

Michael: "What the...? Why are we in my world!?"

Zoe: "Shh, calm down, Michi. It's not real. It's just a dream. I thought it would be best to change the scenery."

Michael: "Wait, this is my dream, isn't it? Why are you in control of it?"

Zoe: "Nope, it's not yours, it's ours. We're sharing a dream right now and we both have control over it. It's a ritual couples do on Xenonan when they really, really, and I mean really love each other!"

Zoe licked his cheek before getting up and examining Michael's room. She sniffed his things and looked more closely at the items on his shelves and desk.

Zoe: "I really like this place. It's cozy and everything has your scent on."

Michael ignored her for a moment as he was deep in thought.

In a dream... With full controll... Can do what I want?

Michael: "Uh, Zoe?"

Zoe: "Yes, dear?"

Michael: "Now that we have control over this dream, does that mean we can actually do anything we want and no one can stop us?"

Zoe: "Mhm."

A smile appeared on both of their faces.

Zoe: "I'd say let's have some fun?"

Michael: "Yes!"

There were actually a few things Michael wanted to do on his homeworld that weren't done yet, and since he dreamed of his homeworld and had full control over this dream, he would definitely take this chance.

The scenery changed and the two of them were sitting on the roof of a beautiful family home. The sunset in the distance looked beautiful, and the sun's rays were falling between the buildings in the distance. There were streets with many cars driving by.

Zoe: "Wow... Where are we? I've never seen anything so beautiful."

Michael: "Well, it's about to get even more beautiful."

Michael spotted a familiar person walking by on the street. It was the girl who had smashed Michael's head on a plate of food in the school cafeteria. It was Jennie, the one who called him terrible things, made him angry, made him feel numb.

(Start of flashback.)

Jennie: "My name is Jennie, by the way. You look hungry. You can have some of my food if you want."

Michael: "R-really?"

Jennie: "Mhm."

Michael: "Th-thank you."

Michael did something he thought he would never do again in his life. He smiled. Just as he was about to take something from the tray, he felt a sudden blow to the back of his head, causing his face to collide with the tray full of hot food. The whole cafeteria pointed at Michael and laughed as if they had just seen the funniest shit in their entire lives.

Michael didn't dare lift his head again. Tears leaked from his eyes as his hope of getting a friend died within seconds. Even though the students' laughter was louder than anything else, he could only hear her voice.

Jenny: "Hahahaha!!! What a loser!!! Did you really think anyone would want to be your friend!!! You're a pathetic excuse for a human!!! A worthless piece of shit!!! Not even an alien would want to lay hands on you!!!"

(End of flashback.)

Michael remembered that day as if it were yesterday. But instead of sadness, anger built up in his mind. He felt a deep hatred for her. It was time for a sweet revenge.

Zoe: "Michi? Is everything alright with you? I can feel that something is... is wrong... Tell me, what is that you're holding right now?"

Michael was holding a strange dark green tube. It was long and looked like it was made of hard material, something Zoe had never seen before.

Michael: "Huh? Oh, that thing I just conjured up? It's a bazooka."

Zoe: "Ba so kaa?"

Michael: "Yeah, that's close enough."

He summoned a missile and loaded it into the bazooka before looking into the scope and aiming it at the bitch who had been psychologically tormenting him.

Now I got you bitch...

Zoe: "Um, what are you-"

Her sentence was interrupted as Michael pulled the trigger. The missile shot out of the bazooka, followed by a loud boom that scared the hell out of Zoe. She covered her ears as she continued to watch. A second later, the missile hit its target and exploded. The force of the explosion almost completely engulfed Jennie, except for some of her bloody body parts that flew in all directions. The shockwave shattered nearby windowpanes, and the plume of smoke rose into the air.

Michael: "YOU GET WHAT YOU FUCKING DESERVE!!! HAHAHA!!!"

Zoe was shocked and speechless. She wanted to share her dream with him because, well, she wanted to do some romantic stuff with him or learn more about his world, but instead she had to watch him cause chaos. It didn't matter anyway, since it was just a dream. Michael had his fun fooling around, and now it was Zoe's turn.

Zoe: "Hmph!"

Michael's laughter died away as he looked at her.

Michael: "What?"

Zoe: "Now that you've had fun, what about me, or us?"

Michael: "Oh, yeah, sorry. I got a little carried away. So, um, what do you want to do?"

Zoe: "Oh, I know. It'll be a surprise!"

She smiled and snapped her fingers. The scenery changed again and Michael was back in his room on his bed, but without Zoe.

Michael: "Uh, Zoe?"

He felt something moving next to him under the covers and glanced inside. There she was, cuddling up to him with a smile. She climbed on top of him and sat up, blushing madly. The covers fell off, revealing the two of them. Realization flashed through his mind. She was naked.

Michael: "Zoe, what the hell!!!? What is this all about!!?"

Zoe held a paw over his mouth to shut him up, and his face turned red as well.

Zoe: "There is something I want to tell you. I want to mate with you, and I want to do it now! Now let's get your clothes off!"

Michael: "Wait! Woah-"

She swung her sharp claws at him, shredding his shirt to pieces and barely touching his skin.

Michael: "Zoe!!! Stop it!!! Bad girl!!!"

Zoe: "Oh, why? Come on, I know you want to fuck me too."

Michael: "I'm not ready for that kind of stuff!"

Zoe: "But it's just a dream, just the two of us! Please. I promise I'll be gentle."

Michael began to sweat, as it was getting very hot. He sighed and looked deep into her eyes.

Michael: "I... I... I-"

Zoe: "Sush! You won't regret any of this, I promise."

She leaned over and kissed him deeply, their tongues fighting for dominance, her soft boobs pressing against his chest. But it a.l had to end when the door to Michael's room flew open and his father entered. His face showed true anger.

Michael's father: "Damn you, son!!! What's going on!?"

Michael's eyes were now wide and he pushed Zoe off of him.

Michael: "Dad!?"

Michael's dad: "You've been gone for a whole week and now I find you here having sex with a dog!!!?"

Zoe: "Michi, what's going on?!"

Michael: "Dad, I swear it doesn't look like that!"

Now Michi's mother interfered as well. Her eyes were red from all the crying.

Michael's mother: "Why did this happen, son? We miss you so much... Please... come back to us... Son..."

Zoe: "Michael! You need to focus! It's getting out of control!"

Michael: "I... I... I can't do anything!!! Zoe, help me! What the..."

Michael looked to where Zoe should be, but spotted Connor instead.

Connor: "Boo!!!"

Michael: "AAAAH!!!"

Michael shrieked like a little girl and found himself in the cave where he had fallen asleep on top of Zoe, who was wide awake now.

Connor: "HAHAHA!!! OH MAN, LOOK AT BOTH YOUR FACES!!! HAHAHA!!!"

Zoe: "You little... come here!"

Michael was flung away from her as she stood up.

Michael: "Woah!"

She growled in anger and bared her sharp teeth Her razor sharp claws extended and she was ready to hack anything to pieces. Connor was still busy laughing his head off and didn't notice Zoe coming towards him.

Zoe: "You've... Ruined... Everything!!!"

Now Connor knew he was in big trouble, because it never ended well for him when he pissed her off.

Connor: "H-hey, I was just kidding, okay? I was just messing with you guys a little bit. No big deal, right?"

Zoe: "YAAAARR!!!"

She lunged at him at full speed and jumped on him. They both turned into a cartoon-like battle cloud with paws and sharp claws swishing around.Michael took out a list and a pen and wrote something down.

Rules for surviving in the wilderness. Rule number forty-seven: don't piss Zoe off. Yep, all done.

(One beat up later.)

The three of them were now standing next to each other, the trap was in front of them. Connor looked at that moment as if he had been in the worst fight ever. He had scratches and bloody marks all over him. In some places his fur was completely missing and he had a blue eye. The three stared at Zak's body, still under the pressure of the logs.

Connor: "So we actually got him?"

Michael: "Looks like it. I can't believe my plan actually worked!"

Zoe: "Oh, God. That must have been very painful."

Michael: "Karma is a bitch!"

Connor: "Well, it can't be any worse than the treatment you gave me earlier."

They both stared at each other, her giving him a cold look. Connor just shrugged his shoulders.

Connor: "What?"

Zoe: "You want a second round now?"

Connor: "Oh, hell no!"

Michael: "Come on, give me a hand here. We need to lift this heavy log."

Connor went to the other side of the log and they both tried their best to lift it as far as they could.

Connor: "Huff!"

Michael: "So heavy... My back!"

Zoe immediately grabbed Zak's body and pulled him away from the trap. After pulling him far enough away, Connor and Michael let go of the log, which crashed to the ground with a thud.

Connor: "Whew!"

Michael: "Now let's see if he's got any valuable loot!"

Michael crouched down and examined Zak's body for clues that might help them find the Red Claw empire.

Zoe: "So, did you find anything?"

Michael: "Yeah, I think I found something."

Zoe: "Really? What is it?"

Michael found a small pouch on Zak's body. He unbuckled it from him, opened it, and put his hand inside. He felt two things and reached for them before taking his hand out to look at them.

Dear... God...

Connor: "What is it? What did you find?"

Michael: "He has a Snickers wrapper and a Durex condom! What!!!? How the fuck did he manage to get those!!!?"

Zoe: "I've never heard of that."

Connor: "What's going on?"

Michael: "What's going on? WHAT THE HELL IS GOING ON!!? This guy somehow got things that you can only get in my world!"

Zoe: "Are you telling me that Zak somehow got access to your world?"

Michael: "Seems so!"

Connor: "Is there anything else in here?"

Michael put his hand back in and looked for more things. Again he felt for two things and took them out. Examining them, he found a shiny penny and an engagement ring.

This piece of stone attached to a gold ring looks damn expensive. I'm definitely going to keep that one, for Zoe.

Zoe: "What exactly do you have for me? Ohh, you got me a present, didn't you?"

Michael: "Um, y-yes. Here you go."

He tossed Zoe the penny, which she caught with both paws, like a cat reaching for a toy above her.

Zoe: "Ohhhh, shiny!"

Michael aggressively put his hand back in, frequently looking for other things in that pouch.

If there's another useless item from home in there, I'm going to snap! Hmm, what's that?

Michael felt a ball of crumpled paper and pulled it out. He tried his best to unfold it without tearing anything. Now that he had it unfolded, he could make out a map of sorts. Some of the things marked on the map looked familiar, like the lake where he had taken a bath with Zoe, in the center left. At the top center was the village where Zak had set fire to everything. In the middle was a small opening where the three of them were right now. There were many more places marked on the map where the three had not yet been, but one in particular caught Michael's eye. In the lower right, away from everything else, there was a larger tree drawn in, even circled. Above it was written "The Mighty Tree."

Michael: "Guys, I think I found something that might help us!"

Connor: "Let's see it!"

Connor plucked the map from Michael's grasp and looked at it closely.

Connor: "Mhh, yeah. I've never been here before. I didn't even know anything like this existed."

Zoe: "The mighty tree. It's even circled. It must be important. Maybe Zak has something hidden there?"

Connor: "How is that even going to help us find the kingdom of the Redclaw? It's probably a trap anyway."

Michael: "But then what are we supposed to do? It's the only clue we have! We have to try!"

Zoe: "I agree with Michi on that one."

Michael carefully walked towards the wooden cage without triggering the three remaining traps. He tore the cage apart and retrieved his smartphone and powerbank, both of which were empty.

I should still have a powerbank in my backpack. I can charge my smartphone one last time....

Michael walked back to Zoe and Connor. The three friends exchanged glances before deciding to check it out. And so they followed the path to the mighty tree, hoping to find clues on how to get into the Redclaw realm.

Meanwhile, they didn't notice a dark silhouette spying them up in the trees.

???: "What a useless imbecile Zak is! Couldn't even start the fight with them! But it doesn't matter anyway! My plan seems to work! Yes, run into my trap! Just like that! The mighty tree will punish you for it and then I will have Zoe all to myself, kill the rest of you and rule over all of Xenonan! Hahaha!!!"

Chapter 18

The sun was high in the sky, casting its powerful light on the forests below to nourish the plants that needed it to survive. Birds chirped happily and flew around in groups, hunting for smaller animals. In the distance, someone could be heard coughing, and the cough echoed through the forest. Zooming in closer, Michael was there on his knees, gasping for air and coughing up slime that blocked access to his lungs.

Connor: "You idiot! I told you before NOT to eat those orange berries! They're poisoned!"

Michael: "I-I forgot."

Michael struggled to give an appropriate response. His voice sounded rough because of the slime clogging his throat. With another forceful cough, he tried to get rid of the slime in his throat, but to no avail. Zoe, worried to death, knelt in front of him and tried everything she could do to make him feel better, while Connor just stood there, not knowing what to do.

Zoe: "We need to get the poisoned berries out of him. If they stay in him much longer, the poisoning will spread and then there will be nothing we can do to cure him."

Michael's stomach began to hurt so badly that he had to close his eyes to suppress the pain a little.

Michael: "I d-don't feel very good. I think I'm a-about to..."

Another strong cough escaped him as he could no longer suppress the urge to do so. As he coughed, a little bit of blood flew out of his mouth and onto the grass below. That was all that caused Zoe to snap when she saw that his lover was hurt. She stood up and forcefully pulled him up, causing him to moan in pain. Next she wrapped her arms around his stomach from behind and squeezed as hard as she could. Michael could do nothing but gag as the pain paralyzed him.

Zoe: "Come on! Get out of him!!!"

With each squeeze Zoe applied, it became tighter until everything in Michael's stomach shot out of his mouth, forming a messy brown and orange fountain mixed with the things he had eaten earlier and the poisoned berries.

Connor: "Gross..."

Michael sank back to his knees and took a deep breath after coughing a few more times.

Zoe: "Are you feeling better now?"

Michael: "Yeah... Thanks to you, Zoe. You're a lifesaver."

Michael wiped the remaining vomit from his face and lowered himself to the grass.

Connor: "Wonderful! Now that you're feeling better, we can continue our journey to the mighty tree!"

Michael: "Please, just ten minutes. I want to stay on the ground and rest."

Connor: "Na ah."

Connor glanced at the map leading to the mighty tree and selected the direction that led to it.

Connor: "This is the way. Follow my lead."

Zoe grabbed Michael by the hand and pulled him along.

I just want to sleep...

As the three friends traveled, they crossed many rivers and climbed many rocks while talking and joking with each other. On some occasions, they took small breaks and ate the food they had collected along the way. They also came across beautiful landscapes, so Michael had to take some photos of them with the three of them also smiling pricelessly. It reminded him of second grade in school when his class went on a field trip to the woods. It was the time he enjoyed the most, exploring new places with his friends. But the good time had to end soon, because a high mountain blocked their way, and there was no way to climb it, because it was too high. The only way to overcome the mountain was to enter the cave that led through it.

Michael: "Uhh... So, through there?"

Connor nodded in response.

Connor: "Through there."

Zoe scratched her ear as she thought about it.

Zoe: "I don't think we should go through there."

Connor: "And why not? Apparently that's the only way that leads to the damn tree we've been looking for for half a day!"

Zoe: "And what if this is all a trap!? It could be a redclaw army waiting for us to enter their lair!"

Connor: "Yes, and!? I don't understand what you mean, Zoe! Our goal is to find this stupid Redclaw Kingdom and kill their leader to end this war once and for all! What do you expect!? No redclaws!? That's ridiculous! Besides, I don't sense anyone in that cave, so it must be empty!"

Michael: "Hey, over there!"

Michael pointed his finger at a wooden sign that stood next to the cave entrance.

Zoe: "Let's go take a look."

As they approached the sign, they could see small, red-colored writing. The sign didn't look very inviting because the letters looked spidery and long. To say it didn't look creepy would be an understatement.

Connor: "So, who wants to read it out loud for the rest of us?"

Michael: "I think I can do it. Ahem! The enlance… enta… Entrance…to…the…What kind of handwriting is that!? It's fucking horrible and I can't make shit out!"

Connor: "Let me try!"

Connor squinted his eyes and zoomed in on the sign as he tried to read the handwriting.

Michael: "So, are you done?"

Connor: "…"

Zoe: "What does it say?"

Connor: "…"

Connor took a few steps back and looked down at the floor, embarrassed.

Connor: "I… I forgot I can't even read…"

Zoe: "Oh. My. God. You guys can be really stupid sometimes!"

Michael: "Ouch."

Connor: "Yo! It's not my fault they didn't teach me to read!"

Now it was Zoe's turn to read what the sign indicated.

Zoe: "The entrance to the cave of the mighty tree. The gateway to another place, a darker place, where the games play with you. Be sure to bring your friends to add to the fun."

Connor: "Sounds very inviting."

Michael: "I don't know about that, comrades. It sounds like a trap to me."

Connor: "Trap or no trap, we're going to go through it. All right, guys! Who's ready for a caving adventure!"

Zoe: "Me! Me! I like caving adventures!"

I certainly don't.

With one paw, Connor conjured a green flame that he used as a light source, and with the other paw he held the map that showed the location of the mighty tree. Right behind him stood Zoe. She had the task of scanning their surroundings for threats with her telepathic abilities, and behind her stood a nervous human who clutched his spear tightly, ready to stab anyone who dared lay a hand on him and his friends. Together they were the three unbeatable musketeers.

Connor: "All right, let's go."

The three entered the dark cave. Connor's flame emitted a green light, illuminating a small radius inside the cave. A crunch could be heard with each step as they stepped on the dry dirt and small stones. Michael clutched his spear even tighter that he could swear it would break soon. The pitch blackness ahead scared the hell out of him, and the small space in the cave didn't make it any better. And the roots hanging down from above.... They looked like they could grab any of the three and tear them to pieces. Now Michael began to tremble with fear. Zoe, who was walking in front of him, noticed his fear and turned around.

Zoe: "Oh, you're scared, aren't you?"

Michael: "Wh-what? Of course not!"

Zoe: "Do you want me to hold your hand?"

Michael: "N-no! I'm fine."

Connor: "Hey! What are you waiting for?"

Zoe: "Michael's scared."

Connor: "Seriously? Pfft! Hahaha!!!"

Michael: "Shut the fuck up! I'm not scared!"

Connor: "Huh? Well, your mind tells me otherwise."

Michael: "Then I dare you to prove it!"

Connor: "Oh yeah, how?"

Michael pulled out his smartphone and held it in front of him.

Michael: "By lighting up the whole damn cave to reveal its dark secrets, because your dim nightlight can't do shit."

Connor grinned, knowing what was going to happen.

Connor: "Hoo, hooo! Let's do this then."

Michael: "Let there be light!"

The second Michael turned on the bright light of his smartphone, he alerted a swarm of bats hanging from above. They were all staring at him with red eyes. Their white, sharp teeth were so long that they hung out of their mouths. Their teeth resembled a cruel smile that reflected in his light. A truly terrifying sight that Michael would never forget.

Dear God...

Not a second later, the bats emitted a suppressed screeching sound and charged toward him.

Michael: "HOLY FUCKING SHIT!!!

Instinctively, Michael defended his face with his arms as the bats flew past his head, flapping their wings and leaving scratch marks on his skin, then all was silent. A few seconds passed before he decided to stick his head out of his arms. Shivering, he shone the light of his smartphone around the cave and didn't see a single bat anymore. He sighed in relief.

I should turn off my light.

Michael immediately turned off the flashlight on his smartphone so as not to repeat his mistake. He looked back at his friends. Connor and Zoe, who were smiling pricelessly, couldn't hold their laughter anymore and started laughing at Michael.

Connor: "HAHAHA!!! You should have seen your face!"

Zoe: "That face you made looked so funny!"

Michael: "Okay, not gonna lie, they got me pretty darn good. But I wasn't actually afraid. Back in my world I witnessed more fucked up things."

Connor: "Yeah, right. Just keep telling yourself that."

Michael: "I'm serious! You know, there's a difference between being jumpscared and being truly afraid of something."

Zoe: "Hm, I guess so."

The three ran further into the cave. The cold and howling wind that blew through the cave made all three of them shiver with cold, Michael of course the most, since he was not wrapped in fur like his two furried friends. The drops of water dripping from above created an uncomfortable atmosphere, the perfect time to tell creepy stories in the dark.

Zoe: "Hey guys."

Connor: "Yeah?"

Michael: "Huh?"

Zoe: "I have an idea how we can make this cave trip more fun.'

Michael: "Turn on the flashlight on my smartphone so I get attacked by bats again? No, thanks."

Connor: "Heh!"

Zoe: "No, no, no. We could tell each other scary stories."

Connor: "Well, I don't have a story in mind to tell right now. Why don't you get started? After all, this is your idea."

Zoe: "All right, I've got one. Have you guys ever heard of..."

She conjured a green flame on her paw and adjusted the angle so the light showed only the top half of her face.

Zoe: "...the mimic creature!?"

Michael: "Na ah."

Connor: "The what?"

Zoe: "The mimic creature. They are known as the most fearsome predators of the night, but no one really knows what they look like. But a few things are certain. When the moon is full, their hunting hour begins. They are always on the lookout for their prey and watch them closely.... and listen for voices to imitate. In this way, they deceive their prey and make them think there is a familiar. No one really knows what these monsters have done to their prey, but the victims have disappeared and no one has managed to find them. Only a few people who escaped after an encounter told the story that the mimic creature mimicked the voices of the missing ones."

Connor began to clap slowly as Michael almost tripped because he wasn't watching where he was stepping.

Connor: "It was pretty decent."

Michael: "My usual bedtime story."

Zoe was annoyed by Michael's response.

Connor: "Really, dude? How about you tell us something a lot scarier?"

Michael: "Yeah, sure. Have you guys ever heard the story of...? The Doom Slayer?"

Connor: "Very original..."

Michael: "Shut up!"

Zoe: "I've never heard of it."

Michael: "Yeah, it's a story from my world. Anyway, now for the story."

Michael took a long, deep breath and let it out.

Michael: "In the first age, in the first battle, when the shadows first lengthened, one stood. Burned by the embers of Armageddon, his soul blistered by the fires of Hell and tainted beyond ascension, he chose the path of perpetual torment. In his ravenous hatred he found no peace, and with boiling blood he scoured the Umbral Plains seeking vengeance against the dark lords who had wronged him. He wore the crown of the Night Sentinels, and those that tasted the bite of his sword named him... The Doom Slayer."

Connor: "..."

Michael: "So, how was it?"

Connor suddenly stopped walking. The map was blown off his paw as his grip weakened. He just stood still and stared ahead, Zoe did the same.

Michael: "Hey, what's the matter?"

Zoe and Connor, both were now shaking for their lives and gasping for air. Their eyes showed true fear. Zoe immediately grabbed Michael's hand, clung to him and buried her head against his chest.

Michael: "Um, guys?"

Connor pointed at something with his trembling paw and whispered to his human friend.

Connor: "W-who is that?"

Michael followed Connor's pointing paw and his eyes widened so much they were about to roll out. Directly in front of them, slightly above them, were bloodshot eyes in the darkness, fully open and staring down curiously at the three of them. Michael reached into his pocket, slowly, and pulled out his lighter. He flipped open the lid and with a loud flick, a bright yellow flame came out, showing the true horror that awaited them.

Oh my god...

Directly in front of them was a thick, dead tree. It had a large, gaping hole with cracks that resembled a smiling mouth. It had no leaves and instead of branches there were a dozen very thin fleshy tentacles moving like crazy. In shock, Michael dropped his lighter and the darkness engulfed them. At the sight, Connor collapsed on the damp floor and curled up into a ball, sucking on both his thumbs at the same time. Zoe tightened her grip around Michael even more, making him wonder if he was going to die of a heart attack or by suffocation.

Mighty Tree: "I am the mighty tree. Welcome to my lair."

The voice echoed through the cave, sounding deep and rough, as if it were the devil himself speaking to them.

Mighty Tree: "Do not be afraid. My intention is not to harm you. Here, let me shed some light."

Suddenly, red flames appeared on all the torches in the cave, emitting a faint red light, revealing the gigantic cave area the three friends were currently in.

Holy shit!

The three friends looked around in fright. They had already forgotten from which direction they had come. Michael felt something wet dripping on his left arm and examined it. There was a small amount of a thick slimy liquid on his left arm, and it smelled terrible. Then he felt it again, but this time on his other arm. He also heard the dripping sound of something landing all over the cave, and concluded that it couldn't be dripstones, but something much worse. Michael looked further up and spotted a huge lump of flesh on the ceiling of the cave, slowly growing and then shrinking. The massive lump of flesh was connected to the huge tree in the center of the cave by a dozen very thin fleshy threads that looked like the tentacles from earlier. The damn thing was alive and even breathing.

WHAT THE FUCK IS GOING ON HERE? AM I TRIPPING BALLS!?

Mighty Tree: "The sight you have before you is horrifying, I know. I can tell by the expression of your eyes, which show what true fear is.... But enough of this talk! It's time..."

T-time for w-what, our d-doom?

Mighty Tree: "It's time... For the games to finally begin!"

Michael/Connor/Zoe: "What?"

Michael: "Um, mighty tree?"

The mighty tree rolled its eyes slowly in Michael's direction. He felt as if they were staring right through him, at his soul. He quickly got goose bumps and felt very nervous. When the tree didn't answer him, Michael decided to keep talking.

Michael: "L-look, we'd all like to play g-games, but we're in a hurry. We found a map that leads to your cave, and we decided to enter it to find clues as to where the Red Claw kingdom might be. B-but if there are no c-clues, then we would all like to leave this place-"

Mighty Tree: "I DON'T THINK THAT WOULD BE AN OPTION FOR YOU THREE!!!"

His outburst scared the hell out of the three friends.

Mighty: "There are rules you have to abide by! I can't just let you guys go like this! You three will play different games with me, and then I will let you do yours. Maybe, just maybe, I will also give you clues that might help you find what you are looking for."

There was silence for a few seconds.

Mighty Tree: "You can't imagine how happy I am to finally be able to play again! The last person left me in here all alone after a few rounds of playing. I think… his name was… Zak, if I remember correctly."

Wait, what!? Zak has been here before!? Something s not right here! Eh, it doesn't really matter. That fool is deac anyway.

Mighty Three: "Oh, where have my true manners gone! I didn't even introduce myself properly, except to give my name. I am the mighty tree, old enough to know the most incompetent things. Yet I do not know how old I am, nor can I remember my true name. I can't even remember what the world looks like from the outside! That's how long I've been living with this curse! But there is one thing I can remember for sure. I was once like you. A walking creature on both legs until he came and changed facts about me."

Cool story, bro.

Mighty Tree: "Anyway, the first game we're going to play now is called "Shell Game," and you, human, will be first."

Great, now I'm getting school vibes. Wait a minute! How does it know I'm a human?

A wooden platform with three empty wooden cups on it, upside down, slid out of the tree's mouth. The center cup floated upward, revealing a small white pearl below. Then the middle cup moved down, hiding the small white pearl, and all three cups moved around with a slow paste. After half a minute, the wooden cups were side by side and came to a stop.

Michael remembered that he used to play this game a lot with his grandpa. His grandpa had a lot of tricks up his sleeve, but Michael was still always right. He was a pro at this game and knew it was used to manipulate others. Unfortunately, his grandfather passed away. Michael really enjoyed playing games with him.

Mighty Tree: "Now guess."

Without hesitation, Michael pointed to the left wooden cup.

Michael: "The left one."

Mighty Tree: "Are you sure about that?"

Michael: "One hundred percent."

The left cup dissolved into thin air, exposing the white pearl.

Mighty Tree: "You did well for your first round. You've earned yourself a prize. Just come a little closer and I'll give it to you."

Michael stood speechless, staring at what he called the mouth of the tree. It looked more like the entrance to an endless void filled with darkness and possible other abominations. He winced as he heard Zoe's voice in his head warning him.

Zoe: "I don't really feel comfortable, Michi. We don't know his true intentions. I think it's best if we leave."

Didn't you hear? It won't let us out until we play its boring ass games! Besides, where should we go then? I don't know where the exit is anymore! Try to read his mind, I bet he's hiding something!

Connor: "That's the problem. We can't read his mind! We can't even sense it! Our powers aren't working against him for some reason! That's why we're so worried!"

What a load of bullshit!

Mighty tree: "Michael, your prize. It's waiting for you. Take it."

He knows my name...

Michael walked closer to the mighty tree, his legs shaking slightly. He looked into the tree's eyes, which stared down at him. The tree couldn't smile, but Michael knew damn well it was smiling inside.

Mighty Tree: "Now close your eyes, bend your arms forward, and open your hands."

Michael had a lot of questions, but decided to comply anyway, not wanting to upset the mighty tree. Michael felt some kind of object appear on both of his hands. It was round, thin and long, and it felt like the material was plastic.

Mighty Tree: "Open your eyes now."

Michael did as he was told and looked down at his hands.

This can't be true...

A straw, a simple plastic straw was his prize. The strange thing was that this item came from Michael's world. How had it gotten here in the first place? No one knew.

Was this how Zak got certain things from my world? By playing games with the mighty tree? How did that tree come to get those things?

Michael sighed and stuffed the plastic straw into his pocket. For some reason, Michael's backpack felt a little lighter, like something was missing, but he didn't pay it any mind. Instead, he complained over his useless prize in his mind.

Useless piece of shit! Well, at least it's not made of paper. Paper straws fucking suck!

Mighty Tree: "Now get ready for round two."

Michael: "R-round two? How many more do I have to play?"

Mighty Tree: "Oh come on, boy. Where's your motivation? Aren't you having fun yet?"

To be honest, I'm having more fun jerking off several times a day, even though I know I'm completely self-destructing.

Mighty Tree: "Well, I have an idea! How about I make the games harder for you, and if you lose, I get a prize from you that I pick. That prize would be your soul, human."

The last sentence was whispered in a low murmur that none of the three heard. Michael did not answer, whereupon the mighty tree took this as a yes. Just as in the first round, the middle wooden cup floated upward, revealing a small white pearl below. The middle cup then moved down and all three cups moved around, but this time much faster and longer. After a minute, the wooden cups lined up next to each other and came to a stop. A completely new player, who had never experienced this game before, would have chosen the middle cup. But Michael, who was a veteran of this little game, noticed in a split second that one of the cups contained the pearl and gave it to another cup.

You sneaky bastard....

Mighty Tree: "Now guess."

Michael: "Right cup."

Mighty Tree: "Are you sure it's the right one?"

Michael: "Yes, right one."

The right cup dissolved into thin air, exposing the white pearl.

Mighty Tree: "What!!! How- ah- I mean.... Congratulations on winning the second round. Most people didn't even make it that far. You've earned yourself another prize."

Connor: "Damn it Michael! You're in a row!"

Connor shouted from the background.

Mighty Tree: "Now close your eyes, bend your arms forward and open your hands so I can give you the second prize."

Michael took a deep breath and complied again. This time he felt something heavy on both his hands. It felt cold and metallic. It was also in the shape of an L.

Wait a minute... Could this actually be a... a gun?

Mighty Tree: "Open your eyes now."

Michael did as he was told and felt deeply betrayed. On his hands was a piece of metal that was shaped like a literal L. He cursed softly to himself and put his well-deserved prize in his pocket.

Michael: "..."

He felt it again! His backpack became even lighter. As if something had been taken out.

That's it! I'm going to check!

Mighty Tree: "So, are you ready for round three?"

Michael: "I... Um... I need some time off. But don't worry about it! Zoe wants to play this game too, don't you, Zoe?"

Zoe's ears perk up at the mention of her name.

Zoe: "Huh?"

Mighty Tree: "Ah, Zoe. Come a little closer and play this game with me, will you?"

Michael's backpack slid off his back and landed on the damp stone floor. He crouched down in front of it and opened it up. As he examined the inside of his backpack, he discovered that two things were indeed missing. One was his survival guide book and the other was his powerbank to charge his smartphone. Two things he didn't give a shit about since he never really used the book and his powerbank was already empty.

How had they disappeared? Was this the work of the mighty tree? If I win a prize, does that mean something gets taken away from me? And by something, I actually mean that it could literally be anything. If that's the case, then thank fuck it wasn't the important stuff I was carrying around! And what would happen if I lost in the game?

Michael glanced in Zoe's direction, where he saw that she was already playing the third round. The three wooden cups were moving so fast that Michael couldn't even follow them with his eyes, but Zoe was doing a great job. Her eyes were fixated on one of the cups and her head was moving very fast, just like a cat is fixated on its toy.

Ha, adorable… Wait a minute. Zoe has nothing on except her tribal clothing. If my suspicions were correct, then….

Too late. Zoe had already successfully completed her first game, but for some reason she still had everything on her. That's when Michael remembered that the day before he had given her the shiny penny he had found while looting Zak's body. He sighed with relief that the coin had most likely been taken from her and not anything else.

Whew… That… Could have ended very badly.

With proud steps and a smile on her adorable face, Zoe walked towards Michael.

Zoe: "Hey Michael! Look at my prize! I have a shiny L like you, but much more detailed and bigger!"

Michael rubbed his eyes a few times to make sure he was seeing it all correctly. His mouth stayed open as he still saw the same prize Zoe had won.

Michael: "Zoe… That's not an L… That's a god damn gun!!!"

Zoe: "A gun? What is that?"

That's iiiiiit! I'm going to play this game until I get the hidden blade from Assassin's Creed!

Michael packed all his important stuff in his backpack and left it on the ground, not wanting to risk losing it while playing the game with the mighty tree. Instead, he had the less important stuff on him that he didn't really need right now, like his house keys, the other useless stuff he got from looting Zak's body and his useless prizes from the game he was playing.

Michael: "Hey mighty tree!"

In response, the mighty tree's bloodshot eyes slowly rolled in Michael's direction.

Mighty Tree: "Human?"

Michael: "I'd like to play a few more round."

Mighty Tree: "What motivated you all of a sudden? Anyway, I'm glad to hear that. Now come closer, my friend."

Michael approached the Mighty Tree once again, ready to win some more great prizes.

Mighty Tree: "Are you ready for the really difficulty you're about to play on this game?"

Michael: "Sure, whatever."

Mighty Tree's eyes, which expressed murderousness, glowed slightly red.

Mighty Tree: "Then let it begin!"

For the fourth time, the middle wooden cup floated upward, exposing the pearl for a second before hiding it again. But this time, instead of a memory catastrophe where all the cups moved side by side, only the middle cup containing the pearl swapped places with the left cup.

Mighty Tree: "Choose now."

Michael: "That's it? Well, alright then."

Michael scratched his chin as he thought about his decision.

Michael: "Hmmmm… None of them have the pearl."

Mighty Tree: "Wh-what?"

All three cups disappeared into thin air. The pearl was nowhere to be seen for some reason.

Mighty Tree: "H-how is that possible? How did you know that!!! There's no way you could have known that!"

Silence spread through the cave.

Uh, why am I hearing boss music in my head?

Mighty Tree: "YOU HAVE CHEATED AND THEREFORE HAVE WON NOTHING!!! RULE BREAKER!!! I HATE RULE BREAKERS!!! THEY MUST BE PUNISHED!!!"

With each word, the mighty tree roared in rage, the huge fleshy lump above it that was connected to it shaking violently, making the entire cave shook.

Connor: "Heads down!"

Michael threw himself to the ground, holding his arms above his head to protect it from falling rocks. Zoe and Connor dodged a few falling rocks and threw fireballs at the mighty tree, which hit them successfully.

Now that the mighty tree was on fire, it shrieked and roared even more. In other words, he became even more furious. The fire spread even further upward and to the massive fleshy lump. It lit up the whole cave. A truly horrible and disgusting sight.

Crap! Where's my backpack!!! I shouldn't have left it lying around!

Michael kept looking in all directions trying to find his backpack.

There it is!

He found it half buried in rocks and carefully crawled towards it.

Mighty Tree: "I WILL KILL YOU!!! I WILL KILL YOU ALL AND FEAST ON YOUR FLESH!!!"

The cave rumbled even more as the roots of the mighty tree tangled from the ground. A pair of legs grew underneath him as he fully reared up, stomping the ground frantically and letting out one of his most furious roars.

Oh fuck! Oh fuck!!! OH FUCK!!!

The mighty tree looked towards Michael's direction, seeing him crawling faster than a grandma in her electric wheelchair, and gave him a hateful look. It roared loudly once more before beginning to sprint at the human still crawling on the ground.

Michael just reached for his backpack and kept looking for the eye of Kaltraff that would turn him into an invincible killing machine, but it was too late. With a powerful kick from the mighty tree, Michael flew to the other side of the cave and hit the wall hard, falling to the ground unconscious.

Zoe: "MICHAEL!!! NO!!!"

Mighty Tree: "HAHAHA!!! You thought you little vermin could defeat me!!!? YOU FOOL!!! So who will be my next victim!!!"

Zoe growled in anger and bared her sharp teeth. She summoned green, fiery flames on her two paws and hurled them at the mighty tree. Her arms rotated in the air as she fired her fireballs like a minigun. Just as one of the fireballs was about to hit the mighty tree, two large hands grew on it. With ease, the mighty tree shielded any flame that rained down on it with its large wooden armored hands.

With the mighty tree now aimed at Zoe, Connor took his chance and tried to attack it from behind with his fire. With the help of his two paws, he managed to summon a much larger fireball than Zoe threw.

Connor: "Hey rotten tree!!!"

Mighty Tree: "Who dares to call me names like that!!?"

Connor: "Behind you!!!"

Connor stretched out both paws and hurled the massive fireball against the mighty tree's back. The impact was strong enough to knock the mighty tree off balance and overthrow it.

Zoe: "Yes!!! Down you go!!!"

Just as the mighty tree was about to get up, two more massive fireballs from Connor and Zoe landed on its back, holding it in place.

Mighty Tree: "Argh!!! You're gonna pay for that!!!"

He hit the stony ground with his massive fist, creating many boulders. The mighty tree took a fistful of them and threw them at Zoe, who was able to dodge them just in time with a sideways leap.

Mighty Tree: "You nimble bitch!!!

The mighty tree's eyes now glowed all red as it summoned roots from the ground. They moved as if they were alive and grabbed Zoe and Connor to keep them on the ground.

Connor: "Shit!!!"

Mighty Tree: "I've got you now!!! HAHAHA!!! Now DIE!!!"

Michael opened his eyes and his vision became very blurred. His whole body ached, but it hurt him even more to see his friends being suffocated by the living roots of the mighty tree. His stomach had a deep gash and he was losing a lot of blood. There were bloody scratches everywhere his skin was exposed.

Argh, damn it... So much pain...

He looked at his fist and opened it. In his hand rested the eye of Kaltraff. The crimson pearl glowed slightly, ready to be used. He managed to get it out of his backpack just in the nick of time before he was kicked away by the mighty tree. Michael glanced back at the mighty tree, which was still choking Zoe and Connor. Both were already unconscious.

I have to save them... Without them I am nothing!

With wobbly legs, he stood up, holding his stomach in pain.

Michael: "Hey mighty son of a bitch!!! Why don't you fight someone in your own league!!?"

Mighty Tree: "Huh!?"

The mighty tree turned around and gave Michael a death stare.

Mighty Tree: "Fight with you!!!? Phaa!!! You can barely stand!!! At least your two friends put up a bit of a fight!!!'

An angry look was plastered on Michael's face. He was fed up with so much bullshit, he had enough of it all and wanted only one thing: to see those who stood in his way suffer.

Michael: "Show me, artificial tree!"

Mighty Tree: "All right! Prepare for your demise!!!"

The roots let go of Zoe and Connor and headed towards Michael at high speed. He closed his eyes and took a calm, deep breath. Just before the deadly roots could reach for Michael, he opened his eyes.

You messed with the wrong man!

Just like last time, time slowed down. Michael's eyes glowed ruby red and his vision turned blood red. The blood inside him boiled and he felt his adderdraline level rise to a maximum. He had only one thought in his mind: eliminate the threat in the worst possible way.

With lightning-fast reflexes and the strength of a true superhero, Michael grabbed the approaching living roots with both hands and swung them over him.

Mighty Tree: "Uh-oh."

The entire mighty tree connected to those roots was flung into the air and then crashed to the ground with an unimaginable force as Michael swung the roots back down. Splinters of wood flew in all directions as the powerful impact occurred between the stony ground and the wood.

Mighty Tree: "Argh!!! Pain!!! I FEEL PAIN!!!"

Michael slowly walked towards the mighty tree, his red eyes that expressed pure hatred glowing even more. Now it was the mighty tree's turn to fear for its own life.

Mighty Tree: "N-no!!! P-please! I'm sorry!!! I'M SORRY!!! HAVE MERCY!!!"

But his pleading didn't help, as Michael grabbed all the fleshy strings connected to the mighty tree and the massive flesh above it that resembled his heart.

Mighty Tree: "NOOOOO!!!"

With all his willpower and might, Michael pulled on the strings. The huge heart above him beat faster and faster until it could no longer hold itself in place. A meaty, tearing sound resounded through the cave as the giant heart was torn down from above, spurting gallons of blood in all directions. It fell directly onto the mighty tree, crushing it completely, and then the giant heart stopped beating. Michael's special abilities disappeared and his eyes returned to their normal brown color.

Michael: "That's what you get for fucking with us!"

He looked down at his own hands, which were covered in blood, not from him, but from his enemy. A sick smile spread across his face and a giggle escaped him. Then blackness took over his vision and his whole body went limp as he fell to the ground. After that, the whole cave went silent.

Chapter 19

A pair of massive, medieval-looking doors were pushed open, creaking loudly in the vast, unfamiliar hall lit by torches on the walls. A humanoid, dinosaur-like shadow strode through the hall, walking toward a much larger, human-like dinosaur sitting on a throne of some sort, hiding in the shadows. It was probably three times the size of the smaller one. The smaller one knelt in front of the one sitting on the throne and spoke. His voice was shaky and rather quiet.

???: "General, I... I have news for you."

The taller one growled in disbelief and puffed in annoyance as smoke escaped from his nostrils.

???: "Good or bad ones?"

???: "B-b-b-both, my general."

The tall one, who was known as the leader, slammed his fist against the throne with such force that it nearly knocked the smaller Redclaw off his feet.

???: "Well, what are you waiting for!? Spit out the bad ones first!"

The smaller one trembled in fear as the general, his general, raised his voice.

???: "I-I have been informed that our targets have defeated the mighty tree."

The general rose from his throne. The throne creaked loudly with relief as the heavy weight no longer pressed down on it.

???: "W-well General, before you get any angrier, you haven't heard the good news yet."

The general took a deep breath.

???: "Well, what are the good news?"

The smaller redclaw smiled slightly.

???: "The targets were captured alive, as they were all unconscious."

The tall general turned and stomped towards the massive doors. As he did so, he growled angrily.

???: "Finally! It took you morons long enough! I had my doubts and was this close to doing it myself!"

The general gestured with his claws how close he was to doing it and exited the huge hall, slamming the oversized doors with such force that a cloud of dust fell from above, burying the smaller Redclaw underneath.

Oh man! Not again!

Meanwhile, a frustrated young man named Michael was sitting somewhere in the middle of nowhere, in an endless void full of darkness, but for some reason he could see himself. He could even move and feel his body, which was new to him because the last few times he had spent there he had been completely paralyzed, invisible.

How many times have I ended up in there? I've already stopped counting. As if that mattered at all.

He got up slowly, his legs wobbly because he couldn't see his surroundings, but there was still something holding him from below and that scared him a little.

Alright, I guess I should look around. There has to be something somewhere, right?

After walking a few steps, Michael suddenly felt no ground beneath him, and he dropped down into the endless dark void. Have you ever missed a step on a dark staircase because you thought it was over, even though it was still going on, because that's what it felt like to Michael, only ten times worse. After that, he gasped and sat up, his eyes finally fully open.

Michael: "Damn, that was intense!"

As soon as he got up, he was greeted by a familiar voice.

Connor: "Rise and shine, boy!"

Michael turned to face him. Connor was sitting in a corner, leaning against a wall.

Michael: "Morning, I guess."

Connor: "How are you?"

Michael held his forehead as it hurt a little.

Michael: "I think I'm okay? My head hurts a little bit, but that's it."

Connor: "Well, that's good to hear that you're okay. But you know what? I feel like crap right now!!! I'M NOT FINE!!!"

Connor's outburst echoed through the whole place. The back of his muzzle was folded back, showing his razor sharp teeth as he bared them and growled like a monster ready to commit countless murders. Michael was surprised by his outburst. He had never known Connor to be so angry about anything. But then, he had only met him a few days ago.

Michael: "Buddy, calm down. What's got you so upset... this time?"

Michael's eyes widened as he looked around at his surroundings. The walls were made of mossy and damp bricks. The only way out of the small room was blocked by rusty metal bars. They were all trapped in a cell.

Impossible...

Michael stood up and wanted to go to the blocked exit to see what was outside the cell, but he was stopped by a sudden force. The sound of small pieces of metal colliding against each other like a chain echoed through the cell and his left foot began to hurt. He almost stumbled, but managed to regain his balance. Looking down at his left foot, Michael noticed that it was chained to a wall.

Hah! Just like in that movie SAW! There is no way am I going to amputate my own foot!

Michael: "So, um, what exactly did I miss?"

Connor growled in annoyance.

Connor: "I haven't been awake that long, but one thing's for sure, we got captured by those red-scaled, no-good sons of bitches!"

Only now did Michael realize that Zoe wasn't even here with them. Michael started to panic. Thousands of negative thoughts filled his mind.

Damn it! Where is she!!! Is she okay!? Is she hurt? What if she's...

"Where's Zoe!!!"

Connor: "Damn it, I don't know! I hope she's okay, because she's not here with us! Maybe she got lucky and escaped! I don't know!"

I hope he's right. Maybe she managed to escape in time and is hiding somewhere. I hope you're okay, Zoe. I really wouldn't know what to do if I lost you.

Michael's first reason for leaving his old life was to start over, to get a new chance, and at first it went well. On his new adventure he met Zoe, a loving girl who was not human, well, not entirely. The two grew close and everything was perfect until those red claws showed up. Since then, Michael made it his mission to protect her at all costs. If he failed, he would fall back into his depressed state where he didn't give a damn about himself or the things around him. His mind panicked and he began to sweat. He really cared about her and if something happened to her, he would break his promise to Zalkan, her and himself.

Connor: "Great! We're both chained to a wall, can't get out of here, my abilities don't help against these chains, and worst of all, my sister Zoe could be in danger! That fucking sucks!!!"

What a bummer! Those damn red claws took everything away from me! If only I'd had my pocket knife with my lighter, at least I'd have had a head start! Wait a minute...

Michael touched the top of his pocket and found that it was fully loaded. He smiled slightly and turned to Connor, who was engrossed in his own thoughts.

Michael: "Hey Connor! I don't think all is lost. We may still have a chance to get out of here."

Connor's ears pricked up at the mention of escaping this prison cell.

Connor: "Huh. Really? And how?"

Michael opened both his pockets and took out his lighter and pocket knife. He proudly held them in the air and gave Connor a smile.

Hah! Those stupid red claws probably couldn't figure out how a zipper pocket works! A big W for the zipper pocket!

Connor: "So what about it?"

Michael: "What about it? We can finally leave this shit hole! I say we play a little game called jailbreak."

Michael looked down at his foot and spotted a lock with the chain hanging from it. He sat down and immediately set about picking it. Yes, picking locks with a knife is possible, of course with a proper knife structure and method. This task requires a high degree of skill and precision that a normal knife cannot provide. Michael tried it a few times when he was taken hostage in the village a few days ago, but failed miserably. But now their lives depended on it and Michael had to make it work this time if they were going to break out.

Connor: "What are you doing?"

Michael: "Quiet! I need to concentrate."

Soft clanking metal sounds filled the cell as Michael carefully fumbled with the blade of his pocket knife in the lock. A few seconds later, a click sounded and the lock opened and fell to the floor with the chain, his foot now free.

Nailed it!

Connor rubbed his eyes and blinked a few more times, thinking he wasn't seeing something right. His human friend actually managed to open the lock.

Connor: "What the hell!!! You actually managed to get free without a key! How did you do that? Magic?"

Says the one who can read minds, heal others, and set everyone on fire. Yet I'm told I'm using magic. Ha, how ironic.

Michael: "Heh... I guess I'm the master at picking locks."

Michael took a few steps around the cell to relieve his leg, since it still hurt a little from being chained so tightly.

Connor: "So, are you going to do your little trick with your little magic fingers on me too or what are you waiting for?"

Michael: "Yeah, yeah, sure."

The human walked up to his friend and squatted down. Immediately he started to break the lock with his great lockpicking skills. After a short time, the lock already gave up and opened, freeing Connor's foot as well.

Connor: "Thanks, lad."

Michael: "Now it's time to get the fuck out of here and look for Zoe."

Michael walked toward the gate that blocked their exit from the cell. As he looked at it more closely, he discovered another lock hanging on the other side that was difficult to reach. The metal bars of the gate were tight enough, but the fact that the lock hung on the other side made it even harder for Michael to pick.

Ah, you've got to be fucking with me!

Connor: "Well, what are you waiting for? Open it!"

Michael sighed deeply, visibly annoyed.

Michael: "I would if I could."

A quiet minute passed as they stared at each other.

Connor: "What do you mean you can't? You just made it two times in a row without failing. Why can't you do it this time?"

Michael: "Are you stupid or what!? Can't you see that the lock is out of reach for me!? I can't reach shit from the other side! It's all on me why we're so close to getting out of here in the first place, so why don't you make yourself useful and melt that damn gate down!"

Connor: "I may be able to create green fire, yes, and I may also be fire resistant to it. But the objects and the environment can still hurt me if they get too hot, and even normal fire can still hurt me. Plus, I don't want to suffocate from the lack of oxygen down there since we're somewhere underground, and I don't think you'd want that either buddy."

Michael: "Geez, okay, okay, I get it. You don't have to read me the safety rules out loud from chemistry class! I already know them."

Never followed them though, hohoho!!!

Connor: "Your chemistry what?"

Michael: "You wouldn't get it."

Suddenly, several light thuds rang through the hallways, causing the ground beneath them to shake slightly. Connor's ears pricked up in the air as he listened closely.

Connor: "Hey, you hear that too?"

Michael closed his eyes and held his breath for a few seconds as he focused his full concentration on his ears.

Michael: "Yeah, I hear it too. What is that sound?"

Connor: "Hell if I know."

Those thuds got louder and louder and the ground shook even more as the sound got closer and closer to their cell.

Wait a minute... Are those footsteps?

Connor: "Shit! I'm sensing someone's thoughts! Someone's after us!"

Shit! Okay, think Michael, think!

Connor: "Okay, I've got a plan! We'll just return to our original position and pretend we're still chained to the wall! As soon as we get the chance, we'll strike!"

Michael gave Connor a quick nod. They both sat down where they had woken up and looked at each other. They also hid their feet behind them so as not to expose themselves, since that was the chained body part.

Connor: "Get ready. On my signal."

Connor's mouth didn't move a bit as he talked Michael through his mind.

Signal? What signal?

Connor: "You'll see..."

Damn... I can't believe we're actually going to do it. Well, all right. At least we'll die in battle.

Michael grabbed his pocket knife and lighter and hid them behind him. They both decided to turn towards the locked metal bars when they heard a low growl and heavy breathing.

Oh... God...

Standing in front of the cell now was a redclaw that neither of them had ever seen before. It had a large scar running through its left eye and was much larger and muscular than a normal redclaw, about three times larger to be exact. Its healthy eye was the color of red, expressing true hatred. It also carried a strange golden axe on its claw that looked so sharp that it could cut even the hardest materials there were. But there was something about this axe that caught Michael's and Connor's attention. At the tip was a glowing blue transperent pearl. It looked just like the eye of Kaltraff, only a different color.

Connor: "There's no way. Don't tell me it's the eye of Nibelon!?"

The eye of Nibelon? Is it like the eye of Kaltraff?

Connor: "Yes, it also gives certain powers to the one who possesses it. But I don't know what they are, because everyone else's powers are different."

Wait. So there are more of these things!? All the time I've spent here on this world, so far I've only gotten one of them!? How many are there exactly?

Connor: "Oh, there are quite a few of them, seven in total. The remaining five are the eye of Occulus, the eye of Ralturf, the eye of Gransel, the eye of Rudiger, and the last one I can't remember."

There are seven in total! Heck, there are seven! And I only have one! Well, not really anymore, because mine is fucking gone! I lost it. I can't remember how! Maybe we really are totally fucked. Why didn't you tell me there were seven before!?

Connor: "I... I thought you already knew."

How the fuck should I know!? I'm a fucking alien on this world, I don't really belong here, and you expect me to know the whole lore of your planet!!!? I bet you also expect me to know something about your faith and the true God who created this beautiful world! Well, let me tell you this. I don't have the slightest fucking idea! Maybe it was a guy named Steven who splattered all over the galaxy!

Their argument in their heads died away when they heard an ugly laugh mixed with a horrified growl.

???: "HAHAHA!!!"

Connor: "That must be the leader!"

Connor and Michael looked at the huge redclaw, who pulled a key out of his pocket and opened the cell door. The door made an unpleasant creaking sound as it was pushed open. Michael panicked and lit his lighter behind him. Then he held the blade of his knife over the small flame to heat it up.

???: "Hello, it looks like you two prisoners are finally awake."

Silence fell in the room, only the howling winc could be heard.

General Bigclaw: "Not so talkative, huh? Oh yes, where have my true manners gone? I haven't even introduced myself. I am General Bigclaw, leader of my redclaw tribes and soon to be leader of the planet Xenonan. My mission is to wipe out all who oppose me, including you damn Xenonans! HAHAHAHA!!!"

The general pointed his huge, sharp claw at Connor, which Connor returned with a hateful snarl.

General Bigclaw: "But you... I don't know exactly what to do with such a strange creature."

He glared at Michael and pointed his massive, sharp claw at him. Michael swallowed and mustered the courage to say something, even though his voice was shaky and low.

Michael: "M-m-me?"

The general smiled fleetingly and nodded.

General Bigclaw: "Yes, you! You are something new, something interesting, something I have never seen before! The clothes you wear, the skin and hair you have, the way you fought against my strong and fearless men. You are very special, to say the least! You are smart, fast and strong. I could use someone with such talents in my family. So I'm going to give you a choice. Either you join me and my men, or I will kill you both on the spot!"

Connor: "Nah, he will pass."

General Bigclaw: "Quiet, you furred fuck! So what's it to be, strange creature? Will you join me or suffer a miserable death?"

Michael: "I'm not deciding until you tell me where Zoe is!"

The General snorted and rolled his huge eyes in annoyance.

General Bigclaw: "The princess of Xenonan? You don't have to worry about that crazy fox girl anymore! She won't be a burden to anyone anymore, as she's about to live her last moment."

Her... Last... Moment...?

General Bigclaw: "Think about it and choose wisely. You could be rewarded with tons of treasure every time you fight! You could become much stronger because we will train you hard! You could become the next leader of the redclaw tribe! You could be the true ruler of the Xenonan planet in the near future and have the largest harem with the hottest redclaws out there! You could be..."

The general's words grew quieter by the second and a loud ringing sounded in Michael's head, growing louder by the second.

Z-zoe i-i-is... In her last m-moments...? She i-is dying? I-I faile d...

Michael closed his eyes and clenched his teeth so hard they threatened to shatter. His rage meter literally exploded, for he was long past his limit! He was so damn angry that the limited vocabulary couldn't even describe it.

General Bigclaw: "So, what do you say? Are you in?"

Join you? I have a much better idea that is much more fun. I'll slice that thick throat of yours open and watch the red goop spill out!

General Bigclaw: "Hmm, what's that?"

The General took a few steps closer to Michael and crouched down when he spotted a lock lying around. With his massive claws, he carefully picked it up and looked at it from different angles.

Connor: "Now is the time! He's distracted! Let's finish him off!"

Before the general could figure out why the lock was even there, Michael took his chance and struck first. He attacked the general with his pocket knife, its blade glowing slightly orange from overheating. He stabbed it directly into the general's eye, which was already riddled with a scar. The general let out a tremendous cry of pain and stumbled back. The hot knife stuck in his eye and melted it quickly, while smoke rose from it and blood leaked out.

General Bigclaw: "Argh!!! You pale naked bastard!!! You'll pay for this!!!"

The General gripped his deadly weapon tightly with both claws and swung it at Michael with great speed. Without Connor's help, Michael would probably be dead now, as a green fireball hit the golden axe. The force of the impact was strong enough to rip the axe with the blue pearl from its host's grip. A loud metallic clang rang through the cell as the heavy weapon hit the floor, which was in the corner on the other side.

Connor: "Get it before he does!!!"

Michael ran as fast as he could towards the axe, but was stopped by the redclaw general himself as he pinned him against the wall and choked him. His grip was far too strong and Michael could do nothing but stay awake for a few more seconds until he would lose consciousness.

Oof, his grip is strong!

The general chuckled as Michael struggled for breath. His eyes began to water and his vision became blurry.

Is this how I'm going to die? Will this be the end of my journey? Zoe, if you can still hear me somehow. I love you above all else!

General Bigclaw: "Hehehe... Pathetic..."

A huge fireball hit the general from the side and he was thrown to the other side of the cell. He crashed into the brick wall and the whole cell shook as if an earthquake had occurred.

General Bigclaw: "Ouch!!!"

The general groaned in pain as he got back to his feet. Meanwhile, he picked up his weapon again. He surveyed his own face in the reflection of the golden axe. Michael's pocket knife was still hot and stuck in the general's eye. Blood oozed from it and dripped onto the stony ground.

General Bigclaw: "I'm not done with you rats yet! I will be back!!! And when I come back, I will kill you all in cold blood!!!"

The blue pearl on the tip of the golden axe began to glow brightly until the general disappeared all at once.

Connor: "What the... Where did he go!"

Michael sat on the floor and took several deep breaths to calm himself. He held his throat in pain and coughed a few times. His hand was also completely burned from holding his overheated knife too long. Connor walked up to his friend and knelt down in front of him.

Connor: "Hey lad, you okay?"

Michael: "My throat and my right hand hurt like hell."

Connor touched Michael's throat and right hand with his paws, which then began to glow a little.

Michael: "Thanks. My neck and hand feel much better now."

Connor smiled and stood up.

Connor: "You don't have to thank me. That's what friends are for, right?"

Yeah... Friends...

Michael looked at the floor with a depressed expression on his face. Then he heaved a deep sigh.

Connor: "Hey, uhh... why the long face? Are you okay?"

Michael: "Not really... I... I don't even know what to do right now. I don't think we can beat him that easily."

Connor: "You've got to be kidding me. You already know you managed to hurt him. You messed up one of his eyes and he backed off!"

Michael: "Yes, and!? What does it matter!? First, I hit his eye, which was already fucked up. Second, he can teleport wherever he wants, whenever he wants! Next time he'll come up behind us and knock us down for good! And if we get another chance to hurt him, he'll fuck off like the wimp he is!"

Connor took a seat next to Michael and patted him on the shoulder.

Michael: "How are we even supposed to take him out. I don't have any weapons on me and my knife is gone now! If I had the eye of Kaltraff, we might have a chance against him. My point is, we're both screwed!"

Connor: "And what about Zoe? She might still be here."

Michael: "Zoe..."

Michael paused for a moment. His eyes began to water and a quiet sob escaped him.

Michael: "You heard what the general said, right? She's out there dying and we don't know how much time we have left or where she is. I don't even know if we're going to make it in time."

Connor: "That's where you're wrong, Michi."

Michael: "Huh?"

Connor: "While the General was talking to you before the fight, I caught a glimpse into his mind. Zoe was captured by the general himself before she managed to escape his grasp. She's still out there somewhere, hiding."

That sack full of worthless shit!!! If I find out she's missing even a single hair, I'm going to pull my knife out of his eye and carve out his anal cavity with it!!!!

Michael looked towards the now open metal door, hoping to find Zoe and end this war between the Xenons and those damn redclaws once and for all. Wiping away the tears that threatened to escape his eyes, he stood up and turned to Connor before saying.

Michael: "I'm ready when you are."

Chapter 20

Drip... Drip... and dripping. That was the sound of water drops falling from time to time from the moss-covered ceiling. Everything else was rather quiet, as if the place was completely empty, and that scared Zoe. She had actually expected to fight hundreds of redclaws, since she was in the middle of their dungeon.

But it was better that way anyway, because she didn't want to attract attention, and she had already taken a good beating from the redclaw general himself before she could free herself from his grip. She had only one goal in mind, and that was to find her brother and her alien lover. Together, they surely had a chance to win the upcoming final battle.

Quietly, she followed the brick hallway covered in damp moss and stopped before an intersection. Before she even dared to stick her head out to peek, she scanned her immediate surroundings with her telepathic ability. When she didn't spot anyone, she sighed in relief and took a look. Her white pointed ears were the first to pop out of the corner, ahead of her whole head.

All possible paths led to a long corridor, except for the one on the left, at the end of which there was a wooden door. Therefore, Zoe decided to walk quietly towards it. Arriving at the wooden door, she tried to open it, but the door would not push open. She looked a little further down and discovered a lock. Of course the door would be locked. She growled in annoyance and glanced at her paws. They had bloody scratches all over them and in some places her fur was torn. She sighed before extending her claws and trying to pick the lock with them.

Something cracked in the lock and then she felt an immense pain, she yelped. Blood oozed out as she pulled back her paw. One of her claws broke off and was now stuck in the lock. She considered setting the door on fire, since it was made of wood, but when a thought occurred to her, she decided against it. She didn't want to attract attention.

An excellent idea came to her mind on how to pick the lock. She remembered her prize when they played the shell game with the mighty tree. There was this strange metal object she had won that drove Michael crazy. He told her it was a gun, a dangerous weapon. But he didn't get a chance to explain to her exactly what it was and how it worked.

She pulled it out of her tribal bra and held the cold object with both paws. It had a strange looking handle to hold onto, and a small barrel sticking out from the other end. She took a look inside and saw only blackness. There was another strange metal part there, the trigger. Perfectly shaped for a finger to pull.

She thought about it carefully before pointing the gun at the lock and leaning her claw against the trigger. She counted down from three in her mind and pulled the trigger at zero.

Nothing happened.

Suddenly she heard a distant roar behind her. Now she was worried about Michael and Connor. They could be in danger right now, and worse, they could be dying. Immediately she turned, sprinted to where the roar was coming from, and crossed the intersection again.

After a few minutes of running, she decided to take a little break and huffed. She looked around and realized she was in a huge, long hallway. Chandeliers hung from the ceiling, bathing the entire room in light. On the sides of the hallways were many metal gates, one of which was wide open.

She walked toward the open gate and glanced at the other gates. They looked like prison cells. Some of them had chains on the walls and a table with torture tools. In others lay corpses, redclaws who had betrayed their own kind, and Xenonians who couldn't fight back well enough. The thought that her loved ones were dead or tortured in one of these cells made her weep.

She was now only a few steps away from the open cell door. Her heartbeat quickened and she suppressed the urge to sob. Why was the door open? Was Michael or Connor in there? Had they survived and escaped just like she had in time? She hoped to God they were still alive somewhere nearby.

Arriving at the cell door, she took a peek inside. The first thing she noticed were the drops of blood on the stony floor. The next thing she noticed was that one of the walls was cracked all over, as if something had been pressed against it with full force. Something had happened in there, like a fight. She also noticed the two locks that were on the floor. Whoever was in there had managed to escape.

A faint smell entered her sensitive nose as she crouched down and sniffed one of the locks lying on the floor. Her eyes widened and her ears pricked up as she continued to sniff it. That smell was all too familiar to her, it was Michael's. She smiled weakly and sighed in relief. They had managed to escape and were most likely fine, just like her.

There it was again! The loud and deep roar of a redclaw. It sounded much closer now than before. Immediately she jumped back up and tried again to scan the surroundings with her telepathic ability for any spirits nearby. There were four in all, but she was still too far away to tell which presence belonged to whom. Now she had to be quick, because Michael and Connor might be involved in a dangerous fight.

With that in mind, Zoe sprinted out of the jail cell and made a sharp left turn, nearly slipping. She ran down the huge prison hallway and rushed toward the nearest wooden door, which was wide open.

After stepping through the open door, she found herself in another hallway, but this time it was much smaller and dimly lit. On the floor lay a beaten redclaw leaning against the wall with a small pool of blood underneath. Her emerald eyes glowed green as she tried to read his mind, but she felt nothing. She was too late, for he was dead. There were three spirits left that she sensed, and now that she was closer, she could tell which spirit belonged to whom. One was Michael and the other two were evil redclaws, but Connor didn't seem to be anywhere. That was because the powers of their kind were immune to each other. That meant she couldn't read Connor's mind, set him on fire, or heal him. She hoped Connor was there with Michael, too.

Eat that, you red scaled fucker!!!

Now she could hear Michael's thoughts. She continued to follow that long brick hallway. Michael's thoughts were now made even clearer to her. They sounded angry, full of hate and without a tiny bit of mercy towards the red-scaled, but behind all the anger was fear and anxiety.

She gained speed, panting with every second. She was almost there! Just around this corner at the end of the hallway. She could hear Michael's and Connor's voices now. They sounded like they were fighting, emitting war cries as they threw a punch now and then. A few roars also reached her pointed ears. Judging by the cries of pain and moans, the redclaws couldn't put up much of a fight, which meant they were getting their asses handed to them.

Now that she had finally arrived at the corner, she peered around it and inspected the situation carefully at first. Connor was busy wrestling with a redclaw on the ground. Both were snarling and snapping in anger at each other. Michael, however, had another idea how to fight his opponent. He grabbed hold of the heavy metal chain that held him in the cell with his hands and threw it upward. Like a cowboy, he swung the metal chain in the air and waited for his opponent to make the first move.

Michael: "Come to me you red scaled motherfucker!!!! I'll show you how to fuck someone up right!!!"

The taunting made the redclaw really angry. He growled and showed his monstrous and sharp teeth. With his clawed foot he made a warning gesture like a bull about to charge on his enemy. A loud roar came out of his fearsome looking mouth.

Michael: "Yeah, fuck you too!!!"

The redclaw charged at Michael with its long, sharp claws, ready to chop Michael's head to pieces, but Michael was faster. With all his strength, the young man swung the metal chain at his opponent. The metal chain wrapped around the red claw's throat, preventing it from breathing.

Michael: "Gotcha, bitch!!!"

The redclaw fumbled with its own claws on the chain around his throat, trying to create a little space so it could breathe easier, but Michael couldn't let it happen. He kept the redclaw in a stranglehold, pulling on both ends of the chain as best he could.

At first, the redclaw fought back like crazy, running all over the hallway while dragging Michael behind him. With each passing second, the redclaw grew weaker from the lack of oxygen and after the last cough, it fell to the floor unconscious.

But there was one more problem that triggered Michael a lot. The redclaw was still alive.

Michael held the chain with both hands and swung it at the fainting Redclaw.

Michael: "I AM ABOUT..."

A crack sounded through the hallway as the chain hit the redclaw's head.

Michael: "TO PULVERIZE..."

Another hit. The chain was now covered in blood.

Michael: "YOUR PATHETIC KIND..."

At the next touch, the chain made a sickening, fleshy sound.

Michael: "OUT OF THIS WORLD!!!"

With his last and strongest attack, the chain gave up and broke into many pieces. The redclaw's head was also no longer recognizeable, a pool of crimson blood lay under a pile of red flesh. Connor, who had now successfully completed the fight against this other opponent, watched anxiously what Michael was doing to his enemy.

Connor: "H-holy shit.... D-dude!"

Michael stood there looking angrily at the floor, his breathing deep and loud.

Connor: "H-hey, calm down."

Michael: "I am calm."

He spat out those three words with venom as he stared at Connor, his left eye twitching with anger.

Connor: "Dear God..."

Connor walked toward a wall and slid his back against it into a sitting position.

Connor: "I think it would be best if we took a little break."

Michael: "Very well..."

Michael took a deep breath to calm himself. He turned in Connor's direction and slowly walked towards him. Just like Connor, Michael slid his back against the mossy brick wall and sat down next to Connor.

Damn it... Where are you Zoe? Can you hear my thoughts? Are you all right?

Zoe heard his thoughts loud and clear, but Michael didn't know. His thoughts sounded sad, anxious, full of worry. This hurt her very much. A tear escaped her eye as she sniffled softly.

Connor: "Did you hear that?"

Michael: "Hear what?"

Connor: "I don't know... It was a very quiet sound. It was coming from around the corner here. I... I can't sense anyone nearby."

Michael slowly got up and crept toward the corner. When he got there, he peeked around the corner and saw only that the hallway was clear.

Hmm ... I don't know what Connor has been using lately. No one is he-

Suddenly, someone put his paw on Michael's shoulder. Michael jumped up at the sudden touch and made the hundred and eighty degree turn faster than in any video game with maximum mouse sensitivity.

Michael: "Alright, Connor. Enough with your games... Wait a minute... Zoe!? Zoe is that really you!?"

Before Michael could believe his own eyes, Zoe charged at him at full speed and jumped. Thanks to his quick reflexes, Michael was just able to catch her. She cried with joy, wrapped her arms and legs around him and hugged him tightly.

For Michael, however, everything happened too fast. He lost his balance due to Zoe's weight and fell to the ground with Zoe on top of him. A great wave of air escaped him as they hit the ground.

Michael: "Ouch, my sternum!!!"

She giggled and playfully apologized.

Zoe: "Ooops, sorry."

They stared into each other's eyes for who knows how long. His dark brown ones into her sparkling green ones, and they both smiled. Then he looked at her more closely and noticed her bloody bruises with scratches. Some of her claws on her paws were also painfully bent or even broken off and covered with dried blood.

Michael: "Z-zoe? What the hell happened? Is everything all right with you? Did he try to-"

She covered his mouth with her paw.

Zoe: "I'm fine, honest. No need to worry about me. Actually, I was more worried about you, you know."

She leaned closer to him, their noses touching, making Michael's cheeks hot.

Michael: "Heh, the same way. I-I mean. I wasn't worried about myself, I was more worried about you, yeah.... Yes... I should shut up, I sound so stupid when I'm a nervous wreck."

Zoe's paws reached for his face and she squished his cheeks.

Zoe: "And that's what I love about you. It makes you look adorable."

Not a second after she finished her sentence, she leaned closer to him and pressed her lips to his. With his hand, he reached out and caressed her fur covered ears as he melted into the kiss full of passion and love.

Meanwhile, Connor watched from across the hall.

Connor: "Yuck, gross! Get a room, you two!"

Zoe broke off the kiss, leaving a trail of salvia behind.

Zoe: "Oh, we will when this is all over!"

She leaned against Michael's ear and gently nuzzled it as she whispered to him.

Zoe: "Am I right, big guy?"

Michael lay under her with his face flushed, not knowing how to answer her properly. Zoe giggled and playfully punched him on the shoulder.

Zoe: "But first we have a job to do."

Zoe got off of him and stood up. She extended her paw to Michael, which he gladly took to stand up. Connor also decided that sitting around was enough and that something needed to be done. He walked up to the two of them.

Connor: "Yeah, we need someone whose head is rolling around.'

Zoe: "Oh Michi, I almost forgot. I have something big for you."

She reached into her bra and pulled something out from between her breasts. Michael gave her a strange look until he realized she had something hidden there. His eyes shot wide open and his jaw threatened to drop when he saw her pull out a firearm, a desert eagle.

Michael: "Holy shit!!! Is it Christmas time here now or what!!!? I've always wanted one of those!"

Zoe giggled softly.

Zoe: "Wait, there's more!"

She squeezed her own belly tightly and gagged a few times until a pop sounded. She pulled out her tongue and a red, glowing pearl lay on top. Connor gave her a somewhat disgusted look, and Michael was even more amazed.

Connor: "Gross!"

Michael: "The eye of Katraff.... I can't believe that."

Connor: "Girls are pretty messed up these days, huh?"

Michael turned to Connor.

Michael: "Dude, if you had to live on my home planet for just one day, you would have put a bullet between your eyes in the first five minutes!"

She handed Michael the red pearl and the weapon, which he gladly accepted.

Michael: "Zoe, you are a keeper! A whole ten out of good!"

Zoe: "Really? Th-thank you. I'm glad I could be a good help."

Michael wrapped his arms around her and hugged her tightly.

Michael: "You were always a good help and you still are. Without you, I'd be screwed. After all of this is over I owe you the world!"

Zoe: "Aww, I'm really glad to hear those words from you."

She gently pulled him by the cheek and gave him a quick kiss. Connor rolled his eyes and cleared his throat to get both Michael's and Zoe's attention.

Connor: "Alright, playtime is over! Now that you're back and Michael has his necessary stuff, we're more than ready to finish what we started."

Michael: "Right..."

A few pops were heard as Michael stretched. Then he unloaded the magazine of his new toy to check if it was really fully loaded, which fortunately it was. Michael had never held a real gun before, but he knew the basics of handling a gun because he had watched many instructional videos on the Internet and played violent shooter games like the evil boy he is.

Zoe: "So...where should we go now?"

Connor scratched at the bridge of his muzzle while lost in thought for a few seconds.

Connor: "Me and Michi have already explored this passage. It leads to an intersection where each path has a locked door."

Michael: "It's basically a dead end. The problem is that fat bastard of a general escaped with my pocket knife. I could have opened any damn lock."

Zoe: "What about that thing I gave you. What did you call it again, a gun?"

Michael: "Yeah, that would work. But first, it's very loud, so it will alert everyone in the building. Second, it has limited ammunition. I don't know how many bullets it would take to take that son of a bitch down, since he's three times our size and built like a tank. And then there's the fact that he can teleport, so I'll probably miss any shots. I don't want to waste any of them."

The three friends looked at each other for a minute before Michael gave up and sighed.

Michael: "All right, fine. I'm only going to shoot one lock. Better hope it's the right one."

The three hurriedly followed the corridor until they arrived at the intersection with the three locked doors. There they stood in the middle and contemplated their options thoughtfully.

Connor: "Only one lock you said. Very well, which one shall it be?"

Michael: "Hmm, good question."

Zoe: "Um, guys. R-redclaws are coming!"

A distant loud roar sounded from the hallway back.

Connor: "Shit! How many? I'm pretty sure we can take them all out with ease!"

Zoe: "I'm not so sure about that. I'm collecting a bunch of their thoughts!"

Connor: "Michael, you need to hurry up! Go ahead and pick a door!"

AH CRAP!!! Now which door should I pick? The door on the right side!? Because the right side is always right!? But what about the left? But I'm not a lefty! And what about the one in the middle? I mean, I'm pretty average, right?

Several more roars rang through the hallway and they got louder and closer.

SO THAT'S IT!!! I choose the middle one!

Michael immediately aimed his new gun at the door's lock and pulled the trigger. There was no loud bang, no recoil, no muzzle flash, and the lock was still in place. The gun didn't even fire.

Why the hell doesn't it work!?

Connor: "Oh man! HERE THEY COME!!!"

Michael turned around briefly to see an entire army of Redclaws charging around the corner and towards the three of them. They were armored from head to toe with heavy metal armor and each of them had sharp weapons like axes and swords.

There was no point in trying to fight them in such a confined space as this corridor, because there were too many of them, and Michael knew that well. Even with the eye of Kaltraff, he wouldn't have much of a chance.

Wait, the safety switch!

With a switch on the side of the gun, Michael turned off the safety. Then he aimed again at the lock and pulled down the trigger. A loud bang sounded as a round was fired from the gun and completely penetrated the lock. The lock then fell to the floor. Connor and Zoe were scared almost to death by the sudden loud noise and covered their ears with their paws, even the redclaws stopped running and stood there for a few seconds before deciding to continue their attack.

Michael: "Quick!!! In here!"

Michael pushed the door all the way open and the three quickly ran through, Michael being the last to enter. After he was through, he slammed the door shut and leaned against it with all his might. Not a second later, a sharp axe bored through the door and stuck, narrowly missing Michael's head.

Zoe: "Michael!!!"

Michael: "Run!!! I'll stop them!!! I have a plan!!!"

Zoe hesitated at first. Her face had the look of fear and worry. She didn't want to be separated from him, not again.

Michael: "Now go on!!! I'll catch up with you!!! I promise!!!"

She gave him one last look that showed a pained expression before running after Connor. Suddenly, someone gave the door a strong kick that almost sent Michael flying away, but he managed to hold on to the door. Michael looked to his left and saw another lock on the door, already unlocked.

A loud and angry roar sounded from behind the door, sending a shiver down Michael's spine. He had a crazy idea and wasn't sure if it would even work, but it was worth a try. It was either that or he had to fight. He reached for his pocket and shoved his hand deep into the dark abyss, much deeper than his mother would with her fancy purse in search of a supermarket coupon or a stick of gum.

Now come on! Please be in here!

He felt something metallic and pulled it out. In his hand was the thing that had started his whole adventure: the mysterious blue key.

Yes!!!

Another roar sounded from behind the door and a sharp blade of a sword pierced the door between his legs. With one hand he grabbed the lock, with the other he rammed the key inside and turned it.

Now please, please work!

The door took more beating by the second and Michael lost most of his strength by keeping the door closed. He took a deep breath and decided to make a speech.

Michael: "All hope abandon, ye who enter here !!"

With these words, Michael jumped away from the door. Not a second later, the redclaws rushed through the door, but instead of a person in a corridor, a bright light awaited them on the other side. After a few seconds, the screaming and yelling finally stopped. With one hand Michael shielded his eyes from the bright light, with the other he reached for the door. Then he closed the door and pulled the blue key out of the lock again. He leaned against the door and let himself slide into a resting position.

Holy shit! It actually worked!

He took a few deep breaths to calm himself. Then he stood up and opened the door again, this time without the blue key. An empty hallway awaited him, not a single redclaw in sight.

Yes, that's right. Rot in hell, you goddamn lizards!

He sighed in relief and continued to follow the corridor, catching up with his friends as if nothing had happened.

Michael: "Guys!"

Connor: "Michael!?"

Michael heard Connor's voice from a distance and put more pep in his step. He was about to sprint, but decided against it when he saw a narrow, circular staircase in front of him leading up!

Ohh man, give me a break, will you?

The human stared up in disbelief and mustered all his courage to walk them up. It felt like time had sped up as he walked up those stairs. Why, you may ask? Because he didn't get anything done in what seemed like ten minutes, just like in school, or at least that's what he thinks.

Step seven hundred and sixty-five.... Step seven hundred and sixty-six... Step seven hundred and sixty-seven...

A gasp escaped him as the boy collapsed on all fours.

What the hell kind of staircase is this!!!? The exact opposite of the staircase from the SCP wikkie, because it goes endlessly up instead of endlessly down!? Oh no... Oh no... I forgot... Now I have to start counting the stairs all over again! Argh, plus my head hurts like I smashed it against a boulder! Maybe I should focus more on getting up there instead of counting, yeah.

A few more minutes passed before Michael finally got to the top. Up there, Zoe and Connor waited patiently, bobbing their feet.

Connor: "That took long enough for such a small staircase!"

Michael: "Small?"

Michael stared down at the stairs and cried inside. It was probably only two flights.

Connor: "So, how exactly did you deal with them? I don't see a tiny bit of blood on you."

Michael scratched his head, trying to think of the best way to answer.

Michael: "They're... gone."

Zoe: "Disappeared or what? What do you mean gone? How?"

Meanwhile, somewhere in the desert, a group of ten redclaws sat in the sand and argued. They were yelling and throwing claws full of sand and dry dirt at each other. The largest of them, the leader of this group, stood up and let out one of his loudest roars, which silenced all the others.

Redclaw: "Silence!"

All the other redclaws stopped what they were doing and looked at the leader of the group, startled.

Redclaw: "Listen, I know we've landed somewhere and no one has any idea what happened, but we have to find a way back!"

All the lower rank redclaws nodded in agreement. The higher rank redclaw looked around and spotted a fence. On the fence was a sign with a symbol he had never seen before. He extended his sharp claw and pointed at the fence.

Redclaw: "All right, soldiers! This fence in the middle of nowhere catches my attention! There has to be something important behind. So we're going to cross it and take a look! Are you ready, soldiers!?"

All the redclaws jumped up and roared as they swung their arms around.

Redclaw: "REDCLAWS, CHARGE!!!"

The leader of the redclaw group sprinted toward the fence and the other nine followed him, roaring loudly. When they reached the fence, they all climbed over it and continued their sprint, ignoring the warning sign.

Redclaw: "DEATH TO XENO-"

Suddenly, there was a loud explosion that came out of the ground, sending dirt and sand flying in all directions. All the redclaws stopped in shock and everything went quiet. When the dust cleared, they could no longer see their group leader.

Thud.

There was his head, landing on the sand, covered in blood. It slowly rolled toward the others and stayed there. Now the situation escalated quickly and everyone panicked. One misstep after another followed, one explosion after another, until all that was left was a pile of limbs and a lake of fresh, crimson blood.

If only they hadn't crossed the fence and read the warning sign that said "Mines!" and the skull and crossbones above it, things might have turned out differently.

Chapter 21

The night sky was covered with thick clouds. No stars were visible, not even the moon. It was raining so hard that it was too noisy to be outside. Lightning struck behind the forest and lit up the whole place for a second, then a loud bang followed. But there was someone standing outside on the roof of a big castle, waiting patiently. He was tall, very tall. And one of his eyes glowed blood red.

Suddenly, the whole building rumbled. A couple of massive metal doors were blown open by a huge green fireball. Several redclaws were carried away by the explosion and flew off in all directions like boneless shreds. Most of them died from the impact. A few others crawled around a bit more until they died because they were still on fire.

When the smoke cleared, three people were visible. A fox, a vixen with a summoned green flame on her paws, and a human. The human who had destroyed most of his armies. The human who had managed to thwart all of his plans! The human he will kill first, right now.

The dark silhouette with the single red glowing eye puffed furiously. Steam poured from his nostrils.

Another bolt of lightning struck behind the forest. The flash of light exposed the redclaw general for a tiny moment. One eye was missing, and dried blood surrounded the empty socket. His other, healthy eye, however, expressed hatred as if he still had both of them. His teeth and claws were long and sharp, and with them he held his golden war axe, in the socket of which rested a glowing blue pearl, the Eye of Nibelon.

Michael hid his weapon in his right pocket. Slowly he reached in and let his hand rest in it. He didn't want to attack yet, because the redclaw general could easily teleport away. He needed a distraction where he had a clear line of fire.

All right, let's get this over with. Connor! Zoe! I need you two to distract him so I can knock him out.

Connor: "I heard you."

Zoe: "Mmm."

They communicated through Michael's mind to keep their plan secret, discussing how and when they would strike. However, the general knew they were communicating behind his back and frowned. He also noticed a glowing red spot on Michael's pocket, which meant he had the eye of Kaltraff.

The three friends tensed and slowly backed away as General Bigclaw slowly stomped toward them. With each step of his the ground shook. The blade of his massive golden war axe scraped across the ground, emitting sparks and an unpleasant sound. With his remaining eye, he gave them all a deadly look that startled them.

Michael: "GO!!!"

The three immediately separated after Michael shouted his command. The redclaw general stopped in surprise.

General Bigclaw: "Huh?"

Zoe ran to the left while Connor ran in the opposite direction. Both began to summon fireballs, which they hurled at the redclaw leader. The redclaw leader clutched his weapon tightly and just chuckled. Then he let out one of the loudest roars Michael and his friends had ever heard. Another bolt of lightning struck the forest and set a tree on fire. The whole place lit up briefly and a deep rumble followed from the thick clouds.

Connor and Zoe swung their arms as fast as they could and in just a second threw a couple of fireballs that created a rain of fireballs heading towards the evil general. General Bigclaw managed to deal with it without breaking a sweat. He deflected most of the attacks with his weapon and sent them back to his opponents. Some of the fireballs came too close, but he simply dodged them. Each fireball that hit the blade of his axe created sparks and a loud metallic impact sound.

Now was Michael's chance! The redclaw general was busy defending himself against the encroaching fire, probably forgetting about the human. Michael had already drawn his weapon and was trying to aim it at his enemy's head. It was a little difficult because his opponent was constantly moving. All he had to do was pull the trigger and hit, and the job would be done.

If that plan didn't work, he would have to go to plan B, which was a little more difficult. Then he would have to rely on the eye of Kaltraff and fight the redclaw leader himself. The problem with this was that the fight would take longer than any other fight he had during his adventure, as the redclaw leader was also in possession of a powerful pearl. The longer the fight would last, the longer Michael would have to lend power from his red pearl, which he would have to repay in return with his life energy. That's why he fainted a few times after a fight, because he used the borrowed powers for too long. If he used them any longer, he could fall into a prolonged sleep, maybe a coma, maybe even death.

But he didn't care about any of that. If it would finish the job, then it would all be worth it and the Xenonan would finally be rid of evil. With that thought in mind, he pulled the trigger. A loud bang sounded. But he did not hit its target. The second Michael pulled the trigger, the redclaw's eyes flashed blue and then he was gone.

Zoe: "Behind you Michael!!!"

Michael turned to face the redclaw general, who swung his axe at him. The eye of Kaltraff in his pocket now glowed brighter than ever. The blade of the axe was too close to him and threatened to cut his nose in half, setting off Michael's crimson pearl.

Time stood still for a moment. At that moment, Michael could feel himself turning into a war machine. His adnerdraline levels rose to a maximum. His blood pulsed. His skin exposed the veins of blood. And finally, his eyes turned blood red with his vision. With this power given to him, he felt unbeatable.

Now that his transformation was complete, time moved on. Immediately, Michael jumped out of the way with only the blade of the axe lightly touching his skin. He then did a backflip and shot a second time at the redclaw general in mid-air. The general managed to deflect the projectile with his weapon. A loud metallic hiss sounded as the projectile struck his axe. He almost lost his grip due to the heavy impact, but managed to hold on to his weapon.

A huge fireball, created by Connor and Zoe, was launched into the air and flew towards General Bigclaw. He noticed it in time and simply teleported back a bit. When the oversized fireball touched the ground, it exploded and covered almost the entire space between them in flames.

Damn! He's invincible with his damn axe! This is not going according to plan at all!

The general growled and slowly circled the burning area, while Michael did the same with his companions. The three stared deadly at the redclaw general as he stared back.

General Bigclaw: "Let me put this message in your head, Michael. You cannot defeat me! NO ONE CAN!!!"

General Bigclaw gripped his axe tighter, his claws scraping across the golden surface.

General Bigclaw: "You can protect yourself very well! But let's see how long!"

He held his weapon with both claws and whirled around like a wild Beyblade. As he did so, he moved slowly toward the three, his axe hot from the desire to cut flesh. The raindrops that landed on the spinning axe were flung in all directions.

Michael: "We need to spread out again now!"

The three friends ran in different directions, keeping a small distance between them. Zoe and Connor threw a few more fireballs at the spinning axe coming at them, but they didn't hit their target. The redclaw leader managed to deflect them all, and the fireballs flew back. Zoe and Connor didn't flinch, as they were immune to their own fire, but Michael still had to dodge them. Two came straight at him. The first he dodged with a leap to the side. At the second, aimed at his head, he bent backward as far as his back would allow. If his gym teacher were there, he would be very proud of Michael and call him the limbo master.

After getting through this stage without any problems, the next one came. The redclaw general teleported from one place to another while still spinning and slicing through the air with his axe. He teleported behind his opponents several times, which they had to dodge. Zoe and Connor were slower than Michael, but they handled it well. They could tell where the general would teleport to next by reading his mind. Michael couldn't do anything like mind reading, but he was incredibly fast and had better reflexes than a condylostyle.

Connor: "Michael! Any plans for our next move?"

We have to separate him from his weapon somehow.

The general teleported behind Michael, who immediately dodged the razor-sharp axe with a leap to the side. If he hadn't been so fast, his head would have rolled around.

After five seconds, the redclaw general teleported behind Connor, who also managed to dodge his attack by rolling away. Thanks to his telepathic ability, he could read the general's mind and saw the attack coming.

Again, after five seconds, the redclaw general teleported away and behind Zoe. But the second he appeared there, she hurled a fireball directly into his face. This surprised the general and he managed to protect his face a bit with his axe. He still got burned though and his remaining eye watered up from the heat. He growled in pain and teleported a few steps away from the three.

General Bigclaw: "Damn you three!!!"

Zoe actually managed to hurt him! I may have a theory on how to defeat him now. I counted the seconds every time he teleported away or to us. Each time there was a pause of at least five seconds in between, which means he can't teleport again until his five second cooldown is up. I have to fire a shot at him immediately after he teleported. If I don't hit him within five seconds, he will teleport away again. I don't think I have much time left. I can pass out at any time. I have to hurry!

The two foxes and the human slowly approached the redclaw general to tense him up a bit, and it worked very well.

The general figured that they had figured out his weakness, that he could not teleport again for five seconds. He growled angrily and slowly backed up as his three opponents rushed at him. Now he had to play this game differently. As long as he didn't teleport to attack, he didn't have to worry about the human shooting at him with his strange weapon. The real problem was these two Xenonans who would make him teleport. The human would shoot at him after that. Teleporting to attack was not an option for him now. Nor would he teleport to a safe place if he really needed to, because that was for cowards, and he was ashamed that he had once done that.

General Bigclaw: "You don't know who exactly you're messing with here!!! You should kneel before me and beg for mercy!!!"

Zoe: "We will never kneel before you!!!"

Connor: "You will pay for all the damage you have done to our kind!!!"

Connor and Zoe conjured new flames on their paws, ready to be thrown. Michael's eyes glowed even redder with rage and the redclaw general clutched his weapon tighter. Then he roared in rage and slammed his fist against his rock-hard chest before calling out to the three of them to attack him with his sharp claws.

Michael made his first move and raced at full speed towards the redclaw leader. General Bigclaw saw him coming and swung his deadly weapon at Michael, but he simply dodged and passed him by sliding on the ground between his legs. Michael then aimed his gun at the general's head and fired from behind.

The shot apparently triggered the effect of the eye of Nibelon, which was in General Bigclaw's possession, and caused him to teleport to another location, but everything was going according to plan. Zoe and Connor had already anticipated it and threw their fireballs at General Bigclaw. The red-scaled beast had no time to react properly and was hit by two hot fireballs. The impact was hot and strong enough to knock him back. He stumbled and landed on his back, dropping his golden weapon. His body was now on fire, burning most of his scales, but he didn't care and fought down the pain. He simply stood up again, as if nothing could knock him down, and reached for his weapon, which was lying on the ground next to him.

But before he could even lightly touch it, a loud shot rang out. The bullet flew toward the redclaw general at high speed and pierced his chest. He stumbled back further and landed on his back with a hard thud, a small pool of blood forming beneath him.

General Bigclaw: "Argh..."

How was that possible? No one has ever managed to beat him so badly. He was known throughout the world as a fearsome leader, an idol of pure evil! And yet, this strange creature from another world managed to defeat him.

General Bigclaw: "NOOO!!!"

He refused to accept defeat and suppressed his pain by mentally screaming at it in his mind. With wobbly legs, he slowly straightened up and turned to face the human, giving him one of his coldest looks.

General Bigclaw: "You..."

Michael: "The game is over, General Bigclaw.... You have been officially demoted."

Michael pulled the trigger again. The bullet whizzed through Bigclaw's remaining healthy eye, creating a bloody mist behind his head. Second by second, he pulled the trigger, piercing his vital organs. A click sounded, indicating to Michael that he had emptied the Deagle's magazine. Blood spurted like a fountain from the general's mouth as he fell backward. The heavy weight of his body crashed to the ground, shattering the bricks beneath him.

A loud rumble sounded and the whole castle began to shake as the bricks began to fall apart under the body of the redclaw leader, creating a hole large enough to swallow him.

And there he falls into the deep, dark abyss below, and may he never see the light again! Rot in hell, you son of a bitch!!!

Connor: "Hell yeah!!! We did it!!! Whooohoooo!!!"

Michael felt himself getting back to normal. He no longer had the rush in his blood and felt weaker. Much, much weaker.

Zoe: "Michi!"

Michael: "Huh?"

Zoe sprinted toward Michael, spreading her arms as she did so, ready to give her lover the biggest hug she had ever given him. He just stood there, not moving, staring at her in bewilderment. His head ached and his vision was a little blurry. It was really strange to see Zoe three times at once, all side by side. He held his hand under his nose and felt some kind of liquid. He looked at the floor and saw drops of blood, his own blood.

Suddenly his legs couldn't hold him up and he fell to his knees and then face down in a puddle and passed out.

Zoe: "Oh my God! Michael!?"

Connor: "Hey! What happened to him? Why did he fall?"

Michael could still hear their voices, but they were getting quieter by the second.

Zoe: "His breathing is getting slower and slower! Damn it, Connor, help me! Don't just stand there and watch! My Michael is going to die!!!"

Their voices were now too low and distant for Michael to understand. He could only make out Zoe's crying, and it broke his heart to hear it. Then there was nothing. Just pitch black. No sounds. Not even his own thoughts.

Everything was silent.

Chapter 22

Have you ever wanted to know what nothing feels like? Like literally nothing? Well, it's an infinite black void with nothing whatsoever. No thoughts, no feelings, no sounds, not even a single soul except the person experiencing it, in this case a young man named Michael. How long had he been in this nothingness? No one could tell, not even himself, since he lacked the ability to do so. His mind slowly regained its sense and he felt himself floating through space.

Suddenly, a voice called out to him.

???: "Michael."

It was that deep female voice again, as if from an older person. Michael could swear he had heard that voice before, but where exactly was it coming from again?

Zahra: "Michael, it's me, Zahra."

Now Michael remembered. It was this strange older woman who had spoken to him once, even before he had discovered this strange world called Xenonan. She also spoke to him a second time when he was in a dark void, just as he was now, and explained that he was in a place called Limbo, a place between life and death.

Was he there again, in limbo, just like the last time? Was he? Was he going to die? So many questions ran through his mind and he wanted to ask them to Zahra. But no sound came from him.

Zahra: "We don't have much time left. I know you have many questions, but I'm afraid I can't answer them all. Therefore, I will tell you only what is necessary."

She appeared before Michael's eyes. He could now see her for the first time. She looked very much like Zoe, a humanoid vixen who wore tribal clothing, and she also had the same fur pattern with color.

Zahra: "You are indeed in limbo. In fact, you were there all the time. For a whole week."

Michael could not process her statement. It did not make any sense. How could he have been in limbo for a whole week? He remembered challenging General Bigclaw, and it seemed like only a few minutes ago. Surely that wasn't a week ago…? Or maybe it was. He couldn't remember the fight itself or what happened afterwards. Had he received too much power from the crimson pearl and gone into a coma? Did he lose the fight and get beaten up pretty badly? Did he even win? He couldn't tell.

Zahra: "I wanted to thank you personally, Michael. Thank you for coming to our magical world and siding with the good people, thank you for saving this world by defeating the corrupted, and finally, thank you for protecting my precious little girl."

A small white square appeared behind her and grew larger and larger. When it was large enough to pass through, it stopped growing. Zahra sighed sadly and looked at the white passage.

Zahra: "I wish I could do more, but this is it. This is where I get off. Goodbye, Michael."

She walked through without looking back, and the white square shrank before disappearing comepletely.

Suddenly, pain filled Michael's body and he felt himself regaining his senses. A smell of alcohol and other drucs filled his nose as if he were in a hospital.

Where am I? I can't open my eyes. I can't move. Everything hurts so much. The pain is the worst I have experienced so far. What exactly is happening? Why do I hear beeping sounds?

???: "He's regaining consciousness, Doctor Harrold. He's finally waking up."

Michael finally opened his eyes and immediately closed them again. The light above him was too bright. It took a few minutes for his eyes to adjust to the brightness. He could make out a white hospital room and four people surrounding his hospital bed. Two of them were his parents and the other two were doctors, a woman and a man.

Hmm, what? What is going on here? Why am I here and how!?

Michael was really confused now. Just a few seconds ago, he had been fighting General Bigclaw. And now he was suddenly lying in a hospital bed with an oxygen mask strapped on.

Michael: "M-Mom? D-Dad? What happened?"

Michael couldn't say much more. His throat hurt and he was coughing a lot.

Michael's mom: "Shh, it's okay. Everything will be okay."

She sobbed. Tears of relief ran down her cheeks as she stroked her son's hair. His father sat in a chair on the other side of the bed, looking down at the floor. The look on Michael's father's face expressed fear at almost losing his son, shame and regret at putting his job before his son, but also relief because Michael had just woken up from a weeks-long slumber.

Why am I here again!!! Why am I back in this... of all places! This fucking place!? It doesn't make any fucking sense!!!

Michael tried to move, but he was in a lot of pain. He wanted to reach into his pocket to get his key out, but noticed that he wasn't even wearing his proper clothes. He was wearing hospital clothes for patients. The pain he felt was unbearable, and he needed to return to Xenonan as soon as possible. Zoe would be able to patch him up with her magic in no time.

Michael's father: "Now is not the time to get out of bed, son. You've been through a lot. You need to stay in bed and rest."

Michael struggled to speak again, ignoring the pain in his throat.

Michael: "K-key!"

Michael's parents looked confused when he mentioned a key.

Michael's mother: "A key? What kind of key?"

Michael: "B-blue k-k-key. Where is it?"

Doctor Harrold cleared his throat to get the attention of the three.

Doctor Harrold: "I apologize for interrupting this conversation, but there are important things that need to be cleared up first. Well, Michael, first of all, a man named Peterson, who was walking his dog by a river, found you floating motionless above the water. He pulled you out and immediately called the ambulance. Without him and his quick action, you wouldn't have survived. Count your lucky stars."

Yes, totally lucky stars!

Doctor Harrold: "No one knows how it really happened, but we have a theory that you somehow fell into a river from a great distance and hit your head on a sharp rock. The accident caused a fractured skull, a broken left leg and a lot of bruises on your body. You fell into a week-long coma due to the amount of blood loss. It was a miracle that you woke up at all. Yesterday, your heartbeat and breathing slowed down even more and....we almost lost hope."

I was in a coma!? For a whole damn week!? But how!? I was in a completely different place! Unless it was all just a dream....

Doctor Harrold: "Anyway, you came through it fine and I bet your parents couldn't be prouder of you. Me and Doctor Grenjin will be by later to run some tests, but for now, enjoy some time with your family."

The two doctors closed the door and left the three alone.

Michael now realized something and he wished he never had. This realization broke his heart and his mind. It hurt him so much inside just thinking about it.

So, everything I've experienced in the last week...? It wasn't real? Was it all just my imagination? Just a dream? The mysterious blue key wasn't real.... The portal wasn't real... My new friend, Zoe, wasn't real.... Zoe... She wasn't real... The love of my life was just a part of my imagination.... The girl who gave me a whole new meaning to life.... No...

His life changed when he found the blue key. He met new friends and the love of his life, Zoe. She changed him. She gave him the hope and purpose to go on with his life. She loved and cared for him very much. He was so happy there. Even though he struggled more than being with Zoe. But it wasn't real at all. It was all just a lie!

Michael just lay there motionless. His mind was completely blank, not a single thought crossed his mind. This realization hit him to the core and broke him completely.

His parents watched his dull expression. He didn't even turn around to look at his parents. He just stared at the ceiling without even blinking.

Michael's mom: "Sweetie, are you okay?"

No...

He didn't react at all and just continued to stare at the ceiling, his eyes not expressing any emotion.

Michael's father: "Son, you have to tell us what exactly happened. Did someone push you off a bridge? You know, the bridge you always use to get home?"

I don't even remember anything like that. How did I end up here in the first place?

An image of himself appeared in his mind, in which he saw himself standing over a wooden fence of a bridge. He had his eyes closed as tears leaked out, and a violent thunderstorm raged in the background.

Shit... Did I really jump?

Michael's father: "Son, you have to tell us.... This is important."

There was silence between them for a minute, only the medical device attached to Michael whirred and beeped softly.

Michael: "I... I did this..."

Both his parents looked at him in confusion. Michael coughed several times and held his throat in pain before continuing.

Michael: "I-I did this to myself."

His eyes watered as tears threatened to escape his eyes.

Michael: "I jumped off the bridge..."

Michael's parents were pulled back by his dark statement. His mother hid her face behind her face as she began to cry uncontrollably. His father's mouth remained open, an incredulous look on his face.

Michael's father: "Why...? Why are you doing this!!! Don't you have any idea how much we care about you? How hard we worked to get the things you wished for and always wanted!!!? Everything would have been for nothing if you hadn't made it!"

If there was one thing Michael truly feared, it was his father raising his voice against him. But in this adventure he had been on, he learned to deal with his fear, and so he raised his voice as well.

Michael: "B-because I don't give a shit about my life! I fucking hate it! I w-was in a d-different world! In a different and b-better l-life! Of course that motherfucker who saw me jump off the bridge had to take me to a hospital and he ruined everything! Bring him to me and I'll rip him in half!!!"

Shock was written all over his parents' faces, for it was the first time he had ever snapped at them so terribly. His voice sounded deep and loud, more like a roar than a scream. At this point, he sounded more like a demon from the pits below than the son they knew.

After taking a few deep breaths, Michael calmed down again. A sad expression replaced his frustrated one.

Michael: "This dream felt so real.... I've never had an adventure like this before. I was so happy. I met a lot of new friends. I even got a girlfriend! Now it's all g-gone! If I had hit my head just a b-b-bit harder, I would probably be sleeping more. If only I had died..."

Michael's mother began to cry harder. It hurt her heart to hear such words from her own son. She didn't understand what made him hate his life.

Michael: "I'm sorry I yelled at you. It wasn't your fault. It's just... I'm not happy with my life now. No friends... Being bullied at school.... Bad grades... Crappy teachers. When I was in coma, everything changed for the better. But it was all just a dream. None of it was real, and I thought it was all real all the time..."

Michael's father leaned forward from his chair and patted his son on the shoulder.

Michael's father, "Don't let this get you down, son. It may take a little while, but you'll get over it."

Michael's mother: "Why didn't you tell us you were so upset? We could have done something, then none of this would have happened."

Michael: "Yeah, like what? Another gaming setup? Don't get me wrong, it's nice, but what I really want is a real friend, someone I can trust with my life, someone I can spend time with, someone I can talk to.... I don't have one."

Michael paused for a moment and sobbed.

Michael: "I didn't tell you about my problems because you were always busy with your jobs and I didn't want to add more problems. I kept it to myself for years, hoping that one day everything would change for the better."

Michael's mother wiped away his tears with her thumb. She had always done that when he was crying as a toddler, and it brought back old memories for both of them.

Michael's mother: "Would you please tell us about your little adventure? It will help you get over it."

Michael: "Well, in my D-dream version, I didn't jump off the bridge. There was a strange voice in my head encouraging me not to. A few seconds later, a crow was struck by lightning and I discovered this b-blue mysterious k-key on its claw. I opened a d door with it and it took me to another world. There I met some anthropomorphic foxes and made friends with them. One of them fell in love with me and I fell in love with her. Even though she was an alien and not human, she was the most beautiful creature I have ever seen. We fought together… survived together… Helped each other… Loved each other… I will never forget her."

Michael paused for a moment and took a deep breath.

Michael: "I was so happy when I escaped my depressed reality…. And of course it turned out to be a dream!"

Michael's mother hugged him lightly to reassure him.

Michael's mom: "Shh, it's going to be okay. We'll make sure you're happy again. We will never leave you alone again. We don't care if we lose our job, because losing our child would be unforgivable."

Michael's father: "We also have a little present! You wished for a friend and now you're finally getting one. This is Zoe. What a surprise, huh?"

Michael's dad gave him a little stuffed animal. The stuffed animal looked just like Zoe. White fur, green front paws, black back paws, green sparkling eyes, and even the tribal clothing looked the same.

Michael: "…"

Suddenly there was a knock at the door and Doctor Harrold and Doctor Grenjin entered.

Doctor Harrold: "I hate to tell you this, but visiting hours are over."

Michael's father patted Michael on the shoulder again.

Michael's father: "We'll be back in the morning. We promise."

Michael's mother kissed him on the forehead.

Michael's mother: "We love you Michael. Good night."

Michael: "I love you too, Mom and Dad... Goodnight."

They both left the room and closed the door.

Michael hugged the stuffed animal tightly and closed his eyes.

Please be real Zoe... I need you...

Epilogue

It was now the middle of the night and Michael was sitting on the hospital bed unable to fall asleep. His parents were gone now that visiting hours were over, but they would be back in about eight hours. He couldn't move properly because of the pain, even with the nurse giving him pain medication, and he was all alone. He hated it, all of it.

If only there was a way to get back to my dream. Do I have to go back into a coma to do that?

A brilliant idea popped into his head. What if he hit his head so hard that he went back into a coma? Would he return to Xenonan and his girlfriend or would he have a completely new experience? Would it be a good dream or a nightmare? After thinking for a while, he decided against it. It wasn't worth the risk.

Curiosity got the better of him when he spotted a drawer right next to his hospital bed. He just managed to reach it and opened it. Inside were some papers, pencils, a remote control for the small TV and the last thing that caught his interest, his smartphone.

It was barely recognizable. There were scratches everywhere, and the display was completely covered with cracks. But it still worked, somehow, when Michael booted it up by pressing the power button. The image on the display was blurry and the touchscreen didn't work properly in the upper half.

If it really was just a dream, would the pictures and videos with me and Zoe have disappeared?

He tapped the gallery icon several times because it was taking too long to open. But when he scrolled through the gallery, there were no recently taken pictures and videos, the last one was almost a year ago when Michael took pictures of the drawings he had done then. He sighed sadly, turned off his smartphone and threw it back in the drawer.

Maybe a little TV will help me feel better. Man, it's been a long time! I hope they still have those old cartoons I loved to watch as a kid.

As soon as Michael hit the on button on the remote, the news started playing on the TV. A man named Steven stood behind his desk holding a stack of papers.

Steven: "Good night, I'm Steven, the news reporter who is supposed to brief you in the middle of the night, and it's now twelve o'clock at night."

There was a pause and the news reporter cleared his throat.

Steven: "A few days ago, an unknown explosion occurred here in this city that took the life of a nineteen-year-old girl named Jennie."

A picture of the girl was shown. Her hair was blonde and long, and she had hazel green eyes. Michael recognized her immediately. It was the girl who had bullied him that day at school. Her appearance caused a shock in him and he clutched the remote control so tightly that the plastic creaked.

That fucking bitch of a whore!

The scene switched back to the news reporter.

Steven: "Today I have a guest on the show with me and he has assured me that he knows more than all of us because he was there when the event happened. Peterson, please explain to all the people watching us right now what you experienced that day."

Peterson… Where have I heard that name before?

The scene changed again, this time showing a man in his mid-forties standing in front of a house. The streets were blocked, the windows of the surrounding houses and cars were broken, and the police were everywhere.

Peterson: "Good night everybody. It's been exactly two days since it happened. I happened to be walking home from work that night. As I turned around the block, I saw this young girl walking on the other side. Suddenly I heard a loud zooming sound, some kind of missile flying towards her. I don't know exactly what it was, but it was coming from some rooftop. It exploded and threw her limbs in all directions, it was horrible! All the windows nearby shattered in the explosion and all the alarms on the cars nearby were wailing!"

Yeah, karma's a bitch, isn't she!!! That's what you get for being a hag!!!

Steven: "Well, considering the fact that you saved a boy from drowning a week ago and are now helping the police solve this mystery, I personally think you should be rewarded with the Medal of Honor."

The TV was turned off when Michael hit the off button and threw the remote across the room. He had clearly seen and heard enough of him and was annoyed as hell.

That fucking PETERSON!!! If only that asshole had minded his own business, I'd still be in Xenonan right now, partying with Zoe!

His eyes began to water as he saw Zoe's face in his mind's eye and heard her gleeful laughter.

No! This was all because of that fucking bitch Jennie! I'm glad she fucking died! At least something to cheer me up a little. I bet none of this would have even happened if she hadn't come up to me that day! I wouldn't be in a freaking coma and I wouldn't have met Zoe! Everything would have been normal and now I'm suffering even more!

Tears started to flow from his eyes when he couldn't hold them back anymore.

If only... If only...

Michael's thoughts were interrupted as the door opened, but instead of a hospital hallway, he was greeted by a bright light and something stepping out of the door. Immediately after, the door closed again.

What the heck just happened? Now I'm seeing things too!

Michael reached for the light switch, since it was dark outside. When the light came on, he was amazed and shocked at the same time. In the middle of the room stood Zoe with a big grin on her face.

Michael: "Z-zoe!? B-but how!? I thought..."

She waved her paw at him and showed him the blue, mysterious key.

Zoe: "You remember this key, don't you? After all, it brought you to me. Now it's the other way around."

She walked slowly toward his hospital bed, giving him the bedroom look.

Where had she gotten it from, anyway? I'm pretty sure I had it all along.

Zoe: "Oh, I guess it fell out of your pocket while you were fighting with General Bigclaw."

How did she hear it? Did I say it out loud?

Zoe giggled delightedly.

Zoe: "I can still hear your thoughts, silly. What, you've forgotten about me already?"

She playfully made a sad face and gave him the puppy dog look.

Michael: "No, not at all! It's just... I don't know. Right now, I don't know what's real and what's not. I'm confused as hell."

She sat down next to him on the bed and eyed him a little.

Zoe: "Oh my God! What happened to you? You look terrible!

Michael: "Pfft, thanks."

Zoe: "Oh, you poor thing."

Michael: "It's hard to explain, really. I doubt you wouldn't fully understand."

Zoe: "Well, shoot."

Michael was silent for a minute because he was deep in thought, thinking about how to explain everything to Zoe without confusing her.

Michael: "The thing is, Zoe, I never left my world. I've always been here in this hospital bed, well, my body to be exact. The Michael you met was probably my ghost."

Zoe: "Huh?"

She tilted her head in confusion, one of her ears flopping down forwards.

Michael: "And as for my injuries. Well, I have a fractured skull, a broken leg, lots of bruises and a hell of a headache, plus I lost a lot of blood too. The truth is that I bungee jumped off a bridge without a rope and fell into a coma. I slept for a whole week, and during that time I dreamed about you and Xenonan."

Zoe: "So you're telling me that I wasn't real until now?"

Michael: "No, what I'm telling you is that in my dream, the dream me version, I somehow got into another real world. And when I was about to wake up from the coma, I was brought back to my real world."

Another pause arose between them until Michael suddenly began to chuckle.

Zoe: "What's so funny?"

Michael: "Ha! Zoe, I think we broke the game!"

Zoe: "Broke the game?"

Michael: "Yeah, because you probably shouldn't have that key and now you've broken the barrier between my world and your world!"

Zoe: "I don't understand."

Michael: "I was in my world the whole time. I was in a coma and dreaming about the blue key that led me to your world. When I was brought back, you were in possession of that key and you were able to leave your world and enter mine! Now it's the other way around."

Zoe: "Ooooh.... Wait, does that mean I'm in a coma right now and this is my ghost form!? Did General Bigclaw manage to put me down?"

Michael: "You know what? Forget it. I'm just glad we're both real and reunited!"

Zoe gave Michael a seductive smile and leaned forward.

Michael: "Don't give me that dirty look!"

Zoe: "Come on... I know you want to do it too."

Michael: "Not really. What I want to do is sleep. I'm tired as hell."

Zoe whimpered at his answer.

Michael: "Okay, maybe until I'm all healed up."

Zoe: "Promise?"

Michael: "Fine."

Zoe was about to give him a big kiss when she spotted his stuffed animal of herself and giggled.

Michael: "What's that?"

Zoe pointed at his stuffed animal.

Zoe: "It looks just like me. It's soooo cute! I bet you had so much fun with it!"

Michael blushed at her statement.

Michael: "Shut up..."

Zoe interrupted Michael and kissed him deeply. She lay on top of him and hugged him. Her whole body glowed slightly greenish as she began to heal him with her powers. This time it would take some time, as Michael's injuries were more severe. Still, it would be much faster than his own healing process.

Zoe: "I missed you so much.... You scared me to death when you suddenly disappeared."

Zoe began to cry.

Michael: "I missed you even more. I... When I woke up, I thought you weren't even real. I thought I had lost you forever..."

Zoe cried even more and gave him a few more kisses. After Zoe calmed down, Michael asked her.

Michael: "So, what happened on Xenonan after I was brought back?"

Zoe: "After you killed General Bigclaw and left, we freed some of his slaves and destroyed his entire castle. The remaining Redclaws who were still alive allied with our kind and were happy because they no longer had bad leadership. After that, I tried to convince my father to join your world. I had a strong feeling that you would be there, and I was right."

Michael smiled even more and closed his eyes. At least Xenonan was free of his corruption. He had made it.

Michael: "I'm glad you thought so."

Zoe: "So, do you mind if I stay with you in your world?"

Michael: "Absolutely not! I forbid it!"

Zoe: "But why?"

Michael: "For your own safety. My world ticks differently than yours. If the government found out about you, they would capture you, experiment on you, torture you, and worse, the furries would go crazy for you!"

Zoe: "But I can hide quite well! Don't you have a house where I can hide?"

Michael: "Yes, I do..."

Zoe: "Then what's the problem?"

Michael: "My parents..."

Zoe: "I'm pretty sure they would be proud if I cured your sadness and depression, just like my dad was proud that you saved me."

Michael: "Can we just go back to Xenonan and live happily ever after?"

Zoe: "Hey! You had your adventure and explored a whole new world. Now I want to explore your world with you."

Michael: "Alright fine! But if my parents don't play along and we get caught, you'll have to go right back to your world! So, in conclusion: Always have the key with you!"

Zoe: "Okay, but I'll drag you along."

Michael: "Fair enough."

Zoe kissed him goodnight and Michael scratched her over both ears.

Zoe: "I love you, my dear human."

Zoe whispered in his ear, which made him shiver for a moment.

Michael: "I love you too, fur ball."

They both fell asleep immediately, snuggling up to each other to keep warm for the night.

SEEKING SIMON

RESCUED HEARTS OF THE CIVIL WAR ~ BOOK 4

SUSAN POPE SLOAN

PROLOGUE

RANDOLPH COUNTY, ALABAMA
AUGUST 1858

Between the rows of unpicked cotton, the girl stood silhouetted by the sinking sun. She lifted her skirt to keep it from dragging and continued her trek through the field. Her walk was a siren's song that enchanted Simon McNeil and drew him to her, the object of his affection.

After months of trying, at last he had attained Pansy's attention, and his reward was at hand.

The difference in their stations mattered little to sixteen-year-old Simon. By accident of birth, she'd been born a slave on the farm Simon's father had inherited. Only, Alabama law declared them unequal and prohibited Simon from courting her openly while his father's law demanded respect for everyone under his protection. Which meant no dalliance among its inhabitants.

But who could bridle the heart of a young man? Simon didn't bother to disguise his interest in the cook's helper, so Pa had consigned Pansy to the fields when she returned from helping in a neighbor's kitchen. As if a few acres would dampen Simon's ardor. It merely meant he had to find ways to sneak a glimpse of her golden beauty.

She looked over her shoulder and smiled, then ascended the three wooden stairs and sashayed into her mother's cabin. Liza, her ma, would be staying in the Big House tonight to help Ma tend to both Pa and his youngest brother, Troy, who had sickened after supper. It was an opportunity Simon couldn't pass up.

Not bothering to hide his intention, Simon followed Pansy through the open door and closed it behind him. She whirled around at the soft sound, her eyes round as if his appearance surprised her. Two steps took him close enough to inhale her scent, a muskiness mixed with the perfume he'd given her last month.

Her sultry voice belied her words. "Simon, you oughtn't be in here."

"You knew I was following you. Did you expect me to wait out there for the gift you promised when I know you're in here alone?" Another step put them toe to toe. Simon lifted his hand to her face, let it drift from her jaw to her shoulder and over her bare arm. She shivered and watched as he leaned closer. Her breath quickened, and desire drove him.

His lips descended on hers, gently at first, then seeking and demanding. Her hands crept up his chest and gripped his shoulders, sending him near the edge of control. Wrapping his arms around her, he pressed closer. "You taste sweet, like Etta's pecan pie." He angled his head and nibbled her lips. "I've been dying to kiss you for months."

Her soft chuckle sent warm breath across his cheek. "I'm glad you didn' perish 'fo' you got one. You shoulda come sooner."

"You know I have to live by Pa's rules." Why did he say that?

The reminder nagged at his conscience. His current actions defied those rules.

She turned her head and whispered in his ear, "If we was to run away together, you could kiss me all the time."

He focused on the latter part of her suggestion. "Mmm. I'd like that, kissing you all day…" He moved to match action to his words.

Pansy put space between them. "Then we have to make plans."

"What plans? How to meet every day so I can—"

"Plans to run away together."

Simon frowned, his passion ebbing away. Where did that come from? Didn't she know about the laws? No, of course, she didn't. But surely, she should realize they'd need money to live.

He scrubbed a hand across his face, searching for words that never came. The door behind him slammed open and bounced against the wall as his older brother tackled him to the floor.

Pansy squealed as Simon fought against Paul's hold.

"Blast it, Simon! What d'ya think you're doing?'

Icy anger drove Simon. He swung his fist and connected with Paul's chin. His brother's head snapped backward, but he returned with a jab to Simon's midsection. The pain further enraged him. Where did Paul get off trying to govern his behavior?

Simon used his legs to flip their positions. Paul surged and shoved him back to the ground. Grunts and curses accompanied each change in position.

Evenly matched, they rolled inside the narrow confines, running into a table one way and toward the door another. After trading more punches, at last, Paul pinned Simon against the doorframe.

"Listen to me, you dunderhead." His voice deepened to a

growl. "You think because Pa's too sick to come after you that he'd allow what you did tonight? Following a woman into her home? You flouted all he's taught us about respect and honor. When word of your actions gets out, the McNeil name will be a laughingstock."

Shame sapped Simon's strength. Low murmurs outside the cabin warned him that others watched them. He sneaked a peek over Paul's shoulder. Pansy's gaze went somewhere beyond him, her eyes wide and a hand over her mouth. What did that reaction mean? Had he shamed her as well as himself?

Panting, Paul rolled to his feet. "Before I help you up, do you promise to return to the house quietly?"

Simon nodded and grabbed Paul's arm.

Both dusted the dirt from their clothes and left the cabin together, ignoring the curious glances from the field slaves they passed as they trudged toward home. At the back door of the big house, Simon asked, "Who all saw me?"

"Besides me, Liza and Ma. I don't know who else."

Simon groaned. Ma would tell Pa, which meant Simon's goose was cooked. How had he thought his actions would go unnoticed? With two dozen slaves scattered across the farm, there were eyes everywhere. Though a son, he might as well be a slave too. He expected his punishment would be the worst Pa had ever meted out.

∼

Hall County, Georgia
October 1858

Daviana scoffed at Shakespeare's Juliet for disparaging being a Capulet. That girl had no idea how a proper name set a person apart—and how it hurt to have others ignore it.

Thirteen-year-old Athdara Daviana Spalding dashed away

her tears and stumbled to the log nestled among the fallen leaves. Some of the log's moisture penetrated her skirt and petticoats as she sat, but the afternoon sun warmed her back. This atmosphere of dying vegetation suited her melancholy mood.

Daviana alternately loved and hated her name, but at that moment, she longed to hear Mama say it. She missed everything about her mother, who'd departed this earthly realm two days ago. Only Mama had ever called her by her real name, sometimes the whole mouthful when she wanted Daviana's full attention. Mama had refused to follow other folks' tradition of passing the same name to each successive generation. She'd wanted her offspring to have their own identities, along with an appreciation for their ancestors.

Daviana blamed the mutilation of her name on her brother Lionel, six years old when she came along. He couldn't master the "th" sound for *Athdara. Daviana* proved easier, especially when shortened to *Davi*. But Pa's habit of calling her "Daughter" soon turned *Davi* into *Dottie*. By the time she started school, everyone knew her as Dottie, and she'd grown tired of correcting them.

Now the name rankled. Dottie! As if she were as inconsequential as a stray mark on a page—the smallest pinpoint on paper—while Lionel's name called forth strength and power, as her brother often reminded her. Since he'd recently married and soon would be a father, maybe he'd leave off his teasing. It broke Daviana's heart that Mama hadn't lived to see her first grandchild.

Fresh tears overflowed. With Mama gone, who would listen to Daviana's fanciful stories of knights and fair maidens? Lionel made fun of her. Pa gave an indulgent smile and said she'd grow out of it.

She focused on the line of trees that edged her sanctuary, providing a barrier between her and the world. A gray squirrel, her lone companion, darted from a spreading bottlebrush and dashed to the trees. Daviana followed his progress until he disappeared among the scrubby pines. Perhaps he searched for food for his family. She'd left her family at the house, crowded with well-meaning neighbors, to search for the comfort this private place often offered. Peace felt far from her today.

"Well, if it ain't the princess of Spalding farm." The gravelly voice startled her from her misery. She jerked around as Jasper Dunaway ambled toward her, his dark blond hair falling over one eye and his thumbs hooked in his waistband. His strut reminded her of their old rooster.

Though she shared a close friendship with his brother, Kyle, Daviana disliked Jasper, and it seemed he felt the same about her. Having him sneak up on her sparked fear. From childhood, she'd been wary of him, but the more Kyle and other neighbors talked about him, about how he mistreated his slaves and even his recently wedded wife, the more her fear spiked in his presence. She couldn't find words to form a proper reply.

He stopped in front of her, his brows lowered and hands on his hips. Some considered him handsome, but his arrogance ruined the effect for Daviana. While the brothers looked much alike, Kyle's easy-going manner won her favor while Jasper's high-handed attitude did the opposite.

His stony eyes raked Daviana. "What're you doin' on Dunaway land?"

She raised her chin and used what Kyle called her "teacher voice." "This is not Dunaway land. This log marks the boundary. Kyle and I put it here last year when the storm took down the fence. See?" She pointed along an imaginary border. "It's in line with the remaining posts."

"Your pa told me he ain't gonna replace the fence since we're such good neighbors." His smile widened as he winked at her.

Daviana shuddered. Pa just tried to keep the peace, but Lionel didn't like Jasper any more than she did.

Jasper motioned to the log. "If you're waitin' on Kyle, you might as well go on home. He's runnin' an errand for me over to Gainesville. I doubt he'll be back afore dark."

She straightened her spine. "I'll leave when I'm ready. Pa won't care, long as I'm home by supper."

His eyes narrowed and focused on her exposed calves and ankles. "Is 'at right? Well, since Kyle ain't around, I reckon you and me could get to know each other." He sat beside her, so close that his hip brushed hers.

Daviana tugged her skirt over her ankles and scooted to the end to leave a couple of inches between them.

Jasper followed and trailed his hand over her waist-length hair. "Ain't it 'bout time you was puttin' your hair up, now that you're showing signs of womanhood?"

A shudder of revulsion slid from her shoulder to her toes. Fear stole her breath and seized her muscles. She had to get away but couldn't chance making him mad.

In a lightning-quick move, he grabbed her arms and stood, hauled her against him, and pressed his hard mouth to hers. When she twisted her face away, his lips moved to her neck.

Daviana's breath escaped in a gasp. Her heartbeat thudded in her ears. Kyle had confided how his older brother liked to exercise his authority, even to the point of hurting people. Maybe he'd release her if she agreed to leave.

"P-please let me go. I'll go on home."

His twisted smile mocked her. "Nah, you done riled me up now. I need to show you what happens when you tease a man, displayin' your legs like 'at."

She squirmed in his grasp, pushed against his arms, and kicked at his shins, but her skirts hindered. When he attempted to hoist her up against him, one arm holding her legs, the other pushing her head into his shoulder, she dug her heels in, to no avail. Her grunts and cries earned increased pressure from his hands. With her arms trapped between their bodies, she had no defense. Alarm surged white-hot in her veins. Her vision clouded with unshed tears as he moved farther into the trees.

God, help me! Where's he taking me?

Though Daviana knew these woods, she couldn't get her bearings. Dead grass scattered with leaves blurred past as he tramped on. By the time he entered a shallow cave, she'd worn herself out. Released from his hold, she fell in a heap on the ground but struggled to sit up when he advanced.

She scooted backward but bumped into the cold stone wall. "What are you going to do?"

His laugh was ugly and humorless. "Now, a girl smart as you oughtta be able to figure that out. It's your own fault, you know. It's plain you was just waitin' for me to pass that way."

One hand gripped her jaw and held it steady while he pressed his mouth over hers. He pushed her onto the ground while his other hand tugged at her bodice.

Daviana clawed at his shoulders, her strength surging as she realized what he intended to do.

In the cave entrance, a dark figure arose behind Jasper. Her eyes widened as the other man raised a large object over her assailant. The object slammed against Jasper's head, and he collapsed, his hand still gripping her bodice. His weight forced Daviana's breath from her lungs. She struggled to move from under him.

Her dark angel shoved the inert body to one side.

She scrambled to her feet and threw herself into the arms of the Dunaways' oversized slave. "Malachi, thank you!"

He patted her arms awkwardly, shrugging away. "Miss Spalding, you gotta get outta here 'fo' he wakes up."

"Yes, you're right. Let's go." She glanced back at the prone form. "He's not dead, is he?"

"Naw, but he be havin' a powerful headache when he comes to hisself."

She clutched Malachi's arm as he led the way to the cave entrance. When they emerged into the waning afternoon light, he shook off her hand. She stayed close enough behind that she would've barreled into him if he'd stopped. He weaved his way in and out of the trees. How did someone so massive move with such speed and so little noise?

He stopped at the boundary between the two farms. "You go home now. I be watchin' till you get safe."

Daviana started that way but swung around. "How'd you know where to find me?"

"I seen him grab you as I crossed the crick. Waited an' watched to see where he headed." He made a shooing motion. "You go on now. I got to be on my way."

A nervous tic moved his eyelid while his gaze darted back the way they'd come. He'd be in trouble if anyone found them together. Daviana spun around and ran full speed for the house. Before she reached the apple orchard, a figure dropped from a sycamore tree into her path.

"Where you been, Dottie?" Kyle's freckled face scrunched into a worried frown. "I been lookin' for you."

"You scared me half to death, Kyle Dunaway!" Daviana bent over, trying to calm her galloping heart.

Kyle's wide eyes and hurt look made her sorry for yelling at her friend. At fourteen, he hadn't yet displayed the arrogant attitude of the other boys. She opened her mouth to ask when he'd returned from Gainesville, then snapped it shut. Jasper had lied to her.

"Are you all right?" Kyle took a step closer.

She glanced back to see if Malachi had witnessed Kyle's arrival. He was gone.

Which made sense. But why had he been as far as the creek on Spalding property?

What had Kyle said? Something about making sure she was all right.

Aware of her disheveled appearance, she could only nod. Yeah, she was safe now. Thanks to the bravery of a slave who proved more honorable than his owner.

What had the rescue cost him? Had he sacrificed his chance at freedom to save her innocence?

CHAPTER 1

"Nothing like having your horse go lame a hundred miles from home," Simon McNeil said. "Especially when you paid half a year's salary for that horse."

The mare eyed him with a sorrowful look, as if it knew what he'd said and sympathized.

Which was what Simon got for talking to a horse.

He swatted his floppy hat against his thigh and gazed across the lonely stretch of road to the west. He grumbled, his language more colorful than he'd learned at home. Ten years before, his parents overhearing any one of those words would have sent him to the yard looking for a switch. Even with him four-and-twenty, he imagined Ma could still blister him with her scornful eye, which always hurt a lot more than the switch did. Years of living with roughened soldiers had expanded his vocabulary.

His time as a prisoner of war taught him there were times to keep his mouth shut.

He squatted and ran his hand down the mare's right front leg. Assured the bruised hoof was the only problem, he rose. He didn't mind going afoot, but it would slow him down. The horse needed to rest a while, and they both needed food, but he hadn't seen a homestead in an hour or more.

He tugged on the horse's reins and trudged beside her. "Come on, girl. Let's go as far as we can and hope we run up on a house before dark."

Years ago, before the war, Simon would have prayed for guidance. He was probably beyond divine help now, considering he'd killed more men than he cared to count. Some would dismiss it as allowable in a time of war, but that didn't make it right. He had to work his way back into God's favor.

He raised his face to the western sky, where shades of pink and orange streaked across the blue, marking the sun's descent. Unbidden, a verse in Psalms, which compared the sun to a bridegroom leaving his chamber, came to mind.

Simon winced and shook the pain away. Deeply embedded Scriptures refused to leave him alone. How long before they brought comfort rather than conviction?

He turned to the problem at hand. How much farther before he reached the Alabama line? According to his map, he might be close to Gainesville. Beyond it lay Atlanta—or rather, the ruined remains of it. He didn't regret missing that action, as close as it was to home. Instead, he'd been languishing in a Confederate prison, where his fellow Southerners counted him a traitor and singled him out for special punishment.

Maybe he deserved it. All his life, he'd been the misfit, the troublesome child that his parents sent away for his own protection. But he'd changed, and he longed for home.

The road turned south, and trees obscured the sinking sun. Images from the past created a hunger for the stability of family, as sharp as the clawing in his belly for food. Whatever the murky future held, he'd find a place to put down roots, somewhere not too distant from his folks in Alabama but far enough to let him be his own man.

His boot sent a rock skittering downhill. The contact brought Simon back to the present. He'd wandered to the road's edge as the light faded. Best correct his course.

"Hold it right there!" The gruff command erupted from the darkness.

Simon swung his head toward the sound, searching the shadows.

The voice added a warning. "I got a firearm aimed at your head, and I'm a crack shot."

Simon stopped, and the mare butted him. He raised his hands and tried to pinpoint the voice. "I'm unarmed, and my horse is nearly lame."

"Then you're a fool. What're you doin' out here, wanderin' around in the dark?"

It *was* nearly dark, though the sun had set without his noticing. "I'm headed home to Alabama. You know a place where I can get some grub for me and my horse? I can pay in U.S. dollars." What was left of the pay he'd collected after he left Libby Prison and traded his uniform for civilian clothes.

The man, still hidden somewhere in the shadows, said nothing. Simon finally caught sight of the stranger as he stepped onto the road. Several yards behind him stood a couple of structures. A house and a barn? A light appeared in the nearest building, then bobbed as if someone walked with it.

"Pa? You comin' in for supper?" From the pitch of the voice, the second person must be either a female or a young boy.

The man half turned in that direction. "You got enough for one more?" he called.

A moment of hesitation, then, "I reckon we'll manage."

The man motioned to Simon. "We got an extra room you can use for the night, too, since you're not like to find a place in town this late."

Simon stretched out his hand and closed the distance between them. "Thank you, sir. I'm Simon McNeil."

The man shifted his firearm and took a step forward to accept the gesture. "Rufus Spalding. Let's put up your horse, then we'll see what's for supper."

Simon followed, matching the man's shuffling gait. His stooped figure hinted at years of hardscrabble living. With his home close to the road between Greenville and Gainesville, he'd likely had travelers pass by every day. Soldiers would have increased that traffic.

The barn door squeaked when Mr. Spalding pushed it open and led the way to the first stall. He struck a match and lit the lantern that hung on the post. In the lamplight, Simon could make out four stalls and an open area beyond. The loft stretched across both sides. No animal noises greeted them, just the haunting sound of empty space.

Simon stared at the single bale of hay in the stall. Did the family have no more than this? He removed the mare's saddle and blanket while his companion dug into a barrel.

"Oats are gettin' low, but I think this'll do." Mr. Spalding pointed to the brush sitting atop the partition. "Go ahead and brush her down while I get the liniment."

Once they took care of the mare, the old man led the way across the yard to the house, a single-story structure not much larger than the barn. Rather than retrace their steps to the front door, Mr. Spalding chose the back entrance. Knee-high markers outlined a kitchen garden about a quarter-acre beyond the porch. It was too dark to see how it fared or what lay beyond.

An orange tabby cat met them at the open door, winding between first one set of legs, then the other. The aroma of stew and biscuits greeted him and set up a rumble in his stomach. A woman stood at the stove, her back to them. Wisps of brown hair floated where they'd escaped from a bun at her neck. The long apron ties pulled into a bow set off a trim waist. The stiff white bow seemed out of place on the lifeless dress that once might have been blue.

Mr. Spalding set the rifle on a high shelf and gestured to the woman across the room. "This here's my daughter, Dottie. That"—he pointed to the feline—"is Minnow, Dottie's cat. Ornery thing, but he does take care of the mice."

Miss Spalding straightened and placed a hand at her lower back before she turned and acknowledged him. Brown doe-eyes met Simon's, then darted away. The glimpse of emotion revealed there drew him up. Was it pain or suspicion? Or did his own anxiety and guilt feed his imagination? Many Southerners would call him a traitor, but she couldn't know which side he'd fought on. Maybe it didn't matter. Both armies must have tramped through this way, leaving destruction and grief in their wake.

Mr. Spalding slapped Simon on the back. "This young man is Simon McNeil from Alabama." He gestured to the table. "Sit down, son. My Dottie can make the poorest meal taste good."

"Sir, after what I've eaten the last four years, I'm sure this will seem a feast." He paused at the table, trying to remember the basic manners instilled in him back in Alabama. Before he had to leave for the sake of all he held dear. Before North and South separated and the world fell apart.

When Miss Spalding brought her bowl to the table, he pulled out the chair where she stood, then he sat to her left. From the corner of his eye, he watched her to determine his next move. Would they pause to bless the food as his family did? She bowed her head while her pa muttered a word of thanks. When she pulled her bowl closer, picked up her spoon, and dipped it in the stew, Simon mimicked her movements. He prolonged the moment to breathe in the fragrance of onion and some spice he couldn't place.

Minnow sniffed Simon's boots, then trotted off. The cat

must hope to find more interesting items to investigate elsewhere.

The familiar movements of sitting down to a meal released a coil of tension Simon had long carried. What could be better than a roof over his head and a home-cooked meal? Not to mention a lovely woman to share it with. Although each spurned encounter over the years ended in a resolve to avoid all females, that declaration soon fell away like autumn leaves in a blustery wind.

Besides, he'd only be here overnight. He could, at least, enjoy the view.

$\sim$

*D*aviana Spalding stumbled when the visitor pulled out a chair for her. Thank goodness, she ended up on the seat and not on the floor. When was the last time a man showed her such courtesy? Had anyone ever done so? Maybe Lester Cox when he'd tried to sweeten her up years ago. Most of them treated her like a commodity—the means to gain more land.

None of them called her by her proper name. Even Kyle, God rest his soul, had tended to forget his manners around her. Perhaps she was to blame. She pushed away any man who got too close.

She took a bite of her food without giving it proper attention. The heat singed her tongue before she swallowed and washed it down with a sip of water.

"Dottie!"

Pa's voice cut through her muddled thoughts, and she jumped. "Yes, Pa?"

"You got biscuits in the oven?" Eyes wide, his head jerked toward the kitchen.

A slightly pungent smell wafted from the kitchen, a warning that sent anxiety roaring through Daviana's body.

Lord, please help. The simple prayer calmed her.

Biscuits. She couldn't let them burn. The ingredients came at a precious cost nowadays. She scraped back her chair and grabbed a crocheted potholder as she opened the oven door. Heat seeped through the worn cotton barrier, but Daviana held onto the pan until she reached the worktable. She dropped the hot metal and shook out her hand.

"Did you burn yourself again?" His question carried a hint of accusation. She'd meant to add another layer of fabric to that square. She'd grown used to padding it with her apron but often forgot when she was in a hurry. Or daydreaming.

"It just got a mite warm," she said. She dipped the offended hand in the cool dishwater and reached for a platter with the other. "Not enough to blister."

With a flick of the wrist, she transferred the bread onto the platter and set it in the middle of the table. "Here we go. The bottoms got a little dark, is all."

Pa stabbed a biscuit with his fork and dropped it next to his bowl. The stranger kept his head down as he continued to eat his stew. Maybe it'd been a while since he ate. She wanted to ask him a dozen questions, but Pa wouldn't allow it. He hadn't been the same since Albert left them. Her seven-year-old nephew had chosen to go out West with his pa, her widowed brother, rather than stay with them. Lionel refused to remain in Georgia, and Pa refused to move away.

Daviana turned the questions over in her mind and envisioned what the stranger's answers might be. Pa said the man hailed from Alabama. Another defeated Confederate soldier on his way home from the war. He must be eager to see his family after his time away. Though his lean frame indicated months of deprivation, his thick brown hair fell in waves to his collar. His blue eyes sparkled every time he caught her gaze. She chastised herself. Such a handsome man surely had a wife waiting for him.

What did he give as his name? Simon. It brought to mind the Lord's disciple, Simon Peter. A bold man, one who spoke sometimes without thinking.

What was the visitor's last name? McSomething. Didn't that mean his family came from Scotland, where folks lived up in the mountains like Ma's Grandpa and Grandma Campbell? How she used to love to hear those tales of the old country. One of the places she longed to visit if she could ever break free and prove her worth far away from Georgia. A glance at Pa's scowl warned her to reel in her imagination before it got her in trouble.

She cut her eyes the stranger's way and forced down a sip of water when she found his gaze on her. Covering her mouth with her hand, she spoke in a low voice. "You needin' somethin', Mr McEwen?"

"McNeil," he said. "You have any butter?"

"Not since we lost our cow." She shifted in her chair. "I might have a bit of muscadine jelly, if that'll do."

Mr. McNeil's lips quirked. "I wasn't asking for me. I remember Ma sometimes put butter on a burn and thought it might help you if you're in pain."

Daviana stared at him. Did she look like she was in pain? She glanced at her hand. It was a mite red, but nothing to worry over. Maybe she'd grimaced while she concocted Simon McNeil's story. Ma always said she could tell when Daviana was spinning tales by the serious look on her face, a habit she couldn't seem to break.

Her cheeks warmed at her being caught dreaming. "I'm fine, thank you, Mr. McNeil." What would he think if he knew where her thoughts had strayed?

~

Simon sopped the remaining contents of his bowl with the last bite of biscuit and scooped it into his mouth. Three more of the golden orbs remained on the platter, but ingrained manners and caution kept him from taking more. He wouldn't repay his hosts by gorging and then hurling up the victuals they offered.

He pushed his chair back and waited for the others to finish their meal. As soon as Mr. Spalding set down his spoon, Miss Spalding hopped up and wrapped the leftover bread in a towel. Would those come to the table again tomorrow morning?

The old man stood with a groan. "You're welcome to join me on the porch, if you've a mind to. I like to sit a spell before turnin' in for the night." He tottered to the front door and stepped into the gloaming.

Simon carried his bowl into the kitchen, narrowly avoiding a collision with the woman on her return to the table. "Oh, pardon me." He shifted sideways to let her pass.

Instead, she reached for the dish. "I'll clear the table, Mr. McNeil. You go ahead and visit with Pa."

Used to fending for himself, he opened his mouth to argue, but her raised eyebrows warned him to hold his peace. Far be it from him to rile a Southern woman in her own home. He surrendered the bowl and followed his host through the front room and outside.

On the porch, Mr. Spalding sat in a straight-back chair which he leaned against the house with its front legs tipped up. Simon bypassed the other chair, leaving it for Miss Spalding, and sank to the stoop. He stretched his legs across the downward steps. In the distance, a three-quarters moon revealed the undulating shadows of hills and valleys in various shades of purple and gray.

The cat crept next to him and sniffed his hand. Simon stroked the brindled fur. "I expect that's a right nice view in the daytime," he said. "How long have you been on this property, Mr. Spalding?"

"Thirty years or so. My wife's family owned a couple hunnert acres here. I bought sixty-five from 'em, and the rest got divvied up amongst her brothers when her folks died."

He set his chair on the front legs with a thump, then leaned to spit a stream of tobacco juice into the yard. Simon relaxed to the familiar chirping of cicadas with an occasional croak from a nearby bullfrog. The faintest scent of magnolia blooms drifted on the cooling air.

Mr. Spalding wiped his mouth with a handkerchief. "What part of Alabama did you say you're from?"

"Randolph County. It's just over the Georgia line, southwest of Rome. Pa has a hundred and forty acres east of Lake Wedowee. His brothers have small farms there, too, but separated by several miles to maintain the peace." He aimed a conspiratorial smile at his companion. "All the McNeils are opinionated and outspoken."

The older man barked a rusty laugh. "I reckon I know what you mean. You the only son?"

"Oh, no. I'm the second of four boys. I figure Pa still plans on my older brother Paul and me dividing the land between us when he passes on. Paul lost part of his leg in '62, and it'll be years before his boy is old enough to take over, so I guess he'll put up with me hanging around to help with the work."

"What about your other brothers?"

"It's generally expected they'll get Uncle Henry's land since he only has daughters, both married, and they live in town." He turned his head away. "That's assuming all my brothers survived the war and we can resolve our differences. I ain't heard anything from home in a year. I reckon that's mostly due to the destruction of rail lines."

Mr. Spalding twisted his lips to one side. "I'd planned on my boy takin' over here when I'm gone, but the war changed that. He come home in April, then lit out for the Western Territories in May. Took my grandson with him too." He paused for another spit and swipe across his lips. "Guess it'll go to Dottie when she gets hitched. If she can find a man that suits her well enough."

From what Simon had seen on his journey, any woman's matrimonial prospects had dwindled. The comment died on his lips. The less mention of his part in the conflict, the better.

The old man didn't seem to expect a response. He gazed in the distance and kept on talking. "My cousin's youngest boy would marry her, but she won't give him the time o' day. Mighty particular, she is. Foolish female." He aimed another stream into the yard and passed the handkerchief across his lips again.

"Are you botherin' Mr. McNeil with our troubles, Pa?" Miss Spalding stood in the doorway, her apron discarded.

Her father turned as she slid into the other chair. "Nah, just chewin' the fat and watchin' the fireflies. Did you fix up a place for our guest to sleep?"

Minnow abandoned Simon in favor of his mistress. Not that Simon blamed the animal. The woman had a pleasing quality, like a cool breeze on a hot day. "Yeah, I put clean sheets on the extra bed and filled a basin with water."

"I appreciate that, ma'am." Simon rubbed his face to cover a yawn. "If y'all don't mind, I'll turn in now. My days of traveling have worn me out." He stood but clutched the rail behind him as a wave of dizziness struck, and his stomach roiled with nausea. "Whoa."

Miss Spalding surged to her feet, sending the cat to the floorboards. "Are you all right, Mr. McNeil? You're white as a lily."

"I...I guess I just got up too fast. Uh-oh." He spun and tottered to the side of the house, where he cast up the contents of his stomach.

By the time he finished, Miss Spalding appeared at his side

with a wet cloth. She pressed it into his hand as he leaned against the house. "I hope it wasn't something in the stew that made you sick. I can't think what would've done that."

He attempted a smile. "More likely, it's because I ate too much at one time. Don't go blaming yourself, Miss Spalding. I should've used more restraint, instead of gobbling it up like Pa's prize pig."

The moon provided enough light to expose the furrows in her brow, evidence of her concern. She seemed to search his face for a moment, then gave a brisk nod. "All right, Mr. McNeil. If you're feelin' better now, a good night's rest should set you right."

"Yes'm. I believe it will."

She retraced her steps to the porch, and Simon followed, willing away the weakness that warned of the recurring illness. Mr. Spalding's chair was empty, so he must have gone to bed. Simon scooped up his saddlebags inside the back door. His hostess picked up a lantern and led the way to a small bedroom at the back of the house.

"This used to be my nephew's room, and my brother's before that. Pa's is next to it, and mine is across the hall." She blushed. "In case you need anything."

Simon glanced around the space. "I'm sure I'll fall asleep as soon as my head hits the pillow. Thank you."

"I'll bid you good night, then, Mr. McNeil."

He waited for her to turn away, then closed the door and stumbled to the bed. He should wash before he lay down but didn't have the energy. He pulled off his boots and stretched out on the patchwork quilt. For the second time that day, prayer seemed in order. His need overrode his unworthiness.

Father, forgive me for straying and ignoring Your voice. I promise to do better. Please let this be a mild bout.

CHAPTER 2

Daviana closed the door to her room, lit the lamp on the dresser, then slid off her shoes and crossed the braided rug to the single window. With a heave, she raised the framed glass and positioned the pot of rosemary on the sill to repel mosquitoes. The pesky varmints didn't bite as much during these hot summer days, but they snuck in during the cooler nighttime.

She pulled the pins from her hair and tossed them into the clay dish she'd made for Mama years ago. Often, she would sit up and write in her journal, but tonight she didn't even take it from the drawer. She was too busy replaying every minute of Simon McNeil's visit. She conjured up various possibilities to explain his current situation and his kind attention to her.

After trading her dress for a cotton nightgown and braiding her hair, she blew out the lamp and lay on the bed, letting her imagination run free until she drifted into sleep.

Sometime later, she awoke with a headache and a powerful thirst. Her usual cup of water wasn't on the dresser. She'd forgotten to fill it, what with the unexpected visitor.

Minnow lifted his head when she passed him on her way to

the kitchen. She dipped a cup into the kitchen bucket, gulped her water, and headed back to bed. A soft thud in the guest's room prompted her to pause. She put her ear to the door, then eased it open. The rustling of sheets and moans from the bed alarmed her. Had Mr. McNeil's stomach upset foretold a more serious illness?

She'd nursed her nephew through various childhood maladies when this was his room, so she could navigate the small area without the aid of a lamp. She tiptoed across the floor to assess the stranger's condition. His body trembled under the light covers, and a quick touch to his forehead confirmed a fever.

She turned to the basin she'd placed on the stand earlier. She grabbed the cloth beside it and dipped it in the tepid liquid. Without taking time to wring it out well, she placed it on the man's heated brow.

He mumbled something in his sleep, but his thrashing calmed.

Daviana hurried to the kitchen to snag a cup and fill a pitcher with water.

By the time she returned and retrieved the cloth from his head, his fever had pulled most of the moisture from the rag. She wet it again and returned it to his brow. The water she poured from the pitcher filled the cup and topped off the basin.

Half sitting on the bed beside her patient, she slid an arm behind his head and held the cup to his lips. "Here's some water, Mr. McNeil. You need to take a few swallows."

The man's mouth worked as she tipped the cup. Then his eyes opened, and his hand covered hers. "Ma? Am I home?"

Daviana moved her hand to ease him back onto the pillow as she edged away from the bed. "No, Mr. McNeil. I'm Daviana Spalding. You're at my home in Hall County, Georgia. Do you remember stopping here last night? You ate supper with me and Pa."

She waited for him to acknowledge the memory while she set the cup on the washstand.

His glassy eyes met hers. "I tossed it up in the yard, didn't I?"

She bit her lower lip. "I hope it wasn't something in the stew that brought this on."

He turned his head on the pillow. "Not that." His eyelids drifted shut, and he sighed. "Malaria. Had it...last year."

Daviana's heart squeezed. She had no experience with malaria. They had no medicine to give him, and no doctor nearby. How could she take proper care of him?

Oh, Lord, I can only depend on You to show me what to do.

~

Simon fought to open his eyes again, at least until he could alleviate Miss Spalding's concern. "Not to worry. You won't get sick." He pointed toward his saddlebags on the floor. "Medicine in my bag. Put a spoonful...in my water."

He closed his eyes and listened to her rustling as she must've searched his meager belongings. Not much to show for the years away from home.

"Found it. Let me get a spoon. And a lamp so I can see better."

She bustled out of the room. Either moments or hours later, he roused to her voice in his ear. "Mr. McNeil, please wake up enough to take your medicine."

He thought he answered, but she shook his shoulder and raised his head. The cool metal of the cup met his lips, and he swallowed as the taste assaulted his tongue. When she took the cup away, she spread a dripping cloth over his forehead and swiped another across his hands and bare forearms.

The cool water soothed him. He sighed and let the sickness take him under again.

A trickle of water flowed over his face to his neck with cooling relief. So hot, this midsummer. Simon and his older brother lounged under a shade tree, their fishing lines dangling in the water. He spotted Pansy walking through the cotton field that spread to their left. Enchanted by the sway of hips under her shapeless dress, Simon forgot about his fishing pole until he felt a tug on the end of the line.

"Hey, you got somethin','" Paul said.

After a brief tussle, Simon pulled in the foot-long bass. He unhooked the fish and tossed aside the pole. "Guess that was my good-luck charm, Pansy walking by. I'll take the catch to the house, and you can bring the poles when you're ready."

He dusted grass from his britches and snatched the bucket with their haul as the girl passed in the field beyond them, apparently unaware of her audience. Before he could set out to meet her, Paul pulled him back.

"What are you thinking, Simon? You can't be sweet on a slave, no matter how comely she is. And you know how Ma and Pa feel about treatin' everyone with respect."

Simon jerked his arm away. "I ain't aiming to disrespect her. She's a friend of Troy's. Why can't she be my friend?"

Paul stepped in front of him. "You know her and Troy are like brother and sister. Is that the kind of friendship you want to offer her? I don't think it is."

The warning only riled up Simon's rebellious nature. He shouldered his way past Paul. "And I say it's none of your business."

He stalked through the field and caught up to the girl. "Hey, Pansy, you goin' to the house?"

She flashed him a shy smile, then dropped her head.

He lifted the bucket to show her the catch. "Me and Paul caught dinner. I reckon you can help Miss Etta fry it up."

A voice called from afar. Pansy looked away and then vanished as clouds separated them.

❧

*D*aviana leaned over a balcony to hear what the tall, blue-eyed man was saying. Where had she seen him before? Who was he talking to?

The voice changed. "Dottie." Pa's voice pulled her back from the dream. Had she overslept?

Daviana lifted her head and winced at the pain in her neck and shoulders. Neither lying down nor sitting up, she must've stayed in this odd position, slumped over the bed, for hours. She eased her head in the opposite direction and found Simon McNeil sleeping inches from her fingertips.

"Dottie." Pa's harsh whisper came again. "Why are you in this man's room in your nightgown, girl? Have you lost your senses?"

She pushed off the edge of the bed and slid back in the chair beside it.

Pa pointed to her patient. "What's ailin' him?"

Memories of the last night rushed by. Daviana touched the man's head to check for fever. Still warm, but not burning as it had been.

Pa's hand came down heavy on her shoulder. "Answer me, girl. Has he brought sickness into the house?"

"He said it won't make us sick. Said it's malaria and he had some tonic to take for it in his pack. I gave him a dose, and he seems to be better."

Minnow padded in and plopped next to Daviana's chair.

Pa's eyes narrowed. "You been in here all night?"

She yawned and shook her head. "No, sir." She explained how she'd found the man in fever and tried to help him. "I been puttin' cool rags on him to bring the fever down. Guess I fell asleep with the last one."

Pa glared at her. "You been in here half the night in your night rail. It ain't decent."

"He ain't noticed, Pa. He's been near out of his mind." She

shrugged, but Pa continued to stare at her, his frown not easing up. "I'll go change now. Maybe he'll sleep awhile."

"I can watch him, if need be, so you can get breakfast started." He swung the chair around and straddled it. Minnow stretched out between him and the bed as if he protected one man from the other.

Daviana crossed the hall to her room, praying Pa wouldn't go snooping in Mr. McNeil's pack. He wasn't a thief exactly, but he'd adopted the army's philosophy of taking whatever was available to him. He considered anything brought inside the house fair game if he needed it. Like the firearms he'd hidden from a couple of soldiers who stayed with them last year. The crafty old fox hid them so well, those men never did find 'em. She didn't approve of his actions, but she could hardly afford to withstand him.

Maybe she should move Mr. McNeil's things to her room. Thanks to Ma's training, Pa wouldn't invade a female's sanctuary.

～

The dream faded to the sound of shuffling and mumbling nearby. Even sick as he was, Simon had trained himself to sense a change in the atmosphere. Thankfully, getting a dose of the medicine early on had eased his symptoms.

He lifted his eyelids a fraction to judge the situation before he acted. The old man stood at the foot of his bed, wrestling with the clasps on Simon's pack and cursing under his breath. The tabby cat—what was his crazy name? Minnow?—pawed at the metal fastenings, too, hindering his efforts. Simon would have to tell Ma how many times her clever sewing had saved his meager belongings. Slender, agile fingers could work the bindings with little effort, but not the thicker ones of most men.

Simon faked a cough to get the man's attention. "Looking for something?"

Mr. Spalding jerked his head up, a red stain spreading across his cheeks. "Just admirin' the nice needlework. Wonder if Dottie could sew something like 'at?" He dropped the bag at the foot of the bed and stared at Simon with no lingering sign of embarrassment. "Did your wife make it for you?"

The question forced a harsh laugh from Simon. "Wife? Don't have one. You think I'd leave a wife at home while I went off to fight—" He broke off, wheezing, and fought for breath. He should know better than try to talk so much before he recovered. By habit, he started counting as he inhaled.

The old man's eyes went wide, and he whirled toward the door. "Dottie! Get in here, girl."

Before Simon got to twenty, the woman rushed into the room. Her glance bounced from Simon to her pa. She advanced on Simon but halted when he held up a hand. "What happened?" She glared at her father.

"I dunno." The man threw up his hands. "We was just talkin'. He got riled up and stopped in the middle of sayin' something."

She shooed her father out. "Why don't you go check on the coffee, Pa? It should be 'bout done."

Mr. Spalding scuttled away like a guilty child, eager to escape a punishment. The cat trotted behind him.

Concern clouded Miss Spalding's honey-colored eyes and wrinkled her brow. "Are you better now? Can I get you anything?"

He expelled a long breath. "Sorry." He inhaled again. "Sorry to give y'all a scare."

Her gaze swept over the bed. "Did Pa upset you somehow? He can be harsh when he speaks at times."

Now that he considered it, Simon owned up to his fault in

the matter. "I mistook his words. It's easy to lose my wind during these attacks."

She didn't seem convinced but abandoned the subject. "Do you feel up to eatin' a bowl of grits?"

Simon attempted a smile. "I'm of a mind to try."

"Let's go ahead and sit you up, and I'll bring it to you." She grabbed the pillow as he leaned forward, then slipped her arm beneath his shoulder to help him slide back. The close contact brought a pleasant fragrance of rosewater. Miss Spalding must make her own, as Ma did, from rose petals.

She backed up and watched him a moment, giving him time to catch his breath. Her scent, her softness, her easy manner reminded him of what he'd missed lately. Even before his confinement at Libby, close contact with gentlewomen had been rare. In his weakened condition, every sensation penetrated like stinging nettles on tender feet. He'd best beware, or he might misinterpret Miss Spalding's interest and set himself up for heartache, the victim of his own impulsive nature and loneliness.

≈

As she slid her arm behind Mr. McNeil's back, the corded muscles of his upper arms flexed under her fingers. Her breath hitched, and her cheek grazed the top of his head, displacing the coarse curls clustered there. What a contradiction of strength and gentleness this man was.

With sudden clarity, Daviana willed her thoughts to veer away from the intimate proximity of the visitor. It wouldn't be proper to cast him into the role of rescuing hero in her fantasies. He wasn't hers to claim, and he'd be leaving as soon as he recovered from his sickness.

When he sighed, she eased back. "All right?" Her voice sounded strange, all croaky-like. What brought that on?

"Yes, thank you. I can breathe better too."

His answer ought to assure her, but he kept his gaze forward. His cheeks looked flushed. Was his fever up again? Another possibility scorched her own face. Had he discerned her struggle to restrain her fanciful daydreams?

She hurried from the room to fetch his meal. In the kitchen, she found Pa sitting at the table, staring into space. Not a good sign. What was he up to?

She stirred the grits. "Pa, did you say something to upset Mr. McNeil?"

He didn't answer. Daviana transferred a dipper of food into a bowl and added a spoon.

She marched to the table. "Pa," she said loud enough to assure his attention.

He cut his eyes upward. "What?"

"Did you say something to upset Mr. McNeil?"

Pa picked up his cup of chicory coffee and sipped. "'Course not. I wouldn't be so unfriendly to a guest." He sipped again, and Daviana turned to walk away. "I only asked about his wife."

Daviana groaned. *Here we go again.* Although she liked Simon McNeil, might even feature him in her private fantasies, she couldn't have Pa scheming to tie her to him. The idea that he had a wife waiting for him put a skunk in that well.

She choked out her words. "What about her?"

"I took him to say he don't have one."

Her chest eased.

At least she hadn't been spinning tales about a married man. Although having a single man in the house might give Pa ideas, and while *her* fantasies stayed safely tucked inside her brain, Pa's often grew legs and got folks in trouble.

She marched back to the bedroom. Would Mr. McNeil be wily enough to ward off Pa's schemes? Maybe he could give as good as he got. She hoped so, even if it meant her dreams would go with him when he left.

CHAPTER 3

After Simon consumed a portion of the breakfast Miss Spalding brought him, he took another dose of medicine and slept deeply. He lost count of the number of times she crept into the room to administer a dose or to bring some form of nourishment. With each visit, he forced a degree of wakefulness to respond to her questions, then plunged into the depths of sleep again.

Over the days that followed, he regained his health, leaving the lingering weakness as the last hurdle to full recovery. He blessed the Union doctor who'd checked him after his release from Libby. The man had insisted that Simon take a bottle of quinine with him when he left Richmond. Rumor was the South had long ago run out of the medicine.

When he woke at last ready to face the day, restlessness to be up and about heralded a return to normal. He lay awake a long while, expecting Miss Spalding or her pa to check on him. His stomach rumbled, and he wished for a clock or timepiece for a point of reference. Sleep and sickness skewed a person's idea of minutes and hours. Little light crept into the room through the curtain at the lone window, so it could be dusk or dawn or a cloudy day.

A more urgent need forced him to swing his feet to the floor and hope that the woman wouldn't walk in while he tended to the matter. Between the dizziness and the weakness, the simple task took twice as long as it should have and drained his energy. He fell sideways across the bed moments before a brisk knock and greeting announced her arrival.

"Mr. McNeil? Are you awake?" She pushed the door far enough to peek inside. "Oh! Did you try to get up alone? Let me call Pa to help you back to bed."

She dashed away before he could answer.

The old man ambled into the room and assessed Simon's position on the bed. He set the chair flush against the bed. "I'll lift and put you in the chair first." He did so, then plucked Simon from the chair and dropped him on the bed. The old geezer was stronger than he looked. Simon's respect for his host rose despite their earlier encounter. Was that yesterday or longer in the past?

When Mr. Spalding stepped back, his daughter approached with a tray. "Here's a bowl of greens in broth and a pone of cornbread for you. Be sure to drink all the broth. Mama always said it would—"

"Clean the sickness out of your liver." Simon finished the saying for her.

Miss Spalding's smile transformed her face, lighting her eyes and making roses bloom on her high cheekbones. Tendrils of hair curled near her ears, creating a frame for her creamy skin. Dark lashes swept down to hide her eyes as she set the tray on the quilt across his legs. "I reckon everybody's mama must pass down the same sayings."

When her hand brushed his arm, awareness shot through Simon and resulted in a shudder. It reminded him of the rippling effect when he slammed his elbow on a hard surface.

He wouldn't call it pain as much as a sensation that touched every fiber of his being.

Had she felt it too?

He steadied the bowl, which rocked when she backed away.

Her voice sounded breathless as she rushed out the door. "I'll collect the dishes later."

It took him a minute to recover from the unexpected attraction, which he blamed on his weakened state. And it *had* been a long time since he'd been in close quarters with a woman. A comely young woman, at that.

The warmth of the bowl between his hands reminded him he should eat to regain his strength. He dug into the soupy dish, remembering how he used to resist eating greens as a child. The last years' experiences had banished that finicky attitude. Like the biblical prodigal son, he'd learned to be glad for any edible offering. At least the cornbread was filling.

He polished off the meal and slid the tray to his side. He closed his eyes to savor the comfort of a full belly and a real bed in a home that seemed relatively untouched by the war. He hoped his folks in Randolph County had fared as well.

The peaceful atmosphere evaporated with sounds of shouting in the front yard. What was happening? He couldn't make out the words, and he was in no condition to challenge anyone. Surely, Miss Spalding would yell out if she needed help.

～

*P*a's raised voice alerted Daviana as she went to collect Mr. McNeil's dishes, and she detoured to discover the cause. She opened the front door. Pa leaned against the porch rail. Beyond him, a young man used sweeping gestures toward Sulphur Springs, his adolescent voice rising and falling as he explained something to her father.

What was going on?

The youth clammed up when he noticed her standing in the doorway.

Pa peeked over his shoulder and sighed but said nothing to her. Instead, he addressed the other man. "You reckon they'll come so far out in the country as we are?"

The visitor glanced her way and stuffed his hands in his pocket. "I wouldn't put it past 'em. We just thought everybody ought to be warned."

Pa stepped to the ground and put an arm around the young man as he led him away from the house.

Daviana huffed and went back inside. Why did men think they protected women by keeping them in the dark about matters? As if women couldn't handle anything outside household chores. As if they weren't the ones who took care of the sick and injured, figured out how to stretch meager supplies to keep everyone fed and clothed, then had to manage farms and finances when their menfolk trotted off to war.

She stomped down the hall to collect Simon McNeil's supper dishes and knocked sharply on his bedroom door. Her irritation warred with her caution about walking in on a man who wasn't kin. The poor man might get the brunt of her ire just by being there.

His voice sounded stronger when he called, "Come in." His eyes sought hers when she pushed inside. "I heard raised voices. Is there a problem?"

"Might be. You'll have to ask Pa. He thinks women don't have the sense to step outta the path of a runaway wagon." She rounded Simon's bed to pick up the tray of dishes he'd set aside.

"You'll notice I consumed all the broth as you instructed." His eyes sparkled when she glanced back. "In my family, we were taught to obey the woman of the house."

Daviana's mouth twitched at his obvious attempt to lighten

her mood. "Well, it's good to know some men can appreciate our value, Mr. McNeil." She lifted the tray and walked to the door. "I'd imagine Pa will tell you what happened out there if you ask him. Then maybe you'll let me know if there's anything to be concerned about."

"I can do that, Miss Spalding, but only if you'll call me Simon. It's hard to feel dignified enough to be called 'mister' while I'm lying here, dependent on you to nurse me back to health." His eyes closed and opened again as if he struggled to stay awake, but the corners of his mouth turned up.

A strange warmth filled her bosom and seeped into her face. Why couldn't more men show such consideration for the women in their lives? She offered a smile in return. "I will try to remember that, Simon McNeil. Get some sleep, and I'll check on you later."

Lordy, she was going to have a hard time keeping that man out of her dreams.

~

The next morning, Simon experimented with returning to normal activities. If he hoped to make it home in time for Ma's birthday in September, he couldn't let sickness hold him here too long. That goal had kept him going many days during his time in prison when he'd been tempted to give up hope. He wanted to see her face light up when he walked in. She would deflect all the attention to him, of course, as she always did, since his birthday fell just a couple of days later.

He replayed scenes from several of those celebrations over the years. Summertime meant hot days in the field but pleasant nights on the porch with family. A good deal of teasing and laughter. That was, if they could steer clear of subjects on which they didn't agree as Simon and his brothers grew older.

The war had scattered them, even pitted them on opposite sides. With the South defeated now, a deep desire for family drew Simon homeward. He expected the first meeting to be rough, but they would soon get beyond their differences. He hoped.

From the bedroom door, he chartered his path, using furniture to provide support. Miss Spalding had brought him a bowl of grits earlier and let him know she'd be working in the garden, but her pa would remain close by in case he needed anything. Simon aimed to visit with the man awhile and negotiate the payment for putting him up for a few days.

Letting go of the doorframe, he crossed the hall and kept one hand on the wall as he inched forward. When he reached the dining table, he stopped and leaned on it. Encouraged by his success, he shuffled to the sofa, then dared to take three strides without support to the front door. He paused at the threshold to catch his breath.

Mr. Spalding looked up from where he whittled on the porch and shifted a chair closer to where Simon stood. "Glad to see you up and about, young man. Take a seat and rest a bit."

Simon sank onto the cane-bottom chair. "Much obliged." A weak laugh escaped. "I just hope I don't have to spend the night in this chair."

The sun had just crested the hilltops, announcing its arrival with streaks of crimson and orange peeping through the clouds that stretched across the horizon. A pair of birds called to one another from the leaf-covered limbs of a white oak at the edge of the porch.

Simon drank in the luxury of sitting outside, his eyes closed. The scrape of Mr. Spalding's knife across wood sent a faint whiff of fresh shavings his way.

After several minutes, Simon roused himself to ask about the previous evening's visitor. "Thought I heard company come by the house last night."

Mr. Spalding snorted. "It weren't company exactly, just a neighbor passing along information about goings-on down at Sulphur Springs."

Not wanting to appear overly curious, Simon waited. When nothing followed, he said, "Nothing serious, I hope." He peered through narrow slits to find his companion shooting a considering glance his way. Was he suspicious?

At length, the older man answered. "Seems a couple of Federal men are scouting the area, tallyin' the size of farms and lookin' for former slaves who need work. Some folks fear they'll lose their land."

Simon shook his head. "I don't think you have to be concerned. Your farm is small, and you don't appear to have anyone else on the property." He forced his remark to sound casual, adding, "Did you ever have slaves here?"

"Nah. Never needed any and couldn't afford 'em, anyway. Dottie's grandpa didn't hold with people ownin' their fellow man. We all pitched in and helped each other when it was called for." A spate of coughing interrupted Mr. Spalding. He wiped his mouth with his handkerchief and folded it into his pocket. "My worries over the land come from a closer quarter. I reckon the Federals might have to wait in line if they aim to take it."

"You mentioned a relative you thought Miss Spalding ought to marry. I guess he's after the land?" As much as Simon disliked the practice of marrying to secure a home, he acknowledged it still happened. Especially in families with several sons who wanted land of their own, like his.

"Him and a half-dozen others." Mr. Spalding resumed his whittling. "That is, if they survived the war. I ain't seen but one come home since Lee handed over his sword."

"Maybe they decided to go elsewhere. They could be over in Texas where the fighting's still going on."

"Could be." He jerked his chair around to face Simon. "How would I find out?"

"You would need to know which units they served in, then find out where the unit was last located."

He shook his head. "Don't know how I could do that. With hardly any mail gettin' through, not even these fellas' closest relatives know where they are."

Simon scratched his chin. "Newspapers are a good source, if you can get a recent edition. If the Union army is in the area, an officer might have information about the last company locations for both sides. I'm guessing those men served in the Confederacy?"

Spalding's look of surprise warned him to tread carefully. "There are Union sympathizers all over the South, Mr. Spalding." He shrugged. "You know your neighbors best."

"I don't reckon any of 'em would be foolish enough to go against their Southern upbringin' and join the Federals." The old man tapped his fingers on his knee. "Even though it could serve 'em well now that the South's beat down. No tellin' how things will play out around here."

"I'd say you're right."

The discussion was cut short when Miss Spalding approached from the side of the house. She carried a basket in one hand and a short-handled spade in the other. Her eyes went wide when she saw Simon. "I wasn't expecting to find you here on the porch, Mr. McNeil."

He gathered his feet under him and started to rise.

She stayed him with an outstretched hand. "Please don't get up on my account."

He sat again, willing the dizziness to end. "I figured I'd better get back on my feet if I'm going to make it to Alabama by the end of August. My full recovery might take longer than any of us would like."

He might have missed the tremble to her lips if he'd looked

away. Did she dread the extra work his presence made for her? Or could it be she hated to see him leave?

When he'd set out from Virginia, Simon had determined to let nothing keep him from getting to Alabama in time for Ma's birthday this year. He hadn't planned on being waylaid at a Georgia farm by sickness and a woman who stirred his interest. What was that poem Ma loved to quote, something about plans going awry? Then Pa would answer with one from Proverbs—"'A man's heart devises his way, but the Lord directs his steps.'"

Simon was tired of running. He'd let his heart lead him far from home, full of idealistic enthusiasm. Seven years later, he'd left his lofty arrogance behind, buried somewhere on the battlefield near Cedar Creek. Despite his dreams and plans, did the Lord direct his steps now? Even in his waywardness, Simon never doubted that God knew where he was. The way he figured it, the Almighty had let him run until he couldn't run any more. Every prodigal ran out of road sooner or later.

CHAPTER 4

The thought of Simon McNeil leaving hit Daviana like a blast of cold air, snatching her breath. She would miss having someone other than Pa to talk to. How had she grown so accustomed to having Simon here in such a short time? Despite her attempts to rein in her imagination, his face and voice often intruded upon her thoughts. Was she beginning to believe her daydreams could become reality? But why would he want to stay here or whisk her away like a knight of old?

She forced a smile. "I reckon that's true, but don't push yourself. You might bring the sickness back on."

At the sight of Simon's raised eyebrows, she hefted the basket in her hands. "I'd best get these vegetables washed and cookin' if we want to eat tonight." She pulled her skirts closer as she passed between the men's chairs and entered the house.

Thankful for the privacy of her kitchen, Daviana hummed a comforting hymn while she gathered leftovers for the noon hour and started preparing a substantial meal for the evening.

She couldn't shake the reality of Simon leaving. In a matter of days, she'd come to anticipate seeing him, talking with him.

He made her feel as if she mattered, acted as though he enjoyed being with her. Even when he'd been terribly sick, he'd seemed to consider her feelings—unlike most of the menfolk she'd encountered in the last few years. Even Minnow approved of his presence. The finicky cat didn't take to many folks.

She set the table, reflecting on how Simon's presence made her want to put more effort into appearances. The meal, the house, and her looks in particular. A glance at her hands made her shake her head. So much for trying in that area. Grubbing in the dirt for potatoes didn't help any. Farm work was hard on hands.

After cleaning up as well as she could, she removed her apron and rushed to her bedroom to fix her hair and apply some rose water before the men came inside. A man who put her concerns above his own was worth the extra effort.

When she left her room, the conversation at the table caused her steps to falter.

"So if my cousin's boy files a report to say I'm not right in the mind, he can take the land from us?" Pa's voice carried a note of worry.

"That's what it boils down to," Simon said. "Of course, the law might be a little different here in Georgia, but you ought to find out before somebody tries it." Simon's voice softened. "However, if your will names Miss Spalding's children as heirs, that could change things. Is there no one she would consider marrying?"

Daviana's heart pounded. Why were they discussing her and her marriage prospects?

Pa's snort erupted into a cough. Finally, he said, "Nah. Silly female sets herself above most of the local boys, just because she had more schoolin' than most and reads ever'thing she can get her hands on."

The problem with the local *boys*, as Pa called 'em, was they had no desire to do anything different, to learn more, or to see anything outside of Georgia...and they couldn't understand why she would. Plus, they were pushy.

"O' course"—Pa's voice dropped lower—"the war took some of those men out of the picture, includin' the only one she ever considered marryin' up with."

She'd heard enough. She pulled her bedroom door shut with a distinct snap and marched down the hall. Both men turned her way, but Daviana breezed past them to lift the water pitcher and set it on the table with a thump.

Pa sat in his usual place. Simon stood by her chair and pulled it out. Caught off guard again, she raised her eyebrows in question. An unruly hank of hair fell across his clear brow. His blue-green eyes met hers straight on, with no evidence of embarrassment. Did he think she hadn't heard them? She sank into the chair and regarded Pa, who fiddled with the napkin next to his plate.

Her face burned. What must Simon think of her and Pa? Imagine Pa asking a stranger for advice on how to get her married so the land wouldn't go to her relatives. A smart man would figure Pa might be exploring him as a prospect for her husband. The draw, of course, was the land. According to the locals, getting a wife in the bargain was a questionable bonus. In her case, there was no question.

She was an unfortunate piece of the deal, just as Leonard Cox had announced at the last county dance before the war started. Her "uppity airs" made her unattractive.

If only she could get away as her brother had. She'd been tempted to go with Lionel, but a daughter's duty lay with her parents until she married. Even if she'd gone with Lionel, she'd still be doing the same thing—cooking and cleaning for her menfolk—except in a different place. And if Lionel remarried, which he certainly would someday, then Daviana wouldn't be needed. It was too bad she didn't live near a large town where she could meet more people. Where she wouldn't feel tethered to the land. Where she might be recognized as a person of worth on her own merit.

She bowed her head as Pa uttered a brief blessing over the food. Daviana prayed silently for help to endure Pa's scheming and bear the shame of not being winsome enough. For all her fanciful ideas involving Simon McNeil, she didn't want to be foisted upon him like unwanted baggage.

As the men dug into their meal, she nibbled at hers. She missed her brother for another reason. When he was here, the family enjoyed conversations at the table, which had given her the opportunity to listen and contribute. That was another strike against Lionel for abandoning them, taking with him her dreams of leaving Georgia.

*W*restling with the uncomfortable feeling of having given advice in a situation where he had no experience, Simon maintained silence at the table. He could offer legal advice, but even that varied from state to state.

No one else seemed inclined to speak either. Mealtimes with Mr. Spalding were so different from those back home, where everybody had something to say.

Miss Spalding ate little, and Simon's appetite had yet to return to normal. A glance in her father's direction proved that man had no problem with consuming his meal. Perhaps he was working on a plan of action to secure his property. Simon hoped so.

When Mr. Spalding rose and left the table without a word, seeming lost in thought, Simon laid his fork across the plate. Before he could thank Miss Spalding for the food, she touched his hand. "Did you find out what happened last night?"

Her words dissipated like steam on a hot stove as he was captured by the odd thrill running from her touch to his chest.

She jerked away. A rosy color brushed her cheeks.

Uh-oh. What had she asked him?

"What happened last night?" he asked, scrambling to catch her meaning.

She pursed her lips. A sign of annoyance? "You know. What did the fellow from Sulphur Springs say to Pa?"

He dragged his eyes from her lips to the hand resting close to his. Slender fingers tapped the table. No ring adorned them. She had no protection beyond an old man who hid his sickness from her and worried about losing the land.

Puzzle pieces slipped into place. Rufus Spalding wasn't worried about the farm. His concern involved his daughter losing her home or being coerced into a marriage she didn't want in order to keep it.

Simon folded his napkin into a square. "There're Union men in the area, moving this way, making note of who owns the land. He wanted your pa to know so he'd be prepared if they come here."

She frowned. "What will they do? Surely, they have no reason to take it from us."

"Not unless you're convicted of crimes against the government."

Her eyes went wide. "What kind of crimes? We heard the Federals arrested women who worked in the cotton mills over in Roswell. Put 'em on trains going north. If they consider making cloth for the Confederate army a crime, they're like to convict all of us for feedin' the men who stopped by our houses —not always by choice."

The Spalding farm's location would have put them in jeopardy. "Did that happen often?"

"Often enough that we learned to hide some of our food. Some would pay for it, but not everyone could. We didn't mind sharin' with those." She traced the rim of her cup with a finger.

Her voice dropped. "A time or two, though, they just barged in and took whatever they could find."

Simon's hand crept over hers, curious to see whether he'd feel the same rush as when she'd touched him before. A tingling warmth spread from his fingertips. "I'm sorry you experienced that. Away from the calming influence of women, men sometimes forget how to act in a civilized manner. I saw it in both armies."

When she raised her eyes to his, Simon's breath hitched at the swirl of emotions there. They beckoned him. Her lips parted in a silent question. Did he lean closer? Maybe she did. Either way, the clatter of a fork dropping to the floor broke the spell, causing both to jump and sputter awkward apologies.

She picked up her plate and hurried to the sink. Simon stacked Mr. Spalding's plate on top of his and followed. Before he could say anything, the old man rushed inside.

"Group of riders comin' this way. Dottie, pull the curtains and go to your room."

He grabbed the blunderbuss and turned to Simon. "You can do what you want, hide or stay put. I hope you'll take our part no matter what happens out there."

Simon eyed the weapon. "I think you ought to give that to Miss Spalding. It's best we don't give the appearance of trouble."

She spun from the window and pulled the firearm from her pa's hands. "He's right. Let's hope we don't need this, but I'll be prepared."

She headed back to her bedroom as Simon followed Mr. Spalding to the front door. And here he'd thought the war had ended.

~

*D*aviana dropped the weapon on her bed and jerked open the bottom bureau drawer. She'd hoped never to need her dagger again, but peace seemed to be in short supply. She slipped the knife in her skirt pocket, then set the bag of gunpowder on the dresser.

She stared at the short-barreled weapon and mentally rehearsed the steps for loading it. As weapons went, she could wish for better, but it would do. Remembering how they came to have it brought a smile to her lips.

That Confederate sergeant who'd stopped by last year had proved to be as wily as Pa. When he and his friend passed through the first time, Pa hid their rifled bayonets where they couldn't find them. The next morning, after searching the property without success, they went on their way to Marietta. About a week later, they stopped at the Spalding house again as they headed back to their unit in Virginia. Only then, they brought a horse and the blunderbuss to offer in trade for the return of their weapons.

Pa had nearly swallowed his tobacco wad in surprise. "Where in the world did you come by this fine mount, Sergeant? I can't believe he didn't get confiscated long ago."

"I rescued him from a Union cavalry officer in Marietta." The man sent a wink toward Daviana as he slid from the dun gelding's back.

She wandered over to pet the horse's nose. "Without a saddle? Can't the Union army afford to outfit their horses properly?"

The private spoke up then. "Seth left the saddle at my house, thinking it best not to have that evidence with us in case someone stopped us on the way."

"We decided to leave this fine animal here with you, Mr. Spalding," the sergeant said. "You've got that lush meadow beyond your house where he can graze, and he'll provide a means of transportation if you should need it."

Pa sputtered. "I ain't got nowhere to go that I need a horse. And no fence to keep him inside that meadow."

"He's trained to be ground-tied." The sergeant dropped the reins and walked away to demonstrate. "And you have a good-sized barn there. But if you don't want to keep him, I imagine he'd bring a mighty good price in a trade."

Sergeant Morgan removed a sack from the gelding's back and pulled out the blunderbuss. "I also brought you this firearm my pa left me, so's you have a means of protection. It's old but in good condition."

Pa walked around the horse to examine it. "What're you wantin' in return?" He licked his lips, a sign he'd been caught in his own trap.

"Our weapons that went mysteriously missing last week?" The sergeant framed it like a question. "I don't suppose you might've found 'em?"

After that conversation, they ate a meal together, and Pa surrendered the purloined rifles and ammunition. When the soldiers went on their way, Daviana swatted Pa's arm. "I reckon that'll teach you not to hide things you shouldn't keep."

"I don't know, Dottie. I thought it turned out right well for us." He thumbed his suspenders and grinned.

"Yeah," she'd said, "as long as the Union army don't come lookin' for their missin' horse."

~

Outside, Simon hung back, lounging near the door while Mr. Spalding greeted the two visitors. From the insignia on their uniforms, they were a corporal and a private, probably both about Simon's age. On this side of the Mississippi, most higher-ranking officers had cashed out, except for the career military men who had stayed. Dealing with lower-ranking soldiers should bode well for his host.

"Afternoon, gentlemen," the corporal called. He urged his mount to within a few yards of the house and leaned forward in the saddle. The private pulled a notebook from his breast pocket. "Who's the owner of this property?"

Mr. Spalding remained on the porch, establishing a defensive stance where his eye level matched that of the riders. "I am. Rufus Spalding. Been here some thirty years. You fellows got business here-about?"

Simon contained his smirk. He had to give it to the old man, stating his position right away. He'd been on the property before either of them had been born.

The corporal answered. "We're here on behalf of the United States government and the Bureau of Refugees, Freedmen, and Abandoned Lands. Our duty is to help the former slaves and other unfortunate folks in the South get resettled. How many acres do you have here?"

"Sixty-five. A good portion of those are unplowable hills and small creeks when we get enough rain." He spoke in a calm, clear voice, without any hint of emotion.

Minnow padded to his side as if prepared to offer his feline defense.

Leather creaked as the corporal shifted in the saddle. "We heard you might be looking to sell and move on."

Mr. Spalding huffed. "I don't know where you got that notion. I'm near sixty years old. Too old to be startin' over some'eres else."

The corporal squinted, putting Simon on alert. What was his scheme?

"Who all lives here?"

"At present, me and my daughter," Rufus said. 'Wife passed away seven or eight years ago. My son took a gander to see the West. Don't know how long he'll be gone."

"Was he or you a member of the Confederacy?"

Rufus deflected the question. "You don't think I'd be fool enough to take part in a losin' proposition at my age, do you?"

At a nod from the senior officer, the private made a note in his book.

The corporal tipped his chin at Simon. "Who are you?"

Simon pushed off the doorjamb and took his time stepping up beside Mr. Spalding. "Simon McNeil, lately a lieutenant of the Second Army Corps and occupant of Libby Prison. Before that, my family sent me to study law in Cincinnati."

He tensed for a possible outburst from Mr. Spalding. Those names might not mean anything to the old man, as apolitical as he seemed and with both places being far north of Georgia. But the corporal would recognize the message in them. Perhaps Simon risked losing his new friendships, but he owed these folks for taking care of him these last few days.

A glimmer of respect appeared on the soldiers' faces while his host didn't react at all.

The corporal cleared his throat. His eyes darted between Simon and the old man. "But you don't live here, sir?"

Simon slanted a smile and grasped Mr. Spalding's shoulder. "Not yet. I just arrived a couple days ago, and my intended says she needs a few more days to prepare for our nuptials."

Rufus Spalding snorted, not missing a beat. "You know how funny women can be about those things. I expect she's in there now, sewing on her dress."

The soldiers exchanged glances and lifted their horses' reins. "Well, as soon as she sees fit to let you move in, Lieutenant, I'd suggest you transfer the deed to your name. It'll save us all some trouble. Good day to you." He and his companion turned their mounts around and cantered away.

Mr. Spalding waited till they disappeared around the bend to face Simon with raised eyebrows. "Did you just claim my daughter as your bride, Simon McNeil?"

Simon shrugged. "It seemed the quickest way to get rid of them. I'm glad you caught on and went along with the scheme."

"I appreciate you coming to our aid. What I want to know is if you're gonna be here when they come back, askin' why you ain't claimed the land?"

A remnant of the spark he'd felt when his hand touched Miss Spalding's coursed through Simon's veins. A vision of those full lips, the bottom one snagged between her teeth, and her eyes, wide with awareness.

Simon sighed. *In for a penny, in for a pound.* "I'd say that's up to Miss Spalding."

CHAPTER 5

"You told him *what*?" Daviana's breath whooshed out as her body went cold, as if she'd dunked in the creek in wintertime. Then when she glimpsed Simon McNeil's crooked grin, she flushed hot all over.

She directed her ire at Pa, poking a finger in his chest. "You put him up to this, didn't you? You're so afraid of losin' the land, you can't wait for me to find somebody and get hitched."

Claiming innocence, Pa's hands went up in the air. "Dottie, I promise it weren't my idee."

Simon stepped between them, daring to grasp her shoulders as if he had the right. "It was my idea, Miss Spalding. I should've asked you first, but it seemed important to let them think we were already courting." His hands slid along her arms until her fingers nestled in his. All her energy pooled in her fingertips. Simon's blue eyes pleaded. "Please forgive me."

She looked away from those hang-dog eyes. His contrition undermined her anger. "All...all right. But I don't see how this solves the problem." Her thoughts threatened to spin into panic. "If anything, it's made it more difficult. Don't you see?

They're bound to come around again and ask why you're not here or why you haven't put your name on the deed."

"That's not going to happen. I plan to take care of the paperwork unless..." He stumbled to a stop, and his brow puckered. "Are you're turning me down?"

Daviana pulled her hands from his, crossed her arms, and hardened her heart to his woebegone expression. "I don't recall being asked anything, Mr. McNeil. You're so clever, seems to me you would have figured that out."

In a swirl of skirts, Daviana stormed back to her room and shut the door with an emphatic click. *Men!* Always so sure she'd jump at the chance to marry up with just anyone. She'd thought Simon McNeil was different, but they were all the same. Did he expect her to go along with his plans without even consulting her? Why had he even concocted such a scheme? He must see it as a chance to grab the land, just like all the others.

She sniffed back her traitorous tears. Why did she always come in second to the land? If she had anywhere to go, she'd leave now. Then what would they do?

A timid knock on the door accompanied Simon's voice. "Miss Spalding, please. Can we talk about this?"

When the plea came a second time, she gave in. Might as well let him say his piece.

She opened the door, crossed her arms, and set her jaw in a mutinous stance, though it offered little defense against his charm.

Simon pushed his way into the room and left the door ajar behind him. Daviana backed up a step so he wouldn't loom over her.

He hooked a hand behind his neck. "I reckon I messed up, didn't I? Fact is, I'd just realized I'd like time to get to know you better and see if we might agree to consider a permanent relationship. Then, before I could say anything to you or your pa, our visitors arrived."

"Hmpf. You didn't have to go out there at all. Pa could've turned 'em away without you jumpin' in." She rubbed at the ache beneath her collarbone. Arguing gave her heartburn.

"I don't think so." He paced away and turned back. "Those men are with the Freedmen's Bureau, which aims to redistribute land in the South so the former slaves have a way to make a living. Now, I don't have a problem with that, but I don't want to see y'all lose your farm either."

Daviana's ache increased. "Could that happen? Would they just come here and turn us out of our home?"

He lifted his hands and let them fall. "I hope not. But your brother did fight with the Confederacy, and your pa seems to be one who might resist cooperating and get them riled up."

"You're right. Pa wouldn't let go of the land for nothin'. It means more to him than anything."

Simon closed the distance between them. "I understand why you'd think so, but I believe you're wrong. You're his main concern, Miss Spalding. Would you permit me to use your Christian name? I hope we might come to an agreement, and I already asked you to call me Simon."

How had her situation changed so quickly? Was Simon like the other men, after all—ready to grab the opportunity to enrich himself? Could she afford to turn him down, with the farm in jeopardy? Perhaps she should give him the opportunity to prove his sincerity.

"I reckon that'd be all right." She lowered her head so he wouldn't see her flaming face. It wouldn't do for him to know that was how she'd referred to him in her journal. "Dottie is what most people call me." Daviana wouldn't share her true name with him just yet. She'd hold it close to her heart until she felt he could be trusted with it.

He touched her chin and guided her face up. "I appreciate

the privilege. Would you agree to consider a courtship? I understand your hesitation, but time works against us."

She swallowed, willing her heart to quit galloping. "How much time do we have?"

Simon shrugged as his hand drifted to her shoulder. "I figure a week or two before those men come around again. Meanwhile, we'll try to come up with another plan if you feel it won't work between us."

Her lips twitched. "I reckon I could abide havin' you here that long." *And maybe longer.* In spite of his high-handed ways, she rejoiced that he wasn't leaving yet.

He eased closer and bent his head toward hers. "I'll be on my best behavior."

Oh. Did he intend to kiss her? She held her breath.

A pounding at the door intruded. "Hey, y'all come on outta there now." Pa's voice boomed from the hallway. "We got work to do and plans to make."

Simon dropped his hand, and Daviana stepped back, her face burning. How shameful she'd become, wishing for a kiss from someone she hardly knew. What would Ma think of her if she could see them? *Could* she see them?

And just why would wedding Simon make a difference in whether they kept the farm? Hadn't he been in the Confederate army too? Why hadn't she thought to ask? Was it because he'd been in the prison, some kind of code soldiers honored? Too many questions muddled her thinking.

*D*on't rush your fences, boy. That was what Pa would tell him—had told him on numerous occasions. *You take off and rush headlong, without thinking things through, when patience would help you reach your goal sooner.*

Simon backed away from those tempting lips with a shaky

smile. "I guess I'll see what your pa needs me to do." He motioned to the blunderbuss on the bureau. "You can put that away for now. I hope you'll take a walk with me after supper."

Her blushing nod gave him a surge of pleasure and fortified his resolve. He planned to get that kiss before they bid each other goodnight.

Mr. Spalding waited in the hallway when Simon exited the room. "I thought maybe we'd walk the property so you have a proper appreciation for the prize."

As the old man led the way, Simon glanced back at Miss Spalding and winked. "Oh, I think I have a pretty good idea of what it is." Her wide eyes and pink cheeks made him chuckle.

He caught up with her father and gave his attention to the man's description of each area they covered. Much of the land would need to be cleared after years of neglect and occasional abuse from armies passing by. Bramble bushes had sprung up around stumps that testified of trees toppled in haste. Wild grass encroached on fields where rows of crops once grew. The most promising sight was a small apple orchard in the farthest acre.

As Mr. Spalding had told the men from the bureau, the land included hills and streams, neither of which lowered the value. In fact, they could add to it, depending on how the land was used.

"What did you grow here before the war?"

"A little of everything. Corn, potatoes, okra, squashes. Got a good number of fruit trees, also pecan trees here and there."

Simon envisioned the fields with rows of crops. "My family had a sizable garden and raised a few cows and pigs, but mostly we grew cotton. How many people you reckon it would take to work the whole farm?"

"Depends on what you plan to do with it."

As the old man rambled, conversations during Simon's army career and his time in prison filled his mind. Conversations that opened his eyes to how diverse farming was across the country. Now that he'd committed himself to stay here, he needed to learn how to make it profitable. It would require more than two or three people to do that. He'd need to hire workers, too, so he could devote some time to a law practice.

Mr. Spalding erupted into a coughing spell, and Simon gazed toward the opposite field, giving the man time to catch his breath. When the older man recovered, he took up where he'd left off his commentary. Was he determined to act as if his interruption had never happened?

Simon gave him a pointed look. "How long have you been sick? And when do you plan to tell your daughter?"

A harsh laugh accompanied a shake of Mr. Spalding's head. "You don't miss much, do you?"

Simon crossed his arms, refusing to drop the subject. "I've noticed blood on your handkerchief a time or two when you spewed your tobacco waste. And your coughing has woken me up more than once."

"I had the first spell about a month after Lionel left to join the army in '62. Albert—that's my grandson—he helped me keep it hid from Dottie while he was here. With the warmer weather, it ain't so bad, but I fear the next winter might be my last."

"Did your son know you were so sick? Why didn't he stay around?"

The old man ran a hand through his hair. "Lionel lost his wife to a similar sickness a couple years afore the war. He didn't want his boy to have to watch another family member die. I reckon he done seen enough death on the battlefield hisself."

An ugly word slipped past Simon's lips, giving vent to his anger. "So, he left y'all here without regard for you or Miss Spalding."

"I reckon he figured it would force Dottie to choose someone to marry."

If Simon ever got his hands on Lionel Spalding, he'd have some choice words for him. That would be after he put his fist to the man's jaw—mild punishment for cowardice in his eyes.

"Mr. Spalding, you need to tell her. From what I've seen, she's a strong woman and deserves to know the truth, but she needs time to prepare herself. I'll do my best to hurry things along with the courtship, but I don't want her to feel pushed into marrying me. She already feels as though she comes second to the land."

"What?" The old man stumbled back. "Don't she realize I'm tryin' to secure her future? I ain't got much to leave her besides the land. War came along about the time she should've been gettin' married. The only boy she spent time with—our neighbor's youngest—well, he decided to join up and got killed in a battle last year."

Mr. Spalding huffed a guilt-laden sigh. "He wanted to marry her afore he left, but I held out against it. Didn't want him to leave her with a child on the way, not knowin' what his fate might be."

Simon released the breath he'd drawn. "I'd say that proved to be a wise decision, since he didn't come back."

"Maybe. But it took Dottie a long time to forgive me. I didn't think she cared so much for young Dunaway, but she cried and carried on, then refused to speak to me for a while. Acted like he was her last hope. I reckon I've been tryin' to make up for it ever since, pushin' her to consider every eligible man around here."

"She undervalues herself. I'll do my best to make sure she knows I hold her in great esteem."

They strolled through the apple orchard toward the eastern boundary at a leisurely pace. Mr. Spalding plucked a sprig from an apple tree and sniffed it. "If we're gonna be kin soon, I reckon you ought to call me Rufus from here on out."

"All right, Rufus. I'm good with that."

With a sudden chuckle, Rufus turned to Simon. "Did I tell you about the two soldiers who stopped at our house twice last year?"

"No, sir. I don't recall hearing about it."

Had Rufus tried to match his daughter with some other soldier passing through? The thought brought a surge of anger —or was it jealousy?

Not that Simon had a right to either. He was little more than a stranger to them, and he'd ramrodded his way into their lives, with Simon getting the better part of the deal.

After Rufus finished his story and they headed back to the house, Simon vowed he'd see that neither of them would regret their trust in him.

He had enough regrets for a lifetime. Now it was time to build his future.

~

With the men away from the house, Daviana kept her hands busy mending Pa's socks. Her mind, however, hovered over the same subject, trying to decipher her feelings about Simon's proposal. The prospect of marrying such a man was like a prize she couldn't have anticipated.

Was it too good to be true?

Why would Simon come to their rescue on such short acquaintance? Perhaps he thought he owed it to them for taking him in and helping when he was sick. But what of his plans to arrive in Alabama by the end of the month? Would he forsake that goal?

What about his family? From what he'd said about his home, he was second oldest of four brothers. Dividing a small farm among that many sons could prove difficult. By marrying her, he'd gain his own property and thus provide his brothers with a larger portion. A selfless act, or did he have other reasons? Could it be that he really cared for her as he'd implied?

Something about him inspired her trust, in spite of the sudden proposal. It was as though he gave her room to breathe.

After an hour, Simon and Pa still hadn't returned. She checked the greens simmering on the stove, slid a pan of corn-bread into the oven, and stirred up a batch of ginger water. She poured herself a cup, then sauntered to the porch to wait.

The approach of a rider forestalled her relaxation. She set her cup beside the chair and waited for the person to draw closer.

The figure stirred a long-buried memory. When the man swept off his fedora, her fears were realized.

Jasper Dunaway.

For years, she'd avoided him, and it seemed he'd been careful to keep his distance from her. Perhaps he feared she'd report his reprehensible behavior, but she'd heard enough to know how he would turn the tables on her. Only Kyle had known about it—except the part about Malachi being the one who rescued her—because she trusted him to protect her from Jasper. Kyle had threatened to expose his brother if he ever bothered her again.

With Kyle gone, she'd kept her distance from the Dunaway farm, and Jasper had no excuse to nose around Spalding land. What did he want?

She steeled herself and prayed Pa and Simon would hurry back.

"Afternoon, Miss Dottie. I trust I find you in good health."

Jasper swung off his horse and walked it close to the porch, where he flipped the reins over the railing. He flashed a grin.

If he thought he could charm her, he could quash that idea. She'd learned the miscreant's true nature long ago. He was the one who'd encouraged Kyle to join the Confederate army, using his wife and children as his excuse to stay at home.

Kyle was lost forever, while Jasper had escaped with nary a scratch.

Careful to neither encourage him nor enrage him, she kept her voice neutral. "I'm fine, Jasper. And you?"

He propped one foot on the bottom step and crossed his arms on the raised knee. "Well, now, I'm doing fairly well. Finally gettin' over the loss of my loved ones and ready to take up my responsibilities again."

Loved ones? Ha! The only person Jasper loved was the one in his mirror. Well, maybe he loved his young'uns. It'd be a poor father who didn't love his own offspring. Not so the woman who'd birthed them, from what Daviana could tell. He'd run her into the ground for years, if not physically abusing her, then making her life miserable with his rough treatment and tales of his philandering, if the rumors could be believed. Daviana didn't know what exactly had happened, but Jasper's wife had passed away last year at the age of twenty-six.

He glanced around the house and yard. "Your pa some-where about?"

Daviana wasn't foolish enough to let him catch her alone again. "Pa's here, just not in the house right now. I expect him back from the field any minute."

Jasper's eyebrows shot up. "Well, now, I've a mind to wait a bit." He straightened and advanced to the top step. "I've a matter of importance to discuss with him. Somethin' that might interest you, about renewin' the proposed union of our families that would've happened when Kyle came home. Since he ain't here..." He lifted his hands, palms up.

He had to be jesting. Surely, he didn't mean... But this was Jasper. Nothing he said or did should surprise her. She feigned innocence. "I'm sure I don't know what you mean."

His gaze traveled down her body and back again, his eyes sparking with intent. "Why, I mean you and me, Miss Dottie. With both Kyle and Deborah gone, it makes perfect sense for us to hitch up. You know Kyle would want me to take care of you, but I couldn't hardly do much while I was married to Deborah."

Not that he hadn't tried.

The smirk on his lips dared her to mention it.

"Anyway," he said, resuming a serious demeanor, "now my mournin's past, and my boys need a mother, so I figured it made sense for us to wed."

Daviana bit back the anger building in her chest, scrunching her skirts in her fists. She wouldn't give him the pleasure of witnessing an outburst. "This is quite unexpected, Jasper. As you mentioned, Pa would have to give his consent, and he's got other plans."

Voices from the side of the house saved her from further explanation.

Thank God.

Minnow raced from the yard onto the porch, and Daviana's breathing eased. God bless Simon McNeil for arriving at the right time. He might be her salvation in more ways than one.

When Pa rounded the house, Jasper turned to greet him. "Well, here's Rufus now."

Pa reached out a hand to welcome his neighbor. "Jasper, I'm surprised to see you. Been a while. What brings you over this way?"

While they shook hands, Simon glanced at her, and Daviana gestured for him to join her.

He brushed past the other men and mounted the stairs.

Pa asked Jasper something, but the man's reply faltered as his attention followed Simon, who took his place at her side.

"Pardon my dirt," Pa said to Jasper. "I been showin' Simon around the farm so we could see what to plant."

"Oh, are you hirin' help now?" Jasper's voice came across as disdainful.

Daviana threaded her fingers with Simon's and tossed him a

smile before focusing on the interloper again. "No, Jasper. How foolish that would be. Simon will be managing the farm from now on. As I was about to tell you, he's my betrothed." She squeezed Simon's hand and prayed he'd get the message.

~

*B*etrothed?

Simon's gaze sought Dottie's when she claimed him as her future husband. Had she decided, then, or was she using his proposal as a barrier against unwanted advances? Either way, he enjoyed the way her hand fit in his. He smiled and raised their joined hands so he could plant a kiss on her knuckles, pleased at the blush that stained her cheeks.

When he had returned from the field to find a stranger standing so close to her, Simon's sudden surge of jealousy had surprised him. The man's demeanor set Simon on edge. A glance at Daviana had told him she didn't welcome the attention—and wanted him to step in. Which he was happy to do.

Focused on the woman he planned to marry, Simon had nearly missed the man's snide remark dismissing Simon as a hired hand. Her answer mitigated his annoyance.

Rufus chuckled, but the visitor didn't find it funny.

"What? I ain't heard nothin' about her bein' betrothed to anyone." Turning his attention to Rufus, Jasper demanded, "Who is this man?"

Without releasing Dottie, Simon stretched his right hand toward the outraged visitor. "Simon McNeil. I'm guessing we'll be neighbors?"

The man barely gave his outstretched hand a glance and made no move to meet it.

"You will," Rufus said. "This is Jasper Dunaway. His farm backs up to ours on the south side." To Jasper, he said, "I don't reckon we seen you since your wife's funeral, Jasper. You and the kids doin' all right?"

Dottie didn't wait for the neighbor to answer. "Why don't y'all sit? Simon can help me bring out some cups of switchel for everyone."

She squeezed Simon's hand and led him into the house, and he followed her like a well-trained pup. Even when she broke contact, he stayed close. "What's going on? Is there something about this fellow I ought to be aware of? Does he cause y'all problems?"

"You might say that." She pulled a pan of golden cornbread from the stove and set it aside. "Like a lot of men around here, he's land hungry. Lost his wife six or seven months ago." While Dottie talked, she poured liquid into three cups and pushed two of them into Simon's hands. She picked up the third. "Now I reckon he's looking to add our farm to his holdings."

Her high color had nothing to do with embarrassment. Her dander was up, and Simon guessed at what she didn't say outright.

"Meaning he came looking to court you?"

"Meanin' you got to convince him that ain't gonna happen."

Simon transferred one cup to her free hand and wrapped his arm around her waist. "That's an assignment I'll look forward to doing." He ushered her to the front door. "You just go along with whatever I tell him. We'll send Mr. Dunaway packing in no time."

CHAPTER 6

Daviana pressed her lips together and kept her eyes on Simon. It wouldn't do to let Jasper see her anxiety.

Back on the porch, Simon handed Jasper a cup, then took the two she held and gave one to Pa, who'd claimed his usual chair. Still wearing a frown, Jasper leaned against the porch rail.

Simon positioned himself between her and Jasper. "Seeing as we're going to be neighbors, I reckon we ought to get to know one another. You been here long, Dunaway?"

Jasper smirked. "All my life, just like Dottie here. She was promised to my younger brother before he went off to war and got hisself killed."

"You didn't join the fight?" Simon sipped from his cup but held Jasper's gaze. If Jasper's comment surprised him, he didn't show it.

Jasper's glower returned. "No. Kyle was rarin' to go, and one of us had to stay and mind the farm. I had a wife and children, plus Ma to provide for."

Daviana checked the urge to roll her eyes. His idea of caring for his family didn't sit well with her.

"I guess everyone's not as fortunate as my brothers and me," Simon said, "to have both our parents still living and able to run things. My older brother lost part of a leg in '63 and went back home. Younger brother spent some time as prisoner of war, as I did."

Jasper glanced around. "Never did hear you say where you was from, McNeil."

Simon spread his arms. "I got family scattered from the other side of Atlanta and into Alabama, where Pa's farm is."

"That's quite a ways from here. How'd you come to meet up with these folks?" Jasper motioned to her and Pa.

Daviana steeled herself. How would Simon answer without making Jasper suspicious of their sudden betrothal?

He wouldn't be the last to ask. They needed to figure out how to tell the truth without inviting disapproval from folks.

Simon glanced at Pa and grinned. "Didn't Rufus tell you about the soldiers who left their weapons here last year?" He reached out to pull Daviana to his side. "Since I first saw her, I couldn't get this woman off my mind. Bringing that horse a week later made for a good excuse to see her again. When I arrived and learned she wasn't promised, I hurried to claim her as mine as soon as I could. I'm sure glad she was agreeable to my proposal."

Simon turned an adoring smile her way, creating dimples in his cheeks. When he winked, heat rushed into her face. How did it occur to him to use the story of the confiscated weapons to make Jasper believe they'd met before? Glad as she was for the help in turning aside Jasper's attentions, it made her uneasy.

Did Simon always spin tales so easily?

Had he used half-truths to win over her and Pa?

"Well, since you ain't from here, I guess you'll be moving

away after the weddin'." Jasper glanced at Pa. "Don't know how Rufus will manage without Dottie here to look after him."

Simon must have seen the speculation in Jasper's eyes that Daviana did. "Oh, we plan to visit my folks for a few days, but we'll be back. Didn't you hear Dottie say I'll be running the farm? We couldn't run off and leave her pa to tend it by himself."

Jasper chewed on that information as he swallowed the last of his switchel. He placed his cup on the porch rail. "Well, it's been good seein' you folks. I reckon I better get on back to my place." He clomped down the steps, picked up his reins, and swung onto his horse. "I expect to be invited to the weddin' now. I wouldn't want to see Dottie abandoned again this late in life."

He turned and rode away before she could come up with a response to his comment. As if she were in her dotage and couldn't hold onto a man! She certainly didn't plan to settle for a polecat like Jasper.

Simon called after him. "No worries about that, Dunaway. I know a good woman when I find one."

When Jasper disappeared over the hill, Simon removed his arm from Daviana but stayed nearby. She missed the warmth and security his closeness offered.

"What do you think?" he asked. "Will he be back? He didn't seem to expect me to stick around."

She huffed. "I wouldn't be surprised if he tried to stir up trouble. He'd like to expand his holdings any way he can." She wouldn't consider that there might be another reason why he wanted her.

Simon stroked his chin. "Does he have enough workers for that? Did he have slaves?"

Pa slumped in his chair. "Yep. He couldn't keep up his place without help. I believe an older couple stayed on with him, but the younger field hands lit out quick as they could. I don't know how he'd manage if he had more land. O' course, he don't want to *buy* it. He saw Dottie as a chance to get more land for nothin' and secure a new mother for his young'uns all in one swoop."

"I don't know exactly how the Freedmen's Bureau plans to help the freed slaves, but I've heard they promised 'em a chance to own property." Simon leaned against the porch rail, his arm brushing hers. "Property from abandoned lands, the newspapers said. That's why I made sure the Union men who came by knew your land was well occupied."

Pa whistled through his teeth. "Whew, they're gonna have quite a job with that. Might take years to get it done."

They fell silent for a moment. Simon pushed off the rail. "Rufus, any chance Lionel is coming back?"

Pa grunted. "I don't expect it to happen, at least not anytime soon." He looked right at Simon as if sending him a private message.

Was he inviting Simon to take charge of the farm? Daviana held her breath. Was Pa sicker than he let on? He kept saying his cough was a cold that wouldn't let up.

"After supper," Simon said, "I'll show you two my ideas about the land. Make sure we're agreed on a few changes I'd like to make. Right now, I believe I'll go lie down for a while."

He swayed and grasped her arm to stay upright.

Alarm shot through her. "Are you gettin' sick again?"

He yawned. "Just tired. But I wouldn't mind it if you walked with me." He draped his arm across her shoulders when they entered the house. His beard brushed her cheek. "This is one benefit I'm glad to claim."

His breath lifted the short curls across her forehead and raised goosebumps on her arms. Could she trust this silver-tongued man, or was he setting her up for a heartbreak?

*H*aving Dottie at his side felt natural, as if she belonged there. More and more, Simon had the sense that he'd met his destiny at this farm—at a time and place he'd least expected it.

Their steps slowed at the door to his room. Aware that Dottie bore a large part of his weight, he shuffled toward the bed. This cursed malaria robbed him of his energy and stung his manly pride. How long would it keep coming back? What if it had the lasting effects that the doctor had mentioned? Back then, the possibility hadn't concerned him because marriage didn't figure into his plans. With the change in his situation, perhaps he should research the matter.

For now, he shoved the matter aside. He wanted to collect the kiss Rufus had prevented earlier, but his strength had flown. He concentrated on making the last few steps without kicking the cat that danced around their feet.

As soon as his knee bumped the cot, Simon fell onto the mattress.

Caught off-balance, Dottie landed on his chest. She pushed away and scrambled back.

"So sorry." He grasped her hand to keep her from leaving. What did her wide-eyed alarm mean? He couldn't find the strength to ask.

She glanced at their hands. "Is there something I can get you? Your medicine or maybe a bite to eat?"

"No. Just need to rest. Wake me in an hour."

The worry eased from her expression, but her gaze roamed his face as if searching for answers there. "I'll check on you in a bit." She bent forward and kissed his brow. "Thank you for dealing with Jasper."

He caught the blush on her cheeks. Her fingers slipped from his, and she fled the room.

He sighed. Too bad he'd worn himself out this afternoon walking the property, else he might've got a proper kiss.

Sometime later, he awoke, refreshed in body but troubled in mind.

How could he expect Dottie to marry him when she knew so little about him? As much as he dreaded it, he had to tell her the truth and let her decide whether his past made him ineligible to be her husband. The way things had developed since he arrived seemed a blessing from heaven for him—the chance to have his own farm and a place to put his legal training to use only a few days' travel from where he grew up—but she might not view it as a gift.

He sat on the side of the bed for a minute before standing to test his balance. After a warning rap and call, the door opened enough for Dottie to peek in.

"Oh. You're awake. How're you feelin' now?"

He met her at the threshold. "I feel like planning a wedding, but we need to talk first. Will your pa let us walk to the garden after supper?" His hands slid from her shoulders to her wrists. "I want you to know all about me, and I want to know about you."

"Pa won't mind so long as we stay within sight of the house."

He touched his forehead to hers. "Thank you. Now I guess you better get out there before Rufus shoots me with that blunderbuss."

She grinned.

He released her hands and opened the door wider. "I hope you came here to tell me supper's ready."

She nodded. "How does squash and potatoes sound?"

"After what I've eaten the last four years, your cooking is like manna from heaven. I'll help you clean up the kitchen when we're done."

"Simon, you don't have to do—"

"Nuh-ah." He set a finger to her lips. "Don't argue. That way, we'll get to take our walk sooner and be back before dark."

~

With the dishes washed and put away, Daviana and Simon left Pa on the porch as they meandered past the vegetable garden. She led the way to a fallen tree trunk where they could face the house and have a peek at the sunset in a while. She sat, and Simon propped one foot beside her, leaning on his raised leg.

Assailed by memories of a similar posture—her sitting on a log while Jasper stood over her—she forced her gaze upward. This was Simon. He didn't deserve her fear. To hide her trembling hands, she clasped them in her lap.

The sun revealed auburn and wheat-colored strands peeping through the brown in his hair. Long fingers tapped an anxious rhythm on his knee as she waited.

Daviana shifted on her rough seat and directed her gaze away from Simon. At the end of the log, a line of ants marched toward a distant bush. She took a deep breath, and a faint scent of onion seeped from the ground, but she concentrated on the more delicate peach fragrance wafting from the trees behind her.

Minnow nosed around the log, then deserted her to chase a butterfly.

Simon cleared his throat and directed his gaze to his linked hands. "I, uh, realize the things I said to Dunaway weren't exactly the truth. For that matter, neither was what I told the Union men when they were here. You must wonder if I'm in the habit of lying, and I want to assure you that I'm not. In both of those instances, my primary concern was to protect you and your interests."

Daviana searched his face. A slight rosy tinge dusted his

cheeks, and his eyes reminded her of a stormy sky. "Very well. I believe you."

With a sigh, he sat beside her and took her hand. "The strange thing is, I've always been truthful, often to a fault. More than once, Ma had to remind me I should find a kinder way to speak the truth or else say nothing."

"How could telling the truth be a problem?"

"People don't always want to hear it. They might expect you to agree with their opinion and then get upset when you don't." He rubbed his thumb over her palm. His touch did strange things to her, made her want to squirm.

"Take your hands. A gentleman is supposed to overlook your calluses and, instead, compliment your eyes or your hair. Many women would hide their calluses with gloves and take offense if someone mentioned them. To me, though, those represent your love for your family, so I commend them."

He lifted the one he held and placed a kiss on her knuckles. "But back to what I wanted to tell you. I haven't been completely honest with you about something." His grip tightened as his gaze lifted to hers. "I didn't fight in the Confederate army."

A frisson of alarm ran clear down to her toes. "You didn't?" She started to pull her hand away, but he kept ahold of it. "You told Pa and those Union men—"

"I told them my name and rank and that I'd been a prisoner of war. All that was the truth." Simon threaded his fingers with hers. "Did you ever hear of Libby Prison?"

What did that matter? "I don't know. Maybe. Where is it?"

"In Virginia. That's where I spent the last several months. It's a Confederate prison for captured Union soldiers."

"You fought with the Federals?" Her heart pounded. She pulled her hand from his grasp, and this time, he didn't stop her. "I don't understand. Aren't you from Alabama?"

Everyone she knew in these parts had supported the

Confederacy. Both her brother and Kyle had fought for "the cause," though Pa had tried to convince them to stay out of it.

"My family was divided. While two of my brothers joined the Rebel cause, a few of us supported the Union. Unusual, I know, for the section of Alabama where we lived. Even more so because my family had slaves."

He wasn't making sense. Had the fever affected his mind? "I don't understand. Your family had slaves, but you fought to set them free?"

He scuffed his boot heel over an exposed tree root. "The slaves were there before I was born, some before Pa was born. They came with the farm when my grandpa settled there, and the law made it illegal for free people of African descent to live in the state."

Snatches of discussions between Kyle and Pa about Georgia laws pricked her memory. Laws that prohibited the slaveowners from setting their slaves free, which had struck her as cruel. Why should the politicians in Milledgeville keep people enslaved when their owners wanted to free them? It seemed Alabama's laws made no sense either.

"So the slaves could be set free, but they had to leave the state?"

Simon scoffed. "Sure, but they had to be gone in something like thirty days. After that, if they were caught in Alabama, they'd be punished and enslaved again by someone else. Pa figured the best course was to keep our folks with us where they'd be treated well. He said he lived within the law but acted according to his Christian conscience."

Daviana wanted to muddle over his words, but he took a deep breath and continued.

"There's more you should know. When I was a youth, maybe fifteen or sixteen, one of the girls on our farm caught my fancy. She was a mulatto, the daughter of our Nanny Liza." He picked up a dried limb and peeled away the crumbling bark. "I was angry that I couldn't court her because she was a slave, and Pa had strict rules about showing respect to everyone, no matter their status."

Simon dropped his head. "I came close to destroying our good name when I visited Pansy in her cabin one night. She wanted me to run away with her, but my brother kept me from making that mistake."

He directed his gaze toward the house. "Pa had already warned me about sharing my abolitionist views and getting into a few fist fights. Ma worried that I'd get myself killed that way, so they sent me to a school up north when I was sixteen. I studied law so I could learn how to argue for ending slavery. When the war came, I joined the Union army to fight for the cause."

Daviana swallowed and pushed past the heaviness in her chest. "You haven't been home since you left? That's been what, four years? Six?"

He tossed the remains of the limb aside. "Nearly seven." His voice carried a world of regret.

"Seven years away from your family?" She couldn't imagine staying away from home that long. Pushing past her discomfort, she voiced her primary concern. "The girl you wanted to court, is she still there on your parents' farm?"

He answered with an emphatic shake of his head. "She married not long after I went north, and they have a couple of children now. In the last letter I had from Ma, before I was captured, she said she expected that family to leave as soon as the war ended. They'd already planned a route to take, knowing Pa wouldn't hold them back once they could leave legally."

The knot in Daviana's stomach eased. At least she wouldn't have to wonder whether Simon expected to reunite with his first love when he went to Alabama. Perhaps that was why he'd jumped at the chance to set down roots here, so he wouldn't be reminded of the girl he'd lost. No matter the years that passed, they said a person always remembered the first object of their affection.

Did the same go for a person's first encounter with licentious behavior? She'd never forget what happened to her six years before, though no one else knew about it. Except Malachi and Kyle, who'd kept her secret. With both of them gone—Malachi to find his daughter and Kyle to the world beyond death—that secret detail of her life was safe. As long as Jasper kept his distance, there was no need to relive that shameful day. Would Simon view her differently if he knew?

~

*D*ottie's silence disturbed Simon. What was she thinking? Was she trying to figure out how to send him on his way but still keep her land? Maybe she found Dunaway's offer more appealing.

The notion made him ill.

Though he hadn't thought of Pansy in months, maybe years, his confession brought to mind that long-ago summer when he'd first experienced the stirrings of desire. She had enchanted him with her sparkling eyes and shy smiles, which he'd imagined as reserved for him alone. Youthful infatuation made everything seem possible.

He now could admit the truth that he didn't want to face then. His jealousy and frustration had driven his adamant stand against slavery. His exile had fueled his fury. Ignoble emotions, for sure, but they'd served the purpose of making him study and work harder.

A touch on his arm turned him to face Dottie. "Sun's settin' now," she said. "We best get back to the house."

Simon searched her eyes. "Please tell me what you're thinking. I don't want to spoil my chances with you, but I felt you ought to know these things before we make firm plans. Do you despise me for fighting with the Union? Will your pa refuse to let us marry? Should I pack my bags and be on my way?"

"No, Simon. No to all your questions. That is, I don't believe Pa will oppose us marryin'. He didn't support the war. In fact, he tried to talk Lionel out of takin' part, said the federal government was never gonna let the South go."

Simon caught a strand of her hair that slipped its binding and tucked it behind her ear. "But it's clear you have some concerns. What are they? Maybe I can set your mind at ease."

His desire for her to accept his suit created a physical pain in his chest. He'd grown to care for this woman more in a week than he had for others he'd known for years. Had he just blown his chance?

⁓

Daviana contemplated his words, finding comfort that he honored her with the truth at the risk of driving her away. The fact that he'd fought for the North instead of the South. That he'd loved a slave girl and had to leave his home because of his views.

He'd heaped a whole barrel of truth on her. The side he'd fought on didn't matter to her, but his reasons for choosing to fight did. Did he still pine for that girl?

It wasn't her mind that needed easing. It was her heart.

Simon McNeil, with all his gentleman's manners and quick wit, could sweep her off her feet without trying. Tarnation, she was half-gone already. Would she let what he'd revealed about his past come between them? It wasn't as if she didn't have secrets of her own.

And therein lay the trouble. Considering his desire for honesty, would she eventually feel compelled to tell him everything?

"I just need a little time to think on what you told me," she said. "Let's plan to talk again tomorrow, all right?"

He grinned as he stood and offered his hands to help her up. "I like that plan. In fact, I think it's what we ought to do every evening."

She allowed him to hold her hand while they strolled toward the house. "How long will it take to go from here to your home in Alabama?"

"On horseback, I'd guess about four days if the weather's good and there's no trouble on the road. To be safe, I'd like to leave by the end of the month." He stopped and faced her. "Would you be willing to get married before then and go with me? My parents would be thrilled to have you."

The prospect set her heart to beating faster, but she shook her head. Despite her dreams of leaving, Daviana's practical nature kept her grounded. "I couldn't leave Pa here alone, not even for a couple of weeks. Besides, we both need time to consider whether this is truly what we want. Can't you just add your name to the deed? We don't have to wait for the wedding to do that, do we?"

Simon's brows created a deep V in his forehead. "You're right. We can add my name on the condition that we marry and set up Rufus's will to say the same. Still, I don't like the idea of leaving you here to fend off Jasper's advances."

Though Simon had shown her nothing but kindness, the idea of giving a man control over her brought a wave of panic. She needed to be sure he wouldn't change. She pulled her hand from his and crossed her arms. "How would he know you're gone? If he comes by again, I'll just say you're in town or in the field."

When Simon didn't answer, she peeked at his face. His eyes seemed to offer compassion.

"Dottie, I'm sorry if you felt I was pushing to a quick wedding. It's an unfortunate trait of mine to plow straight ahead." With slow movements, he lifted his hand to caress her cheek. "Perhaps you're right that we need more time to consider. My concern about Jasper was that he didn't seem to believe our betrothal was real."

Calmer now, she nodded. "What if we announce our betrothal in church and set a wedding date for the fall? With the whole community knowing, maybe that will keep Jasper away." It was all she could offer him for the moment.

"I'll go along with that. I suppose we can take care of the paperwork on Monday, then I'll head for Alabama on Tuesday. The sooner I leave, the sooner I can return."

She couldn't stop the thought that plagued her. *If he returned.* How would she live it down if he didn't? It was a chance she had to take.

CHAPTER 7

Simon took Dottie's hand again and held it until they reached the porch where Rufus reclined in his usual chair. He stood as they climbed the steps. "About time you young folks got back."

Simon grinned as he ushered Dottie inside to the kitchen table and pulled out a chair for her while Rufus claimed another. "Let me get some paper so I can show y'all my ideas."

When he returned, he spread out the paper and set the oil lamp on one corner. "This is my understanding of how the land lies." With his pencil, he drew a heavy line near the edge to represent the farm.

Rufus peered at the drawing. "It's pert near what's on the deed. You got a sharp eye."

"I took some cartography classes in school, figured it might come in handy with farming if not with practicing law." Simon paused to study the outline. "My mentor at the law office where I worked said to always have something else to fall back on, in case of hard times."

He named each section as he marked it and wrote a word or letter to identify it. "I'd enlarge the garden to accommodate a few more rows of vegetables. We might try increasing the corn for animal feed, and I think we ought to expand the apple and peach orchards year by year. The fruit from those will be our main product for sale."

"What's this box here for?" Dottie pointed to a blank square not far from the one marking the house.

"That's where I want to build *our* house. I'll start on it this winter, so maybe we can move in next spring." Her eyes widened in surprise, and he smiled. "We'll be close to your pa, and he'll have room for Lionel or Albert if they come back."

"Or if Pa decides to marry again." She flashed a teasing grin at her father.

Rufus huffed and pointed to a section where Simon had written *FB*. "This here's the farthest portion. It's laid fallow a couple of years. What're you doin' with it?"

Simon locked eyes with him. "I figured we'd designate that as a donation to the Freedmen's Bureau. That should keep them from looking too closely into which side you supported during the conflict. It's about a tenth of the property, and it's near that old cottage that can be used for housing. We'll give it to help resettle some of the freed slaves. They can work with us or someone else to get started."

Simon would not negotiate on this point. He'd watched comrades die and lose limbs for the cause. All his schooling, his military training, and the last four years of his life had brought him to this place.

He sensed Dottie holding her breath beside him while Rufus pondered the idea.

When he dipped his chin in a quick movement, she released a sigh, then broke the silence. "Well, everything looks fine to me. What do you think, Pa?"

"I'm agreeable, I reckon. Once y'all move into the other house, I hope you'll do some cooking for me from time to time."

"Of course I will," she said, but her smile trembled. Was that because she realized she'd be leaving her childhood home? Had she figured out her pa's illness might be more than he pretended?

She stood and paused beside Rufus. "I won't let you starve, Pa. I'm sure some of the local widows would be glad to bring you a few meals, too, maybe in exchange for some of our vegetables."

Simon chuckled at the panicked look on the older man's face and hastened to divert his attention. "Dottie and I discussed how we should proceed with our...relationship. While I am eager to visit my folks in Alabama, I also want to make the changes needed to secure the farm. As an attorney at law, I believe you should file a will that includes Dottie and any children she has in the future. Shall we plan a trip to town on Monday to take care of that?"

Rufus and Dottie exchanged glances. "I'm glad you know how to take care of all the legal matters. You plannin' to set up an office hereabouts?"

"I thought I'd see what might be available along those lines." Simon didn't miss the glimmer of respect that bit of news garnered. "Dottie would like to wait until I return from Alabama to plan the wedding, but I'm concerned that Mr. Dunaway might try to press his advantage while I'm gone."

When Rufus started to protest, Simon held up a hand. "I know you'll watch out for her, Rufus, but Dunaway's presence perturbed Dottie, and I don't want her to have to deal with him."

"We've decided we'll have Pastor Benson announce our betrothal at church tomorrow," Dottie said. "That way, everyone will know and perhaps it will keep Jasper from coming around."

Rufus pushed back his chair and stood. "Sounds good to me. I won't complain about keepin' my girl at home for a while longer." He swiped at the hint of moisture in his eyes. "I believe I'll check on Minnow's whereabouts afore I turn in."

Dottie watched her pa lumber away, her brow furrowed. She pushed the chair close to the table. "I have some sewing to finish, so I'll say goodnight." She turned away.

Unable to decipher her attitude, Simon grabbed his paper and caught up with her at the bedroom door. "Dottie, wait." He braced an arm against the doorjamb and kept his voice low. "Maybe I could postpone my trip and just send my folks a letter for now."

Her eyebrows lifted in surprise. "Why should you do that? No, Simon. It's been seven years since you've been home. I won't be the cause of you staying away longer."

The whine of a door opening made Simon look back in time to see Rufus shuffle to his room and close the door behind him. "I guess your pa's retired for the night. Dottie—"

She laid her hand on his arm. "Please, don't call me that."

"But you said—"

She put a finger to his lips. "It's not my name. It's what everyone calls me, but that's because Lionel had trouble with my real name when we were young. Pa always addressed me as 'daughter,' and from that, my brother started calling me Dottie." She shrugged. "I guess everyone else thought it was easier too."

"But you don't like it, I guess." Why would she tolerate a name she didn't like? "What would you like me to call you, then? Will you be all right with *darling* or *sweetheart*?"

His teasing suggestions brought the color to her cheeks.

"My proper name is Athdara Daviana." She said it with a touch of reluctance, as if she feared he might laugh or recoil. Her lashes lowered, then lifted as she gauged his reaction. This felt like a test of their fragile relationship.

"Athdara Daviana." He tasted the name as he would a new flavor.

"I'd like to go by Daviana or just Davi, if you like it better." She offered the alternative as if she feared he'd reject the longer name. The way she pronounced Davi, he could see why folks might think it was Dottie.

"Athdara." The name seemed strangely familiar. "Isn't that Scottish?"

Her smile warmed him. "Yes. My grandmother's family came from Scotland in 1810. She convinced Ma to name me after her grandmother."

"Athdara Daviana. I like it." He shifted a step closer. "Almost as much as I like you."

He held her gaze and lifted his hand to her jaw, giving her time to pull away. Her breath hitched, but she didn't back up. Simon slanted his head and touched her lips with his. Like a spark on dry leaves, warmth spread all the way to his toes.

~

She shouldn't allow him to kiss her. Pa would have a fit if he knew. Although he must have seen Simon at her door when he retired, so maybe he figured it'd be all right for them to bid each other goodnight with a kiss.

Daviana gave herself up to the experience, sliding her hand to his shoulder as he pressed closer. The paper he held slipped to the floor when he gripped her waist and deepened the kiss.

Too soon, Simon pulled away, his breathing harsh as if he'd just run up a hill. "Oh, my, D—um, Daviana. We'll either need to marry soon, or I'll have to start sleeping in the barn. Your room is entirely too close to mine."

Her face warmed. "Why Simon McNeil, I hope you're not suggestin' you'd behave in an ungentlemanly fashion before we stand in front of the preacher."

He growled and poked her side. "What I'm saying, Miss Athdara Daviana Spalding, is you're entirely too tempting, and you need a good Scottish surname to go with Athdara Daviana. The sooner, the better."

She chuckled at his rendition of the Celtic accent, then tilted her head. "Daviana McNeil. It does have a nice ring to it."

Simon blanched. "Ring? That's something I'll need to remember while I'm in Alabama. I believe Ma saved one of my grandmothers' rings to pass on.

She shook her head. "I have my grandmother's ring too."

"We're all set, then." He touched his forehead to hers. "As much as I am loathe to bid you goodnight, my dear, I suppose I must so you can get some rest. I'll go to my lonely bed and dream of you."

Ah, this man could talk birds from the trees. His way of cajoling instead of demanding dismantled her usual resistance. She eased from his embrace and took a step backward into her room. "Good night, Simon. Remember we'll ask the preacher to announce our betrothal at church. You know tomorrow is Sunday."

He winked. "And the next day is Monday. I'm looking forward to it." He tapped her nose, then sauntered across the hall. Daviana closed the door before she could give in to her temptation and call him back.

Minnow meowed at her feet. Daviana picked him up and stroked the soft fur. "Simon said he's looking forward to Monday, but first, he has to get past Sunday. I wonder if he has any idea what he'll face at church."

~

Simon forced a smile as he settled Daviana's hand on his sleeve. She wore a simple green dress with a white collar that reminded him of Ma's doilies scattered through the parlor. Her hair was pulled into a low bun, and her smile radiated joy at the prospect of attending church this warm Sunday.

Walking between him and Rufus, she spoke with fondness of the people she expected to see. Could she detect his nervousness? The sweat on his brow owed more to his anxiety than the building summer heat.

How long had it been since he'd stepped into a church? Four years or five, not counting the services he attended during the war, and those few and far between. He'd been angry with God for the condition of the world, blamed Him for letting evil run rampant and bad men succeed while good men toiled without progress. Ironically, prison became the instrument that first challenged his thinking. When he witnessed men attack others for their own failures, it made him squirm. Why did people not accept responsibility for their own actions? Facing his own guilt had been Simon's first step forward.

Not that he'd mended all his fences with the Almighty, but at least he allowed room for dialogue. And he had a feeling that would be crucial to his new life with Daviana.

He intended his marriage to be a good one, which meant he and his bride must establish harmony on important matters, such as justice. In his years away from home, observing his friends and associates had shown him what a solid marriage his parents had, though they didn't always agree. Simon could find no better man to emulate than John McNeil.

Using Pa as his standard to judge men, Simon frowned at the one standing in the church yard when he and the Spaldings arrived. Something about Jasper Dunaway rubbed him wrong. It could be simple jealousy, but experience had taught him to trust his instincts.

Dunaway turned from the man he stood near to greet them. "Mornin', Rufus, Miss Dottie." His gaze lingered on the woman too long for Simon's peace of mind.

The other man greeted them and reached a hand toward Simon to introduce himself. "Joe Thompson."

Before he could answer, Dunaway said, "Simon McNaught, wasn't it?"

"McNeil." Rufus darted a reproving glance at Dunaway. To Thompson, he said, "Simon's just come back from the war a few days ago. He and Dottie will be marryin' soon. We thought the preacher might introduce him to everyone this mornin'."

Mr. Thompson broke into a smile and pumped Simon's hand. "Congratulations. You're gettin' a fine gal in our Dottie."

"I agree." Simon grinned at the blush on her cheeks. "Couldn't ask for a better woman than Daviana."

Dunaway pinned Simon with a questioning glare. The ringing of the church bell prevented further conversation, and they all headed for the door.

Inside, eight backless benches lined each side of the center aisle. The wood's sheen and faint odor of some kind of oil attested to someone's care. Light streamed through the plain glass windows on the eastern side and illuminated the wooden cross behind the pulpit. No organ music welcomed worshippers, but a man near the pulpit sent out tentative notes as he adjusted the strings of a violin.

A stout man in a simple black suit stepped from the front row to greet them. "Rufus, good to see you and Miss Dottie."

Rufus shook his hand. "Reverend, this here's Simon McNeil. He's recently returned after several years away fightin'. Him and Dottie plan to marry in a few weeks, and we thought you might want to introduce him to the congregation, since not many know him."

The preacher's eyebrows went up, but he offered Simon a smile and a hearty handshake. "Congratulations, young man." A strident note from the violin made him glance back. "I've been warned it's time to begin."

While the preacher strode to the pulpit, Rufus led the way to the third pew on the right. He picked up one of the worn hymnals and passed it to Simon. Did he discern Simon's unease, or did he merely offer it as a courtesy?

The song leader announced the first hymn, and Simon relaxed to discover it was familiar to him. With each song and prayer, his awkwardness faded. These country folks sang with gusto and prayed with simple sincerity. Beside him, Daviana sent an occasional glance his way, her self-conscious smile warming his heart. By the end of the service, he felt sure God had led him to this small community. The notion humbled him.

The preacher's closing prayer immediately changed into an announcement. "Before everyone rushes into the yard, I've been asked to introduce Simon McNeil. He's come home and won the favor of our own Miss Dottie Spalding. Y'all stand up so everyone can see y'all. Rufus tells me they'll be marryin' soon, so I reckon he's given his blessing."

Before he finished speaking, members of the congregation converged on them. The ladies gushed over Daviana's news, and the men either shook Simon's hand or pounded him on the back. Moving into the aisle and toward the door required patience and persistence, much like treading water upstream. Simon breathed easier when they stepped into the summer sunshine, but folks lingered in small groups with no one in a hurry to leave.

He'd forgotten about the slower pace of Sunday in the South. They'd be fortunate to get to the next meal by midafternoon.

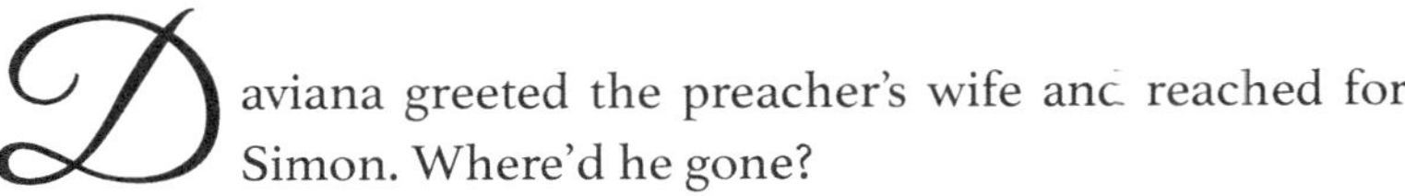

*D*aviana greeted the preacher's wife and reached for Simon. Where'd he gone?

"Daviana." His voice came from behind her. He weaved past a group of giggling girls and finally regained her side.

After so many years of answering to "Dottie," it was strange to hear someone else speak her given name. Growing up, she'd gone through spurts of hating it and creating stories about it. When Simon said it, some of her girlish fantasies came back to her—the ones in which only her handsome knight knew her secret name.

Reverend Benson raised his eyebrows, and his wife gaped. "Daviana? Not Dottie?"

"Dottie's a childish nickname I couldn't seem to outgrow." She flashed Simon a smile but spoke to the older couple. "Like Paul said in First Corinthians, I figured it was time to put away childish things."

Simon squeezed her waist. "Besides, we thought one good Scottish name deserved another. I like the sound of Athdara Daviana McNeil."

The name rolled off his tongue with an affected brogue. His accent sounded much like her grandmother's. He must have practiced it.

"Well…" The minister rocked back on his heels. "Since we've made the announcement, how soon do you young folks want to have the ceremony? We should give the women time to plan a proper celebration."

Daviana shook her head and opened her fan. "Oh, pastor, that's not necessary."

Mrs. Benson shut down her protest. "Now, you know the ladies would never forgive us if we don't give them time to plan a little party. We ain't had much to celebrate lately, and everybody would want to honor you. Besides, we want to make your young man feel welcome."

Daviana forced a smile, though Simon stiffened beside her. He must wonder whether they'd welcome him if they knew he'd fought with the Federals. Well, the truth would come out sooner or later. She prayed it would be after folks learned what a good man he was.

They promised to decide on a date for the ceremony and parted ways with the reverend. Shading her eyes against the bright sunshine, Daviana gazed around the churchyard. Folks were gradually clearing out. To her dismay, Jasper lounged against the bed of his wagon. He straightened and sauntered their way.

"I see you folks walked to church and thought I'd offer you a ride home. Even with the clouds, it's gonna be a hot one." His words sounded innocent enough, but the way his eyes swept her made her skin crawl.

Pa glanced at her and Simon, then turned to Jasper. "I'd be pleased to accept the offer, Jasper, but I think these young folks would rather walk. They can enjoy a spell without this old man hearin' their conversation."

Jasper frowned, but Pa grasped the buckboard's side and pulled himself up to the bench. "I'll meet y'all back at the house. See you don't dawdle."

"Thank you, sir." Simon nodded at the other men. "We'll be there directly." He turned Daviana toward the road and bent his head to her ear. "Your pa's a wily one, ain't he?"

~

As Dunaway's wagon rolled from the yard—its owner scowling at his lack of success for whatever he'd planned—Simon matched his steps to Daviana's shorter stride. He appreciated Rufus's clever maneuver, but it pricked his conscience to set the man at odds with townsfolks. Maybe Dunaway wasn't a close friend, but he was a neighbor, one Simon must learn to deal with.

In his attempt to help the Spaldings hold onto their land, Simon might have put them in an uncomfortable position. When the neighbors found out he'd been on the Union side— and he had no doubt they would eventually—the community might feel Rufus had betrayed them. He should have come clean with the old man last night. Daviana accepted him. Was Rufus desperate enough to see her settled that he'd overlook Simon's political history?

His betrothed nudged him. "I think we're supposed to be havin' a discussion Pa shouldn't hear."

Simon chuckled. "I'm not sure you're ready to hear all I want to say to you."

Her cheeks turned pink as he'd expected, and she set her fan in motion again.

He patted her hand. "I'll save it for later. Are you pleased with the announcement about the wedding, or will the extra attention upset you?"

"I'd just as soon avoid a big celebration, but Mrs. Benson is right. The ladies will be hurt if we don't let them get involved."

"Do you think Dunaway will try to cause trouble for us? He still seems to think he can convince you to look his way."

She shrugged. "I never know what Jasper will do. He can be hurtful or helpful, dependin' on what serves his purpose."

Something about her voice stirred Simon's curiosity. What kind of history did she have with Dunaway, beyond being his prospective sister by marriage? Did it figure into why she'd accepted Simon so easily?

He didn't have time to explore those questions now, but he'd keep them in mind. The best he could do today was to make it clear he wouldn't tolerate Dunaway's interference, no matter what tactics he used.

Simon pulled his betrothed closer as they approached the house. With her softness flush against him, he breathed in the sweet scent of roses. "Will your pa feel obligated to ask Dunaway to join us at the table?"

Daviana met his gaze. "Obligated? No. Pa does as he wishes, without thought for what might be expected."

A glance toward the farm showed Rufus and Dunaway

occupied the two chairs on the porch, and his wagon was nowhere in sight. Daviana sighed. "That doesn't mean he won't extend the invitation. If he thinks it will serve us somehow to feed Jasper, I guess we'll just have to go along and exercise our patience."

Her nearness made for a welcome distraction. Simon almost wished the man would stay to visit so he'd have an excuse to demonstrate his affection. Would that convince Dunaway to drop his campaign for Daviana's attention and property, or would it perhaps rile him all the more? Though Simon didn't like the man, he didn't consider him a real threat. Any man who sent his younger brother to war while he stayed home—and then moved in on the brother's promised bride—didn't elicit Simon's respect.

CHAPTER 8

*D*aviana's dread diminished as Simon placed a protective hand at her back. Maybe having Jasper stay for the meal would prove beneficial if it meant Simon stayed close to her. She'd have to put another pan of cornbread in the oven to add to the one already made, but she could make that work to her advantage.

She kept her voice level as they reached the steps where Pa and Jasper waited on the porch. "Simon, will you join me in the kitchen for a minute? I need to add to our meal."

His crooked grin set off the flutters in her belly. "Of course, sweetheart. How can I help you?"

Jasper sent a sour glance her way when she passed by. Like a pouting child, his mouth compressed into a frown as he glowered at them. Warnings went off in her head. *I've learned not to push him too hard,* Kyle had told her more than once. Jasper could strike out like a cornered bobcat if things didn't go his way. A fact she'd witnessed and Malachi had paid dearly for. At least her rescuer had been able to get away when the war ended.

Every thought of Kyle brought an ache. How she missed her

friend. He'd been her constant companion since she went with Mama to visit the Dunaways when his grandfather died. While their mothers had arranged dishes in the kitchen, she and Kyle had slipped out the back door to see a litter of newborn pups. In the years after, since their properties shared a boundary, it was easy to meet after they finished their daily chores. Then they'd found a common purpose in protecting others—particularly slaves—from Jasper's wrath.

Simon called her name, and she snapped back to the present. "I'm sorry, Simon. What did you say?" She backed out of the pantry with the nearly empty bag of flour.

He moved closer and twisted a stray strand of her hair around his finger. "I hope you were dreaming of our wedding." When she blushed, he chuckled. "You don't have to tell me. I asked what you wanted me to do to help."

They got to work and had the meal on the table by the time Rufus and Jasper came inside.

As usual, Simon helped Daviana into her chair, then sat next to her. Jasper grabbed the chair on her other side, which put him across from Simon.

Minnow settled on the floor between her and Simon, a good place to retrieve any crumbs that fell.

After Pa blessed the food, Daviana aimed for polite conversation while everyone filled their plates. "You went to church alone this morning, Jasper? I hope your children aren't sick."

"Aunt Lou took 'em to stay at her house for a while. Said it would give me time to find somebody to watch 'em since their nanny run off."

Ah, that explained why he'd developed a sudden interest in "renewing the proposed union" between their families. He must've figured she would fall in with his plans without any protest. Counting on her relationship with Kyle to pave the way —or a distorted account of his attempted conquest—he must not have even considered she might turn him down.

She prodded further. "When did Lily leave? I thought most folks had promised their help a wage to stay."

Jasper shot her a disgruntled look. "She said old man Simpson offered her more than I did, and that way, she could be with her man."

Daviana despaired. Should she give up trying for polite conversation? With Pa engrossed in his meal, Daviana slanted her gaze in a silent plea to Simon, who took the hint.

"I take it Lily was your housemaid?" Simon asked. "You should check with the Union men at the Freedmen's Bureau about finding a replacement. I understand they can help with those things. They're also supposed to provide some seed and food staples for anyone who needs 'em."

Jasper narrowed his eyes at Simon. "Yeah, I heard as much. The United States government ain't wastin' no time in taking charge after they tore up the country with their guns and stripped the ground clean."

Daviana cringed.

But Simon continued chewing and swallowed the bite of beans he'd taken before he answered. "Somebody's got to take charge and clean it up. It's a pity how destructive marching armies can be." He held Jasper's gaze for a few seconds, then casually returned to his meal.

Anxious to divert the conversation, Daviana rose. "Does anyone need more water, or should I put some on the stove for a cup o' chicory?"

Simon, true to form, stood and offered to help. Maybe he figured to give Jasper time to find another topic of conversation.

~

Chagrined that his comment had backfired, Simon rose when Davi did. He'd meant to offer Dunaway a solution, one that didn't involve the other man pursuing Daviana.

To say Dunaway resented anything Simon said would be an understatement. Simon had best steer clear and keep his mouth shut for the present. Pa always said not to poke a rattlesnake.

In the kitchen, he redirected his attention to more pleasant thoughts. In a few days, he'd be on his way to Alabama again. He'd have a good visit with his family, then return to settle into his new life, hopefully dividing his time between a decent legal practice and making this farm work.

Daviana turned and pressed a pitcher of water into his hands. "Take this, and I'll heat up more for the chicory."

"Sorry I got Jasper all stirred up in there." He kept his voice low. "I'll watch my words from now on."

Her bosom rose and fell with a blustery huff, but she spoke softly. "I'm afraid Jasper's in a mood to be riled, no matter what you say. Maybe he won't stay much longer. Go on, now. I'll be back when the water's hot."

Simon kept his promise for the rest of the meal, answering questions with brief and polite blandness. Daviana served the bitter substitute for coffee. She must have used the last bit of real coffee last week. Odd that they'd even had coffee beans in their pantry, when other places on his trek home had none to offer. In fact, the Spaldings seemed to have fared better than some whose homes were less conspicuous to passersby. How had they retained their commodities?

The story of the soldiers' missing weapons came to mind. Did Rufus wrangle something from everyone who stopped at his house? Come to think of it, Simon had caught the old man trying to pry into his knapsack while he was lying ill. Rufus was a sneaky one, all right, but he'd be hard pressed to deal with an entire company of men, so how did they still have a few items most folks ran out of long before? Maybe they'd bartered away other things. Davi did serve some interesting meals, and the bread lately lacked its usual flavor.

Rufus and Dunaway scuffed back their chairs and mumbled they'd continue to visit on the porch.

Simon settled his hand on Daviana's. "I'll help you clear the table."

"No, you can go on out with Pa and Jasper. I'll have this finished before Minnow can lick his whiskers." With Dunaway out of earshot, she said, "Jasper may try to get more information out of you."

"I think I can handle Dunaway, darlin'. Just don't take too long in here." He kissed her forehead and sauntered out to the porch, set on asking Daviana a few questions himself after Dunaway left.

The porch was empty. When he continued down the stairs and around the house, he found Rufus and Dunaway gazing at the top of a birch tree.

He wandered closer. "What's so interesting in that tree?"

Rufus pointed to an object on a far branch. "Got a decent beehive back there. I wonder if we ought to consider addin' honey to our future crops?"

Shading his eyes and following the line of Rufus's finger, Simon spotted the busy hive. "My Aunt June used to raise bees, but she died a couple of years ago. Maybe someone back home can tell me how to retrieve the honey."

Rufus pulled a handkerchief from his back pocket and wiped his sweaty brow. "Jasper was askin' how our side of the creek looked, so we started that way." He took a few steps toward the far property line and tottered.

Simon caught him by the arm. "You might want to get out of the hot sun, Rufus. Go on back to the house, and I'll show Jasper around."

"Sure enough, Rufus," Jasper said. "Get into the shade. We won't be out here long."

The older man shambled toward the back stoop. Simon

waited to be sure Rufus wouldn't pass out, then turned to Jasper. "To the creek? Is that what you want to see?"

With a shrug, Jasper started toward the back acres, setting a pace Simon easily matched. "Since we're alone, I ought to tell you a few things about the Spalding family most folks don't know."

"Really? I'm surprised you're so concerned about my well-being." Simon wanted to roll his eyes. How did Dunaway figure he could sway Simon with what would undoubtedly be lies? He must've spent the previous day cooking up tales to scare the Alabama boy away from what he considered his territory.

With a firm grip, Dunaway tugged Simon's arm. "Surely, you've seen how Rufus can manipulate folks to get what he wants. Well, let me tell you, so can Dottie. She ain't as innocent as she seems. It's her fault my brother ran away to the army."

"Is that so?" Simon asked, feigning interest. How far would this man go to convince Simon to tuck tail and run? Though Dunaway didn't inspire Simon's trust, this discussion might provide some insight into his future family.

~

Cradling the dishpan on one hip, Daviana opened the back door and drew up short at the sight of her father sitting on the top step. Dishwater sloshed over her hands. "Pa, what are you doin' here? I thought y'all was on the front porch."

Pa wiped a trickle of spilled water from his ear. "Simon insisted I get outta the sun, and this was the closest spot. Throw that water on the rosebushes before you douse me anymore."

She stepped past him and used the cup she'd brought to portion the water across her plants. A cardinal flew to a higher branch in the dogwood tree while Minnow batted at the shedding rhododendron blooms. With her task finished, Daviana set the pan in the grass and plopped on the stoop beside Pa. "Where did Simon and Jasper get off to?"

He motioned toward the back of the property. "Jasper wanted to check out the creek on our side of the boundary. Said he's worried it might dry up again if we don't soon get some rain."

"Hmpf. You think that's really what he wanted?"

"I reckon he's lookin' for a chance to bend Simon's ear 'bout something."

She looked in the direction he'd indicated. "Yeah. He'd love to spew some tales that might cause Simon to leave." A passing cloud blocked the sunlight overhead as dread spread its gloom in her mind.

Pa glanced her way. "Quit worryin' that bottom lip with your teeth. Your ma would smack it, you know."

Daviana smiled at the memory and leaned against him. "You'd think I'd outgrown such things." Memories of Mama blurred in the face of current circumstances. "Seems like we always go from one trouble to another, don't we? You reckon Simon will heed Jasper's lies?" Much of it would only be a twisting or stretching of the truth. He was clever that way.

Pa grunted. "I think not. He's a sharp one, Simon is. Looks beyond the surface and makes up his own mind, I'd say. Besides, I wager he's got a secret or two of his own he ain't shared."

She plucked at the dark spots on her skirt, testing whether they might be stains or merely drops of water. It was too bad she'd cut up her last apron to patch Pa's shirt. She turned Pa's statement over in her mind, debating how much to share.

"As to that," she said, "he did tell me a little something last night. I think he plans to tell you before he leaves for Alabama."

"Is 'at so?" He stuck two fingers into his shirt pocket and pulled out a plug of tobacco. "Was it something that troubles you?"

Daviana shook her head but continued to face forward. Minnow padded close and lay beside her. "Not really. You might be surprised but not alarmed."

In the distance, two figures emerged from the stand of pines along the western boundary. They neither hurried nor seemed reluctant to end their meeting. As they drew closer, the difference in their movement distinguished the men. Jasper's slouch and grasp of his suspenders made his elbows stick out, while Simon walked with an easy stride that reminded her of the confident strut of a bobcat.

"He really is a fine figure of a man."

Pa's head jerked her way, and she covered her mouth. Had she said that aloud? His grunt turned into a chuckle, drawing out Daviana's smile.

"At least he won't be hard to look at every day over the dinner table," she said.

CHAPTER 9

Catching sight of Daviana sitting with her pa on the back porch, Simon's anger dissipated. He kept his gaze on her and ignored the sulking man who walked beside him.

Did Dunaway's irritation stem from the fact that he hadn't roused Simon's ire to the explosive level? Lord knew, the man had tried hard enough, spouting one tale after another designed to shock Simon or at least turn his interest away from Daviana and the Spalding farm.

Was Dunaway so desperate to latch onto the Spalding homestead? Or was Daviana the real draw? It never seemed to occur to the louse that the more he pushed to drive Simon away, the more determined Simon was to stay.

Rufus and Daviana stood as he and Jasper drew near. She picked up a dishpan. "Why don't we all go around to the front porch?"

With a quick movement, Simon took the pan from her and clasped her hand. "Sounds good to me. Looks like rain's coming from the west. Maybe it'll cool things down."

Rufus fell in behind them, but Jasper balked as they reached the front yard. "I better head on home, in case that builds into a storm." He veered off toward the barn to collect his horse and wagon.

Like a good host, Rufus shuffled that way as well, but Simon waved him off. Holding back a sigh, he shoved the pan onto the porch and trotted after the unwelcome visitor.

In uncomfortable silence, Simon helped Jasper hook up the horse to the buckboard, then stepped back. Jasper climbed aboard and frowned from his perch. "You think on what I said, McNeil. You're in for a world of hurt if'n you stay here."

With those parting words, he clicked the horse into motion, rode into the yard, and headed down the hill.

Was that a threat? Was he planning some retaliation? Simon didn't fear for himself, but he worried over Daviana and Rufus.

He crossed to the house and joined them on the porch. Funny how a body could grow so close to folks in such a short time. He settled on the planks between their chairs and reached for Daviana's hand, threading her fingers with his.

Rufus shifted his weight to face Simon. "Did Jasper satisfy himself about the condition of the creek?"

Simon barked a harsh laugh. "Ha! All the way there and back, he ran his mouth about how I ought to get on my horse and leave. He doesn't seem to think too highly of you folks." He canted his head toward Rufus. "He claims you ran Lionel off when he came home, and Davi was the cause of Kyle joining the army."

Rufus didn't seem surprised. "Figured as much. Jasper tends to interpret things in a way that favors him. He accused my grandson of destroying an old shed on his property the week Lionel returned home. Lionel didn't take it well, and we all got into a shoutin' match. The war was hard on my son. He decided he'd do better away from here."

"I can understand that." Simon gazed into the distance. "He

gave up years of his life for a cause he believed in, and the outcome didn't meet his expectations."

Confession time. "I felt much the same way. And I was on the side that prevailed."

Distant thunder rumbled.

Simon gave Rufus a moment to process his statement. Daviana's fingers tightened on his.

The old man shifted to face him. "I sorta figured that when you stood up to those Union men last week. I reckon you had your own reasons, as every man did, whatever choice you made."

Simon snorted. "I can't claim my reasons were so noble. I was against slavery, but I also wanted to prove that I was right and others were wrong. Life has a way of teaching a man what's what. I learned you can't force men to change their thinking. Only God can do that."

"You're right, son. I got caught up in wrong thinking myself, not on account of slavery or states' rights or such." Rufus spat into the yard. "My problem centered on provin' I could handle everything by using my brain to outsmart everyone who came by."

"Like that story you told me about hiding the soldiers' rifles?" Simon grinned at Daviana. "Sorry I appropriated it for myself, but it proved right timely to get rid of Dunaway."

Daviana twisted her lips. "For the time being, anyway."

Minnow returned from his wandering and stretched out beside Simon. He stroked the cat's fur absently as he addressed Rufus. "I assume you also used your gift of bargaining to secure coffee beans and other items?"

Rufus scratched his scraggly beard. "Yeah, and we got some good places to hide valuable items in them caves back o' the property. I'll have to show you sometime."

When Simon's hand jerked and fisted in Minnow's fur, the cat batted at him. "I don't expect to have to hide anything away.

Besides..." He directed a smile at Daviana. "I have all the treasure I need right here." *And I'll protect her with my life if necessary.*

~

The sun neared its apex, blasting its rays from a hazy sky that held no sign of yesterday's rain clouds. The morning's dew had dissipated in the rising heat while Simon and Rufus waded through the legal process of securing the farm. Though she was not a participant, Daviana had accompanied them and occasionally asked Simon for clarification. He admired her quick grasp of matters that some men had trouble with.

"If you don't mind waiting here a few minutes"—Simon gestured to a bench in the high-ceilinged lobby of the Hall County courthouse—"I want to ask about renting some office space."

They agreed, and Simon climbed the stairs to the second floor. The smell of lemon wax permeated the stairwell, and the railing gleamed as testimony to a recent cleaning. He pulled open the door at the landing and peered in each direction. His footsteps echoed in the hallway as he approached the secretary stationed in the antechamber. The young man didn't pause his writing but spared Simon a brief glance.

"Excuse me." Simon stepped closer. "The clerk downstairs said you might have a room to rent?"

The pen kept moving. "It won't be ready until next month."

"That's fine. May I look at it?"

One arm pointed down the hall. "Second door on the left."

Simon reined in his irritation. This was no time to start an argument. He strode to the indicated room, opened the door and peered inside. It needed a good cleaning, but it would serve.

Back at the secretary's desk, he asked about the payment, which proved satisfactory. "I'll pay half that amount now as down payment for you to hold it for me," Simon said.

When he offered the money, the secretary dropped his pen and stared at the Union currency. Confederate and state-issued money had been demonetized, but greenbacks must be rare here. The clerk's eyes went from the offered payment to Simon and back again. He reached for the bill, but Simon pulled it back. "I will need a receipt."

With everything settled, Simon returned to the lobby and held the main door open for Rufus and Daviana to exit the courthouse. "Well, that went rather well."

Rufus grunted. "Bunch of legal round-about talk if you ask me. I'm glad you knowed what they was talkin' about." He wiped his brow with a checkered handkerchief, then returned it to his back pocket. "So we got to come back tomorrow and sign the papers, then it'll all be done?"

"We'll wait until later in the day, to be sure we allow enough time for the clerks to write out all the copies." Simon guided Daviana around a puddle in the road then toward the mercantile where they'd parked the borrowed wagon. It was an excuse to touch her, of course. Soon he wouldn't need an excuse—in public or private.

Gainesville had escaped the worst of the war, thanks to General Sherman veering south to capture Savannah after he left Atlanta in ruins. The courthouse stood at one side of the square, with shops, a hotel, and a church marking the other sides around the green common area. If soldiers had come through the town, at least they'd left the buildings intact.

Daviana peered around her bonnet. "Why did you ask for extra copies? Wouldn't the one at the bank be enough?"

"That was what my former boss thought until a strong storm caused a fire that destroyed half the town where he lived. His onetime partner took advantage of the missing documents to claim Mr. Townsend owed him for half the business he'd built."

"How terrible." She wagged her head. "But why do we need three copies?"

Her questions were his reward for choosing a smart woman. Like Ma, she didn't hesitate to ask questions. Maybe most women were like that, despite how some of his fellow soldiers had disparaged them.

He stroked her hand on his sleeve, glad she didn't feel the need for gloves. "I'll take one when I go to Alabama. I'll have my father keep it in case anything happens to the copies here. I want to stash one at the house, so we'll have it handy in case your brother comes back. Or your nephew might return when he's older and demand his share of the property."

"I gotta give it to you, Simon," Rufus said, "you sure think ahead on matters. Sets my mind at ease that you'll make a good provider for Dottie and any little'uns that come along."

Simon grinned and cut his eyes toward Daviana in time to see the rosy color splash across her cheeks.

"I appreciate your confidence, Rufus. I plan to do my best." He pushed aside the niggling doubts of his ability to provide those children because of his recurring malaria.

Raised voices across the street drew their attention.

Two men and a woman stood outside the Freedmen's Bureau office where the United States flag fluttered over the door. Otherwise undistinguishable from the other businesses that lined up beside it, the office occupied the end of the block across from the courthouse. The alley beside the bureau headquarters provided convenient access to the rear of the building for deliveries. Simon pulled Daviana behind him to shield her in case trouble erupted from that quarter.

Rufus hemmed her in from the other side. "What's goin' on there?"

Simon couldn't make out the words. Of the three people,

the larger man, whose voice rose and fell along with his gestures, seemed overbearing. The other two stood as if frozen. A Union soldier emerged from the building, and Simon breathed easier. Perhaps the officer would settle the matter.

"Seems to be a disagreement of some kind. I think the Federal man will handle it."

"Oh." Daviana clutched Simon's arm. "That reminds me. We need to go by there and see what kind of foodstuff they have."

"No," Rufus wagged his head and tugged Davi the other way. "We don't need their charity, Daughter."

Daviana twisted her mouth and lowered her brows. She propped her fists on her hips. "Have you seen the state of our pantry, Pa? We're scrapin' the bottom of the barrel on pert near everything."

The old man's eyes flicked from her to Simon and back. If he thought Simon would side with him against Davi, he could relinquish that thought.

"We got vegetables in the garden we can pick," Rufus said.

Her head bobbed in agreement. "As long as the rain and sunshine cooperate and the critters don't get into it, but we've got no wheat for flour or corn to mill for bread." Her voice grew more intense as her pa's expression darkened.

Simon stepped into the dispute before they outdid the folks across the street. "Rufus, did you forget? I have Union currency, and I owe you for my room and board until Davi and I are wed. Why don't you go have a seat on the bench at the mercantile while Davi and I go see what we can buy?"

The older man huffed but gave in. "I guess I can do that. Glad we borrowed the preacher's wagon so we don't have to walk back in this heat. Especially if we got to tote groceries."

Daviana's eyes narrowed with concern as Rufus tottered away. "He doesn't look so good, does he? Maybe I shouldn't have pushed the matter, but we need provisions."

Skirting the subject of her pa's health, Simon turned her toward the bureau office. "It's hard for a man to let others help him at times. But you know best about what's needed in the kitchen—and the rest of the house, for that matter.'

They passed the disgruntled man who'd been arguing earlier. Simon offered a polite nod, but the stranger didn't acknowledge them. Maybe he'd find a place out of the heat to calm down.

Daviana squeezed Simon's arm where her hand rested. "Thank you for offering to pay, but I thought we might work out a trade with the Union men—our vegetables for some of their wheat and corn."

"I'll ask about hiring some workers too. I'll feel better knowing you and Rufus have help on the farm while I'm gone."

"But how will we pay them, Simon? We can offer food and housing, but they'll expect more than that after a while."

He patted her hand. "You let me worry about that." If all went well at home, he'd have enough to see them through the next few months.

~

The door to the office stood open, serving as a welcome as well as letting in fresh air. Like many of the buildings in town, it was twice as deep as it was wide, with another door a dozen yards beyond the desk and waist-high counter. A long bench sat opposite the counter, and Daviana tensed to see the couple who had been involved in the recent argument seated beside an older man.

Simon removed his hat and whispered, "This is the corporal who came by the house."

The lanky soldier nodded at their approach. "Good afternoon. I'm Corporal Ewing. How can I help you folks?"

Simon accepted his outstretched hand. "Simon McNeil, and

this is Miss Spalding, my bride-to-be. I met you last week out at the Spalding place. I wanted to let you know we've arranged to get my name on all the farm documents, which should secure it without problem."

"Ah, now I remember. You're the lieutenant who was at Libby, right?"

"That's right. Miss Spalding and I will be marrying—"

"I knew it!" Another voice overrode Simon's, and Daviana clutched his arm. Cringing, she dared to look over her shoulder as Jasper staggered toward them.

He pointed a finger at Simon. "This man was a Yankee spy."

Gasps issued from the people on the bench. Their wide eyes swung from Jasper to Simon.

Corporal Ewing stepped beside Simon and faced Jasper. "Sir, I must ask you to leave since you appear to be intoxicated. There are ladies present."

Jasper's arms flailed. "It's the ladies I'm tryin' to protect from scum like him who'd sell out his own countrymen."

Simon's face darkened. "Dunaway, you're making a scene with your wild accusations. I never spied for anyone, and I served my country during the war, unlike you."

Jasper swung a fist toward Simon, but he blocked it and twisted Jasper's arm behind him.

Murmurs near the door indicated they had an audience. Had Jasper brought his buddies to witness this?

With help from the corporal, Simon pushed Jasper, still spouting accusations, toward the exit. When they reached the small crowd of men, Corporal Ewing eyed Simon. "I suggest you wait inside until I send these men on their way."

Daviana welcomed Simon's embrace when he came back to her. From a door at the rear of the building, another soldier carried two baskets of dry staples. The private gave them to the folks who'd been waiting on the bench, and they left with wary glances toward Simon.

The private addressed Simon. "Can I help you folks with anything?"

"As a matter of fact, Miss Spalding wanted to see if we might barter some of our garden produce for a measure of grain you have on hand."

The man's gaze shifted to Daviana. "I'd be happy to do so. We've proposed that to a number of folks, but few seem ready to deal with us."

~

Simon had feared as much. Other men would express the same opinion as Rufus had. If he and Daviana led the way and let others know what was available to them, perhaps more women would convince their menfolk to do likewise.

Corporal Ewing returned, and the private offered to let them survey the food distribution area.

"You go ahead," Simon told Daviana. "I want to see about hiring some workers."

The corporal pointed to the counter where a book lay beside some loose papers. "We have a list of folks we've interviewed, along with their particular skills. If you see any you want to try, we'll contact them and send them to you. You're the first to ask about hiring, so you can take your pick."

He shifted through the papers at the counter, which were blank contracts. Curious as to what he'd done about Dunaway, Simon said, "I hope you sent my troublesome neighbor home."

The officer snorted. "Him and a couple of others who started drinking too early in the day. You'd think they'd save their carousing for evening." He handed Simon a book with names of potential workers.

Simon reviewed the list of and selected two brothers, Jude and Titus Granger, whose skills included construction.

Corporal Ewing pointed to one of the contracts. "Once you and the workers come to an agreement, we'll fill out copies for each party to keep and file one here, in case there's ever a dispute."

Simon looked it over. "Is this all the legal documentation you require?"

"Yes, sir. If we need anything else, we're to seek legal advice from the man in Dahlonega or the colonel in charge of the North Georgia area down in Athens."

Undecided whether to mention his training just yet, Simon merely nodded, but the corporal narrowed his eyes. "You know someone closer by who might be of assistance?"

Simon smiled, hiding his surprise at the other man's perception. "Perhaps. I've arranged to rent an office in the courthouse starting next month, after I return from a short trip. You'll know where to find me if needed."

"Yessir. I daresay we might be seeing each other from time to time in the future."

While establishing connections with the Federal men might not sit well with some of the locals, Simon breathed easier afterward. He relied on them to help keep the peace. Perhaps he'd mention that to Daviana, in case she needed them while he was gone.

Besides, it made good sense to seek out folks with mutual goals. How did the Bible put it? *Two are better than one, because they have a good return for their labor.*

In his present circumstances, he'd take all the help he could get.

CHAPTER 10

The rain that Pa had predicted Sunday finally arrived early Tuesday morning. It pounded the earth with ferocious downpours, accompanied by lightning flashes that sent Minnow scurrying under Daviana's bed. During a short interval when it let up, Daviana grabbed a rubber raincoat to make a trip to the garden.

Simon caught her at the door. "Tell me what you want brought in, and I'll get it. I need to check on the mare in the barn, anyway." He transferred the slicker from her hands to his.

"Some onion and a carrot, at least. And anything that looks like it's taken a beating."

He darted a glance toward Pa's door, then held the raincoat over their heads and leaned in for a quick kiss. He chuckled when she gasped and bit her lip at his cunning.

"Get used to it, Davi. I plan to collect a kiss whenever the opportunity appears." Then he stepped into the storm.

By late afternoon, the rain had slacked off, and the sun threatened to return even hotter than before. The phenomenon of rain and sun together amazed her, but Pa considered it a bad omen. He complained of a headache, and Daviana convinced him to lie down until suppertime.

Simon tugged her onto the porch. He moved chairs close together and motioned to one. "Sit with me, and we'll watch the rain together."

Daviana laughed. "We might get soaked, even on the porch." The drops angled onto the wood and bounced. "It is a sweet sight to behold, ain't it?"

Simon reached across the space between the chairs. "Tell me about this woman I plan to marry. What does she enjoy doing, besides watching the rain? What does she hate? What are her dreams?"

"That's a tall order, sir." Her face warmed as she shook her head. "I can't imagine you'd find them anything but silly. Are you sure you want to know all those things?"

"Absolutely. I need to know how to make you happy." He raised her hand and kissed her knuckles. "Once we're wed, that will be my primary concern."

Daviana shook her head. "I thought it was the other way around. I'm supposed to apply myself to making you happy."

He pressed her fingertips. "You already do that. I find I know so little about you, and I want to know everything."

"I hardly know what to say."

"Start with the easy stuff. Your age, your birthday, favorite color or flower, your favorite person named Simon..." He wiggled his eyebrows.

She laughed. "I bet you were a handful growing up."

"You have no idea." He flashed the grin that made his dimples wink and her heart melt.

This was new territory for Daviana. She'd never had anyone express interest in getting to know her on such a personal level. Simon's sincere admiration made her feel treasured and hopeful for the future.

⁓

Granny McNeil's voice echoed in Simon's head. "It's because he's the second child," she'd told Pa when he apologized for Simon's rambunctious nature. "He'll demand your attention so you don't overlook him."

It had taken him years to tame his impulsive streak. It still popped up at times, as evidenced by his unprompted response to the threat on the Spaldings' property. The opportunity to help them also carried the possibility of gaining something for himself, made more enticing by his attraction to Daviana. Without her, he might never have made the offer.

"If you won't tell me," Simon said. "I'll have to make up the answers. Let's see. You're eighteen." Always err on the side of caution, Pa would say.

Daviana shook her head. "Twenty, just turned back in—"

"Nah-huh. This is my story. Your birthday is April ninth."

Her jaw dropped. "How did you know?"

He chuckled but otherwise ignored her question, not yet ready to reveal his own secrets. "Your favorite color is blue."

"Close. It's lavender, like the flower, but my favorite flower is—"

"The rose."

"Daisy."

He shrugged. "Well, at least I got one right, and now I know the real answers."

"Ah, but do you remember them?" The sassy smile she presented cranked up his heartbeat. She had no idea how much she intrigued him.

Thankful for his excellent memory, he rattled off the answers. "Daisy, lavender, twenty, April ninth."

"How did you guess my birthday?"

He leaned forward as if to whisper a secret. "I looked in your family Bible, but I couldn't tell if the year was forty-three or forty-five." Grinning, he sat back. "As for your dreams, you were simply waiting for me to come along and marry you."

Pink dusted her cheeks. "Close enough."

So engrossed in their conversation was he, Simon hadn't noticed the rain had stopped. Nor had he noticed a wagon rattling close. A call rang out. "Hello, the house!"

Daviana pulled her hand from Simon's grasp, and both stood to watch a young man clamber over the side. He hefted a sack from the wagon bed and took slow steps toward the house as the wagon drove off. Straggly hair cleared the top of his ears, and his chin sprouted a reddish beard. A loose-fitting shirt hung above trousers held up with a rope. Hopping over and around puddles, he focused on his booted feet until he halted at the base of the steps.

When he lifted his head, Daviana's hands flew to her face. "Kyle?"

She sagged, and Simon moved fast to brace her. Closer inspection revealed the same wide-set eyes and square jaw as Jasper Dunaway possessed. Alarm blazed through Simon's body.

Daviana stammered. "But we thought...Jasper said you were..."

The stranger grimaced. "I know. There was a mix-up. I still can't cotton there was another Kyle Dunaway in the Army of Virginia, same division as me. I met his family—but time to talk about that later. I wrote Jasper last month to let him know I'd finally recovered and was ready to come home. Didn't he tell you?"

When Daviana only stared in shock, Simon took charge. As much as it pained him to welcome a rival for Daviana's affection, he reached out a hand in greeting. "Welcome home, Dunaway. I'm Simon McNeil, Davi's fiancé." Best to lay out the matter right off.

The man's eyes widened. His gaze darted from one face to the other. "Fiancé?"

"Yep." Simon dropped his outstretched hand, which the other man had ignored.

"Dottie?" Kyle looked as if he'd barely registered Simon's words. Instead, he searched Davi's face. "Is this true?"

She nodded, then managed a shaky, "yes."

Simon tried to ease the awkwardness. "Pardon our manners. You must be worn out from traveling. Come onto the porch and have a seat. I suppose Davi must be overcome with surprise to see you."

"Yes, Kyle, stay a while and visit." Her voice wavered, but she motioned to the chairs.

Kyle blinked as if waking from sleep. "Nah, I need to get on home. Just wanted to stop by and say hello since the road runs right past your house." He edged away from the porch. "Maybe I'll come over tomorrow for a spell." He nodded toward Simon. "Glad to meet ya, mister, uh…"

"McNeil," Simon said. "Same here, Dunaway. I reckon we'll get to know each other soon, as we'll be neighbors." As long as the man didn't try to reclaim Daviana.

"Yeah, guess so." He headed toward the side of the house, then looked back. "All right if I cut through the woods there?"

"Of course," they answered in unison.

Kyle slung his knapsack over his shoulder and trudged toward the shortcut. They watched his progress until he disappeared into the trees. Simon's concerns over one Dunaway had multiplied. Which would prove the greater threat to his and Davi's future?

*D*aviana turned her face into Simon's chest and heaved a deep sigh. Like a violently plucked string, the shock of seeing Kyle alive still reverberated through her being. How wonderful to see him again, but his reappearance was bound to create ripples of unease for everyone.

Simon's hand stroked her hair, dislodging a few strands. "Are you all right?"

His chest rumbled beneath her ear when he spoke. Such a comforting sensation. Like his slightly musky odor and his arms around her. Here was a shelter where she could hide until she felt ready to move on.

The worn fabric of his shirt caressed her cheek when she tilted her face up to look at him. "I'm so glad you're here."

Simon's brow cleared, and his eyes lightened to a clear blue. He tucked his chin and kissed her brow. His husky voice deepened, and his chest rumbled again. "So am I."

A clatter near the door preceded Pa's throat-clearing warning. "I thought you young folks had more sense than to spark on the porch in the daytime."

Reminded of her lapse of decorum, Daviana pulled away, but Simon kept his hold on her. While embarrassment warmed her face, he chuckled. "We're trying to recover from the shock of a dead man come back to life."

"What? I didn't sleep *that* long." Pa rubbed his face as if to verify his beard hadn't grown.

"You might want to sit down," Simon said.

When Pa sat, Daviana dropped to her knees beside his chair. "Kyle's alive, Pa. He came by here on his way home."

Pa's face paled, and he gripped the sides of the chair. "How can that be? His name was listed in the paper, killed in the battle at Cedar Creek last year." His expression changed from confusion to alarm. "Does Jasper know?"

"Kyle said he wrote to him, but I wonder if Jasper got the letter. The mail still ain't reliable. I guess he must've been sick for a while. He did look a mite puny. Thinner." She struggled to figure out what else had changed. "His hair was much different, not thick and curly anymore. Like maybe he'd shaved it and then let it grow back." She sought Simon's gaze. "Would the army do that?"

"I never heard of it, except maybe for an infestation of lice. Could be he had a head injury or sickness that caused it to come out. He did say he'd recovered from something."

She grabbed the chair arm to brace herself, and Simon assisted her to her feet. "I guess he'll tell us one day, when he's ready. Right now, I ought to put together some dinner."

"Need any help?" Simon asked. He followed her to the door, his eyes more gray than blue under his furrowed brow. Did he worry that she'd renege on her promise to him?

She dredged up a smile.

"No, you stay here and visit with Pa. I've got vegetables simmering on the stove. I'll stir up some bread to go with them." She preferred to be alone while she sorted through her jumbled feelings.

In the kitchen, she stoked up the stove, mindful of keeping her clothing clear, then brought the flour and lard from the pantry. Thankful for the powdered milk from the Freedmen's Bureau, she mixed a small amount with water.

The change in Kyle's appearance stayed on her mind while she worked the biscuit dough. A couple of years away and the experience of war would account for much of that. It wasn't only his looks, though. Something about his manner. Was it the way he moved or the tone of his voice?

Although he'd been surprised to learn she and Simon planned to marry, he seemed more puzzled than upset about it. What did that mean, and why did it bother her? It wasn't as if her and Kyle's match could be called the great romance of the county. He was the only male, outside her family members, that she'd felt safe with. They'd been friends so long, everyone expected them to marry when they came of age.

The onset of the war had intervened, and Pa refused to countenance the notion of a hasty marriage. At first, she'd been hurt by his firm stand, but as the war raged on, the wisdom of his edict became apparent. Some of her friends who'd rushed into marriage now wore widow's weeds. With Lionel leaving her in charge of his son, and having to help Pa with the farm, she'd had enough responsibility to handle.

She placed balls of dough on the pan and pressed them with her fingers. After checking the temperature of the oven with her hand, she slid the pan inside, then returned the dry ingredients to the pantry and put the used dishes in the sink.

Now, Kyle had returned from the grave, as it were. He'd said he wrote to Jasper. Had Jasper received such a letter and not mentioned it to her? And here she was betrothed to Simon, who'd ridden into her life only a week ago. Life surely could get complicated.

The sound of boots on the floorboards brought her head around. Simon stopped short of approaching her. His smile wavered, and his eyes seemed full of questions. Hands tucked in his back pockets, he lingered near the kitchen door.

His unusual hesitance stirred her compassion. He must feel as uncertain as she did.

"Supper will be ready soon."

"Good. Since the rain has stopped, I thought I'd ride into town and see about the workers we hired. Your pa also asked me to get our copies of the documents we filed yesterday."

She turned from the stove and studied his face. "All right. You'll eat first, won't you?"

"Of course. We've still a few hours of daylight left."

The scene from yesterday's visit came to mind. "And you'll be careful? Although I expect Kyle's appearance will keep Jasper at home, so he shouldn't be a problem."

He reached out to trace her jawline. "I appreciate your concern, but I'm not worried about Dunaway." Though he said it almost flippantly, his voice wavered.

He blinked and withdrew his hand. "I'll be back before you turn in for the night."

That meant no evening walk to discuss this new complication in their relationship. Daviana hid her disappointment. Perhaps Simon meant to give her time to adjust, which she appreciated, but she didn't like the awkwardness between them.

~

Simon's guilt smote him. He'd lied to Daviana. He was worried about one Dunaway, but it wasn't Jasper. From their previous conversations, she'd considered Kyle more of a close friend than a romantic partner. Many people created decent marriages from friendships, of course, and that may have been all she expected. Did her feelings for Kyle run deep enough to rescind her commitment to Simon?

Her manner had been subdued since Kyle's return. Which was to be expected. He'd feel the same way in her situation. But doggone it, why did the man have to show up now?

All the way to town, Simon mulled over the turn of events. He'd been so sure he was finally on the path God had planned for him. Despite his neglect in the past, even his careless disregard for his soul, the sense of divine watchfulness had been constant. Now that he'd begun to try to "walk worthy," as Pa would say, complications cropped up.

When he reached town, the streets were quiet. Most folks

had likely wound up their business and headed home. Simon retrieved the documents from the courthouse clerk in a matter of minutes, then crossed the street to the bureau office.

Corporal Ewing paused in the act of closing the door when he saw Simon coming his way. "Good evening. Mr. McNeil, isn't it?"

Simon removed his hat as he followed the man inside. "Sorry to come in so late, Corporal. Just wanted to check on whether you contacted those workers."

The soldier pursed his lips. "I'm afraid the storm kept most folks away. I'm heading over toward Dahlonega to investigate a complaint, so I'll pass the word to the Granger family about your interest. You can probably expect them to show up in a day or two."

"I'll be on the lookout for them." Simon replaced his hat. "I won't hold you up any longer. Once we work out our agreement, we'll bring you the paperwork for your records."

"Much obliged." The corporal shut the door behind them and turned his face toward the sky. "At least it's cleared up enough to give us a little moonlight for our ride. See you in a few days."

Glad to have his tasks completed, Simon mounted the mare and turned her toward the farm. The thick envelope in his breast pocket crinkled with promise. Having his name on the papers tucked inside it created a swell of pride and gratitude. Simon cast aside the doubts that had plagued him on the ride into town and rehearsed the blessings on his life.

With the rising moon to guide him, he set the dun to an easy canter. No sense risking a tumble by going faster. He needed the horse healthy for the journey to Alabama.

As he crested the last hill before the farm came into view, a shrill whistle jerked his attention to the right. Something slammed against his left side and knocked him from the horse.

No sooner had he gained his feet than a body barreled into him.

A voice he didn't recognize punctuated punches with curses and vile names. "We don't cotton to strangers...comin' in here... hookin' up with Federal men...hirin' Butler slaves ...throwin' your money around."

Fists pummeled Simon's head and shoulders. The taste of blood galvanized him.

With a roar of anger, Simon launched himself at one attacker. He spun around and slashed the other assailant's neck with the outside of his flat hand. The first man tackled Simon from the back and wrenched his arms backward. A fist plowed into his belly. Seconds later, pain exploded in his head, and darkness descended.

~

*D*aviana set a lamp in the front window as a beacon for Simon. She'd expected him to have returned by this time. Worry niggled.

Pa had gone to bed, and Daviana settled in the chair next to the lamp. She picked up the Bible. "Lord, please protect Simon and help him get the workers we need. Keep him from harm and bring him safely home. Thank You."

Leaning her head against the chairback, she closed her eyes. Moments—or hours—later, a thud startled her. She sat up straight. The Bible had slipped from her lap, and the lamplight danced erratically. What time was it? Where was Simon?

She rose to peer out the window, but shuffling near the back door propelled her that way. When the door swung open before she reached it, she gasped, and her heart dropped.

Kyle stood there with a disheveled Simon, his head hanging down and his arm draped across Kyle's shoulders. "Had some trouble gettin' him on and off the horse. If you can help me get him to a chair, I'll go put up his horse."

Simon's one eye was swollen beneath his brow crusted with dried blood. A rip in his shirt nearly separated the sleeve from the rest of the garment, and dried mud spattered his trousers. Daviana shook off her alarm and moved to support him on the other side. She detected no hint of spirits, only the manly odor of sweat from heat and exertion. When she pressed against him, he gave a low moan. Together, the three of them hobbled to a chair at the table. Simon dropped onto the seat and laid his head on his folded arms as if he'd go to sleep.

"Oh, Simon. What happened?" Daviana glanced from him to Kyle, who shrugged.

"I'd walked to the road, lookin' for my nephew's puppy that wandered off. Found him"—Kyle nodded to Simon—"sprawled in the road a couple hundred yards away. He came to when I tried to roll him over. Put him on the horse and brought him here. Don't know who would've done this."

Suspicions kicked up Daviana's ire. As much as she hated to distrust her longtime friend, she couldn't let Kyle go without being sure. "Let me see your hands."

His brow furrowed. "What? You think I did this?" He raised his hands, turned them palms up, then down. "Why would I bring him here if I did it?"

Mollified, she waved him off. "Sorry. I had to ask. Jasper wasn't happy to hear about our engagement. Yesterday, he accused Simon of being a Federal spy, so I thought maybe he'd told you and you got angry..." She let her words hang as she went to grab a cloth and bowl of water. Kyle was standing in the same place when she turned back. "Thank you for helping. If you'd take care of the horse, I'd be grateful."

He edged toward the door. "All right, then. I'll come over tomorrow and see how he is. We need to talk, anyway."

She turned her attention to Simon. "Can you sit up and let me see where you're hurt?"

With a fair amount of groaning, he shifted in the chair. Blood oozed from a cut at his hairline, and the skin beneath the swollen eye had turned purple. She dabbed the wet cloth at the blood, then positioned it over his injured eye. "Hold this on your eye while I gather some medicines."

Before she could step away, he grasped her wrist. "I'd rather hold you."

A strangled sound, part cry, part chuckle, broke loose. "Honestly, Simon. You must not hurt too badly if that's where your mind is turning." Once she located more bandages and ointment, she worked at cleaning away the dirt and blood from his face. "Where else are you hurt?"

He presented his battered knuckles, which she treated. "Now tell me what happened."

"Somebody was waiting to ambush me. I guess they saw me on the way to town, then chose a spot to jump on me."

"But who was it, and why would they go to so much trouble?"

He shook his head. "No idea, but it was at least two men. I heard a whistle, then somebody pushed me off the horse. Another started hitting me. I fought back but"—he raised a hand to touch his head and hissed—"got a knock on the head for it. Guess that's when I passed out."

He stood and draped an arm over her shoulder, leaning against her. "Let's forget about it for now. I think I'll go lie down. We can talk more tomorrow."

"All right." She gestured to the items on the table. "I'll clean this up later."

Simon didn't say anymore, but he winced in pain and groaned with every step as they shuffled to the bedroom.

He may not know who devised the attack, but she could guess why. Jasper's accusation likely got picked up and repeated. Forgiveness didn't come easy to some people, and others wouldn't even consider that an option. It would be a long time before he could prove to the community that he was more than a former Union soldier. She should have refused his offer of marriage and sent him straight to Alabama. At least there, his family could protect him somewhat.

Would he be in constant danger here? How would she bear it if the worst happened?

CHAPTER 11

Whoever planned the attack meant to scare Simon either into leaving or from working with the Freedmen's Bureau. That person or persons could not know it had the opposite effect. Simon had run away once, due to pressure from his family who only wanted to protect him. He would not flee again.

While Daviana prepared breakfast the next morning, he sought out Rufus.

His father-in-law gaped at Simon's battered face. "What happened to you?"

"Someone attacked me on my way home from town last night. I plan to ride back in and see what anyone knows. From something one of my attackers said, it could be they're upset about folks working with the Freedmen's Bureau. Maybe I can rally a few men to stand with me against such attacks. If our workers show up before I get back, you might give them a tour of the farm or get them to start cleaning out the old cottage."

He'd awakened during the night and considered his options. Since running away was out, he could either pretend it hadn't happened, or he could enlist help. What he needed most was the strength of influence. He'd start with Sheriff Moore and Reverend Benson, but a stop at the Freedmen's Bureau also might be worthwhile.

Daviana set a bowl of grits on the table and peered at Simon's face. The swelling around his eye had gone down enough for him to examine the results in the shaving mirror this morning. The cuts were minor, but the left side of his face would sport changing colors for a while. He was thankful none of his teeth had been jarred loose.

With gentle fingers, she examined the damage. "Well, you ought to get a load of pity when you show up, if nothing else."

Simon waited until Rufus offered a brief blessing over the food to respond to her teasing remark. "It's not pity I'm after, but I figure seeing the damage might convince others of the seriousness of the situation. They need to be alert to the danger."

Rufus set down his coffee cup. "Then you don't think it had anything to do with you bein' a former Union officer?"

"Not completely. One of the men made a crude remark about me hiring former slaves who used to work the Butler farm. From what I gathered from Corporal Ewing, nobody besides us has even asked about hiring workers or using the contracts to help bring in their crops."

Daviana set her mouth in a grim line. "You think they mean to discourage the rest of the community from hiring those folks."

At his nod of agreement, she tapped her fingers on the table. From her lowered brows and compressed lips, she was planning something. "I think I'll go to the ladies' sewing group next week. Maybe it's time to use some gentle persuasion."

"Now, Dottie, don't go stirring up trouble," Rufus warned.

She put on an innocent face, widening her eyes. "Why, Pa,

how would you think I'd do that? I just mean to let the women see how they can support the community by encouraging their menfolk to hire workers."

He shook his head. "It's liable to start an argument. Might even make a few enemies of them women."

Simon's gaze went from Rufus to Daviana, as he attempted to decide which one to support. If the women could sway their husbands to stand against vigilantes, it would help his cause. But he didn't want Daviana exposed to any negative repercussions.

He phrased his words with care. "How do you propose getting them to offer assistance, sweetheart?"

"Why, Simon dear…" She continued her innocent act. "Have you not read any of those newspaper articles about the suffragist women? They have several suggestions for ways to persuade their husbands."

Some inner voice cautioned him to tread carefully. He finished his coffee, stood, and kissed her cheek. "I believe you'll have to tell me about it later. Right now, I'm off to wage my own campaign."

A low chuckle from Rufus followed him to the door. It had the peculiar ring of "coward" in Simon's ears.

~

Dew sparkled on the grass Thursday morning as Daviana stepped outside to determine whether the fair weather looked to hold long enough to do laundry. Beyond the pink streaks that accompanied the sun's rising, no clouds dotted the sky. The ever-changing song of a mockingbird drifted from the topmost limbs of a sweet bay magnolia where its white blooms scented the air.

Her spirits rose to heaven on a prayer. "I'm mighty thankful for the grains we got, Lord. And for the bounty from the garden. You always find a way to provide what we need. Thank You for protecting Simon. I pray that more folks will be open to trade with the Freedmen's Bureau so we can all heal and be one nation again. You know what it will take."

Simon had met with Jude and Titus Granger after his visit with Sheriff Moore yesterday. Despite the beating he'd taken for it, his pride and pleasure showed as he led them around the farm. They'd cleaned up the old cottage to make it habitable until they could erect more suitable housing for the men's family.

Humming the chorus of "Solid Rock," she reentered the kitchen to start on her chores. She pushed up her sleeves and stuffed wood into the stove, then grabbed the largest pot for water to heat. Heavy footsteps made her glance back a moment before Simon lifted the pot from her hand.

He took advantage of her upturned face to press a kiss to her cheek. "Good morning. I'll fetch the water so you can get started on those biscuits you promised."

"Thank you, kind sir. I'm going to need that pot filled a few more times after I get the coffee and grits goin'. Then you can put your dirty clothes in the tub outside and set it on the firepit so I can do the laundry."

"My, my." His eyebrows went up along with the corners of his mouth. "Fill the lady's larder, and she becomes a tyrant for housework."

Daviana smirked. "Oh, you just wait, Simon McNeil. I'll be sure to find a few more things for you to do around here, now that you're on the mend."

He leaned close and kissed her nose. "I'll look forward to it." He headed out the door, whistling.

After breakfast, Pa and Simon went to meet with Jude and Titus to discuss the day's work arrangements. Soon as Daviana cleaned up the kitchen, she started on the laundry.

Simon wandered by as she struggled with wringing out the larger items from the rinse water. "Here, let me help."

"Gladly. These big coveralls are always hard to handle." Sneaking glances at Simon as he wrung out the garments, she admired the play of muscles in his hands and arms.

He smirked when he handed her the last item to hang on the line. "I hope I've convinced you that I can be handy to keep around."

She turned away to hide her smile. "Maybe. As warm as it is now, these things should be dry in a couple of hours." She ran her hands along the clothes on the line.

A familiar figure emerged from the woods, a black-and-white spotted dog trotting beside him.

Simon must have seen him too. "Looks like we've got company." His gaze flitted to Daviana. "You might want to put on a fresh dress or apron. That one looks as though it should be hanging on the line."

Her face warmed at his chuckle. She crossed her arms over her chest and hurried into the house before Kyle got close enough to call a greeting.

$\sim$

*S*imon lowered the sleeves he'd rolled up for the laundering, his eyes following Kyle Dunaway's progress over the bare stretch of ground near the barn. Pa's advice rang in his ears. "Show respect to everyone, but don't trust 'em with your valuables."

Because of Kyle's history with Daviana, Simon would be neighborly, but he'd watch the man. He didn't seem as hostile as Jasper, and he had helped Simon get to the house the other night, but he might be sore about losing the woman he'd planned to wed. Even as a friend, he wouldn't take kindly to a stranger usurping his place in her affections.

"Morning, neighbor," Simon called when the visitor came within hearing distance. "What brings you out so early?"

Kyle stopped several yards away. Was it so he wouldn't be obliged to shake hands with someone he considered his— what? Rival? Adversary? Enemy? If he only knew how true that had been in the past.

The little dog came close enough to sniff the hand Simon offered, then trotted off to sample the grass surrounding the garden fence.

Although Kyle's demeanor didn't hint at belligerence, neither did he offer a smile. "I wanted to come while Jasper's occupied elsewhere. I feel I owe Dottie an account of what happened to me, same as y'all should tell me how *you* came to be here, proposin' to marry the girl who was promised to me."

Simon let the slight jab pass. "Sounds reasonable. Davi went inside to repair her dress. We can go inside or sit out on the front porch."

Kyle shrugged. "Whichever seems best to you."

Deciding to establish his role as host, Simon gestured to the back door. "I believe there might be a cup of coffee left from breakfast if you'd care for some." He recalled from his studies a quote by some Greek philosopher, something about circum-stance being what determines whether a person is considered a friend or an enemy. Perhaps he and Kyle could come to an amiable agreement, which would please Davi.

They made their way to the back door, and Simon entered first, calling out to warn Davi and Rufus. "Hey, y'all, Kyle's come over to visit. Is there any coffee left?"

His fiancée hurried from the hallway and greeted them, her eyes bright with curiosity. "Hello, Kyle. I'll put on a fresh pot. Why don't y'all sit at the table?" She bustled to the stove while Simon gestured for Kyle to take a chair.

Rufus shambled from the front room to join them. He

reached to shake the visitor's hand. "Mighty glad to see you made it back, Kyle." He sat in his usual place and traded remarks with the neighbor about conditions and folks in the county while they waited for the coffee to brew.

Simon drifted closer to the kitchen. Davi pushed a basket of leftover biscuits and a jar of jam into Simon's hands, then turned back to the stove. He put the items on the table but remained standing until she brought everyone coffee and took her seat.

When she did, they turned to Kyle, everyone waiting to hear his story.

He toyed with his cup handle. "Well, what happened is, I took a bullet to the shoulder and couldn't lift my rifle. So I retreated to tend to it, to stop the bleedin', you see, and got turned around in the woods where I was hidin'." He dropped his head. "I guess I passed out."

"Blood loss will do that." Simon broke a biscuit open and added a dollop of jam. "Especially if the person hasn't eaten in a while. I saw it happen often enough."

Kyle sipped his coffee. "When I woke up, I was in someone's cabin, lyin' on a mattress on the floor. A woman and two girls tended my wound. They'd found me and somehow managed to get me in the house. At first, I didn't remember much. It was like I had to think backward through time to figure out what'd happened and even where I was from."

Kyle spoke with his head down most of the time, seeming to struggle with his story. Why did he feel it necessary to go into such detail? Simon's gaze veered to Daviana.

Other than polite attention, her expression gave no indication of her feelings.

"When was that, Kyle?" Rufus asked.

"December, just before this last Christmas."

"The second battle for Nashville?" Simon asked.

When Kyle nodded, Davi gasped. "But Jasper told us the army reported you'd been killed at Cedar Creek in September. It was in the Macon Telegraph."

"That's where the mix-up occurred. It was the other Kyle Dunaway at Cedar Creek. I didn't know about the report till I finally got back to my company in March."

"You were laid up that long, from December to March?" Simon shook his head.

Color suffused the man's clean-shaven cheeks. "The wound got infected, and I ran a fever for days. If it weren't for Myra—the woman who took me in—I likely would have died in that little cabin. All the medicine she had was home-grown remedies. They'd already been reduced to one meal a day, plus taking care of me, when her grandpa showed up to take her and her sisters home."

Davi glanced from Kyle to Simon and back. "I don't understand. I thought you were already at their house."

"It was a one-room cabin, like a huntin' shack in the woods near her grandparents' farm." Kyle glanced around the table. "Mr. Carson took the womenfolk there before the fightin' commenced. For their safety. When it was over, he came to retrieve 'em. I was still awful sick, but I heard him arguin' with Myra to leave me there. She refused to go and stayed to nurse me till I was well enough to walk on my own."

The reason for Kyle's lengthy confession became clear. If the woman tended him, they would have stayed in the cabin together for a prolonged time. Whether she was single or married, her reputation would be shattered after being alone with Kyle for more than a few hours.

Rufus cut his eyes to Daviana, who raised a hand to cover her mouth. "What happened when you improved enough to leave?" Rufus asked.

"Myra's grandfather insisted she had to marry me, since we were both single." He shot a swift glance to Davi. "That's why I had to come see you right away, Dottie. To explain why I can't marry you, seein' as I'm already married."

Relief coursed through Simon's bones even as Davi placed her hand over Kyle's. "I understand, Kyle. As you can see, we gave up hope you'd ever return when the reports said you'd been killed."

Simon stretched an arm behind Davi, making clear his claim with a touch on her shoulders. "I'm sorry for what you endured, Dunaway."

After removing his hand from beneath Daviana's, Kyle picked up his coffee cup. "Now it's your turn. How'd you two come to meet?" He focused on Simon. "Jasper said you're from Alabama, and he'd never met you before."

"It's true that our acquaintance is rather recent," Simon said, "not unlike yours with your wife." He paused to let that truth resonate. "You must know that dozens, even hundreds of soldiers passed by here on their way to report for duty or return home, just as I did."

"And not all of 'em as pleasant to deal with," Rufus said. "Some so bold as to take our provisions at gunpoint."

Daviana spoke up. "Then there was the visit from the Federal men, asking about the land." She leaned into Simon's side. "I don't know what would've happened if Simon hadn't been here."

Simon took her hint to skip to the end with the truth. "How glad I am for that. It gave me the opportunity to forgo days or weeks of courting Davi's favor and to move right on to the proposal."

Kyle regarded each of them again, convincing Simon of his sincere concern for his friends. "I reckon everything worked out for the best for all of us."

Simon grinned. "It certainly worked out best for me. I can't imagine what my life would be without this woman. Though I hate it took a war to bring us together." The vision of countless lives ended or forever changed marched through his mind. "The war reshaped the future for everyone, especially in the South."

"But, Kyle," Davi said on a gasp, "where's your bride? Surely, you didn't leave her in Tennessee, or do you plan to return there?"

His face pinkened as he pushed his chair back "We had a little trouble on the way home, ran out of money, and I had to continue alone. Travelin' wore Myra out, so she stayed with an older couple down in Cumming to rest until I get back there. I'm headin' out to get her now."

Simon spared a moment of sympathy for the poor girl, left in a strange town without the means to complete her journey. Kyle must have walked and begged rides whenever he could.

When Kyle ambled toward the door, the others followed. He turned to Davi. "I just wanted you to know what happened first before word gets around. Thank you for the coffee."

"You bring Myra over to meet us soon as you get back." Davi shook her finger in his face. "She'll need a friend here, and I aim to be the first one."

In the open doorway, Kyle faced them. "I'd hoped to make it there and back by tonight, as long as the weather holds. Best I get back to the house and hook up the wagon, or that ain't gonna happen. We'll come over sometime tomorrow. G'bye, now."

Davi waved him off, then nudged Simon in the side. "That was a surprisin' turn of events, huh? Imagine, Kyle's here, alive, and married."

Rufus snorted as he wandered toward the kitchen to finish his coffee. "Days of miracles never end."

Simon squeezed his woman and waggled his eyebrows. "I'd rather imagine you and me married. Tell me again, why did we decide to wait?"

"Because you need to visit your folks in Alabama, and I

need to stay here with Pa. Besides, there's no reason to rush. I'll be here when you get back."

He held onto those words. Maybe some time away would work to his advantage. If she missed him, she'd welcome his return. It was a chance he had to take, as difficult as it was for a man of his impulsive nature.

CHAPTER 12

With her sewing in hand, Daviana sat on the porch to enjoy an hour of quiet. Her lavender dress still bore a faint scent of the sachet from her cedar chest as she added tucks in the waist for a better fit. After a thorough investigation of the fabric, Minnow curled up near Daviana's feet for a nap.

She was halfway done when the sound of wagon wheels alerted her. Kyle waved as he drove into the yard. Daviana folded the dress and set it inside the house before calling out a welcome. The woman with him wore a brown dress and bonnet. Kyle helped her from the buckboard and held her hand until they reached Daviana.

"Dottie, you wanted to meet Myra soon as we got back, so here she is. Myra, this is my good friend, Dottie Spalding."

As tall as Kyle, the newcomer displayed the bearing of royalty—or the way Daviana had always imagined it. She must come from a well-to-do family. Daviana grasped her hand. "Myra, I'm so happy to meet you. Please have a seat. Kyle, why don't you bring out one of the kitchen chairs so we can all sit and visit?"

The women each took a chair while Kyle hurried to do Daviana's bidding. Myra's curly red hair peeped from a brown bonnet that covered delicate features set in a porcelain, heart-shaped face. Long fingers plucked at her brown skirt, which had once been fine but now wore a sheen, indicating its age and frequent wear. She licked her lips, and her pale blue eyes darted from the wagon to the front door.

Davi touched Myra's hand. "Now, I know Kyle said my name is Dottie, and that's what most folks have called me for years. However, I'm asking my closest friends to use my true Christian name, which is Daviana, or Davi, if you prefer, as my fiancé does."

"I don't think I've heard that name before." Myra's light eyebrows rose. "It's lovely. Why does Kyle call you Dottie, then?"

Kyle returned with the third chair and positioned it between the women. Daviana glanced his way. Did he think he'd need to maintain the peace between them? Too bad they couldn't send him to join Pa and Simon, who'd taken the new workers to view the farm and clean out the old cottage.

He balked at Myra's question. "I've always called her Dottie, just like her brother and her pa."

"My brother copied Pa, who called me Daughter, but it turned into Dottie."

"Daughter, Dottie, Davi," Myra repeated. "Oh, I see how that would happen." She leveled a look at Kyle. "We will remember to use her proper name, won't we, Kyle?"

He tossed Daviana a grin. "Soon, you'll have another new name to go with it." He shook his head. "Daviana McNeil. I'll try to remember, but don't blame me if I forget."

Myra sat up straighter. "Of course, my grandmother would say we should call you Mrs. McNeil."

Daviana laughed. "Now that would make me feel old. Even the pastor's wife asks to be called Mrs. Evelyn. We're quite informal around here. I hope you don't mind if we use first names. Now I want to hear about you, Myra. Kyle didn't get to tell us much about you while he was here, only that you saved his life."

Myra's blush nearly matched her hair. "Oh, I only did what I could. It was the Lord's will for Kyle to live. And my sisters were there too. They helped me drag him into the cabin. He didn't come to his senses until the next day."

Simon and Pa rounded the corner of the house, returning from their exploration. Kyle jumped from his chair to offer it to Pa. "Sit here, Mr. Rufus. Should I bring another chair or two outside?" His glance went from Daviana to Simon as Pa sat.

"Only if you want one." Simon lowered himself to the floor beside Minnow, who uncurled and claimed his lap. "I'll just sit here on the porch and visit a few minutes. I want to get our hired help started on the plans for their cabins."

Kyle's eyes widened. "Hired help, you say? Where did you find anyone?"

After a glance at Pa, Simon answered. "The Freedmen's Bureau. They help to find work for the former slaves. We've hired two who can help in the fields and orchards, but they're also experienced in construction. Later on, I hope to get more to assist in building a new house for my bride." He slanted a grin in Daviana's direction.

Myra clapped her hands. "How wonderful! Am I correct in assuming that would be you, Daviana?"

"Oh, where are my manners? Forgive me." Daviana touched Simon's shoulder. "This is Simon, and that's my pa, Rufus Spalding. I'm sure you men have guessed this lovely lady is Kyle's wife, Myra Dunaway."

Both men expressed their welcome.

"And I haven't even offered anyone a cup of tea or water." Daviana poised on the edge of her chair, prepared to rise. "I'm a poor hostess, indeed. What can I get y'all?"

"Oh, nothing for me." Myra waved away her concern. "And don't worry, dear. I expect you're all a-flutter with plans for your wedding. When will it be?"

Not sure how much to reveal, Daviana hedged. "Sometime this autumn. We have to work around the different harvesting times."

Simon intervened. "I'm planning a trip to my home in Alabama right away, hopefully so I can be there for my mother's birthday. Once I return, we can decide on a more definite date."

He narrowed his eyes and seemed to come to a decision. "In fact, Kyle, I hope I can depend on you and your bride to check on Davi and Rufus while I'm gone. There are some around here, I'm afraid, who would take advantage of my absence to finagle their own plans. I trust you know what I mean?"

Daviana's gaze went to Kyle, who gave a slow nod to Simon. "I feel privileged to be asked. You may trust that I'll honor your confidence. When do you expect to leave?"

"If I can finish up my projects today, I'd like to leave early tomorrow."

A heavy weight settled in Daviana's stomach. Time apart was what she'd insisted on, but hearing Simon announce his departure gave her apprehension rather than relief.

"Please..." He looked at each one. "Keep this information to yourselves. The fewer people who know, the better. If all goes well, I should be back in a couple of weeks."

Kyle moved to Myra's side. "With that in mind, I suppose we ought to be mindful of your time and leave so y'all can tend to your preparations."

Myra nodded and took his hand, and everyone stood.

"I'm so glad to meet you, Myra. Since we'll be neighbors," Daviana said, "I hope you'll feel free to call on me for anything you might need."

"The same goes for me. It's good to have a friend close by."

Daviana waved as Kyle and Myra drove away, then turned on Simon. "You plan to leave tomorrow?"

He glanced away from her. "If I plan to be back for the apple harvest, I'll need to take my journey now. This soon after the attack, you can excuse my absence from church by saying my injuries are keeping me abed. Maybe I'll be back before anyone figures out I'm gone."

~

*S*imon secured his saddlebags on the mare and turned to say his goodbyes. In the pale light of dawn, Daviana and Rufus waited to send him on his way.

Two steps brought him to Rufus, who extended his hand. "You remember the cutoff I told you about, to miss goin' through town?"

"Yessir." Simon tapped his forehead. "Got it right here. You let Jude and Titus do all the heavy work now, while you supervise. If any problems arise, Davi has the information for sending me a telegram. There's enough traffic between Pa's farm and town that I'll get it without delay. Of course, you can call on Kyle too."

Rufus nodded and backed away. "Reckon I'll go finish my coffee, then. See you in a few weeks."

As he went inside the house, Daviana stepped forward. Barefoot, with her hair barely contained by a ribbon, Daviana reminded Simon of a waif he'd assisted in Gettysburg. Was that forlorn expression a sign of regret? Did she wish, as he did, that she were going with him?

He grasped her shoulders, and she slid her arms around him. They held each other for a long moment before Simon drew away. If he didn't get on that horse now, he'd end up staying.

"Be sure to send a wire to let me know you arrived safely."

She ducked her head as if hesitant to say more. "Don't forget to come back."

"Darlin', I'll be thinking of you every day. How could I forget?" He tipped her chin and pressed a chaste kiss on her forehead. "You stay safe and be ready to set a date when I get back."

Without waiting for an answer, he swung onto the mare and nudged her with his heels. At the road, he couldn't resist a glance backward. Davi waved from the porch. He doffed his hat.

"Lord, keep her safe until I return." Two weeks had never seemed so long before.

CAMPBELL COUNTY, GEORGIA

Simon's second day of travel took him through Atlanta, where a Union soldier directed him to an inn that offered meals and the possibility of a fresh mount in exchange for the mare, which he would reclaim on his return journey. Eager to press on, Simon struck a deal with the hostler, loaded his knapsack with ham and cheese biscuits, then prayed the spirited gelding would make it to Aunt Lydia's house in Campbell County by sunset.

With less than an hour of daylight left, he crossed the creek leading to the Sweetwater Mill. Charred bricks and beams marked the place where the mill used to stand. Simon took a deep breath to keep from expressing his outrage. He should be used to such sights by now, having witnessed the carnage in numerous places, but each area of devastation struck him with a fresh wave of remorse—this one the worst.

Perhaps it was because he'd known people who lived here —his Aunt Lydia among them—on what the family called

Granny McNeil's farm. Or maybe it was the lack of rebuilding that made it harder to bear. The areas around Atlanta bustled with the activity of new structures going up. Train tracks showed signs of repair work, and the early days of harvesting, meager though it might be, kept farmers busy in the less-populated areas. In this area of Georgia closer to the Alabama line, there was no evidence of such recovery.

Maybe it was good that Davi hadn't come with him. How heart-wrenching it was to see so much destruction and know what it had cost in lives on both sides.

Abandoning his contemplation, he glanced farther afield. He must've lingered longer than he meant to. The horse had taken advantage of the loose reins to nose the grass springing along the roadside.

As soon as he topped the next hill, Aunt Lydia's house came into view. He slowed the horse, looking for signs of habitation Someone on the porch rose from a chair and watched as he cantered closer. Was that Cal Gibson? But no, Ma's letters had said Cal was lost in the battle at Chickamauga.

Simon rode closer, and the man on the porch gripped the post. "Simon Pieman?"

The voice was deeper, but only Troy called him by that name. "By all that's holy, Troy, when did you get so tall?"

Simon dismounted. Before he could loop the reins over the porch rail, Troy assaulted him, wrapping him in a fierce hug. He wasn't sure which of them was choking the other while trying to speak past the emotion.

Simon groused to cover his sentimental display. "Dang, Troy, let me breathe, will ya?"

"About time you came home, old man." Troy blinked back the moisture in his hazel eyes as he pushed Simon back to arms' length.

Amazed that his baby brother now matched his height, Simon took a minute to survey the man before him. Under the dark hair, he found the old scar at Troy's left eyebrow where Simon's hammer had grazed him when it slipped while fixing a wagon. At ten, Simon had worried he'd killed the six-year-old who dogged his steps.

A woman's voice called from the doorway, "Well, don't just stand there. Troy, let him come in the house and rest."

Troy stopped at the base of the steps. "Millie, you remember Simon, don't you?"

The grown-up version of Millie Gibson, stepdaughter to his Aunt Lydia, stepped onto the porch. She'd been a sassy little girl who tagged after Troy whenever they visited.

With a saucy smile, the blonde glanced their way. "I remember someone putting a frog in my shoe...."

Simon raised his hands in defense. "Wasn't me. I'm sure I was too old for such pranks." He poked his brother's side. "Sounds like something Troy would do. He always was sweet on you."

Troy grinned. "I cannot deny it, and I finally got her to give up and marry me. Hey, I'll take care of your horse and bring in your baggage. Go on inside with Millie. I'll be right there."

Simon slapped his brother's arm. "I appreciate it. I pushed the horse pretty hard, and it's been a long two-day ride."

In the parlor, a braided rug covered the pine floor between a worn sofa and the unlit fireplace, flanked by two mismatched chairs. Millie scooped up a toddler from the rug and continued past the scarred dining table on to the kitchen. She chatted all the while.

"We just finished supper, but there's a wedge of cornbread." She shifted the child to one hip and picked up a plate from the worktable. "And a bowl of peas I was going to toss in the scrap jar. I can warm those up if you like." She set the dish on the stove.

Simon trailed her. "Whatever you have is fine as it is. But tell me, whose child is this?"

She spun away from the stove, laughing. "I forgot you wouldn't know about Amy. She's mine and Troy's, of course." Millie thrust Amy into his arms. "Here, Amy, go to Uncle Simon. You two can get acquainted while I fix you a plate. Would you prefer coffee or tea or maybe some of that powdered milk?"

Unaccustomed to children, Simon grasped the toddler awkwardly, expecting her to put up a squall to be so close to a stranger. Instead, she grinned and patted his cheeks above his beard. Simon bounced her a bit.

"Unca, unca, woo," she jabbered.

Simon chuckled. "It sounded as though she tried to say 'uncle' just then."

Millie peeked over her shoulder while she worked at the stove. "It did sound like it. I believe she thinks you're Rupert. There is a strong resemblance, and we were at Henry's until last week while Troy worked with the Freedmen's Bureau there. Amy took to Rupert right away."

Mention of his brother and uncle distracted him from Amy's babbling. "How is everyone? I'm headed that way, of course, so I trust all the family is well."

Troy came in, and Amy reached for him, leaving Simon empty-handed. "They're fine. Always wondering about you and your whereabouts. I finally asked General Swayne to see if he could find out whether you'd stayed in the army, and we learned you'd turned in your colors this past May. What's kept you away so long?"

"Let the man eat first, Troy." Millie set a plate on the table and pointed Simon to a chair. "I need to get Amy nursed and ready for bed. Just leave your dishes when you finish, and I'll clean them later. Water's heatin' on the stove if y'all want coffee or tea before I return." She swept Amy from Troy's arms and headed down the hallway.

Simon broke off a piece of cornbread. "So you and Millie live here now? Where's Aunt Lydia?"

"Up in Kentucky. I guess you know that General Sherman sent the workers north when he ordered the mills burned? Well, Lydia and Millie got caught in that."

While Simon finished his meal, Troy told him about events that happened during his years away, especially the last two when letters from home had been scarce. As he listened, Simon tried to determine how best to explain his current situation, which might sound strange to someone who hadn't lived it. His thoughts drifted to Daviana and stalled. No matter what other people might think, no matter how Jasper and others tried to run Simon off, he intended to return.

Troy stopped talking and stared at him. "Are you even listening? You look as though your mind is a thousand miles away."

Simon couldn't stop the grin spreading across his face. "Not a thousand, but a good many miles east of here, in the North Georgia mountains."

Millie sauntered back into the room and perched on Troy's lap. "Amy's asleep. Did I miss any important information from Simon?"

"I think you're just in time," Troy said. "Something happened in North Georgia, or maybe it's *somebody* he's thinking of."

"Her name is Daviana Spalding, and I've asked her to marry me."

CHAPTER 13

Taking time away from farm chores was a blessing, even if it meant the person had to work a little longer and faster the following days. Daviana's attendance to the ladies' group had been sporadic over the last year, as she'd found it hard to hear the other women talk about their men when she had no one. Now she had a handsome fiancé and also a friend her age to accompany her.

Myra was eager to be included and agreed with Daviana's concern, since the attack had occurred so close to their homes. Kyle also planned to hire workers at the bureau. He just had to convince Jasper of the notion.

No one had mentioned Jasper's name in connection with Simon's attack, but that didn't rule him out in Daviana's eyes. The elder Dunaway brother could be crafty.

In the Bensons' parlor, more than a dozen women worked on a quilt while others kept their hands busy with crochet or knitting projects. One small girl sat beside her mother, winding yarn on a ball while an infant slept in a basket, oblivious to the chatter around him.

At the first opportunity, Daviana paused her needlework to speak up. "I don't know if you heard, but Simon was attacked after leaving town the other night."

Before she finished describing what had happened, Mrs. Fuller made a clucking sound. "That reminds me of what happened to my Harvey back in '61." That got her started, and she launched into a detailed account of the long-ago incident.

With as much tact as she could muster, Daviana tried to bring the conversation back to her point. "I just wanted to alert everyone to be on guard and watch out for each other."

Mrs. Benson offered her a kind smile. "I saw your poor Simon's face when he came by to speak with the reverend. If you need it, I can give you a jar of salve to help speed the healing."

Her offer sparked a discussion of the best types of medication for different ailments. And on it went. Every time Daviana or Myra directed the conversation to the need for binding together to protect the innocent, another woman turned the subject. The morning flew by without another opportunity to garner any tangible support.

As everyone gathered their fabrics and sewing notions in preparation to leave, Mrs. Benson approached them. "So glad you came today, ladies. I hope you'll become regular members of our little group. It's good for women to get away from the work at home for a while. Our menfolk, God bless their hearts, just don't understand how much goes into running a home."

Daviana exchanged a glance with Myra and nodded. "We'll certainly try, Mrs. Benson. Thank you for the invitation."

"And don't you worry about your young men. I heard Reverend Benson speaking with some church council members about keeping their eyes open for any questionable activity."

So the preacher had followed through on his promise to

Simon. A burden lifted from Daviana's shoulders. "Thank you, ma'am. We appreciate that."

The two of them tied their bonnets and stepped into the bright sunshine. Reflection from a metal object made Daviana squint as someone called to Myra from a buckboard. Daviana shaded her eyes to find Jasper hastening their way. Why was he here? Kyle had promised to come for them.

He held out his hand to Myra. "I told Kyle I'd fetch y'all since I had business nearby. Much to my disagreement, he's still talking with those Federal men."

A quick glance at Myra's puckered brow confirmed her own misgivings. Daviana would rather walk than ride with him, but she didn't intend to desert her friend, who could hardly refuse her brother-in-law. Besides that, there was no telling what Jasper might tell Myra to disparage Simon and Daviana. According to Myra, he'd already dropped hints to discourage her and Kyle from associating with Simon.

Jasper turned from helping Myra aboard and grasped Daviana about the waist. His harsh whisper assaulted her ear. "You, too, Dottie. I wouldn't want anything to happen to my *closest* neighbor."

With her hands clutching her sewing basket, she could only squeak out a protest as he boosted her to the bench seat. She settled for glaring at him and hoped Pa would be close by when they arrived at the house.

All the way home, she clung to the edge as Myra pressed close to her and away from Jasper on the other side. When the wagon rolled to a stop, Daviana handed her basket to Myra, then gathered her skirts in one hand and used the wheel to balance on her way down.

She reached up to retrieve her basket from Myra and slammed into Jasper as she turned around. His hands gripped her arms with so much pressure, she would have bruises.

His hard stare seared her. "Don't think your Yankee suitor is gonna keep me away forever. I got plans for you and for this farm."

With a sinister grin, he released her, and Daviana ran on shaky legs into the house and shut the door without a backward look.

CAMPBELL COUNTY, GEORGIA

Simon woke to the tantalizing smells of coffee and ham cooking in a frying pan. How had he slept past sunrise? He and Troy had stayed up later than usual, catching up on each other's lives, but he'd been used to short nights during the war. Travel fatigue must have done him in.

After dressing and gathering his baggage, he made his way to the kitchen. Primed to apologize to Millie for having to feed him again, he found Troy at the stove. "I didn't expect to find you making breakfast, little brother."

Troy gave him a lopsided grin. "It's what you do if you like to eat. Millie made the biscuits and put them in the oven, but some cooking smells still make her sick."

Simon's puzzlement must have shown on his face.

Troy transferred the ham to a plate and set the pan in the sink. "I forgot you've not yet experienced the joys of having a pregnant wife. Women in the early months of that condition tend to have sensitive stomachs."

Oh. That was why Millie appeared heavier than he remembered. But it'd been years since he'd seen her. A vision of Daviana's slender curves rose, bringing a notion of how those might fill out in such a situation. The pleasant warmth accompanying his fantasy vanished. He might never know that experience if the army doctor's warning proved true. Cursed malaria could have far-reaching consequences for some men.

Troy's voice intruded on his thoughts. "Best eat up if you want to get on the road soon. We can wrap up what's left for you to take with you."

As Simon poured himself a cup of coffee, Millie came into the room with Amy on her hip. "Did you stir the grits and dish up some to cool for Amy? Good morning, Simon. Please, be seated. Amy, can you say, 'good morning' to Uncle Simon?"

Millie bustled around the kitchen, filling plates and cups, still holding Amy.

Simon sent a questioning look to Troy, who merely shook his head. "I guess she's fine now."

They all sat, and Troy asked a blessing on the food and on Simon's travels. He spooned grits onto his plate. "You're still a day and a half away from Pa's. I know the route well, having traveled it a few times. I took the liberty of writing a note of introduction for you to the preacher in Carroll County, the one who helped me hide from the Confederate conscription scouts. He'll put you up for the night, then you'll be close enough to Henry's or Pa's to get there in four or five hours."

Millie handed half a biscuit to Amy. "How long do you plan to stay? Troy plans to make a trip over in a few weeks to check on the Freedmen's office there. Since he was the first representative in that area, some folks prefer dealing with him over the current officer."

Simon set down his coffee cup. "I'll probably leave before then. I want to be back in Hall County in time for apple gathering. Can't take a chance on Daviana forgetting me."

He smiled, but his concern was real—not for her forgetting him but for her running afoul of his enemies.

Hall County, Georgia

*L*ike the endless summer heat, the hours dragged as Daviana marked the fifth day of September, the fourth day of Simon's absence. He should have reached his home by now, if the weather along his route had been as clear as it was here. Farm chores kept her busy as ever, but she found excuses to do more outside because Simon had left his impression everywhere inside. How had he become so important to her in such a short time?

She turned to the other recent addition to her life, Myra. With new circumstances in both their lives, perhaps friendships could be forged amid common tasks.

"Why don't you get Kyle to bring you over whenever he comes this way?" Daviana had suggested on Sunday. "We can visit while we work on the day's tasks, perhaps even share our garden collections."

Myra had agreed. "I'd like that. Jasper's boys are with his aunt this week, and I'd just as soon not be in the house without Kyle there."

A late-afternoon sprinkle of rain eased the day's heat, creating a pleasant atmosphere on the porch. Daviana stood and poured her pan of shelled beans into the bowl sitting on the porch between her and Myra. "This chore is so much easier to do when I have someone to talk to." She filled her apron with three more handfuls of pods from the basket before she returned to her chair.

"It sure is, especially when the company is pleasant." Myra used her thumbnail to split a pod, then raked out the green lima beans. "Thank you for suggesting to do this at your house. I don't know which is worse at our place, Jasper or his young'uns. They all complain about everything."

"The children haven't had a good example to follow since Jasper's wife and mother passed last year. I'm sure you and Kyle will be a much better influence on them."

"I hope so. The older boy saw me drawing a picture yesterday and said he liked to draw but his pa made fun of him."

"How sad. I think we should encourage children in anything they're interested in doing," Daviana said, "as long as it's not dangerous. My mama thought so too. She always listened to my outrageous stories and dreams of traveling to distant places."

Her thoughts drifted to her most recent daydreams. This morning, Pa had caught her staring out the window and guessed she was wondering where Simon might be. He hadn't been far off the mark, though she was closer to wishing she'd gone with him. How would his family react to meeting her? What sights might she see along the way?

Myra dropped her hands into the pile of bean pods. "Well, I hope you'll feel free to share your stories and dreams with me. I'd love to hear them, might even draw a picture or two to go with one."

Startled at the idea, Daviana laughed and stared at her friend. "What for? Are you suggesting we could put together a book like *McGuffey's Reader* or a children's primer?"

"Why not?" Myra's gaze veered from Daviana to some faraway place. "We could work on it during the winter, when we have more time on our hands." She bounced in her chair and grinned. "Let's do it. It'd be fun, even if nobody else ever sees it."

Her enthusiasm pricked Daviana's. "It would help to pass those dreary winter days. We could see if Miss Taylor, the schoolmarm, might like to use our stories." She chuckled. "When I was a girl, I thought she was so old and maybe I'd take her place teaching when she died."

"But she's still at the school, huh? You could still do that someday. How old is she?"

Daviana tried to keep from laughing but couldn't contain

her mirth. "She told me her great secret last year at the children's Christmas play. She's only thirty-eight."

"Oh, my, such an old woman." Myra chuckled and shook her head. "'Tis a wonder she can hobble around, much less keep up with a dozen children."

As their laughter faded, Daviana brushed her hand over Myra's. "I'm so glad you're here, Myra. Whoever would have guessed that Kyle's unfortunate injury would lead to your coming here and becoming my friend?"

Myra's smile belied the moisture in her eyes. "Only God, my friend. Only God."

Despite their pleasant agreement, her countenance darkened. "Before I forget, I want to warn you about Jasper. We heard how he accused Simon of being a spy, and he still complains about Kyle and me visiting you."

"I think he's always resented my friendship with Kyle." More than once over the years, Jasper had tried to come between them, but she'd put it down to simple jealousy.

"He told Kyle he's courting a woman over in Sulphur Springs, but I think he's lying. No man goes to court a woman without sprucin' up a bit. And when Jasper returns, he smells more like smoke and spirits than perfume. I'm telling you, he's up to no good."

Perhaps if Jasper found someone to marry, he'd concentrate on his family and abandon his crusade against Simon. But Myra was right about his suspicious behavior. It wouldn't do to let her guard down when it came to Jasper.

Randolph County, Alabama

After four days in the saddle, Simon was ready to put his boots on the ground again. He'd crossed into Alabama about midmorning, so home was near. Other than the occasional late-summer shower, the weather had been good. September could be unpredictable, but for now, it continued hot and dry with occasional breezes.

He was thankful that he'd found good resting places along the way. Future travel would be easier since he could plan his stops at those stations. Finding Troy at the old McNeil farm in Campbell County had been an unexpected treat that encouraged him and provided his next stop.

Last night's visit with the preacher in Carrollton had been enlightening. Reverend Dan Holt and his wife had given a safe place for Troy and other men trying to avoid the Confederate conscription as well as a few runaway slaves over the years. They'd shared about how conditions in that area of the South had deteriorated as the war progressed, despite the conflict not reaching them until the last year.

"Troy was here the day before the Federals burned the Sweetwater Mill," the preacher had said, "and I drove him partway there. If I'd've known he was gonna be arrested and sent north, I never would've left him." He'd shaken his head, then smiled. "But the Lord's plans are always best, even when it doesn't seem so. It opened up the way for him to get beyond the Confederate army and catch up with Millie."

Contemplating that thought, Simon had to agree. Sometimes it seemed as if circumstances thwarted a man's plans, but God oversaw it all. The verse from Proverbs came to mind. *A man's heart deviseth his way, but the Lord directeth his steps.*

The strident call of a crow jolted Simon out of his pensive mood. He sat up straighter and took in the view. The familiar fork in the road meant he'd come to the last mile before he reached Pa's farm. He gave the gelding a gentle kick to pick up his speed, and Simon's heart did the same. Eagerness overcame his trepidation as the home place came into sight.

The two-story, white-washed dwelling that had sheltered three generations of McNeils stood strong among the oaks and pines. The paint peeled in places, but its brick pilings held firm. As a child, he'd fancied the upper-story windows combined with the wide porch created a smiling face. The image evoked a warm invitation.

Simon halted the horse at the front porch, slid from the saddle, and tossed the reins over the rail. The door stood open, so he leaped over the steps two at a time and stopped abruptly when he saw Ma at the threshold.

She gave a shriek of joy and launched herself into his arms. After a long embrace, she held him at arms' length. "Simon Patrick McNeil, look at you. I can hardly believe you're here."

Tears coursed her cheeks, and Simon wiped the telltale moisture from his own face. Beyond her, three women of various sizes and color clustered with a little girl.

Paul's wife stepped forward to give Simon a brief hug, her petite stature barely reaching his shoulder. Her dark hair was drawn back with netting rather than the ribbons she used to wear, but otherwise, her looks hadn't changed. "Welcome home, Simon. This is my daughter, Lucy." The little girl clung to her mother's skirts, alternately hiding and peeking at him.

Simon nodded. "Hello, Lucy. Jane, thank heavens she looks like you." He turned to the older women, the former slaves who'd loved but often despaired of him. "Etta, Liza, good to see you both."

Etta grabbed him, oblivious to the fact she still held a dripping ladle in her hand. "Glory, hallelujah, chile! Good to see you too."

She released him and dabbed her eyes with her apron as Liza took her place. "I knew you'd come back once the way was clear. Glad you made it." She shook her finger in his face. "Just see you behave yo'self."

The familiar admonition elicited a chuckle. "I'll do my best." Simon glanced around. "I guess the men are out in the field, huh?"

His question set the women in motion. Etta and Liza scuttled back to the kitchen area while Ma took his arm and led him to the parlor with Jane and Lucy trailing behind them.

Ma grinned up at him. Her hair showed streaks of gray, and lines creased her face, but her eyes still sparkled when she smiled. "John and Paul took P.J. to check out the fields from the late planting. I reckon you know what that means." She sat in the corner of the worn settee and patted the place beside her. Besides a rag rug on the floor and newer pillow coverings, the room looked the same as he remembered.

Simon guffawed as he accepted Ma's unspoken invitation to sit beside her. "In other words, he's pickin' cotton." Soon as the words left his mouth, reality intruded. "That means you fared well enough to plant a crop, then. Do y'all have any field hands left, or did everyone pick up and move away?"

"They only planted about half the usual crop. We have enough workers for what came in, thanks to Troy's work at the Freedmen's Bureau. We're blessed that a few stayed with us, the older ones. I don't blame the young folks for wanting to spread their wings and see what's in the world. I just pray they don't find out how cruel it can be."

Simon veered away from that sobering subject. "Well, I'm glad Liza and Etta stayed." He raised his voice so it would carry through the house. "I've been craving red-eye gravy."

A voice floated down the hallway. "I hear you."

From the front door, a deeper voice called, "Hey, what kind of fool leaves a horse standin' in front of the porch?"

Simon stood and strode to the parlor threshold. Pa was

crossing the porch, his steps slow as Simon moved closer. "The kind that hasn't been home in seven years."

Pa halted at the front door, then rushed forward to embrace Simon. "Dear God. I thought we'd lost you for good."

Emotion clogged Simon's throat, and he couldn't speak. Standing behind Pa in the doorway, Paul gripped the shoulder of the boy beside him. So like Paul at that age, the boy had to be his son.

Simon released Pa, stretched out his hand, and grasped his brother's. A tug brought them closer for an embrace. When they broke apart, Simon regarded Paul's upright stance. "Good to see you haven't slowed down any, Paul." Too many men had lost limbs in the conflict. Thank God that doctors had found ways to attach artificial legs to maintain their mobility—and thank God Paul had submitted to the procedure.

Paul pounded Simon's back. "Good to see you alive, Simon."

They regarded each other a moment longer, then Simon nodded to the boy. "This must be Paul Junior, also called P.J., who I've heard about. How old are you?"

Solemn-faced, the boy met his gaze with steely blue eyes. "Six and a half."

A nudge from Paul elicited the obligatory, "Sir."

Simon gave an abrupt nod. "Well, P.J., how are you at brushing down a horse? If I don't put up that gelding proper-like, Pa's liable to tan my hide."

Interest lit the boy's countenance. "I can put him up." He turned to his father. "Can I, Pa?"

When Paul nodded, P.J. skedaddled out the door and leaped off the porch.

Simon couldn't contain the grin that broke forth as he soft-punched Paul's arm. "He's your son, for sure."

"He is that." Pa gestured to the parlor. "Let's go join the ladies until supper's ready. We've got a lot of catchin' up to do."

Simon took the lead and returned to the seat he'd left. The unspoken question was how long would the peace last? Could the prodigal son find his place again in the family circle?

Water from the outside pump trickled over Daviana's hands and the last of the summer squash she'd harvested from the garden. Her anxious gaze drifted again to the eastern fields where Pa supervised the early apple picking. From all accounts, the apple crop promised to be better than expected after a rather dry summer. She'd already started collecting the worst of the bruised and stunted ones to press into cider or turn into apple butter.

She startled at the sound of hoofbeats behind her. She chided herself for the hope that rose before she turned around. It was much too early for Simon to be back.

Kyle halted the horse and waited for Myra to slide off behind him. She called a greeting to Daviana. "I hope you don't mind if I visit with you while Kyle goes into town."

"Of course not." Daviana released the pump and tossed the squash into her basket. "Come into the kitchen, and I'll fix us a cup of tea. We'll use the water I was heating for the vegetables."

Myra followed her inside, untied the ribbons of her bonnet, and removed it. "I didn't want to stay at the house with Jasper in one of his foul moods, but neither did I want to wait for Kyle to take care of his errands."

"Is he applying for extra help for the harvest?"

Myra nodded. "One of the many things he and Jasper argue about."

"I'm sorry you have to put up with that." Daviana scooped tea into a straining cloth for each cup, then added hot water.

Myra accepted a cup, carried it to the table, and sat. "Oh, arguing in general doesn't bother me. My sisters and I seemed to always be disagreeing about something."

Daviana joined her. "Tell me about your family. You have two sisters, right?"

"And two brothers still living at home." Myra removed her soaked cloth of tealeaves and stirred in a dollop of honey. "I thank God they were too young to fight."

"I always wished I'd had sisters and maybe even another brother."

Myra's brow puckered. "Did your mother die at a young age?"

"She was nearly forty years old, so not too young, I guess." Daviana swished her bag of leaves, watching the water grow darker. "She had trouble carrying some of her babes, though. I hope it's not a family tendency. I'd love to have a houseful of young'uns."

"I don't think your mother's condition will necessarily carry over to you." Myra lifted her cup and tasted it before she answered. "My pa was a doctor, and he had a theory that past diseases might be the cause of some conditions we blame on our family."

"I haven't heard that before. What kinds of diseases?" Daviana set aside her bag of leaves and sipped the cooled tea.

"Measles, smallpox, malaria—"

"Malaria?" Daviana's sharp gasp interrupted the list. "I wonder if Simon knows about that."

Myra shook her head. "Unlikely. I don't know how many doctors agree with the theory, so it's not common knowledge. Pa had planned to do more research with a group of physicians, but he got sick himself and died in '59. It may be years before we know more."

"I'm sorry for your loss." She laid her hand over Myra's. "And not only yours, but the world's. We need more people dedicated to learning about diseases and how to heal them. We should add that to our prayers."

Daviana's conversation with Myra came back to her later in the day while she and Pa sat on the porch, listening to the sounds of nature as the day wound down. Pa's troubling cough had not lessened but seemed to be worse. She said as much, but he shrugged off her comments.

Not willing to be put off, she shifted in her chair. "Myra told me today that her father had been a doctor," she told him as she sifted through her sewing basket. "He had a notion that some of our family health issues might come from diseases we had earlier in life. Were you sickly as a child?"

His brow wrinkled in thought. "No more'n most children, I reckon. I always took longer to recover than my brothers, but Ma said it was 'cause I was so skinny."

She threaded her needle and measured the length before she clipped the thread. "I wonder if Simon's malaria will have any ill effects later on."

"An army doctor told him it might hurt his chances of having children." A spate of coughing kept him from saying more.

Panic threatened to rise in Daviana's chest, making it difficult to take a full breath. So Simon had been warned that his bouts of malaria could render him sterile?

When Pa recovered his breath, Daviana leaned forward. "Simon discussed this with you?"

"Not discussed, just mentioned it in passing, kinda like how you and me are talking now. Nothing in this life is for sure, Daughter. We all learn to take what life hands us and make the best of it. We gotta trust that the good Lord knows what we need and what we can handle."

"You're right. None of us is promised another sunrise."

Still, the thought rankled. Why hadn't Simon mentioned this to her? Did he think it an inappropriate subject to discuss with a female, or did he find it embarrassing to admit to an imperfection?

She should have suspected something, with Simon swooping in to save her and the farm. Didn't most good things in life come with a tradeoff, a sacrifice of sorts? She'd have to decide whether she'd let this knowledge affect her relationship —and her commitment—to Simon.

RANDOLPH COUNTY, ALABAMA

*E*arly the next morning, Simon wandered around the farm. Every acre brought back memories. Climbing into the hayloft to hide from Pa, tumbling down Loblolly Hill in the springtime, and crawling through the high grass to shoot birds in the autumn. He ended up—as he likely intended to, though he never would say so—near the creek that separated the slave cabins from the Big House.

Only a couple of people moved among those wooden structures. An old man sat outside on the stoop of the nearest cabin while a slender woman fastened clothes to a line. For a moment, he imagined the female could be Pansy, though it was the wrong house. Her hair was bound in a kerchief. Her dress hung loose on her slight frame.

Then she turned toward him and waved. In a high-pitched voice, she called a welcome.

Simon startled. How had she seen him, deep among the trees as he was?

At her call, another voice answered from the meadow to his left, not far from his position. Ma's familiar figure strode purposefully toward the woman. When she reached the house, both women went inside.

Simon shook himself. Why had he come here? It wasn't as if he could change the past, and there was no one left he felt comfortable asking about what'd happened after he departed. He'd let them all down somehow. No threats or punishment from Pa or Ma or his old nanny could curb his impulsiveness.

Unfortunately, he still tended to rush in when wisdom dictated caution. Sometimes the best course of action was no action. And in this case, he should leave the past right where it was—buried deep.

The moment he stepped out of the trees to head back, Ma exited the cabin. Her gaze seemed to zero in on him, so he yielded to his fate. She always could see right through any excuse he offered.

When she drew even with him, he fell into step beside her. "You still nursing everyone on the farm?" he asked.

A smile flitted, then disappeared. "What are you doing out this way?" Her eyebrows rose, her eyes drilling him before she glanced away.

He tried to shake off the guilt. He'd done nothing wrong, unless looking for answers was forbidden. Forcing a careless air, he threw his arms out. "Just getting reacquainted with the land. It's been a long time."

"Seven years." Her gaze darted back to him. "You could've come back, you know. When you finished your studies, I mean."

"I had a good job at the law office, another life. I wasn't ready. And then..."

She heaved an unhappy sigh. "The war called your name."

"It was a cause I could get behind. And I couldn't live here again until things changed."

Ma stopped and faced him, worry clear in her eyes under her puckered forehead. "Why are you really out here, Simon?"

He could hedge, but Ma would know. As he scrubbed the back of his neck, his gaze wandered beyond her to the dormant cotton fields. "Looking for answers."

Her arm swept wide to include the woods and meadow where they stood. "There are no answers here that will bring you peace." She patted his chest. "This is where peace is found."

A knot formed in his throat. "I'm not the prodigal son now, Ma. Somewhere in Northeast Georgia, God knocked some sense into my head, and it found the way to my heart."

She flashed a grin, the action deepening the grooves beside her mouth. She took a few steps toward the house, then stopped when he didn't follow. "Simon? What is it?"

His chest ached, and pressure built behind his eyes. "I just need to know what happened when I left here. How bad did I mess up?"

"Oh, Simon. Have you been carrying that burden all this time?" Her work-worn hands gripped his shoulders as she shook her head. "Perhaps you weren't the one who messed up at all. It was the rest of us."

A flock of geese flew overhead, their honking the only sound Simon registered as he stared at the woman who loved him as her own. The woman Pa had chosen to mother his three sons when his first wife died.

"What do you mean, the rest of you messed up?" He paced away so he wouldn't have to see the disappointment on her face —again. "I was wrong to go into Pansy's cabin that day. I knew Pa would have my hide, but I didn't care. I tossed aside every teaching y'all instilled in me and let my desire overrule my head." Tears pricked his eyes as he turned her way. "I never even bothered to say I'm sorry—not that day nor later in my letters. Regret ate at me, but I figured it was too late. The damage had been done, not only to her but to everyone on the farm. By ignoring Pa's rules, I hurt the family name, maybe reduced his authority with the slaves and his influence in the community."

Ma closed the gap between them and settled her hand on his shoulder. "Now that you've had your say, let me have mine. There's a good reason your pa is so strong about respecting everyone, regardless of color or status. I should say, several reasons, one of which is the way he was raised. Another is his deep faith."

"I know, Ma, and nobody is more respected in these parts than John McNeil."

She held up a trembling hand to stop his words. "One more reason is what happened to me before we married. You deserve to know the truth as the others do now." A deep sigh escaped before she continued. "John isn't Troy's biological father."

Stunned, Simon tried to get beyond her words. Pa's first wife, Mary Catherine, had died when Simon was so young he didn't remember her. Had Ma been married before too? There was another possibility. "Troy is adopted?"

A sad smile played on her lips. "In a manner of speaking, I guess he is. By your pa. Troy is *my* son by another man I fell in love with before your pa and I married. When I discovered I was carrying a child and had no word from that man and no way to contact him, I ran to John."

Attempting to process this new information, Simon started toward the house again. Ma strolled beside him, giving him time to come to terms with what she'd revealed. "But why would a man leave you, knowing you were—"

"He didn't know, and he'd planned to come back for me

when his job allowed. I learned only recently that he was injured and unable to travel until much later. By that time, John and I were married, and I loved your pa as much as I thought I'd loved Ethan."

"Why'd you choose Pa? Aren't y'all distant cousins?"

"Yes, and we were friends. He needed a mother for you boys, and I already loved y'all."

A fresh appreciation for his father washed over Simon. "Pa never treated Troy any differently than the rest of us."

"No, he didn't. From the moment we said our vows, John claimed Troy as his own. Now maybe you can understand why your pa was strong on those rules."

His mind worked its way back to her earlier statement. "You said y'all might've messed up. What did you mean by that?"

"A couple months after we sent you off, Pansy asked to speak to John and me. She admitted she'd set you up, knowing how you were drawn to her. What she'd hoped was you would run up north with her and marry her when she told you she was with child."

Alarm sizzled through his veins. "With child? But, Ma, I never—"

"I know, I know. She said you didn't, but she was hoping you would give in that day. Then she could claim the baby was yours."

From hot to cold. Simon froze and demanded, "Whose was it?"

Ma pressed her lips together. "I promised not to say, but I believe your pa will tell you if you ask him."

HALL COUNTY, GEORGIA

*C*hores kept Daviana busy Wednesday morning. The especially small load of clothes to be washed taunted her about Simon's absence—as if she needed the reminder—so she took down all the curtains and added them to the wash.

Pa observed her actions and stayed out of her way until the midday meal. By then, she'd exhausted her need for activity. She sank into her chair at the table. "I'm sorry for my surliness this morning. You don't have to stay out in the hot sun to avoid me this afternoon."

He patted her hand. "Good to know. I don't expect your mood had anything to do with Simon bein' gone, did it?"

"Of course not." She busied herself shredding cornbread into her greens so she'd avoid Pa's gaze. "I just took a look around the house and realized how much needed to be done."

"Uh-huh." He grinned but said no more during the meal. When he finished, Pa drummed his fingers on the table. "Come sit with me on the porch a few minutes. The dishes'll wait."

The serious tone of his voice, coupled with the anxious flutter of his hands, guaranteed Daviana would comply. She set the dishes in the sink, wiped her hands on a towel, and followed him out the door.

Outside, the clear blue sky offered no respite from the sun's heat. Summer wouldn't release its hold on the county for another month or more. Daviana slid her chair an inch closer to Pa's and tried to shake off her apprehension.

Pa clutched the arms of his chair and smashed his lips together, as if battling to keep the words from being said. He shifted in his chair and faced her. Her heart turned over at the glimmer of tears.

"Simon wanted me to tell you the truth about my sickness. He said you're a strong woman, and I believe he's right. You've held up under losing your mama, taking care of Albert when he lost his mama and Lionel went off to war, then losing them both when they lit out for the West. I wanted to spare you, but I reckon there's no way to shield those we love from sorrow. It's part of life."

Daviana clenched her hands in her lap. "What about your sickness? Have you had a doctor examine you to determine what's wrong?"

"I saw a doctor last winter. You remember when we thought Albert might've broke his foot 'cause the swellin' wouldn't go down?"

She gave a single nod. "That's when I was laid up with a cold, and you wouldn't let me go with you. So you let the doctor examine you then?"

Pa huffed. "I didn't *let* him do nothin'. He held my grandson hostage until I agreed to it."

Wise doctor. "And what did he tell you?"

"He said not to expect to get better. I've likely got a cancerous growth around my lungs. That's why I've lost weight and spit up blood at times. The thing is, doctors don't know what causes it or how to cure it. Doc said I could live another ten years, or I could go tomorrow."

Willing away the tears that threatened, Daviana reached for his hand. "Then we'll pray for as many years as the Lord will give you."

He squeezed her hand. "That night Simon stopped by, not an hour before, I'd asked God to send someone to take care of you, in case my time is short. I could hardly believe it when the answer came so quick. I reckon God was already working on that before I asked."

The approach of a rider prevented Daviana's answer. Rather than Kyle riding the familiar gray horse, however, Jasper brought the animal close to the porch. The way he lifted his hat and grinned put Daviana in mind of a traveling salesman who'd come through the area last spring, promising miracles from the elixir he sold.

"Hello, Rufus, Dottie. I brung you a gift for your stew pot." He dismounted and unhooked a string of fish from his saddle. He held it aloft, admiring the silvery catch.

Pa groaned as he left his chair and tottered to the porch edge. "That's right neighborly of you, Jasper. Where'd you find such good specimens?"

"Oh, I got a secret spot not far away." He surrendered the catch to Pa and shot a glance at Daviana. "We all have our secrets, don't we?"

Ignoring the comment, Pa shifted so as to put himself between her and Jasper. Daviana held her breath. Pa wouldn't leave to clean the fish or invite Jasper to stay, would he? It was the neighborly thing to do, but this was Jasper.

Jasper peered around Pa. "Where's that Yankee feller you called your fiancé? Haven't seen him around the area in a while. Did he run off and leave you?"

Ready for the question, she answered easily. "Simon has taken a room in town. He spends some time each day setting it up to use as an office."

"Is 'at so?" Jasper's eyes narrowed. "He don't come around to help with the farm work every day? Not much help, is he?"

Pa transferred the string of fish to his other hand, close enough to Jasper's face to capture his attention. "Simon's been a big help, and he's hired two good workers. I suspect it'll take him a few days to get his law office set up in town."

"Law office? What's a Union soldier know about law in the South?" He spat into the yard to punctuate his comment.

Daviana lifted her chin. "I expect he knows plenty about Federal law, and we'd all do well to remember that Georgia is now under their jurisdiction."

With a step backward, Jasper muttered under his breath and adjusted his fedora. "Well, I reckon you folks got plenty of work to do, so I'll be goin'." He swung onto his horse and grinned. "Enjoy the fish."

As he rode away, Pa asked Daviana, "What was that he mumbled?"

"I didn't catch it, but I doubt it was complimentary. Now, are you gonna clean those fish or toss them to Minnow?"

"I'll clean 'em. Might feed one to Minnow as a test, though. I can't see Jasper offering us anything without some hidden motive."

CHAPTER 15

Ma's revelations of that morning kept playing through Simon's mind. He waited until midafternoon to approach Pa in his office. Paul Senior had gone to work in the field, Ma and P.J. were at the new school in town, and Jane was teaching Lucy to crochet.

Coffee cup in one hand, Simon knocked on the frame of Pa's open office door. The room was so small, Simon hesitated to enter. He'd avoided close places since his time at Libby. He gripped the cup in both hands and inhaled a fortifying breath as he stepped inside.

Opposite the fireplace, a square window revealed a blue sky beyond the dark-green leaves of Ma's favorite magnolia. A desk sat in the middle of the floor with neat piles of papers stacked on top and chairs of varying style and age positioned to face it.

Pa sat in the worn leather chair that caused a variety of memories to skitter through Simon's mind. Standing in the corner while Pa administered lashes for misbehavior. Sneaking in here to avoid his brothers finding him during a game of hide and seek. Even sitting in Pa's chair to pretend he was the one in charge.

The difference in reasons for his last session and this one wasn't lost on him. His father must have had the same thought.

"You're a bit beyond my chastisement anymore." Pa beckoned him forward. "But you seem to be working through some serious questions these days."

Simon sat on the opposite side of the desk and sipped his coffee before answering. "Ma told you about our conversation."

"You knew she would." Pa waited as he drank from his own cup.

Raising a hand, Simon hurried to explain. "My only aim in coming home was to reconnect with you and Ma, and my brothers. Being here, though..." He shook his head. "It stirred up those questions."

Pa leaned back in his chair. "A natural occurrence, I think. You left in a time of turmoil, and none of us knew everything that was going on at the time."

"I guess I should start with an apology for causing you and Ma such grief."

Pa heaved a sigh. "I'm afraid the blame for what happened falls on me."

Simon scoffed. "I don't see how that could be."

"The details are fuzzy now, but I recall we had a busy harvest the preceding season, so some folks were caught shorthanded. It wasn't unusual for neighbors to lend our field hands or household help to others now and then. When Asa Russell asked for help in the house after his wife fell ill, I sent Pansy over for a few days to work in his kitchen. As far as I knew, he'd never mistreated any of his people, so I wasn't concerned for her safety. She spent the week and returned to us to take up her duties here. She never gave an indication of bein' abused."

This wasn't at all what Simon expected to hear. "Are you

telling me that Mr. Russell took advantage of her? And she never said a word about it?"

Pa nodded, grief etched into his face. "He was crafty. He threatened her, said he'd throw the blame on you if she told anyone. You hadn't bothered to keep your feelings for the girl secret, and Asa had never been known to abuse anyone in his employ, so his threats worked."

Revulsion rocked Simon. Bile churned in his stomach. He stood and paced to the window, edging aside the curtain to reveal clouds scuttling over the fields. "Pansy was protecting me? But the day Paul caught me coming from her cabin, she'd talked about us running away together."

Pa's chuckle held no humor. "I reckon she figured it to be her only chance to get away. She was smart enough to know he'd come after her again if she stayed here. However, that all blew apart when Asa's wife shot him."

Whirling around, Simon stared at his father. "She what? How did that happen?" One surprise after another. His memory of both the Russells only conjured up a mild-mannered couple with no children.

"According to what Mrs. Russell told the sheriff and the judge, she caught him attacking another girl, and she shot to injure him so he'd stop. Her aim wavered, and the bullet hit his spine and paralyzed him. He lingered a while, long enough to confess his sins, which included forcing Pansy and a couple of others over the years."

"What happened to Mrs. Russell?"

Pa's fingers tapped the desktop. "She sold her place and moved away. The doctor testified that Asa's cause of death was from the infection that set in, which he said could have come from the bullet wound or the deep fingernail scratches on his body."

Simon chewed on his bottom lip. "Not enough evidence to

convict her." He tried to imagine how the shocking news had spread in the community.

Pa drained his coffee cup and set it down. "Soon as Pansy heard he was dead, she told your ma what'd happened."

"But why did no one write to me and tell me then?"

Pa stood and looked him in the eye. "You were settled in and deep in your studies. Pansy and Jem had married, and she was content. With Asa dead and you far away, there was no need to rehash all that in a letter. We *all* thought it best to leave the matter settled."

"I see." From his current perspective, he could understand their concern. He'd been a volatile youth, passionate to extreme on some matters. They must've feared he might hie himself to Alabama and create even more havoc.

Still, though Pa offered to accept responsibility, the blame lay squarely with Simon for his indiscretion. He was man enough to admit it.

Unfortunately, some of those who could grant him forgiveness had moved away. Could God help him move beyond such condemnation?

HALL COUNTY, GEORGIA

Sultry weather made for a miserable day. Daviana had traipsed between the kitchen and the back yard a dozen times, eyeing the sky for a sign of relief. None had showed up yet.

Neither had any word from Simon to announce his safe arrival on his trip. He'd been gone six days, surely long enough to have reached his home, unless he'd been waylaid.

Unable to sit still enough to sew, she'd taken the discarded portion from her sourdough batter and started making an extra loaf of bread. It was easy to spend her frustration on the pitiful lump of dough.

"Should've known he'd forget." She pounded the dough. "Men always do. 'I'll think of you every day,' he said." She pounded the dough. "Hogwash. Good thing I put him off till— oh, Lord, what if he had another spell of malaria?"

She paused her muttering and kneading as another sound caught her ear. What was that wheezing and whistling outside? "Pa?"

A clatter on the back porch overrode the whining. Daviana rubbed the clinging dough from her fingers with some loose flour and stepped outside. A gust of wind pushed her skirts to one side and sent loose tendrils of hair across her face. Dark clouds billowed in the west, roiling and speeding in her direction. The relief she'd prayed for might be worse than the heat.

She left the porch and headed toward the field where Pa had said he and the hands would be working. Nobody should be outside when the storm hit. Wind was bad enough, but it could bring dangerous lightning and hail with it.

"Lord, please protect us all, and if You would, limit the damage to our crops. We need them to sustain us through the fall and winter."

She had to press against the wind now. With her head down against the onslaught, she ran straight into Pa's outstretched arms.

"Get back in the house," he shouted.

"What about Jude and Titus?"

"They're takin' shelter in the cave over by the creek. They'll be fine. We'll have to ride it out here."

Pa hooked his arm around her, and together they hurried as the wind first drove them, then switched tactics and hampered their progress. At last, they reached the back porch. Pa grabbed the door and forced it closed behind them right as the first hail stones hit.

"I'll get the chairs in off the front. Get a blanket off your bed and sit in the hallway."

"But Pa, what about—"

"No time to argue, Dottie. Do as I say."

Fear clawed at Daviana's throat. They'd had bad storms before, and Pa always took them in stride. Something about this one had him worried. She pulled the quilt from her bed and carried it to the hallway. The eerie wailing of the wind conjured up images of ghosts and headless riders while the hail and the banging front door sounded like those monsters asking to come in.

With the quilt over her head, she paced between the bedrooms, silently urging Pa to hurry. One loud bang reduced the noise level and announced Pa's success.

Like a shadow in flickering lamplight, he wavered where the front room merged with the dining area. He started her way, then stopped and crumpled to the floor.

RANDOLPH COUNTY, ALABAMA

Simon inhaled a long breath of sweet, rain-cleansed air. It echoed the cleansing that forgiveness brought to his soul. Yesterday's discussions had been painful but beneficial.

In the rocking chair beside him, Ma seemed to read his thoughts. "Nothing like the freshness after a storm, is there? I bet you didn't get to sit on the porch and watch storms up in Cincinnati, did you?"

He chuckled. "Sure didn't and couldn't have. You'd hardly have room for a rocking chair on the porch where I lived. Plus, my room was on the third floor above the law office."

"City living has its advantages," Ma said, "but I much prefer the country life, even with the problems it brings. Such as John and Paul having to round up the piglets from that crazy sow."

"P.J. seemed to enjoy it, even if it did mean an extra bath." Simon gazed out over the yard. "I'm glad the horses were already put up when the lightning struck. I'd hate to have to spend my time here raising a new barn."

Ma reared back in her chair and stared at him. "What d'you mean, your time here? You planning to leave again?"

Simon stopped his rocking and tried to contain his smile as he faced her. "I've been waiting for the right time to tell you. I met this girl on my way home."

"I see." She narrowed her eyes. "Exactly where on your way home? Don't tell me you'll be going halfway across the country to see her every month or two."

"No, ma'am, not too far. She lives in northeast Georgia. It only took me four days of good riding to get here from there."

"I suppose that's where your mind has been when you get that faraway look in your eye." Her mouth twitched with the glimmer of a smile. "So you're seriously thinking about courting this Georgia girl?"

"I've asked her to marry me." Simon's chest warmed as he said it. "If not for her father, I would've married her and brought her with me."

A frown brought her eyebrows down. "Is he against the marriage? Just how long did you tarry in Georgia before you decided to come home?"

Simon rushed to assure her. "No, Rufus is fine with us marrying, but he's not well, and there's no one else to help but Davi. Well, there're the workers I hired before I left, but that's not the same as family."

"How long were you with them? What did you say her name was?"

He sighed. Trust Ma to demand the full story. "Her name is Athdara Daviana Spalding. What happened was I had a spell of malaria the night I stopped at their house, and Davi took care of me. I was there about ten days."

"And you asked her to marry you after ten days? Simon—" She broke off, stood, and paced to the end of the porch. She turned around with her arms crossed, her back against the porch rail. "I'd hoped you'd outgrow your impulsive nature as you matured. It seems that's not the case. I can only pray it doesn't bring you more trouble and sorrow."

Simon tensed. Seeing Ma, his constant champion, upset over the matter was not what he'd expected. It didn't offer much hope that Pa and Paul would take the news well. He'd better prepare for a battle of wills, especially when they learned his plans for his share of the farm.

~

HALL COUNTY, GEORGIA

The quilt fell from Daviana's shoulders as she rushed to her father's side. "Pa, what happened? Where are you hurt?"

She knelt at his side and ran her hands over his face, his arms and legs. Water seeped from his clothes onto the floor. His gray hair looked dark plastered to his head, and trickles ran into his ears and beard. She could find no evidence of injury in her cursory examination.

A moan brought her back to his face. His eyes fluttered and focused on her.

Relieved at the signs of consciousness, she sighed and patted his chest. "Where do you hurt, Pa? I don't see any blood, and all your bones seem intact."

He blinked and lifted a shaky hand. "Head."

"Hmm. Must've got hit on the back. Can you sit up?"

She helped him struggle into a sitting position where he

could lean against the sofa. With little light filtering through the window, she'd have to rely on her fingers to find the problem. In moments, she found a lump and the stickiness that indicated bleeding.

"Pa, I need to get a wet cloth and a lamp so I can see how to treat it." She touched his shoulder as she rose. "You stay here and rest. I'll be right back."

In the kitchen, she filled a bowl with water and dropped in a cloth, her lips moving silently in a litany of prayer for her father's health and her own abilities to care for him. When she returned and found him nearly prone on the floor, she couldn't stop the cry of anguish. Had he passed out?

Daviana shook his shoulder, and he lifted his head. "Here, Pa. Let's get you on the sofa."

He moved slowly, touched a finger to his brow, and muttered, "Dizzy."

"All right, just take it slow." After a couple of tries, they got him on the couch, and Daviana lit the lamp on the side table. As tenderly as she could, she dabbed around the goose-egg-sized swelling, wiping the blood away. At least the bleeding seemed to have stopped.

When she started to move away, Pa grabbed her wrist and vomited into the bowl she held. "S-s-sorry. Sick."

"It's all right, Pa. I'll throw this out and bring you a clean cloth for your mouth."

She hurried to the back door and tossed the waste into the bushes. Warm rain fell in gentle sheets like a blessing. When had the hail ceased and the wind stopped howling? Preoccupied with Pa's injury, she'd failed to detect the change.

Ah, if only he hadn't gone outside to get those blasted chairs.

RANDOLPH COUNTY, ALABAMA

When Ma called his name from the barn door, Simon turned from saddling the chestnut gelding. Riding over to see Henry and Rupert would give his parents and Paul time to adjust to his announcement about making his home in Georgia.

"Take this jacket to Rupert, please. I fixed the tear in the pocket. He's liable to need it soon. And tell Henry we'll expect them both to come for Sunday dinner after church." She turned to go, then stopped. "I'm sorry if you felt as though you were on the witness stand last night, having to defend yourself. I should've kept your news to myself."

Simon sighed. It was just like Ma to take the blame for last night's clash of opinions.

Pa didn't hide his disappointment that Simon wouldn't be staying to work his portion of the farm, especially after being gone so long.

Paul's reaction bordered on anger, criticizing Simon's tendency to rush into a situation without careful analysis. Although Simon offered to work out an agreement on the division of land, Paul wasn't mollified, and the atmosphere remained tense.

Simon crossed the hay-strewn floor to where she stood. "It's not your fault, Ma. It was bound to come up sooner or later, and I wasn't surprised by Paul's attitude. A day at Uncle Henry's was always part of my plan, anyway."

She nodded, but the worry lines still furrowed her brow. "You have a good visit. Will you be back for supper?"

"More likely, it'll be tomorrow." He mounted the horse. "I need to go by town first, as I should've already sent Davi a telegram to let her know I got here safely."

Half an hour later, he wrote out his message for the telegraph operator to send. The young man peered over his spectacles at Simon and tapped the note. "Where is Gainesville, Georgia? I heard yesterday's storm hit pretty hard on some of the areas east of Atlanta. Wires might be down in places, but I'll give it a try."

Simon silently scolded himself for procrastinating. "Gainesville is about fifty miles northeast of Atlanta. I have business at the bank, so I'll check back with you later."

The news about the storm stayed on Simon's mind as he made his way to the bank. Mr. Gilford, the bank president, fiddled with his keys at the door, then swung it open.

"Morning, Mr. Gilford."

The older man turned and eyed him. "Rupert?"

Simon shook his head. Why did so many people mistake him for his brother? "No, sir. I'm Simon McNeil, the one who's had half of my paycheck deposited here every month." He waited to see whether Southern loyalty would outweigh the man's shrewd judgment for business.

A broad smile stretched across the banker's florid face, and he stretched out his hand in welcome. "Well, good to meet ya, Simon. You've grown up since I last saw ya. Come in, come in." The businessman led the way, leaving the door open as he lit a lamp on a nearby table.

Another man passed Simon on his way inside and scurried to man a service window. Mr. Gilford waved him off. "I'll take care of this one, Dabney."

Good. Simon wouldn't have to explain himself twice, and he trusted the bank president to handle his request properly, despite the fact Simon planned to move a large portion of his funds to Georgia.

Hall County, Georgia

A loud banging on the back door alternated with someone calling her name. Daviana sat up and stared at the mess scattered about her in the front room where she'd spent the night. Light filtered through the curtains, announcing an end to her solitary vigil.

Her gaze went to Pa, and she scooted over the floor to check on him. His forehead was warm, but he must be sleeping deeply if that noise didn't wake him.

"Dottie. Rufus." The call came again. "Are y'all in there?"

God bless Kyle for coming to check on them. Daviana pushed to her feet and stumbled to the kitchen. When she opened the door, Kyle sagged against the wall. Full daylight revealed a blue sky behind him, with scattered limbs and small puddles as evidence of yesterday's storm.

"Thank heavens." He put one hand to his chest. "I was afraid y'all might've been blown away." His eyes raked her in a hurried assessment. "What happened here?"

Unbidden tears filled Daviana's eyes. "Oh, Kyle. I didn't know what to do. Pa's hurt. I couldn't bear to leave him and take a chance on him gettin' worse."

"Where is he?" Kyle pushed his way inside, and she pointed to the front room.

"On the sofa. Something hit his head during the storm. He passed out, then he was dizzy and sick, and he started runnin' a fever."

Kyle peered at the sleeping form. He touched Pa's forehead, then laid his hand on Pa's back for a moment. He turned to Daviana with a frown. "I'm goin' for the doctor, but first, I'll go by home and get Myra. She can come and sit with Rufus while you get cleaned up."

Daviana glanced at her dress, rumpled and stained where she'd spilled tea during the night, in addition to spots of blood, and shook her head at the sight. She reached to touch his arm, then pulled back so as not to share her filth. "Thank you, Kyle. Thank you for being such a good friend."

As soon as he left, she did what she could to set the room to rights, moving quietly lest she disturb Pa. Ma had always said sleep was good for healing, but doubt crept in. Hopefully, the doctor would have some answers.

When Myra arrived, she helped Daviana move the chairs back to the porch and sweep up the dirt and mud tracked inside. Then she shooed Daviana to her room. "You go wash and change. I'd say you should lie down and sleep, but I know you won't rest until you talk to the doctor."

Thankful for her friend's understanding, Daviana hurried through her morning ritual and returned to the room. "Has he stirred at all?"

"No," Myra said. "Moaned a little, but that's all. Hey..." She dug into her reticule. "I brought you a couple of boiled eggs. It's all I could grab before Kyle rushed me out the door. You should eat."

Daviana accepted the thoughtful offering and turned to the kitchen. "I'll make us some coffee."

Nearly two hours later, Kyle showed up with Dr. Meadows. Kyle and Myra stayed with Daviana while she answered the doctor's questions. Pa awakened, and the doctor asked them for privacy to examine his patient.

A quarter hour passed before Dr. Meadows met them in the kitchen, placing his black bag on the table. "Whatever struck Rufus on the head hit him hard. He has a concussion. There's not much we can do for a head injury, but that's not what worries me. With the illness he's had for a while, he'll be more susceptible to infection."

Daviana swayed. "What can I do for him?"

"Keep a close eye on him. Don't let his fever get too high. And pray." He gave her a half-full bottle of medicine. "That's for the pain. Just put a teaspoon of it in a glass of water." He picked up his bag. "I'll check back in a couple of days, but send for me if he seems to be going downhill."

Myra hugged Daviana while Kyle walked outside with the doctor. "I'm so sorry this has happened," Myra said. "You know that Kyle and I will help you take care of Mr. Rufus."

"Thank you." Daviana sniffed and wiped her wet cheeks. "Did y'all have much damage at your house? Oh, Myra, what about Jude and Titus? I haven't even checked on them. And where is Minnow? I'm so negligent."

And why hadn't she heard from Simon? Could he be lying somewhere hurt and unable to return?

A week ago, even yesterday, her life had been simple, the future promising. Now her plans were falling apart. That lovely future wouldn't exist without Simon or Pa. One fast-moving storm had ripped off more than a few tree limbs. For her, it had changed everything.

CHAPTER 16

Simon's stomach rumbled on the way to Uncle Henry's house. He should have gone to the hotel and eaten there, but he didn't want to spend any more time in town. He'd lost a good hour roaming the mercantile while he waited to hear whether his telegraph had gone through.

Now he was as hungry for welcoming faces as he was for nourishment. The sprawling, single-story house that'd been like a second home spread its wings in welcome. Aunt June's flower beds looked to be thriving. Someone other than Uncle Henry and Rupert must tend to that. Despite the McNeil men's talent for farming, they didn't bother much with flowers.

Several yards away, the lanky brown frame of a young boy dropped from a stout hickory tree and scampered toward the house. "Horse 'n' rider!" he called.

Rupert came around the corner of the house the same moment that Simon dismounted. Rupert skidded to a stop, then lunged for him. "By all that's holy, Simon! When did you get here?"

The squeak of the barn door interrupted Simon's answer. They both turned to greet Henry, who lumbered toward them with a cackle. "Hoowee, lookee there! Ain't you a sight to behold, boy?"

Simon loosened his hold on Rupert and greeted his uncle with a handshake and hug. The years had taken a toll on Henry —or maybe it was the loss of his wife two years ago that had brought the change. His hair had turned pure white, and his gait seemed slow and uneven.

"Should you be out here working? I heard you gave everybody a scare not long ago."

Uncle Henry's bushy eyebrows lowered. "You know better. I plan to work until the day the Lord calls me home."

Behind Uncle Henry, a large black man of indeterminate age emerged from the barn, joined the boy from the tree, both watching the reunion. Simon tilted his head toward the two. "That's some lookout you got there, Henry. We could've used him in the army."

"You're right about that." Uncle Henry gestured between them. "The scout's name is Levi, and that's his grandfather, Malachi. And this here"—he gripped Simon's shoulder and addressed the other two—"is Simon, Rupert's brother who's been away a long time."

With the introductions and handshakes done, Uncle Henry pointed to the porch. "Let's go in the house and visit over some good food."

"Then I guess somebody else is cooking besides any of us?" Simon asked.

Rupert chuckled. "That would be Jewel, Levi's mother, and she lives up to her name."

"Y'all go in and warn her while I put up the horse." Simon grinned at Malachi's grandson. "Maybe Levi can help me?"

The boy's face brightened. "I be a good helper."

Once they settled the horse, Levi escorted Simon into the

house and back to the dining table. Henry sat at the head with Rupert to his left on a bench. The aroma of turnip greens and cornbread drifted from the dishes in the center.

The tall black woman greeted Levi and Simon as she laid out an extra plate and utensils. Levi grabbed her hand. "Mam, this be Mistah Simon. Don't he look just like Mistah Rupert?"

Simon laughed. "I've been told so a couple of times recently."

Jewel shook her head, but a smile played about her lips. "Mind your manners, Levi. Now go wash up and git to the workin' folks' table. You want buttermilk or tea, Mistah Simon?"

"Buttermilk, please." He joined Henry and Rupert at the dining table.

Uncle Henry prayed over the food, then passed a bowl of greens to Simon. "I suppose you stopped by your folks first. Everyone all right there?"

"Yes, sir. I was already there when the storm hit. Thankfully, it didn't do much damage. How did you fare?"

"Had a couple of weak pine trees come down, is all," Uncle Henry said.

Conversation gave way to simple table requests and comments on the delicious meal for a while.

Rupert, always first to finish, pushed his plate away and studied Simon. "You and Paul get along all right?"

With studied nonchalance, Simon took a sip of buttermilk before he answered. "For all of two days. Until I told everyone my plans."

Rupert raised his eyebrows. "You have plans?"

Uncle Henry stifled a chuckle, then leveled a serious gaze at Simon. "I guess you've grown up, then. What about your plans?"

Simon shifted. "On my way home, you see, I met this girl— young woman, I should say...."

"Oh ho!" Uncle Henry chortled. He traded smiles with Rupert and winked. "Now we know why it took you so long to make it home. But where is this girl?"

"She lives in Northeast Georgia, Hall County, a little farther than a day's ride from Atlanta. Her pa has a small farm, which she'll inherit, at least in part, since her brother headed west when the Confederates cut him loose. I plan to marry her and settle down there."

Uncle Henry lifted his plate toward Jewel, who waited at the doorway between the dining area and the kitchen. "I can't see anything wrong with that plan, but I can see how your folks might not agree. You just got home after several years away and tell 'em you're leaving again. But tell us about this girl. What's her name?"

Simon grinned. "Athdara Daviana Spalding."

Jewel gasped and then clapped a hand to her mouth. "So-sorry, I was just lookin' to see if y'all was finished." She pinned Simon with her stare. "Did you say Dottie Spalding?"

He didn't point out the difference in the names. How did this woman know Davi? "Yes, ma'am."

Jewel carefully stacked empty plates on the table. "She live next to a family called Dunaway?"

"That's right." How strange to meet someone who knew Davi here, so close to his home. "Am I to understand you knew Davi?"

"It's where me and Pap was 'fore I was sent to Macon." She turned to Henry. "That's how we got separated, you see."

Anger surged through Simon on behalf of the family he'd just met. "The Dunaways sold you away from your father? When was this?"

She slanted a look toward the kitchen where she'd taken her meal with Levi and Malachi. "Nine years ago when Old Dunaway found out I was carryin'."

"Malachi set out to find her as soon as he could move freely in Georgia," Rupert said. "Took him about three months because Jewel got traded again during those years."

Simon worked his jaw to contain his anger at the injustices these people had suffered. When he could speak again, he tried to offer a smile. "Well, I'm glad he finally found you."

"About Miss Dottie…" Jewel licked her lips as if afraid to ask again. "You really aimin' to marry her?"

"Just as soon as I make it back to Hall County. If she'll have me."

"Good. You take care of Miss Dottie, please. My pap'll tell you. Keep her away from that no-good Jasper."

Simon took the woman's message to heart and went in search of Malachi while Henry and Rupert gabbed with a neighbor who dropped by. Levi directed Simon to the barn where he found the older man mending a harness in the last stall.

"Hey, Malachi. Mind if I ask you about your experiences back on the Dunaway farm in Hall County?"

Malachi's eyes rounded, and Simon hastened to explain. "You may not have heard us during the meal talking about my engagement to Miss Spalding. My only reason for asking is so I can protect her. Jewel said I should ask you about Jasper." Simon upturned a wooden bucket and propped one foot on it while he leaned against the stall partition. "You have nothing to fear from me, sir. I just need to understand the situation. Davi —Miss Spalding—does everything she can to avoid Jasper, and yet she's good friends with his brother, Kyle, who just returned home."

Surprise lit Malachi's weathered face. "We heard Mistah Kyle was dead. He's alive?"

"I saw him and talked to him myself before I left. The reports confused him with someone else."

Malachi shifted on his chair and set aside the harness. "That's good. Mistah Kyle watched out for Miss Dottie after she tol' him 'bout Jasper takin' her to that cave, and her hardly more'n a chile."

Simon's indrawn breath hissed. "What happened?"

"The Good Lord allowed me to see 'em. I followed, quiet-like, picked up a big rock and—" He cupped his hands and swung them downward. Grief colored his voice when he continued. "A hard knock on his head was mild punishment for what he done to my Jewel." His focus jerked back to Simon. "He always wanted the women, 'specially the young ones, and the land. Don't trust him to do right by either one."

Simon straightened and offered Malachi his hand. "Thank you for telling me. I'll be on guard." Hopefully, Kyle would resume his protective position while Simon was gone, but already, Simon was considering returning sooner than planned.

~

HALL COUNTY, GEORGIA

Hours passed in a haze as Daviana tended to Pa and did what little she could to keep the farm going. What a blessing to have good friends like Kyle and Myra, who checked on her a few times each day. Kyle conferred with Jude and Titus about the farm work, relaying messages back and forth, while Myra helped with the housework and cooked up vegetable broth for Pa.

Reverend Benson and his wife came Sunday after church to pray for Pa, having learned of his condition from Dr. Meadows. At the end of their brief visit, Daviana walked outside with them.

Mrs. Benson gently chided Daviana for not calling on the church folks for assistance. "You know we take care of our own, so you can expect a few of the ladies to bring you a meal or offer to help with your laundry or other chores."

The pastor made a show of glancing around the homestead. "Where's that young man of yours? I heard he'd claimed a room in the courthouse for an office, but I haven't seen him around in a week or so."

Caught off-guard, Daviana stumbled over her answer. "Simon had to go over ...toward Atlanta. He wasn't here when the storm came through...might've run into it on his way. I can only pray he got somewhere safe, so he's not delayed in returning."

Mrs. Benson patted her hand. "Ah, no wonder you're distressed, worryin' about him and your pa. We'll keep him in our prayers too."

They drove off, and Daviana leaned against a post on the porch, searching for a measure of peace in nature's calm. A red bird flew from a tree branch to the juniper bush and flitted in first one direction, then another, as if he searched for something. How wonderful it must be to take flight and go anywhere, concerned only for one's daily food—and predators, like Minnow who also watched the cheery fellow.

Beyond the tree, fluffy clouds floated across the sky, its blue reminding her of Simon's eyes. The crushing weight of sorrow nearly took her breath. What would she do if Pa died, if Simon never returned?

The door opened behind her, and Myra came to the rail beside Daviana. "He'll be back, Davi. I know he will."

The old feelings of insignificance gave way to despair. "How can you know? He's not tied to me. I wouldn't agree to the wedding until he'd gone home. Maybe he decided returning was too much trouble, even with the promise of the land." Or maybe he'd found someone who restored a lost dream. Dreams didn't die easily.

Myra turned to lean against the rail. "I think you should let

Kyle send him a telegram, so he'll know what's happened. Simon seemed quite fond of Mr. Rufus, and I think he'd want to be here, especially if your pa doesn't pull through."

"But I don't know for sure he made it home. He hasn't sent me word as he promised to. What would his family think to get such a message?"

"And so you'd punish Simon for that oversight by not attempting to contact him."

That did make it sound as if she was pouting like a spoiled child.

Myra continued her persuasion. "At least if you send him word, he can't blame you if he misses saying goodbye to your pa."

Daviana sighed and embraced Myra. "You're right. What did I do to deserve such a good friend as you?"

With a pat of approval, Myra led her inside. "Let's go tell Kyle. He can go to the telegraph office first thing in the morning."

Daviana went back to check on Pa. He'd fallen asleep again after the Bensons left. The fever had abated, and he was resting more easily than before.

Why did the men in her life always leave? Kyle, Lionel, Simon. Not only did they leave, they seemed to drop out of her life without further contact.

But Kyle had come back. Maybe another miracle would take place. She could surely use one.

~

RANDOLPH COUNTY, ALABAMA

The prospect of Sunday dinner with most of the family gathered had produced as much anxiety as anticipation in Simon. He'd reminded himself it could be several months before such an opportunity came again, so he should make the best of it. Also he needed to smooth the way before he brought Davi to visit.

After church, Simon shook hands with half the congregation. Some extended a hearty welcome, but others seemed wary of his return. At least no one accused him of betraying his heritage, as Paul had once implied they would.

On the ride with Uncle Henry and Rupert to his parents' house, Simon mentioned one noticeable absence. "I didn't see Uncle Ellis nor any of his young'uns today. Don't they still come to church here?"

"No," Uncle Henry said, "they started going to the new Methodist church in town. It's a mile closer for them, and I believe his oldest boy is courtin' one of the preacher's daughters."

"Do you reckon they'll come to Pa's for dinner?" Simon tried to act unconcerned, but Uncle Ellis had been in the Confederate ranks and, according to Troy, had spent time in the Union prison at Camp Chase. If he showed up, keeping the conversation off the war would be even more challenging. Any discussion might again spiral into a general disapproval of Simon's past and his current plans.

"Not likely." Rupert maneuvered the wagon around a puddle left from the recent rains. "I think Uncle Ellis has his eye on the banker's widowed niece."

Contrary to Rupert's prediction, Uncle Ellis drove his buggy into the yard minutes after their arrival. He turned the reins over to his younger son and headed straight for Simon. "I heard news in town that my missin' nephew had showed up."

Uncle Ellis looked much the same as Simon remembered. His and Aunt Lydia's mother had been Grandpa McNeil's second wife, so Ellis was several years younger than Pa. The McNeil traits tended to overpower the others, with their distinctive blue eyes and brown wavy hair, so the resemblance was strong. Of the older McNeil brothers, Ellis was the most sociable one, the charmer. That hadn't changed either.

When Simon offered his hand, Uncle Ellis ignored it and embraced him instead. "I had to come see you for myself, invited to dinner or not."

Pa called from the porch, "Ellis, you know you have a standing invitation, especially since we're celebrating Connie's and Simon's birthdays. We heard you're keeping busy elsewhere."

To Simon's surprise, color rose in Uncle Ellis's face as he shook his head. "Didn't think you listened to idle gossip, John. But it's just me and Bubba today. The others stayed with friends in town. We wouldn't turn down a piece of Etta's cornbread."

All the men gathered on the porch to wait for the call to dinner.

Uncle Ellis bumped shoulders with Simon. "Now tell me all about your adventures since you left us."

Simon snorted. "Don't know about any adventures, Uncle Ellis. I did a lot of studying to earn a law degree while I worked for my room and board. Then the war started." He shrugged, unwilling to delve into that subject.

"Yeah, I reckon it was near impossible for you to get back then." Uncle Ellis glanced at the others and didn't press him. "But here you are, home again. Good to have you back."

"Don't get used to it. He won't be here long," Paul said. Simon couldn't tell from Paul's tone of voice whether he'd accepted Simon's choice to leave or still disapproved of it.

Rupert draped an arm around Simon. "That's what happens when a man rescues a woman and gains a farm. He winds up leg shackled."

Amid chuckles, Uncle Ellis turned to Simon. "What's that? You're gettin' married? But where's your girl?"

"Unfortunately, she's several days away in Georgia. She couldn't leave her pa alone on the farm because he isn't well."

"And what's this about a farm? You're not going to bring her here to settle down?"

Ma came to the door and saved him from answering by announcing dinner was ready. Simon slapped Uncle Ellis on the back. "It's rather a long story that the others have already heard. Let's eat first, then I'll be glad to tell you all about it."

Thanks to Uncle Henry's subtle direction, the mealtime conversation centered on stories from Simon's childhood and featured other family members as well as him. When Uncle Ellis prepared to leave, Simon walked with him to the barn and told him about Daviana.

Uncle Ellis stopped beside his wagon. "I guess you know our family has a history of inheriting properties through our womenfolk. It's how Grandpa McNeil came to have land in both Alabama and Georgia, how Henry got his farm and I got mine. Ain't nothin' wrong with that. In fact, it's biblical." He slanted a grin at Simon's surprise.

"Biblical?"

"Read about the daughters of Zelophehad in Numbers. Of course, they had to marry their cousins to keep the land that passed to them. My advice is, don't let Paul give you grief over it. Find a way to resolve it to make him happy."

How unexpected to find an ally in Uncle Ellis. His son scampered aboard the wagon, and Simon stood clear. Rupert and Uncle Henry meandered toward the barn while Ma and Pa waved from the porch as Uncle Ellis drove away.

"What did Uncle Ellis have to say about your plans?" Rupert asked.

Simon grinned. "He said marrying into land was a family tradition."

Uncle Henry cackled, and Rupert shook his head.

Their shared humor died away as a buggy barreled into the yard, rolling past the men and leaving dust in its wake. A thin woman in a dark blue dress and bonnet scrambled from the seat, calling, "Mr, McNeil! I need to see Mr. John McNeil!"

With Simon closer to the wagon than anyone else, his quick steps rounded the wagon and brought him behind her. "Is there something I can do for you, ma'am?"

"Mr. John—" She whirled toward him and stared, mouth ajar. "Simon?"

Simon froze in mid-step. The voice was familiar, but the face had changed. "Pansy?"

The clamor brought Ma and Pa to the yard. Pansy turned their way, her gloved hands nervously clasping and unclasping. "Please, Mr. John, we need your help. They's holdin' Jem in the jail and says he has to pay or give thirty days' service."

Pa deftly moved to replace Simon, and Ma maneuvered to Pansy's other side.

Pa captured the woman's flailing hands in his own. "Slow down a minute now. Exactly where is Jem?"

"At Two Springs in the jail." Her voice rose in a wail on the final word.

"Why did they put him there?"

"The sheriff said on account of vagrancy. Said he must be up to no good since he ain't got a job anymore."

Other than the sigh that escaped, Pa showed no sign of distress. "What's the fine?"

Simon broke in. "Did they offer him a lawyer?"

Pansy shifted her attention to Simon. "Said he could have one if'n he could pay for it. They know he can't. They bound to keep him like they done the others. Please, can y'all come help me get 'im free?"

While Pa collected all the information from Pansy, Simon tried to recall what he knew of Jem. Nothing stood out beyond a quiet young man who fit in well with the others. Pa would do what he could to help—that was his nature. But Simon's history with Pansy could make for an awkward party if he were asked to join the effort.

CHAPTER 17

"'My life is cold, and dark, and dreary.'" The words of the poem whispered to Daviana from long ago. Words learned as an assignment but often repeated over the years—when Mama died, when Lionel marched off to war, now sitting by Pa's bed.

There was another part of the poem, something about the sun still shining. Maybe Myra could recall it and help dispel this gloomy mood.

Daviana touched Pa's forehead again. Was it cooler now? Certainly not as hot as before. Maybe he would pull through despite all her fears.

He opened his eyes and smiled. "Don't fret, Daughter. I'm still here."

"Thank God for that. Do you feel up to eating a bite?"

"In a while maybe. Need to talk to you. Sorry if I pushed you about marryin' Simon."

"It's all right, Pa. I know you were worried about leaving me alone."

He sighed. "I still believe he's the answer to my prayer, but you do what you feel best."

A knock at the front door prevented her answer. "I'll go see who that is. Might be one of the church folks. Do you feel up to company?"

"I'll try. If they stay too long, you come and send 'em away."

She promised to do so and checked her hair and clothes in the mirror. Not much could be done about the circles under her eyes and her pale face. When the knock came again, she hurried to open the door.

Surprised to find Kyle there, she stepped back. "Since when do you come to the front door, my friend? What's wrong?"

His eyes rounded. "Nothin's wrong. Just figured I ought to be more respectful."

His answer didn't ring true, but she wouldn't argue. "Come in, then. Say hello to Pa."

She led the way and stopped at the door while Kyle greeted Pa. She retrieved a dust rag from the kitchen and ran it over the furniture. Keeping the house ready for visitors had taken precedence over her personal time, but the activity kept her from dwelling on unhappy possibilities.

In moments, Kyle retraced his steps, treading softly. "He's sleeping."

Daviana kept her voice low as they returned to the front room. "You got the wire sent?" She sat on the sofa, and Kyle took Pa's favorite chair.

"It went through, and"—he reached into his coat pocket and pulled out a paper—"I found a telegram waitin' there for you. It must've come in too late on Saturday. Dwight had just found it when I got there."

Daviana took the paper with trembling hands. She stared at it. What if it held bad news?

"Aren't you gonna open it? Oh, should I turn around to let you read it in private?" The twinkle in his eyes teased her.

"No, silly. I'm sure it's—Did you read it already?" At her sudden query, he shrugged and she huffed. "So is it good news or bad news?"

"Open it."

Trusting that Kyle wouldn't tease her if there was cause to worry, she unfolded the message.

Dearest Davi, arrived well. Forgive my delay. Miss you. Simon.

She read it three times before she refolded the paper and slipped it in her skirt pocket. "He got home okay. That's a relief, but why did he wait so long to let me know?"

Kyle tapped his chin, mocking concentration. "Maybe the trip took longer than he expected. He was tired. The telegraph operator was sick. A storm knocked down the lines."

She chuckled. "All right, I get the idea. Thank you for bringing this and for helping so much. If not for you and Myra—"

"And Jude, Titus, and the Bensons." He pointed a finger at her. "You would do the same for us. It's what friends and neighbors do." His face clouded with concern. "There's something I should tell you because I'm not sure how it will affect you and your pa."

Daviana swallowed. There *was* bad news. Her premonition proved true. "What is it?"

"I was in the mercantile with my back to the door when I heard it open and someone call out a greeting. Both men moved to the back, and I couldn't distinguish their voices at first. They came closer after I paid and started to leave. That's when I heard their names, along with some remarks that didn't set well with me."

"Kyle? Who was it?"

"It was Lionel. I think you should be prepared. He didn't seem happy to be back."

RANDOLPH COUNTY, ALABAMA

oisture hung heavy in the air, and clouds scudded across the sky in the morning breeze as the small party set out the following day to rescue Jem. From Pansy's description of the distance, if all went well, they should return before nightfall. At first, Simon had declined to go along, but Byron Harris, the local lawyer and Freedmen's Bureau representative, had taken ill so he couldn't travel.

Ma had sensed Simon's reasons for hesitation. "I don't believe you're tempted to renew your youthful infatuation with Pansy. Are you afraid helping her would be disloyal to Daviana?"

"I wouldn't want either of them to get the wrong idea about my involvement. For some reason, Davi has a hard time believing she's more important than the land that comes with her."

"Do you think she'd encourage you to help a friend in need?"

"I know she would."

"Then go help your friends and spend the rest of your life convincing Davi of her true worth."

No one else expressed any doubts about Simon joining them. The general feeling was the McNeil family took care of its own, with no deference to color. Pansy had been born on the farm the same as Simon and his brothers. Jem had come later, rescued from a harsh master by Pa's shrewd bargaining. His cheerful manner had soon captivated everyone.

Simon inhaled the fresh air as he cantered on horseback beside the buggy Pansy had borrowed. Liza rode with her while Pa drove the buckboard. They would need the larger vehicle to transport everyone on the return trip. Paul had volunteered to send a wire to Troy to meet them in the small town of Two Springs, which was due north and closer to his location. In the event he didn't get the message in time, they'd have to rely on Simon's legal knowledge and work with any Bureau representatives there.

A couple of hours away from the farm, they stopped to rest and water the animals. Liza distributed the food the women had packed for the journey. Simon accepted his portion and slipped away to prepare himself for what they might face in the legal realm.

He sauntered to the creek and fed the horse an apple. His thoughts bounced from their current situation to cases he'd studied years ago to conversations with Pa, and a couple with Rufus, about people using the law to oppress others. Witnessing the abuse of power firmed his resolve to stand against it whenever he could.

The sound of his name jerked him from his musing.

A stone's throw away, Pansy stood as if reluctant to approach him. Neither of them spoke for a moment. Simon studied her face, finding it the same and yet—not. The girl was gone, just as the boy he'd been had grown, leaving behind faint impressions of the past.

Folding her arms across her middle, she lifted her chin. "I jus' want to apologize for breakin' in on y'all's Sunday visit."

He waved away her concern. "No reason to apologize. In fact, it's probably the best time you could've arrived, with all of us gathered there so we could give Jem the best defense."

"Yeah, I guess the Good Lord did that." She plucked a leaf from a sour gum tree near the water's edge. "But I'm sorry, too, for what led up to you leavin' home so long ago."

"Pa explained what happened. It's probably best that I did leave, and really none of the blame can be laid on you. I hate you had to endure what you did." He wouldn't mention the man's name nor any details from that time.

She took a step closer. "But I was ready to involve you, hopin' to get away so it wouldn't happen again. You didn't deserve to be blamed for what you didn't do or even know about."

Simon grabbed the horse's bridle and led him away from the creek. "I reckon you were desperate, and I was a willing candidate. Who knows how it would have ended if Paul hadn't hauled me outta there? I guess we're both fortunate things turned out as they did."

A slight smile lifted her lips. "I don't know if I could've carried through when my heart was already turnin' to Jem. Then I found out he was ready to marry me, even knowin' the truth."

Pa's voice carried from the hill where he stood. "Time to get goin' again. We want to arrive around noon."

Pansy half turned to go, then paused and looked over her shoulder. "No matter how this turns out, I 'preciate you comin' along to help."

Simon grinned, feeling lighter about his decision to join the mission. "That's what friends do."

A few minutes later, his horse pranced as Simon mounted. "You're ready to get this over, too, huh? It shouldn't be much farther."

An hour later, the women drove through town and on to retrieve Pansy's children. Troy waved to them from the local Bureau office. They'd start there before confronting the sheriff.

Troy and Pa headed for the office while Simon tethered the horses. "I want to check the dun's shoe. He may have picked up a stone." And it wouldn't hurt to get a quick glance around, see who might be watching them. Only a handful of shops lined the street, and most of the people appeared to be simple folks —farmers and the like.

One skinny fellow glared at Simon as he passed, then crossed the street and entered the barber shop. A minute later, he emerged again with a heavier man in tow. The larger man settled a black bowler on his head as he walked, sporting a burgundy vest with fancy stitching over his white shirt.

Simon straightened and prepared for a confrontation. He forced a grin. "Afternoon, gentlemen."

"I'm Councilman Digby," the big man said. "Noticed you rode in with an empty wagon. You lookin' to make some purchases?"

"Might be. My pa wanted to check here at the Freedmen's Bureau first." Simon rubbed his belly. "We heard they might have food to hand out. We'll need extra to feed any workers we can get."

"Oh, you folks lookin' for laborers?" The councilman pounced on Simon's statement. "We have an arrangement with the sheriff to hire out the vagrants he arrests. For a donation to the city, you see."

Simon continued the ruse. "I'll let my pa know. He'll want to send a message to Ma about our situation. Is there a telegraph office here?"

The man pointed to his left. "Two doors down, next to the mercantile. Y'all come on over to the jail when you're done."

"Thank you. We'll do that."

The councilman tipped his hat and strode in the direction of the jail, his skinny friend in tow.

Simon burst into the bureau office without knocking. "These people are determined to destroy the state with their clinging to old ways."

Pa's eyebrows went up. Beside him, Troy motioned to the bureau representative. "That's what Sergeant Colton just learned. Sergeant, this is my brother, Simon McNeil, formerly a Union lieutenant."

With determination, Simon forced his hands open to accept Colton's handshake. Of average height and stature, he didn't present an imposing figure. "Do you mean this unlawful arrest of innocent citizens has been going on behind your back?"

The sergeant offered a bland smile. "Pleased to meet you, Lieutenant. As to the nefarious activities you mentioned, my superiors heard rumors about illegal dealings last month. It took a few weeks to secure the office, and I arrived last Thursday. I've been trying to get a feel for the place before I start banging heads together."

As Colton spoke, Simon's doubt must have slipped past his guard because the sergeant's eyes narrowed. "I assure you, sir, General Swayne has given me the authority and expects me to report back by the end of the month." His voice rang with confidence. "Do I understand that you're offering legal representation to any of the accused?"

Simon nodded. "I'm here to serve as needed."

"Very good. With your expertise and my fellow bureau representative here," the sergeant said as he grasped Troy's shoulder, "I believe justice shall prevail without delay."

Colton's words proved prophetic. He gave a note to a boy who ran to alert others to join him and the McNeils at the jail. The deputy protested when they entered and Colton announced his intention. "I'm authorized by General Swayne of the United States Army to replace you with a man who will uphold the law."

After a few minutes of arguing, Colton turned to Simon. "I've brought in a U. S. attorney who has offered to represent the men you hold free of charge."

Simon cleared his throat. "You should know that the U. S. Senate has already passed an amendment to the Constitution abolishing slavery. That includes *de facto* slavery, such as you are operating here. There are other amendments in the works which this state must adopt before it will be readmitted to the Union. Until that time, Alabama will remain under military law. Is that how you want to live, with soldiers posted around your town?"

At the sound of whispers behind him, Simon turned. People had pressed inside the jail to observe the confrontation. The whispers grew to outright demands for the deputy to release the prisoners and resign his office.

One face caught Simon's attention. Councilman Digby dabbed a handkerchief across his perspiring forehead as the deputy removed his badge and pointed a finger at the councilman.

"I told you, Digby," he said. "I told you it wouldn't last once the Freedmen's Bureau came in." He handed his keys to Troy, who went straight to the cells and released the six prisoners while Colton designated another lawman.

Pa elbowed Simon and canted his head toward the door. "Well done, son. We'll meet Troy and Jem outside. I'm ready to head home."

The pride on Pa's face erased Simon's seven years of alienation. And Davi would surely approve as well.

∾

HALL COUNTY, GEORGIA

Wavering between joy and concern, Daviana struggled to predict how Lionel's arrival might affect her situation. On the one hand, having her brother back would make Pa happy and give her some relief. Between keeping a close eye on Pa and overseeing the farm work, she'd not had a minute to rest and renew her energy.

On the other hand, Lionel could be easily riled, which would disrupt the peaceful atmosphere. And how would he react when Simon returned?

She clutched the paper in her pocket as if it could prepare her for what came next. "Kyle, what were the disparaging remarks you heard? Did they come from Lionel or the other person?"

Kyle pressed his lips together as if he didn't like to repeat the words. "It was Lester Cox. You know how he is. He spouted off about you being engaged to a Yankee soldier. You can imagine your brother's reaction to that announcement."

She could, and the image wasn't pretty. "Did you say anything to them?"

"I thought the wisest course of action was to leave without saying anything. Not knowing whether Lionel was aware of my reported death or return to life"—one side of Kyle's mouth lifted in a mocking way—"I didn't want to cause a scene there in the mercantile."

She stood and tiptoed to Pa's room, then grasped the door and pulled it nearly shut. As she returned to Kyle, a new concern gripped her. He hadn't mentioned Albert. "What about my nephew? Was Albert with Lionel?"

Kyle's brow furrowed as if he searched his memory. "Not inside the mercantile. There was a boy in a wagon parked outside, but I couldn't say for sure if it was Albert. He was still a tyke when I left home, you know."

How good it would be to have Albert back, but other considerations brought on dread. How would he and Lionel react to seeing Pa so ill? As for her engagement to Simon, Lionel was sure to stand against it, and he'd raise all manner of outrage about the changes to the deed. Could Lionel's return and his reaction to those changes cause a decline in Pa's health?

When Kyle stood and walked to the door, Daviana snapped out of her troubling thoughts. She followed him. "My goodness. Lionel could be here any moment." Her heart picked up speed. "Please don't go yet." Maybe Kyle's presence would keep

Lionel's anger in check for a while. The shock of seeing someone he'd thought dead should help.

Kyle turned, his eyes sympathetic. He shook his head. "I don't think it will do much good for me to stay. Myra will—"

The clatter of wheels over the rutted yard interrupted his answer. "Oh, here's Lionel now."

Joy eclipsed Daviana's worries at the sight of her brother and nephew. Albert leaped from the wagon as soon as it stopped and launched himself into her waiting arms. She cried and hugged him, then held him away. "You've grown taller since you left. Oh, I missed you so much." She covered his face with kisses until he turned away. She'd forgotten a seven-year-old boy could take only so much display of affection.

"Missed you too. Where's Grandpa?" He wiggled from her arms, but she drew him back.

"Grandpa is very sick, Albert. You must be quiet when you go into his room."

"Pa's sick?" Lionel had parked the wagon and came up behind Albert. His hair, the same muddy brown shade as Daviana's, touched his collar, and his clothes needed laundering. Just as thin as when he'd left, Lionel slumped at the mention of Pa's illness. His gaze went to Kyle, and he blanched. "Kyle? Is that you? Heard you'd been killed in battle."

Kyle edged away from Daviana's side and offered his hand. "It's me, Lionel. Good to see you."

Lionel's gaze darted from Kyle to Daviana and back, his brow creased. "Are y'all married, then? I heard crazy rumors in town that my sister had lost her senses and—"

"Kyle is married to a sweet lady named Myra." Daviana blurted out the answer to stop Lionel's accusations. "He only came by to bring me a telegram from Simon, my fiancé." She turned to Kyle. "Thank you for doing that, and please tell Myra I'll expect to see her this afternoon as usual."

Like old times, Kyle understood her plea to go along. "I'm sure she's looking forward to it. I'll go through the fields and check on things with your workers." He brushed by the three of them. "See y'all later."

Daviana couldn't blame him for his quick retreat. If she could, she'd do the same.

Lionel acknowledged Kyle's departure but trained his eyes on Daviana. "What's this about your fiancé, and how long has Pa been sick?" Though he didn't raise his voice, the tone said he expected answers.

A diversion was in order.

"Why don't you bring in your belongings and get settled? Are you hungry?" She directed the last question to Albert, sure that a growing boy would always be ready to eat. Perhaps Lionel would be easier to deal with after he had a meal too.

RANDOLPH COUNTY, ALABAMA

After riding much of the day, Simon was bone tired. The satisfaction of having used his skills to help someone in trouble offset the dreariness of the return trip home.

Simon rode close to the wagon so he could converse with Pa, who rode in the back. Jem drove the wagon while Pansy leaned on his arm and Liza sat on the other side. The rocking of the wagon had lulled the two younger children to sleep on their blankets, which were tucked near the bench. The older girl leaned against the back of the seat close to Jem. Simon discreetly looked for signs of Mr. Russell in her face and found none. Except for slightly lighter skin tone, she was a replica of Pansy—and Jem's darling.

The familiar song of cicadas accompanied the wagon's creaking as it rolled over the uneven ground. With the fiery colors of the setting sun on their right, the weary group gave a collective sigh when their destination came into view.

Jem drew the horse to a halt in front of the house. Pa hauled himself over the buckboard and rubbed one hip as he lumbered to the driver's side. "Take the wagon on down to Liza's cabin, Jem. Yours is still empty, and you're welcome to stay as long as you need to. Just unhitch the wagon and ask Rudy to tend to the horse."

Jem tugged his cap and drove on to the outlying buildings.

Simon dismounted and led the mare into the barn. Pa tossed hay into the stall while Simon brushed her down, then they trudged to the house.

Ma greeted them on the porch. "It looks as if you had a successful trip. That was Jem driving, wasn't it?"

Pa draped an arm over her shoulders. "Yep. I hope you saved us some supper."

"We did. Etta took some to the cabins, too, so everyone can eat before they go to sleep." She led Simon and Pa to the dining table and sat with them.

Pa said grace, then gave his report between bites of corn-bread and vegetable soup. "It was much as we expected. One of the town's influential citizens coerced a local deputy into arresting any black men seen in town on a charge of vagrancy. Then he'd take the men to a designated area—which changed from day to day—and leave them for a farmer to put them to work, supposedly to reduce their fine."

Simon grabbed a second piece of bread and took up the story. "If the person requested a lawyer, he was told it would cost a similar amount to provide that representation. So he'd be fleeced either way."

"Our son"—Pa nodded to Simon—"explained how that

kind of activity would jeopardize the state's readmission to the Union and leave us under military law."

Ma gripped Simon's hand. "Those years away had a purpose, which you've only begun to see. God can use that passion inside you to accomplish much good wherever you are."

Paul wandered into the room and leaned against the doorframe. "Uncle Henry has a neighbor who lost some workers last week. He's going to see if Jem and Pansy can work there, at least temporarily."

"Liza will go along and help them get situated." Ma grinned. "Of course, that offer had nothing to do with being able to spend time with her grandchildren."

Simon pushed back his bowl and stretched. "I think I'll turn in early. It's been a long day." He should take a few minutes to write Davi a letter, but it might not reach her before he did. A better choice would be to rest tomorrow and head back the next day.

Paul drew a paper from his breast pocket and shoved it toward Simon. "Before you do that, you should read this. It came in while I was sending the wire to Troy."

A dark mantle of dread dropped on Simon's shoulders. A glance around the table revealed his parents' furrowed brows. He tore into the paper.

Simon, Pa is worse. Please come soon. Daviana.

A ripple of urgency replaced his fatigue. "Rufus has gotten worse. Must be really bad for Davi to wire me. I've got to go back right away."

He started for his room, but Ma's voice stopped him. "Simon, you can't travel in the dark. Too many things could happen. Get some rest and leave early tomorrow."

Pa came to his side. "Both horses are done in too. Yours will serve you better if you wait."

All they said was true, but it chafed to know that his arrival wouldn't be as timely as it should've been. His poor Davi, left to deal with the farm and now with Rufus's relapse. He ought to be with her, to lift that burden.

Could he possibly make it back to Hall County in three days?

CHAPTER 18

ionel's hard stare unnerved Daviana. She deliberately avoided looking his way while Albert helped her set breakfast on the table the morning after their arrival. She shouldn't have offered Lionel coffee while the gravy thickened. It gave him an excuse to sit there and glower like a sullen bullfrog.

Thank heavens for Albert. Not only was he a powerful buffer between her and Lionel, but his presence had also buoyed Pa's spirits like nothing else could. Pa had rallied enough to enjoy a half-hour visit with the boy and to tell Lionel point blank that he would have to wait until Simon returned to discuss the changes to the deed.

So far, Daviana had eluded a long discussion with her brother, but her time was short. Resigned, she sent Albert to watch over Pa after breakfast while she and Lionel took a walk around the farm—far enough away that Pa wouldn't hear their arguing voices.

She took the path that wound around the apple trees. The

sweet scents of autumn floated on a cool breeze, and Daviana pulled her shawl closer. She waved a greeting to Jude and Titus, who worked within shouting distance, gathering the precious fruit.

Sunshine filtered through the leaves of an old oak in a dappled pattern. She chose it as a good place to take her stand. A noisy bluejay griped at their presence there and soon took flight. Lucky bird.

Lionel started right in. "It's about time you tell me what's going on around here. I've only been gone four months, but when I come back, I find everything changed."

Daviana seized the opportunity to turn the tables. "Why did you come back, Lionel? From the way you left, we figured we wouldn't see you till Albert was able to grow a beard."

He reared back, obviously surprised to be challenged. "Well, Albert was the main reason. I couldn't find anyone suitable to watch him while I worked. Not that much work was available that I could do as we moved from place to place." His brows lowered as he paused. "Dang it, Dottie! This ain't about me coming back. It's about you lettin' some Yankee soldier sweep you off your feet and take over our land."

"At least he was here, Lionel, unlike you. And having been a Union officer, he knew how to deal with those men from the Freedmen's Bureau to be sure our property wasn't seized. I shudder to think how that meeting might've gone if he hadn't been here."

"Oh, but it's not *our* property any longer, is it?" Lionel sneered. "It's *his* land because whatever was yours is now his, and you have no legal standing."

She took a deep breath to calm herself. "That's not how it is, Lionel. You only have to examine the deed on record to see the truth."

Lionel blustered. "What good would that do?"

"You'll find it still includes your name as well as mentions any of your heirs or mine. There's a copy in Pa's trunk, but I'll be happy to go with you to the courthouse, if you like, so you can have the clerk explain how Simon and Pa set it up."

She waited while he digested that information.

He paced a few steps away, then turned back. "All right, but we'll wait till Pa is better or this Simon shows up to defend himself. Now you can tell me how you came to be willing to marry a stranger when you'd turned your nose up at all the other fellows who would've taken you on."

"Taken me on?" she cried. "Don't you see what that attitude says about me? Those others only wanted the land I could bring them. Did it even matter to you how they might treat me?" She inhaled again and modulated her voice. "By the way, I'm going by my real name now, and it's Daviana, not Dottie."

Lionel's hand slashed the air. "Don't change the subject. You're supposed to be telling me how this Yankee persuaded you to agree to his proposal."

"His name is Simon McNeil, and he's not really a Yankee. He only served in the Union army because he was against slavery. He was born and raised in Alabama."

Lionel snorted. "That don't recommend him any better. A scalawag." He paced away, then turned back. "So where is this righteous paragon now?"

Feigning more confidence than she felt, Daviana said, "He should have received my wire yesterday and already be on his way here. You would have a better idea of how many days that will take than I do."

Her fervent prayers for Simon's safety and soon return would join with those for Pa's healing. How many miracles could she ask for?

*F*or all his hope of shortening the return trip to Hall County, wisdom warned Simon not to push his mount beyond the animal's endurance, but patience was not his best attribute. He chafed at every delay. The first day, a group of stray sheep clogged the road, and he helped their young shepherd steer them in the right direction. Then a wagon of produce lost a wheel and spilled half its load. He didn't have the heart to refuse the driver who begged Simon for a ride to the nearest farm—two miles out of his way.

The next day, it rained. By the time Simon reached Troy's house that evening, he was soaked and weary of plodding along muddied roads. He took the horse to the barn first, where he found an additional horse and a carriage he didn't recall from his earlier stop.

"It's gonna be cozy in here, y'all," he said to the animals. "Don't get into any fights." He rubbed down the mare, who seemed glad to be back in her usual stall after serving for part of Simon's journey. Using one of the saddle blankets, he dabbed at his wet clothes, then dashed to the house.

Troy answered his pounding on the door. "Simon. You're earlier than we expected. Come in and dry off. We're just about to eat."

A man and a woman emerged from one of the bedrooms as Simon reached the sputtering fireplace in the front room. More concerned with his sodden state, he ignored them until the woman called him by name.

"Simon, so good to see you. Troy told us you'd be by soon. How are you?" Aunt Lydia hadn't aged at all, from his perspective, but she must be close to thirty. She possessed a quiet beauty that glowed from within, not unlike Daviana's, though Lydia was taller and heavier.

She came near for a hug, but he held up his hands in warning. "I'm awfully wet, Aunt Lydia, but I'll collect that hug as soon as I get dry."

"Fair enough." She gestured to the man beside her. "Let me introduce you to my husband, Seth Morgan." The slim man stood a few inches taller than Lydia, his hair and beard nearly the same shade of light brown as hers. "Seth, this is the other Union nephew you've heard about. Simon probably influenced Troy's choices."

Seth offered a handshake, which Simon accepted. "I'll try not to hold that against him," Seth said with a grin. "Having Troy as my guard at Camp Chase worked to my benefit, so I'm at peace with the Union."

Troy turned from feeding more wood into the fire. "Yeah, that worked to my advantage, too, since you knew where to find Millie and Lydia."

Millie came from the hallway with Amy on her hip. "Did I hear someone say Simon was here? It's awfully bad weather to be traveling in."

Simon laughed when Amy repeated his name. "Sorry to barge in on you like this. I didn't realize you'd have a houseful of guests."

"Oh, posh," Lydia waved off his apology. "We're all family, and I'm eager to hear about what's gone on with you since we've been apart."

They squeezed in another chair at the table and visited while they ate. Simon glanced around the house, which seemed smaller than he remembered from his youth, not nearly as large as Pa's. Last week, he hadn't paid much attention while he and Troy shared their stories. But with two more adults there, the place felt crowded. Where would they all sleep?

Millie noticed his frown. "Something wrong with your food, Simon?"

"No, it's fine. I was just wondering where you're going to put us all."

Millie laughed. "Don't worry, we won't make you sleep on the porch. I guess you don't remember about the secret room." She pointed her fork to a bureau pushed against the wall between the dining area and front room.

Simon shook his head, but Seth rubbed his hands together. "I'm eager to see it. Lydia told me how y'all hid Troy away in there during the war."

Soon as everyone finished the meal, Troy led them to the bureau Millie had indicated and pushed it aside.

Simon followed Seth to peer inside the area. "Amazing. I had no idea this was here. This is where you hid from the Confederate conscription scouts?" Visions of Libby Prison swam before him, and he grasped the doorframe.

Troy clutched his shoulder, and his eyes conveyed understanding. "I lodged here and other places between Pa's and southern Tennessee. Staying on the move was my best option. Millie and I will sleep here. Y'all can have the other bedrooms."

Simon nodded. "Thanks, brother. I'm glad you didn't have to endure a hell such as Libby Prison."

By morning, the rain had slowed to a drizzle, so Simon prepared to leave, uneasiness prodding him toward Hall County. His brief conversation with Malachi echoed in his head and urged him onward.

Troy followed him onto the porch and handed him a rubber raincoat. "In case this is just a lull. I can get more through the Bureau. I know it's close quarters here, but you're welcome to stay as long as you like."

"I appreciate it." Simon draped the raincoat across his arm. "I'm worried about Davi being alone with Rufus in poor condition. And I'm sure there's a heap of work waiting for me there." No need to mention the threat Jasper posed.

The others came onto the porch behind him. "I expect you to bring Daviana to meet us soon as possible," Millie said.

"It's too bad the railroads aren't all repaired yet." Lydia leaned toward him for a one-armed hug. "That would make your trip go faster."

Seth hooked his thumbs in his suspenders. "They're in a sad state. The Union army tore them up, now they got to fix 'em. If you ever come by Marietta, you're welcome to visit us."

"Thanks. The roads from here to Atlanta appeared to be in good condition on the way over. As long as the rain holds off, I should fare well enough." He swung onto the horse.

Troy stepped close. "Be watchful. With Atlanta attracting all manner of people, you never know what you might run into. Riff-raff like to hide in cities."

"Unfortunately, that's not the only place you can find 'em." Simon waved and turned the spirited gelding to the road. The horse must sense he was going home—or else he'd missed getting the chance for a good run.

Simon was of the same mind. His need to see Davi went beyond his fear for her well-being. Like a flower seeking sunlight, he yearned to hold her, to hear her laugh and watch her smile bloom when he teased her. Though his nature had urged him to press his suit and forge ahead with the wedding— as he still would if she'd agree—Davi's insistence to wait showed wisdom. The time apart proved his commitment. Now he could prove his love.

Hall County, Georgia

*P*a's improvement began to slip a couple of days after Lionel's return. Daviana yielded responsibility for the field work to her brother and did as much housework as she could while caring for Pa. Albert convinced them he should wait on returning to school until the following week, which suited Daviana. Having him around cheered her as much as it did Pa.

She left her supper preparations to check on her patient and met Albert coming from Pa's room. The boy wiped his eyes and whispered, "He's asleep."

Daviana nodded, clasped Albert's hand, and led him back to the kitchen. The pain in her heart doubled when he asked, "Is Grandpa going to leave and go to heaven like Ma did?"

She wrapped her arms around him and swallowed to dislodge the lump in her throat. "Sooner or later, we all have to go. Your mama was young, and it's always sad to lose someone we love, but especially when they're young. Grandpa would tell you, though, that he's lived a long time and had a good life, that he misses Grandma, and it's time for him to be with her. We'll miss him something fierce, but we can remember the good times we had while he was here with us."

According to the doctor, it was a miracle Pa had lasted this long.

"You know what?" She turned Albert to face her and gripped his shoulders. "I think he knew you were coming back, and he waited to see you so he could say goodbye. It made him very happy to see you." Forcing a smile, she tousled his hair. "Now come and help me set the table."

Perhaps she should have insisted that Albert go to school today. Watching someone you love waste away was hard enough for an adult, but much more so for a child.

They'd put everything on the table, and Albert started toward Pa's room to check on him. He turned around before he got there. "Somebody's in the yard, Aunt Davi."

The squeal of the outside pump told her Lionel's work was done for the day. "It's your pa, washing up."

"No." Albert veered toward the front window. "There's someone coming to the front porch."

Not a good time for company. Daviana didn't bother to remove her apron as she hurried past Albert. The door swung open, and she gasped in relief as Simon strode inside. Dusty and obviously travel worn, he'd never looked so wonderful. Without hesitation, he closed the distance between them and embraced her.

His words rushed over her ear. "I came as quickly as I could. I've missed you so much. I'm sorry I wasn't here for you."

Davi swallowed to contain her emotions. "You're here now. That's what counts." In the safe confines of Simon's arms, her fears subsided. All would be well now.

~

When Daviana relaxed into his embrace, welcoming him, Simon's energy revived. He pulled away enough to gaze at her face, then lowered his lips to hers. With his attention focused on her, the world faded away.

The slam of the back door startled them apart. Simon barely had time to register the presence of a boy and the man beyond him when the latter growled and charged toward him and Daviana.

"Get your filthy hands off my sister, you blue belly."

Simon stepped forward to shield Daviana, but she peeked around him. "Stop, Lionel. Albert, go check on Grandpa."

After a moment's hesitation, the boy scurried to the nearest bedroom door, and the names connected in Simon's mind. Should he trounce Davi's brother now or wait until they were alone? Davi clutched his arm as if she could read his intent. Guess it wouldn't do to start a brawl in the house. Lionel maintained his hostile stance, opening and closing his fists, while he glared at them.

"Simon, meet my brother, Lionel, who showed up a couple of days ago. Lionel, this is Simon…"—she turned back to gaze at him—"who must be exhausted after riding for so long. Supper's ready. Let's all sit down and eat like civilized people."

He shifted and tilted his head toward the barn. "I need to take care of the horse first. Jude's boy took him as I arrived, but I should check that he's fed and bedded down."

Albert, having returned from his task, announced, "Grandpa's still sleeping. Can I go help with your horse, mister?"

Davi pulled the boy close. "You *may* help if Simon doesn't mind." Her eyes met Simon's. "This is my nephew, Albert."

Simon took the hint. "I could certainly use the help."

He ushered the boy outside. Albert's hair, similar in color to Davi's, covered his ears and flopped over his forehead. He had the same honey-brown eyes as his aunt, but his darker complexion either came from his mother or from long summer days spent outside.

"Albert, is it? Like that prince over in England?"

With careless indifference, Albert shrugged. "I reckon, but I was named for my mama's father. Where'd your name come from?"

Simon chuckled as they entered the barn. "Simon Peter, the apostle. My aunt claimed it was prophetic because I used to act like he did before he met Jesus."

By the time they finished in the barn, Simon and Albert had established a relationship based on their mutual care for Daviana—and horses. The boy hadn't offered any information about the months away with his father, and Simon decided not to pry. They washed up at the outside pump and entered the house through the back door.

Lionel sat at the table, already eating. Daviana pointed to their waiting places and gripped Simon's hand as he sat between her and Albert.

"Albert, would you like to bless the food," Simon asked, "or shall I?"

Lionel glared across the table but put down his fork.

Albert glanced at each adult, then responded to Simon. "You do it."

Simon exhaled, releasing his former ire toward his future brother-in-law. Pa's oft-repeated homily came to mind about the beauty of brothers living in harmony. "Father, thank You for family, for safe travels, and for this food. We are so grateful for all Your blessings. Amen."

He squeezed Davi's hand and sent her a smile. Despite Lionel's hostility toward Simon, he'd be one more person to protect Davi from Jasper. Albert clearly adored his aunt and already accepted Simon. More than ever, Simon appreciated Rufus's desperate need to provide for Davi's future. Family trumped all other treasures on earth. How blessed he was to have found this new one and made peace with the former one. *Thank You, God*

CHAPTER 19

Daviana snuggled deeper into her blanket and tried to block out the sound of someone calling her name. In her dream, Simon held her close and whispered—

"Davi, wake up." The scrape of his beard on her cheek penetrated the dream fog. He *had* come back. She opened her eyes and met his blue ones.

He smiled and straightened as he pulled away. "I wouldn't want Lionel to find me here in your bedroom before we've said our vows. He might skin me alive."

Snatches of memory from the previous day galvanized her. Simon had moved the small settee into Pa's bedroom and sat with her long into the night. In low voices, they'd shared about the days apart—how Pa had been injured, how Simon's parents had reacted to his betrothal announcement, among other things. She must have fallen asleep. Narrow beams of light slipped past the edges of her curtain.

"What am I doing in bed?" She clutched the blanket close. Had Simon carried her to her room? She couldn't imagine Lionel doing so.

Simon chuckled. "Don't worry. You're fully dressed as you were yesterday, so come along. Rufus is calling for you."

Her hands went to her hair as she swung her legs over the side. How awful for Simon to see her in such disarray. "I should fix—"

"No, sweetheart." He grasped her hands and tugged her to her feet. "Your pa won't care whether your hair is tumbled. Davi, he's about to slip away."

Sorrow swelled her heart, pushing tears to the surface. She wiped them away and sniffed. Setting a hand to her back, Simon nudged her down the dim hallway. They entered Pa's room, where dark curtains held the sun at bay, and Simon went to the lamp on the side table and turned up the light.

Albert and Lionel rushed into the room, out of breath. Lionel brushed his hands on the sides of his trousers. He must have been in the field already. Simon gave Albert a pat and drew him to stand between Davi and Lionel. Davi gripped Simon's hand and leaned against him.

Pa's eyelids slid open, and his mouth worked a moment before the words came. "Good. All here." A finger wobbled between Simon and Davi. "Hold...together." The finger pointed to Lionel and Albert, then upward. "Fam'ly...first." His hand dropped to the bed, then he wheezed. "Sing, Davi."

How could she sing with the end so close for him? She focused on the ceiling, inhaled, and forced out the first shaky sound. "'My hope is built on nothing less than Jesus' blood and righteousness.'"

Somehow, she made it through the first verse and a chorus. As the last note died away, Simon stepped forward and passed his hand over Pa's eyes to close them. Daviana sank to her knees, releasing the tears. Albert dropped next to her and burrowed into her side. When she felt she could stand, she gently nudged Albert away and reached for Simon's strong hand.

He pulled her beside him. "Should I send Titus for Reverend Benson?"

Lionel gave Simon a hard stare, then headed for the door. "My place. I'll do it. Told him I would when he came by yesterday." He motioned to Albert. "You stay and help Aunt Dottie get the house ready." Then he was gone.

"He's still not bending on our marriage." Daviana stared at the empty doorway. "I don't know how long he'll fight it."

Simon shrugged. "Don't let it worry you. He's dealing with your pa's death too. Everybody grieves differently. What do you need me to do?"

Daviana searched his face, lined with fatigue. He'd let her sleep while he sat up after riding all day. "Go get some sleep. You can take my bed. Albert and I can drape the mirrors and the door. Anything else can wait until Lionel returns."

And then she'd have another talk with her brother—before his overbearing prejudice tore the family apart.

~

After a few hours of sleep, Simon stretched and levered himself from the bed. With this unexpected opportunity, he couldn't resist glancing around the room, Davi's private domain. Across from the bed sat an ancient armoire of cherry wood, all its doors and drawers snugly closed. The lone window wore a curtain of cheerful yellow adorned with flowers. The armoire's matching dresser stood against the wall across from the window, its surface clear except for a brush and mirror set, a book, a pen, and an inkwell. Like the woman herself, the room was tranquil and charming, a place of rest from the outside world.

A knock at the door interrupted his survey. "I'm awake. Come on in." He found his boots at the foot of the bed and pulled them on.

The door opened a few inches, and Daviana peeked in. "I hope you were able to sleep despite the noise of people coming and going." She nodded toward the bureau. "I need to get one of my dresses so I can dye it, else I wouldn't have disturbed you."

Simon covered the short distance between them and fought the urge to pull her close "I'm well rested. If you don't need me for a while, I thought I'd ride into town and set up my office, make sure it's secure. Your brother will be glad to get me out of the way, I imagine."

She wrinkled her nose. "You never know. He might accuse you of desertin' us."

He tapped her nose and lifted her chin with a finger. "I won't give him the chance. I promise to be back by suppertime." A chaste kiss on her cheek was all he could risk as he edged past her.

She grasped his arm to halt his progress. "I put back a couple of biscuits for you. They're wrapped in a napkin on the back of the stove."

Mindful of others in the rest of the house, he mumbled his thanks and moved down the hallway. A talk with the preacher might be in order. Would Daviana's mourning postpone her decision about getting married? So far, she'd welcomed his affection, but was that due more to her need for support than her feelings for him? With Lionel back to manage the farm and Albert to care for, had Simon become redundant?

In the kitchen, which was blessedly empty, he found the bundled biscuits and enough lukewarm coffee in the pot for a cup. Rather than sit, he stood at the stove to consume his meager meal. The swishing of skirts and rattling of cups approaching from the front room warned him of company.

Myra glanced up from the tray in her hands as she neared the sink. "Oh, Simon. I thought Davi said you were sleeping."

He shifted aside so she could set the tray on the worktable, the move revealing Davi in the kitchen doorway. "I was," he said to Myra, "until, in a strange reversal of a popular fairytale, my charming princess wakened me with a kiss."

Daviana's eyes lifted from the clothing in her hand on a gasp. "I did not. Don't listen to him, Myra. I knocked on the door."

Myra chuckled and turned to give her friend a brief hug. "He's teasing you, Davi. My brothers always loved to tease me and my sisters. I reckon you didn't get that much, with such an age gap between you and Lionel."

"Not in that fashion, at least. It was the same for Kyle. I suppose that's why we became friends, to escape our older brothers' badgering."

Simon brushed crumbs from his hands and stepped closer to Davi. "Speaking of those brothers, has Jasper been coming around lately?"

Daviana and Myra exchanged glances. "Jasper's been acting strange," Daviana said. "A few days after you left, he brought me and Pa a string of fish he'd caught. I think it was just an excuse to find out if you were still around."

"He's been leaving the house nearly every day on one excuse after another." Myra removed the bundle from Daviana's hands. "I'll get our new girl to dye this for you, so you can get back to the wake. I'll come back later."

Davi walked with Myra to the back door, then turned back to Simon. "I forgot to tell you. Kyle said he'd speak to you this evening."

What was that about? Did he have information on who Simon's attackers might have been? If the conversation could wait a few hours, it must not be too concerning.

"Good, maybe he can catch me up on what Jude and Titus have been doing since Lionel wouldn't." Should he share Jewel's warning? Would it cause Davi more anxiety or make her more cautious? Since her pa's death meant a constant flow of visitors to the house, maybe Jasper would stay away.

It fell to Simon to keep Davi safe, but he couldn't be with her every minute. The best course would be to advise Lionel and Kyle to be on guard. Despite their relationship to Jasper, neither of them cared overly much for him. With the three of them watching, Jasper would be hard-pressed to cause her any harm.

~

Fickle September favored the gathered mourners with a perfect day for Pa's burial. A capricious breeze played with puffy white clouds that mitigated the sun's heat and sent an occasional whiff from the nearby crape myrtle trees. Only the open wound in the earth next to Mama's grave marred the scene as the small group gathered around it.

Daviana stood between Simon and Lionel, with Albert at his elbow, as Reverend Benson's words competed with the droning of bees in the top of the spreading oak. Behind the immediate family, Kyle and Myra joined Mrs. Benson and several members of the congregation who had been friends with Pa. A murmur went through the crowd as a latecomer arrived, but Daviana didn't look back to see who it was.

The preacher closed his Bible and raised his voice. "It seems fitting to me that Rufus Spalding made his transition from earth to heaven during the time of harvest. A humble man of the earth, he planted his seed and his good deeds in Hall County, and he lived long enough to see his first grandson who will carry on his name. To know Rufus was to appreciate his own brand of humor and honesty. We all will miss him."

After a closing prayer, the family blessed Pa's coffin with handfuls of Georgia red clay. Friends formed a line to offer their condolences, and Myra put her cheek to Daviana's. "Be aware that Jasper showed up. He's at the end of the line. Kyle and I will stay close by."

Simon must have heard the whispered message. He stiffened beside Daviana as she clutched his hand. "It's all right. He can't hurt you. You're surrounded by people who love you."

One of the ladies from church moved from Lionel to Daviana, so she had no chance to reply, but questions assailed her. Why would Simon say anything about Jasper hurting her? As far as he knew, the man had only proved a nuisance. Had Kyle disclosed her long-ago narrow escape from Jasper?

The slow-moving line soon dwindled, and next to her, Lionel muttered under his breath at Jasper's approach.

"So you couldn't make it out west and had to come back." Jasper didn't offer his hand, and neither did Lionel. "Too bad it wasn't in time to rein in your sister."

Daviana held her breath and prayed Lionel wouldn't let Jasper push him into a fight.

"Out of respect for the women and the preacher over there, I won't say what you can do with your opinion, Jasper." Lionel gripped Albert's shoulder and herded him toward the house.

Daviana held herself ready for a similar cutting remark, but Jasper only inclined his head in a mocking nod. "*Miss* Spalding," he said with a smirk, then narrowed his eyes at Simon. "I thought maybe you'd run off after that beating you took, but I reckon you didn't get the message."

Simon's nostrils flared. "What do you know about the attack on me? Were you party to it?"

"Who, me?" Jasper pointed to himself in outraged innocence. "Why, I was at home with my children that night. You can ask my Good Samaritan brother, who was dumb enough to go to your rescue."

"In case you didn't know"—Simon punched a finger in Jasper's chest—"if you have knowledge of a crime and don't report it, you're judged an accessory. Consider how your children would feel if you had to spend time in jail for that."

Jasper snarled. "Don't spout that legal stuff to me, Federal man. There's more than one kind of justice in these parts."

Simon shrugged. "Georgia is under military law until it complies with all the requirements for readmission to the Union, and the U. S. Army doesn't abide vigilante justice."

With a disrespectful huff, Jasper turned and stomped down the hill.

Daviana sagged against Simon. "Do you think he'll consider what you said? He must know we're suspicious of his ways."

"I doubt it. Men such as Jasper think they're justified in whatever they do, regardless of the law. Lionel may not like me, but he has no love for Jasper, either, and we're both watching out for you." They ambled toward the place where Kyle and Myra waited. "As long as we're all on alert, he can't get to you."

She trusted Simon to do all he could to protect her, but anxiety didn't dispel so easily. How long would she have to live in dread of Jasper catching her alone?

~

*S*imon untangled his legs from the blanket he'd added to his bedroll in the office last night. Who knew it would get so cold in September? Weather in the foothills of Georgia shouldn't be that much different from middle Alabama.

He kicked the covers aside and padded across the room to close the open window. The morning's moisture-laden fog obscured the hills normally visible from this second-story viewpoint. By the time the sun burned away the haze, he'd be at the farm, ready to start on the new house and persuade Daviana to set a date for their wedding.

In minutes, he'd stashed all evidence of his temporary sleeping quarters in the large armoire at the back of the room. Filling the empty shelves with his new law books would have to wait until evening. For now, they were tucked out of sight under the battered desk that dominated the space. He dressed and exited, pausing a moment to admire the neat lettering on the door's placard—*Simon P. McNeil, attorney at law*—then hurried to the water closet at the end of the hall.

He reached the farm in time to join Daviana and Albert for breakfast. Lionel must have shoveled his food down while Simon settled the horse in the barn. Simon keeping his distance for a couple of days hadn't softened Lionel's attitude toward him.

"He's still not ready to air his grievances?" Simon asked Daviana as Lionel stalked out the door and into the yard.

Daviana took her seat at the table. "He'll come around—soon, I hope. Something happened while he was gone to make him come home, although he won't say what. Then news of Pa's illness and our betrothal met him head-on the minute he arrived. We ought to give him time to adjust."

Simon waited for Albert to bless the food and start filling his plate. "Are you referring to our wedding plans? He won't adjust any easier with a postponement."

Her hand crept over his. "You're right. I think we would honor Pa by proceeding with the end-of-harvest plan."

Gladness expanded Simon's chest. He shifted his hand to hold hers and gazed into her honey-brown eyes, large and luminous over pink-dusted cheeks. When he leaned her way, she tossed a meaningful glance toward Albert and squeezed Simon's hand as if she read his intention. "Eat your breakfast. I have another proposal for you to consider."

Ah, the woman knew how to negotiate. At the moment, he'd agree to almost anything.

He released her hand and scooped grits onto his plate. "Go ahead."

She busied herself breaking a biscuit. "Myra and I have started a collection of children's stories we want to offer the school here. I write the words, and she draws pictures to go with them. Could you take me to town with you one afternoon so I can show them to the schoolmarm?"

While Simon chewed his biscuit, Albert spoke up. "They're real good stories, and Miss Myra's pictures are funny."

"Well, since Albert recommends them"—he saluted the boy with his raised coffee cup— "I don't see how I could refuse."

Why had Davi been hesitant to ask him for such a simple request? It seemed they needed to have a conversation about expectations.

He sipped his coffee and set down the cup. "Let me see how well our work progresses, and maybe we can make that trip today."

After breakfast, Simon set out for the new home site, which was on a slight rise behind the main house. The location allowed him to observe anyone coming to or leaving the main house. Since he was the one paying the workers and the harvest seemed to be well on its way, he chose Jude to work with him on the house and left Titus to help Lionel with whatever chore he assigned.

That action earned a scowl from Lionel, but Simon didn't back down. "Look at it this way—the sooner my house is finished, the sooner you won't have to see me at meals." Simon gestured to Jude to follow him and started toward the cleared plot of land.

"And while you're eatin' my sister's good cookin'," Lionel shouted after him, "me and Albert will have to do for ourselves."

"So get yourself a wife," Simon answered over his shoulder.

"There ought to be plenty of women who'd be glad to marry you, what with so many widows after the war—"

"Duck!"

The warning from Titus came a moment too late. Lionel pounced on Simon's back, and they both went down. Rolling in the dirt like schoolboys wasn't Simon's idea of a fight, but he had to get leverage to stand before he could gain an advantage. Lionel had rage on his side, and Simon had to ramp his up.

Drawing on long-ago lessons, he rammed a fist into Lionel's stomach hard enough to break his hold. Simon leaped to his feet and crouched the way Uncle Ellis had taught him a dozen years ago. Lionel caught his breath and mimicked Simon's stance.

Without the jeers and taunts of spectators around them, Simon could imagine they sparred as friends in a gymnasium, with the only prize a healthy respect for one another's athleticism. He'd give a fair fight, but one good enough to let Lionel blow off his fury.

They jabbed and circled, clutched and punched each other for longer than Simon liked. Perspiration dotted Lionel's upper lip and forehead, and Simon blinked away the sweat trickling into his eyes. He held back and waited for his opponent's energy to fizzle in the growing heat, but Lionel didn't seem to be slowing down.

Just when he prepared for another round, a shout came that jerked his attention to the left. Lionel lunged and pinned him on his back.

"Give up, Bama Boy?"

The softened slur hit Simon as fully as a fist. What happened to Yankee and Federal man? Was this Lionel's way of making peace? He gave a slow nod, and Lionel grinned.

Kyle's face appeared as he bent over them. "Let him up, Lionel. That's his second 'Welcome to Georgia,' and I think he's feeling welcome enough."

Lionel levered himself to a sitting position and offered Simon a hand. As he accepted, the pain and sight of his knuckles made him wince. "I'm glad we cleared the air, Lionel, but I don't think Davi's gonna be happy with either of us when she sees us."

When both her brother and her fiancé showed up for the noon meal sporting cuts and bruises, Daviana gave them both scathing expressions. Kyle had stopped by an hour earlier to advise her of their fisticuffs match.

"Now don't get all upset," he'd said. "It's clear they both had to work it out of their systems, or at least Lionel did, and Simon let him."

She'd never understand how men thought fighting could solve problems. "Do you think Lionel will accept Simon now? With Pa gone...." She'd pressed her lips together to keep from crying.

"Well..." Kyle's brow had furrowed as he hedged. "It's a beginning, anyway. If Lionel won't give you away at the wedding, I will."

She'd laughed then. "Thank you, my friend. Now, did you bring me some more of Myra's drawings?" Her question had recalled his reason for visiting, and then he'd headed to his own farm.

After Daviana gathered her medical supplies and ordered

both Simon and Lionel to take a seat, she set about doctoring their injuries. "Y'all should've come here immediately after, instead of cleaning off at the creek. Even small cuts can cause a fever."

"We had work to do." Simon hissed as she dabbed ointment on a cut.

"She forgets we suffered worse than this during the war," Lionel said. He examined his knuckles and flexed his fingers.

"That's something I'd like to forget." Simon stood as she finished with him. "Except it did bring me face to face with a blunderbuss and change my future." He winked at her and turned his chair toward the table. "Another couple hours of work, and I'll take you to town, Davi. By the way, did you choose a date?"

She pretended indifference as she bandaged Lionel's knuckles. "Do you think you'll have the roof on the house in another month? If so, I thought the middle of October would be nice. Harvest will be at an end, and everyone will be glad to celebrate."

"That will be my goal." Simon poured himself a cup of water. "Pray the good weather holds and the sawmill has the lumber we need. Otherwise, we may have to sleep in my office."

After she had everyone patched up, she set the meal on the table. They were halfway through when Albert walked in the door.

Lionel rose in alarm. "Is school out already? I thought it went to midafternoon."

"Miss Taylor got a message and sent us home." Albert laid his lunchbox on the table and opened it. "She asked me to give this note to Aunt Davi."

Daviana accepted the paper and read aloud. "'Miss Spalding, I've just received word that my sister has had a fall and requires my assistance for a few weeks. The city council will find another teacher for the regular school, but I need someone to fill in three days a week at the Freedmen's Bureau school, which meets in the evening. Would you be willing to do that? Reverend Benson recommended you, and I remember that you once expressed an interest in teaching. Please let me know. Thank you, Beulah Taylor.'"

Mixed emotions set Daviana's heart to racing. What a shame for Miss Taylor, but an opportunity for Daviana to experience teaching on a temporary basis. Three pairs of eyes focused on her as she set the letter down.

Albert sank into the vacant chair. "I wish you could go to *my* school. You'd be more fun—"

"Enough, Albert." Lionel stared at her. "Surely, you're not thinking about doin' what she asked. It's a long walk to and from town, and in the evening, no less."

Daviana turned to Simon. "What do you think?" Would he stand by her if she decided to take up the offer? His answer would give a good indication of his intentions for their marriage.

"Your brother has a point, especially when we're concerned about your safety." He drew in an audible breath. "However, if it's something you want to do, I think you should." As Lionel started to object, he said, "I will take you to and from town on those days. My office is near the school, so I can work there while you're in class. Does that sound reasonable?"

Though tempted to fling herself into Simon's arms, she settled for clutching his hand and squeezing it. "That sounds wonderful. Thank you."

Lionel snorted. "As long as you're responsible for her gettin' back and forth, I'm agreeable. She's about to be your responsibility for good, anyway. Heaven help us all."

Daviana couldn't stop her spreading smile. Heaven already had helped in more ways than she could count. She'd been loved by wonderful parents and looked forward to a bright future with a man whose actions showed he truly cared for her.

And here was a chance to prove herself outside the farm. Life was good.

~

The next evening, Simon left his office and walked across the street to meet Davi after her first day of teaching. He'd arranged with the livery worker to rent a small buggy for these short trips to and from the farm.

Corporal Ewing greeted him with a handshake. "Haven't seen you in a while. How are your helpers working out for you?"

"I couldn't ask for better workers." Simon leaned against the counter strewn with papers. "Even while I was gone to Alabama, they carried out the tasks I'd assigned, with only an occasional visit from a neighbor. Have you had more people hired out to bring in crops?"

The corporal gathered the papers and tapped them together in a stack. "A few here and there. Some folks just take a while to adapt to change."

"I know that's the truth." Simon lowered his voice as students began to filter through the office from the back room. "I don't suppose you've learned who might've been the scoundrels who attacked me a few weeks ago?"

Corporal Ewing called farewells to the departing pupils then turned back to Simon. "Not enough to warrant an investigation. Mostly just indirect remarks about getting rid of Yanks." He glanced toward the schoolroom. "If you want to collect your lady, I'll get ready to lock up."

Simon grinned and straightened. "You don't have to tell me twice. I'm ready for the day I can collect her for good." He sauntered to the connecting door. A peek into the room revealed Daviana was alone as she pushed a stack of papers into a canvas bag.

He crossed the room and held out a hand. "Let me take that for you, and you can tell me about your first teaching experience."

She passed him the knapsack and tied on her bonnet. "Thank you. It was enlightening. I didn't realize how blessed I was to have learned at an early age. The children catch on much faster than the adults. Thankfully, Miss Taylor had taught them the basics of using letters to form words, so I chose a few simple ones for everyone to practice."

He helped Daviana with her shawl and ushered her outside where Corporal Ewing stood by the door. "Goodnight, Corporal," Simon touched a finger to his hat. "See you tomorrow."

She told him about the class as they strolled to claim the buggy at the livery. The short time they had together on these jaunts would work to his advantage. It was time they discussed a few subjects they'd avoided.

As soon as they left the town behind, he cleared his throat. "I haven't told you about a couple of things that happened on my visit home. Strangely enough, I discovered that Uncle Henry's new employees came from this area."

She tilted her face toward him. "Really? They came from Hall County?"

"More specifically, from Dunaway's farm. A woman named Jewel and her father, Malachi."

Davi stiffened beside him but didn't say anything. He flicked a quick glance her way, then went on. "Jewel has a son named Levi. She didn't give the details, but I concluded that Levi's father is a Dunaway. Then Malachi told me about following Jasper into a cave—"

Davi's sob stopped his words, and he halted the horse. His arms went around her. "Shh. It's all right. You weren't to blame."

She hid her face in his chest. "I should have told you, but I didn't want you to think badly of me."

"I'd never think badly of you. From what Malachi said, you were quite young. I just thank God that Malachi was able to rescue you." He held her close while he considered his own confession. "There's something I need to tell you, should've told you long ago. I didn't want you to see me as weak, but keeping it from you isn't right."

With only a crescent moon for light, she leaned away to peer at his face, waiting.

Simon swallowed. "Because of the recurring malaria, there's a possibility that I can't give you children."

While he'd prepared himself for her anger or weeping, Daviana merely nodded. "I know."

"Your pa told you?" That surprised him, but he hadn't asked Rufus to keep it a secret. If she already knew and was still willing to go through with the wedding, then...."You're not upset?"

"I was at first, but I figured that's in the Lord's hands, like everything else in our lives. So many examples in the Bible demonstrate that God can do the impossible. Why should I worry over something I can't change but He can?"

Amazed at her calm acceptance, Simon cupped her face in his hands. "Athdara Daviana Spalding, you are an incredible woman and a gift I don't deserve." He settled a tender kiss on her lips then drew back. "We'd better get on our way again before Lionel comes hunting us down."

Simon kept one arm around Davi as he signaled the horse forward. Tomorrow would be soon enough to tell her about his search for answers and the trip to rescue Jem.

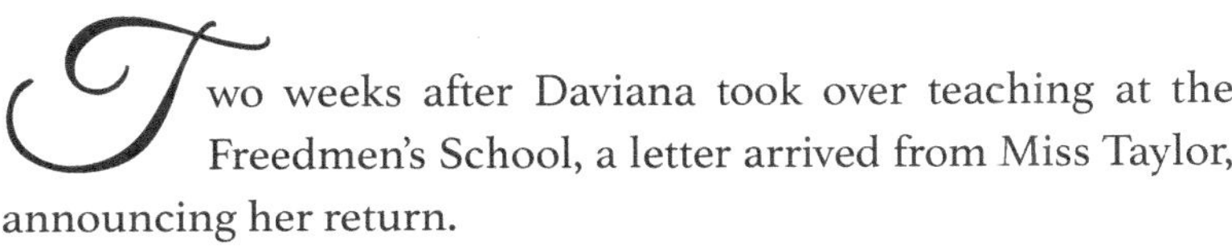

$\mathcal{T}$wo weeks after Daviana took over teaching at the Freedmen's School, a letter arrived from Miss Taylor, announcing her return.

"I have good news for you," she told the class that evening. "Miss Taylor will be back with you next week."

Thankfully, a few groans testified that she hadn't done too badly. While she'd enjoyed the experience, she would need more schooling herself before attempting to do more than fill in.

Besides, she had a wedding to prepare for, as Simon often reminded her. Having the time alone with him on their rides had strengthened their relationship. As Daviana learned more about him and his family, she fell more in love with this man who'd swept into her life so unexpectedly. Even his description of seeing Pansy again revealed his tender heart and passion for justice. How could she not love a man like that?

Though neither of them had called their feelings love, Davi was sure of it. Simon's care and deferential treatment of her said more than flowery words. Her own manner was reserved, so perhaps he followed her lead in not declaring his undying devotion. He proved his commitment in more tangible ways. Perhaps he wanted to demonstrate he'd grown beyond the impulsive young man who had given his family grief.

The last student left, and Corporal Ewing peeked around the door that separated the schoolroom from the front office. "Are you about to leave? I'm going to walk over to the livery and see if my horse is shoed and ready to go."

"I just need to pack my supplies. You go ahead. Simon will be here in a minute."

He nodded. "I'll come back and lock up before I head home."

He retreated while Daviana returned Myra's drawings to her knapsack. Sharing those with the younger children had helped to keep them interested in the lessons.

A noise in the outer room alerted her that either Simon or Corporal Ewing had come in. Only a minute or two had passed since the corporal left, so it must be Simon. She lifted the basket and called, "I'm coming." She went through the door and stared at the empty room. "Simon?" He must have gone back outside to speak with Corporal Ewing.

She pushed the outer door open. Someone jerked her into the alley, and she yelped. A hand clamped a foul-smelling rag over her mouth and pulled her left arm backward. Daviana dropped her knapsack and tore at the restraints with her free hand. The struggle sapped her energy. She took a deep breath and prepared to kick backward, then she slumped. That foul smell…

The sensation of being lifted and carried roused Daviana from sleep. A curse issued from the person who held her as he stumbled over rough terrain. That voice evoked troubling memories.

The air changed from cool to fetid. She forced her eyes to open and blinked. Oh, dear God, how was she back here? Had she only dreamed the passing years…Pa's death…Lionel's return…Simon's proposal? She couldn't draw in enough air.

Lamplight came closer and revealed her captor. Jasper dumped her on the floor of the cave and loomed over her. "This time, there will be no rescue from my brother or yours. You and your land will be mine. No one else will want you."

～

Simon was losing his mind. How could she have disappeared? He'd seen the door open from his second-floor window as he grabbed his coat. Less than a minute later, he'd been striding across the street at the same time that Corporal Ewing led his horse to the door. The corporal's confused glance met Simon's.

"She must've gone back inside for something." Simon grasped at the thin hope.

But a thorough search inside yielded nothing. In the gathering twilight outside, Simon found Daviana's knapsack. Panic robbed him of breath and muddled his thinking. He'd failed to keep her safe.

"Someone's taken her." Grief transformed into rage, and energy surged through his veins. "I'll kill him."

"Now, Mr. McNeil..." The corporal tried to reason with him. "Let's not be hasty. Who would have taken her and why?"

"Jasper Dunaway. He's obsessed with Davi, wants the land that her pa left her. I've got to find her." He stormed to Ewing's horse waiting at the post. "I'll take your horse, if you don't mind, and let you bring mine from the livery." The mare pranced sideways.

Corporal Ewing grabbed the mare's reins as Simon mounted. "I'll do that. Where would he take her?"

Simon groaned. "I don't know, but her brother might have an idea." Desperation urged him onward, but he couldn't do this alone. "You remember which farm it is?" The horse responded to Simon's urgency, tugged at the reins, and circled as he held her back.

Ewing waved him on. "Go ahead. I'll find you."

All the way to the house, Simon prayed for Davi's safety and thanked God for the nearly full moon to guide them. He bolted from the saddle before the horse stopped moving, pounded up the stairs and through the front door.

Lionel turned from the bedroom door. "What's wrong?" His gaze went behind Simon. "Where's my sister?"

"Missing, and we've got to find her."

Lionel advanced and grabbed Simon's jacket lapels. "You're supposed to be guarding her. How could this happen?"

"Jasper must've been hiding in the alley and abducted her when she stepped outside. We found her rucksack there. Where would he take her?"

"Dang if I know! Obviously, not to his house and no place where others would see them." Lionel released his hold.

Corporal Ewing crossed the porch and shook hands with Lionel. "Corporal Ewing. You're Miss Spalding's brother?"

"That's right."

"I found wagon wheel tracks behind the building. It looked as though they might've headed this way, then veered off the road just outside town, but it's getting too dark to see the tracks. We'll need lanterns."

Simon and Lionel set about collecting those. Albert stepped from his room with his table lamp, his eyes wide and tear-filled. "Take this." He handed the lamp to Simon. "Find Aunt Davi."

Simon squatted to his level. "Do you have any idea where Jasper might've gone with her? Any good hiding places around here that you know of?"

The boy scrunched up his face. "Just the woods and caves, but Aunt Davi always warned me not to go in the caves. Bears might be in there."

"Good advice." Simon shuddered at the thought of searching a cave. Surely, no one would.... He stilled. What had Malachi told him about Jasper's earlier attempt on Davi? Didn't it involve a cave?

Simon met Lionel in the front room. "Lionel, there's a short cut from here to Dunaway's, right? I've seen Kyle take it. Can you let him know what's happened and see if he'll come help? He might have insight into where Jasper would go."

After Lionel left, Simon prepared for whatever a rescue might require. "Corporal, do you have a rope on your horse? We might need that. Albert, get Aunt Davi's basket of medicines, maybe tie them in a dishtowel so they can go in my saddlebags. I'll grab the blanket off her bed and tie it on my horse."

Albert helped him saddle Lionel's horse and secure the bundle of medicines. They all loaded up whatever they might need and were in the yard ready to move out when Kyle and Lionel returned to join the search party.

Simon speared Kyle with his gaze. "Do you know anything about Jasper taking Davi to a cave in the past?"

"I guess she told you." Kyle's shoulders drooped. "She didn't want to report it because it would be her word against Jasper's. She refused to tell me how she got away."

Simon's anger surged, clamoring for release. "One of your family's slaves knocked Jasper out." He drew a deep breath. "Do you know where that cave is? I figure he's aiming to finish what he'd planned for her then."

"We used to play pirates in a couple of 'em. I hope I can remember which ones."

"I know of a couple, too," Lionel said. "We should divide up and spread out. Albert, you stay here in case she gets away by herself. Put a lit candle in a couple of windows so she can find the house in the dark."

Simon nodded. "Good thinking. Let's talk about a way to signal each other when we find her."

Kyle's gaze jerked to his. "It may take all of us to bring him down."

Alerted to the possibility, Simon turned his horse to follow Lionel to the back of the property. Would Kyle be able to raise his hand against his own brother?

~

*D*aviana pressed a hand to her aching head, fighting through the mental fog. She had to figure out how to get away from Jasper, or at least delay him long enough for help to arrive. Surely, Simon would come looking for her.

A jug sat near the struggling fire—water or strong spirits?

"Could I have a drink of water? My head hurts."

"Why, of course, Princess." He turned a sickly sweet smile on her. "I even have your dinner ready and waiting." He threw a handful of sticks into the fire and grabbed the jug.

His sudden agreement puzzled her, but after he filled the cup, she reached for it. She sipped, and cool water met her lips. Though her thirst demanded more than a swallow, it might be wise to drink slowly to give herself time to recover and keep Jasper away.

His gaze shifted from her to the bag he was digging through, then to the cave entrance. Though he claimed no one would find them, he didn't seem so sure of that, and it appeared he'd set things up to give him the advantage over any later arrivals.

Blankets lay strewn on the far side of the fire, along with a pillow, saddlebags, lantern, and another jar. How long had he planned her abduction?

Holding the cup in front of her, she asked, "How did you know I was at the Freedmen's Bureau?"

He laughed as he pulled two small bundles from the bag. He unwrapped one and took a huge bite of the sandwich inside. "I've been watchin' you comin' and goin' for weeks. Didn't know that, did ya? Just had to bide my time till that dirty Yankee let down his guard. When you started making those trips to town, I figured that was gonna be the best place to move in."

He handed her the other wrapped sandwich. "You'd best eat while you can. You won't have time later with what I got planned." He sat in front of Daviana cross-legged and smirked. "Your supper is courtesy of my brother's idiot wife, who thinks I'm courtin' some gal over in Sulphur Springs. She never suspected I was usin' her to take care of the young'uns while I got this place ready and made arrangements for other things, like that Yankee's beatin' last month. Too bad he didn't take the hint and stay gone."

She paused in unwrapping the bundle. "You arranged for Simon to be attacked?"

"It don't take much to rile up some of those boys over the

way." He nodded toward the cave entrance. "They was right glad to oblige when I told him he was hirin' all the field hands and payin' em in gold."

"But that's a lie." Davi's protest earned a shrug and an evil smile.

"It worked, didn't it?" He bit into his sandwich but kept his eyes on her.

He showed no remorse or care for his soul, but guilt struck Daviana. When had she prayed for Jasper or offered anything besides begrudging tolerance? Maybe if more people had tried to show him the love of Christ...

She made a tentative offering. "You know lying is a sin." Not to mention the other sinful acts he'd committed. "But the Bible says if we repent, God will forgive us."

His mocking laughter prevented her from saying more. "Now, why would I want to do that? God is for women and cowards. Men make their own destiny." He slashed his hand in the air. "No more talk."

To keep from looking at him, she nibbled at her food. If Myra had made it, she could trust it not to hurt her. Thinking of Myra provided a good diversion from Jasper's presence. In their last story planning, she and Myra had debated on how their lady kidnapped by pirates should react. Would their heroine be calm, waiting patiently for her hero to come to her rescue, or would she pace the ship's hold in agony, afraid the pirates would kill him before he could reach her? Myra had suggested the lady should try to get away on her own. Could she do that?

Daviana's head jerked up. Did Jasper have a weapon on him? Was he hoping for a chance to kill anyone who breached that entrance?

CHAPTER 21

*S*imon stared at the cave entrance. The occasional flicker of a light inside convinced him he'd found the place where Jasper was holding Daviana.

Sweat beaded on Simon's forehead and made his palms slick. He hung the lantern on a stout tree limb and dropped the blanket on the ground. After wiping his hands on his trousers, he checked the knife inside his boot and crouched. His breathing grew shallow as he contemplated going inside that close area, no more than a fissure in the side of a hill. Going in there required more than his own strength. Where had Lionel and the others gone? Simon couldn't even summon the breath to send the signal.

He closed his eyes and directed his silent prayer to the only One who could help. *Dear Lord, I know I don't deserve anything good, but I know You are good, and You love Davi as much as I do, or more. You gave Your life for her and for me. Please give me the courage to go in there and save her from that madman.*

The Scripture about a man finding treasure in a field popped into his mind. Where did that come from? What did it mean? The man sold all he had so he could purchase that field —because he valued the treasure there as worth it.

Simon straightened from his crouch. Davi was a treasure, his treasure to guard and care for. Underserving as he was, God had smiled on Simon when Rufus pointed that blunderbuss at him. He wouldn't let fear hold him back.

He took a breath and sent the signal. Was it loud enough? The second try was louder.

He edged to the cave mouth and listened. Perhaps he could judge their distance by the sound of their voices, if Davi was able to talk. A mocking laugh erupted, and words followed, but he couldn't make them out. The way the sound bounced, the cave must open up farther inside.

He moved into the entrance and took four slow steps while Jasper kept talking. Simon's boot sent a stone rolling along the dirt floor. He paused at the sudden silence that followed, with only the beat of his heart thumping in his ears.

"No, Jasper!"

Davi's cry propelled Simon forward, blinking in the brighter light as he rounded a turn.

He skidded to a stop inches from the knife Jasper held. The man grinned and cackled. "Welcome to the party, Yankee. We've been waitin' for you."

The look in Jasper's eyes made Simon's blood pool in his veins. The man was crazy, and crazy men were dangerous. Simon didn't dare look away from him, not even to assess Davi's condition.

"Give it up, Jasper. I'm not the only one looking for you. Lionel is mad as a hornet. Kyle too."

"You think I care about them? Lionel's lost his claim to Spalding land. As for Kyle..." He spat the name. "My little half brother always got everything I wanted. A pa that stuck around. A ma that wasn't ashamed of her son. When she thought he'd died, she died too. And I couldn't convince her to change old man Dunaway's will to name me the chief heir."

A gasp behind Simon diverted Jasper's attention and gave Simon the opening he needed. He hurled himself into Jasper, knocking him off balance and sending the knife into the dirt.

When Jasper turned and lunged, Simon sent his fist into the other man's jaw. Jasper wobbled but shook himself and launched headfirst at Simon, who sidestepped to the wall of the cave.

Jasper's momentum took him deeper into the cave. He clawed the ground and came up with the lost knife in his hand.

Simon pulled his own knife.

Jasper crouched, and the two men circled each other in the flickering fire and lantern light.

Scarcely a yard separated them.

Simon feinted left to judge how his foe responded.

Jasper jabbed at air.

Simon swiped Jasper's chest, slicing through the fabric and producing a thin red line. Memories of battle scenes threatened, and Jasper's knife grazed Simon's arm. He lunged for Jasper's knife hand and felt the thrust of his blade against his opponent's flesh and bone.

The dagger dropped, and Jasper clutched his bleeding wrist with his other hand, screaming curses.

~

With Jasper's full attention on Simon, Daviana had inched her way to the cave wall, intending to go toward the entrance. She'd changed her mind when the two circled each other with knives. What if Simon were injured? He might need her help.

But Jasper got the injury, and Simon walked toward the enemy instead of her.

Breathing hard, Simon grabbed Jasper's dagger and tossed it into the dying fire.

He pulled a handkerchief from his pocket and thrust it in Jasper's face. "Quit your cussin', or I'll use this to gag you in place of savin' your sorry life." Jasper clutched the fabric to his injured hand.

Daviana used the wall to help her climb to her feet as Simon turned her way. He reached for her, then a crash and burst of light wrenched their attention to the cave exit in time to see Jasper escape.

Flames trailed from the cook fire to the blankets, and smoke billowed, blocking the exit.

"He broke the lantern and set the blankets on fire. We're trapped." Fear held her immobile.

"No, we're not. Come on." Simon draped his arm around her and tugged.

The smoke choked her. She coughed but couldn't move. Old memories erupted with fear. There'd been a kitchen fire when she was a child. Mama's screams echoed in her ears.

Simon's voice jolted her. "Daviana, let's go."

She nodded, but her feet wouldn't move. Simon bent and picked her up, running before she could protest. Though his body shielded hers, the heat wrapped around her. The scent of scorched cotton and singed hair burned her nose and throat. Desperate to escape, she struggled against him. Then strong hands pulled them into the blessedly cool darkness and snuffed out the flames around them. Familiar voices replaced the roaring in her ears.

Lionel took her from Simon's arms and urged them toward a beacon of light. Others gathered around them—Kyle, Myra, Albert. Then Simon collapsed on the ground.

∽

Simon blinked, the only movement he trusted not to bring pain. Full sunlight painted a path across the wooden floor in the limited view next to the bed where he lay prone. Outside, a bird's cheerful song competed with the slosh of water, close but out of sight. Nothing about his current condition evoked a memory—until a skirt danced within his vision and cool cloths soothed his bare back.

He gripped the sides of the bed and lifted his head. "Davi? How's Davi?" He ran his tongue over his lips, seeking to relieve his dry mouth.

"I'm fine, but you must lie still so I can treat your burns." Her voice placated him only for a moment.

"I wanna see you."

Soft footsteps took her away then came back with a chair, where she sat. Now he could see her chin to her waist.

"I like this view fine, but I'd really like to see your face." He couldn't stop his grin and imagined the color of her cheeks must match his shoulders.

The chair slid back, and Davi sat on the floor with a "humpf." A smile played about her lips as she leaned close. "Now are you happy?"

He shifted one hand from the bed rail to her shoulder. "No burns?"

She winced and moved his hand to her jaw. "Only small ones on my right arm and leg, very minor compared to yours."

"The important thing is, we survived." He sighed. "Tell me what happened after we left the cave."

Her brows furrowed, and she bit her bottom lip. "Kyle had come up while you were fighting and heard Jasper complaining how Kyle had gotten whatever Jasper wanted. The news must have shocked him, and he said he froze until Jasper ran out. Kyle chased him and yelled for Lionel to come help. Corporal

Ewing was there too. They struggled, and somehow Jasper got hold of the corporal's gun...."

Tears filled her eyes, and Simon's breath hitched. "Who was hurt?"

"Jasper turned it on himself. He's gone."

Simon blew out a breath. He should mourn a lost soul, as apparently Davi did, but at the moment, relief that Davi was safe overrode his sympathy. "Anyone else hurt?"

Daviana shook her head and swiped a finger under her eyes, then smiled. "Lionel says we might as well go ahead and get the preacher to set a date since having you here has compromised my reputation."

Simon captured her hand. "I'm agreeable. Glad he's finally coming around."

"But first, we've got to get your back healed, so lie still and let me apply this salve."

"Slather it on thick. I'm ready to sit up and see something besides the floor."

After Daviana applied the healing ointment and bandages, she helped Simon maneuver into a sitting position on the bed. She turned away and picked up the shirt hanging over the back of the chair. "Here's one of Pa's old shirts, if you want to put it on." She averted her gaze as she handed it to him.

He chuckled. "I suppose I must, to preserve your modesty."

She spotted the package on the dresser. "I nearly forgot. Lionel picked up a package that came for you. He said it was too light to be a law book."

She hefted the wrapped bundle from the dresser and brought it to him, her eyes alight with curiosity. "It feels as though something soft might be inside. Oh, you'll need something to cut the string." She fetched her sewing scissors. "These should work."

"Ah, it arrived just in time." He took the scissors and patted the space next to him for her to sit. It took a moment to slice through the thick string binding. Dragging out the suspense, he unwrapped the package layer by layer.

When he reached the final layer, he paused, his hand covering all but a corner of green and blue and brown stripes. How close he'd come to losing her, and he'd never told her how much she meant to him. "I don't remember whether I asked properly before, so I thought I should make sure." He affected a brogue. "Athdara Daviana Spalding, I love you, lass. Will you be my wife, take my name, and wear this McNeil plaid I ordered from Scotland?"

Her eyes didn't stray from his as she answered. "I love you, Simon Patrick McNeil. I will, and I'm glad you remembered to ask this time."

He leaned forward and kissed her briefly, then spread the tartan between them.

Her eyes widened, and her lips trembled. "Simon, it's so beautiful. How did you find it?" She stroked the soft fabric, and together they admired the bold representation of an ancient clan. "It contains the color of your eyes." She held it up to his face to verify the claim.

Simon chuckled and mimicked her action. "And yours, so you see it was already determined ages ago that we were meant for each other." He couldn't resist teasing her a bit more. "You know, by Scottish tradition, just claiming each other as mate makes it a legal wedding."

Her brow puckered. "Is that so?"

"Mmm-hmm." He delivered another kiss. "And our house only lacks furniture."

"And a stove for cooking," she said.

He ran a finger down the length of her nose. "There's a fireplace."

She put some space between them. "We still have to face the preacher."

"Hmm." Simon twisted a strand of hair around his finger and drew her closer. "How about tomorrow?"

She bit her lip and pretended to ponder. "Day after tomorrow."

Finally! He framed her face with his hands and gazed into her eyes. "You win. No, I won. I found my treasure." Then he claimed her lips as a promise.

EPILOGUE

*L*eaves scattered across the path between Pa's house and the barn as Simon matched his stride to Troy's, a six-foot-long plyboard held level between them. The morning fog had lifted, the sun warming the air and promising a beautiful autumn day.

The McNeil men followed the same routine for every big gathering—set up the sawhorses and place wide boards over them to create a table. The women would lay cloth over the temporary tables and later top them with various dishes. Smelling the roasting meat as it cooked over the open pit tempted everyone's appetite.

They set the board on the sawhorses, and Troy poked Simon's side. "I guess this might be the McNeil version of the Union's Thanksgiving Day, huh? Did you ever get to attend one of those dinners?"

Simon shifted the board to line it up with the others and scoffed. "Not unless you count having the same meal as I had the day before in the company mess tent, surrounded by the same men I'd been with for months. The ones that survived, anyway. How about you?"

"Yeah, last year at Camp Chase." He shook his head as he set down a sawhorse. "Hard to believe that was just a year ago."

"I read where President Johnson's continuing the day to give thanks—only, he set the date in December this year." Simon lowered the plank and tested it for stability. "Maybe he thinks it should blend in with Christmas."

"I doubt many Southerners will feel like celebrating anything, with so much rebuilding still ahead." Troy gripped Simon's shoulder. "Let's pray the Alabama legislature comes to an agreement on the new state constitution soon. Maybe folks will relax once the military turns over the government to local people."

Simon glanced around, counting the tables. "I think that's the last one. I'm gonna go find my wife." He smiled. He loved saying that word.

"Speaking of your wife," Troy said, "she told us you rescued her from a cave where she was held hostage. You wouldn't even step a foot into our secret room at the house. How did you find the courage to go inside a cave?"

"I remembered a Scripture about giving up everything for a great treasure." He shrugged. "Davi's my treasure."

He found her helping Millie carry dishes from the kitchen into the yard. He took the one Daviana held and set it on a nearby makeshift table. "You don't mind if I steal her away, do you? I see an old friend she might want to greet."

Millie waved her hand over the table. "Looks like we're all set here. Go and say hello."

"Who is it?" Daviana asked.

Simon shook his head and directed her closer to the pit where he'd spotted Malachi helping Jewel add more basting to the roast.

When Malachi turned around, Daviana's eyes widened. "Oh, my goodness. How are you?" She grasped Malachi's hands, smiling through tears as he beamed at her.

"Happy as a pig in slop, Miss Dottie, now that I found my Jewel. You 'member her?" He waved Jewel closer.

"I think so, yes." Her eyes glowed as if prompted by a memory. "She worked in the Dunaways' kitchen."

"A long time ago," Jewel said. "I'm glad to see Mr. Simon brung you with him this time."

"Oh, I've told him he's to make no more trips without me."

"An order I take seriously." He pulled Daviana close and turned her back toward the house. "Looks as though Uncle Henry brought a few neighbors with him. I don't recognize the fellow talking to Troy. Let's mosey over that way." Something about the fellow pricked his memory. Close to the same size as Troy, the man's stance had a military bearing.

As they approached, Troy glanced up and motioned toward them. "Here's another Union man," he said to his companion. "Simon, I've told you about Byron Harris. Byron, this is the brother who spent some time in Libby."

Simon reached across his wife to shake Byron's hand while Troy introduced Daviana. "He also married a Georgia girl like I did."

Daviana dipped a quick curtsy, and Bryon tipped his hat. "Good to meet y'all. Maybe I should ride over the state line and see if I can find a bride, if they're all as lovely as you and Millie."

Troy chuckled. "I'd think your first encounter with Millie would discourage that idea, Byron." To Simon and Daviana, he winked as he explained. "She punched him in the nose."

With abashment, Byron rubbed his nose. "And well she should have, but that's not a story I like to share."

The memory of Simon's earlier discussion with Troy stirred.

"Ah, you're Troy's associate at the Freedmen's Bureau. Good choice wearing civilian clothes today."

"I have Southern roots, too, which comes in handy in our line of work," Byron said. "Do I understand you served as a lieutenant with Burnside?"

Simon inclined his head. "That's right. Until a bout of malaria landed me in prison."

Byron gave a low whistle. "'Tis a wonder you survived."

Any talk of the war didn't interest Simon, especially on such an occasion. Though his struggle with malaria wasn't a topic he liked to pursue, either, it provided a pivot in the conversation. "In all honesty, I'm thankful for one recurrence of the disease." He squeezed Daviana's waist and winked. "It gave me a good excuse to linger in Georgia long enough to win over my bride."

Troy slapped Simon's arm. "I reckon that's like the story of Joseph in Genesis—what could've been evil turned out to be for your good."

"I'd say it was very good," Simon agreed. "Ah, we've put my wife to the blush."

Beyond Davi, Ma crossed the yard to the pole with the dinner bell. "And it looks as though Ma's about to give the signal to gather for the blessing, so we should head over that way."

With the bell's ringing, everyone moved closer to the tables laden with food. In the hush that followed, Pa's voice lifted. "Father God, we're so thankful for this occasion to gather as family and friends to celebrate endings and beginnings. As we near the end of another year, we praise You for an end to the war that divided our nation and our homes. May we all work to secure peace and restoration. We thank You for the new additions who've joined us through marriage and those born or yet to be born"—he paused and cleared his throat as if emotion hindered his voice—"into the family. Thank You for this provision from the earth to strengthen our bodies. May we apply ourselves to doing Your will and honoring You. Amen."

Simon thumbed away the moisture from his eyes, awed and humbled that God had ordered his steps home. Perhaps it took those prodigal years to show him the value of the spiritual truths he'd been taught. What a rich heritage to share with future generations.

Rupert slapped him on the back with a knowing smirk while Millie, on the other side of Davi, chuckled and patted Davi's still-flat belly. The McNeils didn't keep secrets very well.

The joy that radiated from his wife's face echoed in his heart. As he wrapped Davi in his embrace, Simon's glance bounced around the gathered family members, Pa's prayer had touched on every aspect of their lives and put God in the center.

Lord, help me to become such a man, one who will walk with You each day, always seeking Your will.

Don't miss the next book in the Rescued Hearts of the Civil
War series!

Redeeming Rupert
Releasing February 2025

Sunday, March 11, 1866
Randolph County, Alabama

"Ashes to ashes, dust to dust, but the spirit returns to its Creator."

Twittering birds and droning bees provided a pleasant—if contradictory—background to the minister's words over the freshly turned earth where Rupert McNeil's Uncle Henry now lay next to his beloved June. The family burial plot lay a couple of acres from the farmhouse but only a stone's throw from Aunt June's beehives, neglected since her passing two years earlier.

Rupert clutched his handkerchief and pressed it to his brow, wishing Brother Trotter would wind up his comments. Of course, then everyone was liable to crowd into the house for another round of condolences, meaning he'd have to shake hands and accept hugs from neighbors, some of whom he barely knew.

Beside him, Millie, the wife of his younger brother, Troy, swayed in the unseasonable heat. Rupert took a half step closer to assist while Troy's arm circled Millie's waist. Into the pause of the preacher's inhale, Rupert raised his voice in a hearty, "Amen."

Troy nodded his thanks and ushered Millie toward the house, but Brother Trotter's mouth hung open at the outburst before he snapped it shut.

Ma sidled up to Rupert. "Was that you? I don't believe I've heard you raise your voice in years, especially not during a church service."

Warmth filled his face. "I didn't fancy havin' to help Troy pick Millie up off the ground if he kept going." He steered Ma toward the house but kept his pace slow.

"Ah, the poor dear." Ma's gaze followed the couple ahead of them. "The new baby is wearing his mama thin. She should've stayed in bed longer after delivering, but she loved Henry like a father. I'll go see if I can do anything to help."

No sooner had Ma left Rupert's side than his old nemesis and cousin, Wilma Thurman, maneuvered into take her place and threaded her arm through Rupert's. "I'm glad Pa left the farm to you, Rupie. I certainly wouldn't know what to do with it."

Rupert at first ignored her use of the juvenile nickname he hated. Wilma, Henry's younger daughter, didn't need the farm's income, not with her house in Jacksonville and her late husband's vast holdings. She'd put off her widow's garments last year, and according to rumor, she didn't mind flaunting her wealth. How such a selfish, conniving creature had come from Uncle Henry and Aunt June baffled him.

On second thought, he returned the age-old taunt. "Hello, Willie."

When she glowered, Rupert bit his tongue to keep from smiling. "I'm surprised you made it in time for the funeral. Thought you'd gone to Mobile."

"Oh, I left as soon as I got Uncle John's wire. Whatever you may think of me, I did love Pa, you know." She dabbed at her eyes with a lacy square of cloth.

Rupert nodded. "Like all the rest of the family. He was the one person any of us could count on for help when we needed it."

Would the family maintain the tenuous peace they'd achieved when the war ended, or would old hurts and disagreements tear them apart?

Wilma raised an eyebrow. "Your folks seem to have emerged from the war fairly intact. I heard even Simon finally came back and brought you a new sister-in-law."

Rupert's shoulders stiffened at her implication. Did she

mean to stir him up or only to deflect from her own escape of hardship? Her late husband's wealth and connections proved good insulation, even after his demise. With effort, Rupert kept his voice neutral. "Yeah, we did right well. Paul lost half a leg, Simon spent nearly a year in Libby Prison, Troy got carried off to Camp Chase, and I couldn't save my best friend who died from a gut wound."

Perversely pleased to see Wilma's jaw drop, he regretted it a moment later. He had no business antagonizing someone who'd just lost her father. Besides, the cruel reminders bit at his heart. Wilma always brought out the worst in him. As children, she'd bossed and used him to her own advantage until he'd learned to avoid her. Why had she sought him out now?

From her perch in the barn loft, Hannah peeked out the window to gauge the activity below. She should've expected the people to return from the gathering soon, but she'd barely hauled her knapsack up the ladder when voices alerted her to their proximity.

Aunt Ginny had insisted that Henry McNeil lived alone. Of course, he must have workers to help with the farm and the house. Hannah scolded herself for not considering that visitors might be here when she arrived. In most circumstances, she examined all potential problems.

Earlier, she'd knocked at the front door and even walked to the back of the house when no one answered. Perhaps Mr. Henry had gone to town for supplies. She wouldn't dare go inside the house, but she could wait on the porch. The large number of wagons and carriages parked around the barn drew her eye. Too many for a small farm, but no one at the house. Surely, someone had to be nearby. She shied away from meeting Mr. Henry in front of a bunch of strangers, dusty from travel as she was. After Elmer and Esther dropped her off, the walk had been longer than she'd anticipated. She'd gotten directions from a couple of local residents and learned that some folks' estimation of distances fell shy of the truth.

She'd climbed into the barn loft where she might have a better view of the farm. Aunt Ginny would be appalled at Hannah's actions. When Hannah argued for making this journey, she hadn't counted on the sudden bout of anxiety that gripped her. Her parents would never have countenanced such an undertaking—traveling such a distance, the last few miles alone, and risking the Whitfield reputation with her appearance at a gentleman's home to beg his help. No matter that Papa's rash actions had triggered the events that pushed the family close to penury and made this journey necessary. She shoved aside the memories of hiding in her family's barn whenever Papa went into one of his rages, for the weight of her mission lingered.

Of the six barn loft windows, one overlooked the fields and a slight rise where a group of people gathered. A church service, maybe a baptizing in the nearby creek? It couldn't be a funeral—otherwise, the doors and windows would be covered.

Whatever the reason, she'd make her appearance when the others left.

As she peered out the window, two couples separated from the group, one of the women leaning into her companion as if she couldn't make the short trip on her own. Hannah ducked to the side as the second woman deserted her escort and hurried to catch up with the other two. Did an argument brew there, or did she go to lend support? None of them looked toward the barn but continued on to the house.

Relieved they hadn't come to collect a wagon, Hannah resumed her original position. Now a different woman clung to the second man, and the rest of the people followed at a distance. Maybe two dozen, plus a couple of babes in arms. It was more than she would expect to attend a simple farm service in this isolated area. Would any of them remain overnight? She'd have to watch when the visitors loaded their vehicles and figure out how many stayed.

A couple of hours later, with the sun sinking toward the horizon, it seemed everyone had left except some close family members and servants. Six adults and three children, one of them an infant with a strong wail. The sound ripped through Hannah, reminding her of Caleb's long-ago cries of pain, which still crept into her troubled dreams. Though he'd begged her not to go on this journey, at the age of six, her brother refused to cry and eventually accepted her explanation. His inheritance hinged on what she might accomplish.

Hannah riffled in the knapsack for another biscuit. There was none there, only her change of clothes and a sliver of soap wrapped in a rag. At least she didn't have to worry about attracting rodents during the night. As she replaced the items, the scrape of the barn door startled her. She slowed her breath, listening to the movements below and praying the person didn't have reason to climb into the loft.

The quiet of the barn embraced Rupert after a day among chattering people. Inhaling the familiar blend of hay, leather, and animals, he welcomed the cool interior. Bessie's soft lowing called him to the far stall, where he set down the lantern, then situated his stool and bucket to tend to her.

"Sorry to be late, old girl. There's been a passel of folks up at the house, all wantin' to talk to me and ask questions I ain't got answers for."

The soothing rhythm of the chore and the satisfying ping of the milk hitting the bucket eased his tension. With visitors lingering past sunset, he'd missed his evening stroll. Thankfully, his parents had stayed on to help entertain the company after Mille and Troy retired to bed. As much as he loved them all, he'd be relieved when they headed home.

Though he neared his twenty-fourth birthday, had spent a year away from home and fought in a few battles before his capture, his mother worried over him living alone on the farm a dozen miles from where she and Pa lived. He grunted and spoke aloud. "I don't know why Ma thinks it would be any better if I was married. Does she think a woman can protect me or take better care of me than I can myself? Dang! All she has to do is look at Troy to witness how havin' a family has run him ragged."

With the milk foaming close to the top of the bucket, he stood and shoved the stool into the far corner. He rubbed the cow between her ears and thanked her, as he always did.

He shuffled to the aisle and started for the door, moving slowly so as not to slosh any liquid from the bucket. In the lantern's light, a long strip of fabric stuck to the bottom rung of the ladder caught his attention. He set the bucket down and bent to remove the cloth. What was it? A man's neck-cloth? He didn't recall seeing anyone wearing something this color. Someone had lost this—one of the visitors who'd called, though Rupert had no idea who'd been in and out of the barn.

He folded the fabric and stashed it in his pocket. Whoever it belonged to might come asking for it later.

Hannah relaxed the pose she'd held to keep from giving away her position. 'Twas a wonder she didn't faint dead away from trying to hold her breath. She pulled up the hem of her skirt to muffle her laughter. She hadn't dared lean out to try to see Henry McNeil, but she'd heard his mumbling. Only a farmer living alone would talk to his cow. From the sound of it, he didn't care for having his solitude interrupted by visitors.

His conversation revealed that Aunt Ginny had described Mr. McNeil well—gruff and cantankerous but tender-hearted toward his family. Though some of his words had been indiscernible, his tone had come through loud and clear. He preferred to be left alone, which suited Hannah just fine. Having friends and neighbors drop by without warning now could jeopardize her mission and delay her return home.

Of course, neither she nor Aunt Ginny had expected her to arrive in the middle of a church service. With Mr. Henry's preference for solitude, Hannah was surprised he agreed to host it on his farm, but such kindness testified of his helpful nature. For her sake as well as Mr. McNeil's, she prayed the last of his visitors would take their leave in the morning.

Her growling stomach added another vote to that sentiment. She wouldn't sneak into the man's kitchen to steal a quick meal, but hunger could make a person desperate. For now, she concentrated on her plan to approach Mr. McNeil, hoping to block the demands of an empty belly. She'd need all her wits about her tomorrow.

Eventually, her exhaustion overrode other fleshly considerations. Tomorrow would come soon enough and, as the Bible said, bring its own trouble.

Rupert set the milk bucket on the table, leaving it to Jewel to store or use right away. "If Amy's still awake, keep out a cup for her, please."

The cook dipped a ladle into the bucket. "'Zactly what I planned to do, Mistah Rupert."

Standing on his tiptoes, Jewel's son and his niece's favorite playmate peered into the pail. "Enough there for me, too, Ma?"

Rupert patted the boy's head. "I think you better have two cups of milk, Levi. I'm dependin' on you to grow strong muscles so you can help me and Malachi out in the field."

With a hand to his brow, Levi saluted the way he'd seen soldiers at the Freedmen's Bureau do. "Yes sir, Mistah Rupert. I be the best helper you ever have."

Rupert took the cup Jewel handed him and sauntered to the front room.

Ma was reciting a familiar story, her clear voice drifting into the hallway. He slowed his pace, not wanting to interrupt the tale as it reached its conclusion.

With Amy wedged between Pa and Ma on the settee, Pa leaned his head against the high back.

As Ma's voice faded, Rupert couldn't resist joining them and teasing her. "She's not even two, Ma. Do you really think she'll understand or remember those fanciful tales?"

When Ma made as if to swat him, he held the cup aloft. "Don't make me spill Amy's milk."

The little girl beamed her bright smile on him. "T'ank you, Unca Wuper."

Rupert's heart warmed. His niece had charmed the whole family from the first time they met her, when Troy and Millie came back from Kentucky the year before.

"You're welcome, sweetie." He pulled the cloth he'd found from his pocket. "Do you know who might've lost this piece of cloth, Ma? I found it in the barn." He held the fabric where she could see it while she helped Amy with her cup.

"I don't recall seeing it before." Ma wore a speculative smile as she set the cup down. "Might belong to one of the Varner girls. Maybe Becky thought leaving it would be a clever way to get you to visit them."

Rupert snorted as he sank into the chair across from them. "She can scheme until the next century. I ain't got no intentions of courtin' her." When Ma scowled, he knew what was coming.

"You mean you *don't* have *any* intentions of courting her."

"That's what I said." He couldn't hold back a teasing grin. "Her sister, Blanche, might not be so bad. She's quiet most of the time, but she's too young."

A dramatic sigh preceded Ma's reply. "It's a pity there're no more young women nearby. Perhaps this winter, you should visit Simon and Daviana. You might find someone over their way to catch your fancy."

Pa saved Rupert from giving his standard answer of not being able to leave the farm. "Why don't we all make it a matter of prayer?" He patted Ma's knee. "God saw fit to bring all our boys home and provided wives for the others. I'm sure He has someone in mind for Rupert too."

Opening the Bible in his lap, he declared the subject settled. "Listen to what the prophet Jeremiah says. 'For I know the thoughts that I think toward you, saith the Lord, thoughts of peace, and not of evil, to give you an expected end.' The people were going into captivity, but even then, God was preparing for their return to Jerusalem. He had a plan for them, and He has one for each of us."

Rupert caught a silent exchange between his parents. A private, shared memory, perhaps, or an agreement of sorts—one that excluded him.

Though it lasted only a moment, loneliness pierced his heart.

Before Henry passed, Rupert had been content. Helping his uncle around the farm had given him purpose. Now, Henry was gone, and the farm was his. Funny how he felt more alone with so much family around. With all his brothers married now, he was the odd man out, but he'd better get used to it. Marriage didn't figure into his plans. He'd lost too many people he loved and wouldn't risk losing another.

Would Ma and Pa pressure him to visit his brother in

Georgia to find a prospective mate? Didn't they realize that courted only tragedy?

Did you enjoy this book? We hope so!
Would you take a quick minute to leave a review where you purchased the book?
It doesn't have to be long. Just a sentence or two telling what you liked about the story!

Receive a FREE ebook and get updates when new Wild Heart books release: https://wildheartbooks.org/newsletter

ABOUT THE AUTHOR

Born into a family of storytellers, **Susan Pope Sloan** published her first articles in high school and continued writing sporadically for decades. Retirement provided the time to focus on writing and indulge her avid interest in history. Her Civil War series begins (and ultimately ends) in her home state of Georgia with references to lesser-known events of that period. She and husband Ricky live near Columbus where she participates in Word Weavers, ACFW, and Toastmasters.

If you love historical romance, check out the other Wild Heart books!

A Heart's Gift by Lena Nelson Dooley

Is a marriage of convenience the answer?

Franklin Vine has worked hard to build the ranch he inherited into one of the most successful in the majestic Colorado mountains. If only he had an heir to one day inherit the legacy he's building. But he was burned once in the worst way, and he doesn't plan to open his heart to another woman. Even if that means he'll eventually have to divide up his spread among the most loyal of his hired hands.

When Lorinda Sullivan is finally out from under the control of men who made all the decisions in her life, she promises herself she'll never allow a man to make choices for her again. But without a home in the midst of a hard Rocky Mountain winter, she has to do something to provide for her infant son.

A marriage of convenience seems like the perfect arrangement, yet the stakes quickly become much higher than either of them ever planned. When hearts become entangled, the increasing danger may change their lives forever.

Lassoed by the Lawman by Renae Brumbaugh Green

Juliana Duke's dreams don't include ranching.

But as the only child of Oscar and Maria Duke and heiress of the vast Duke Ranch, her job is to marry a rancher and produce a male heir. When Lt. Cody Steves rides onto the scene, her resolve to place duty over daydreams is shaken. Now that her heart's been lassoed by the handsome lawman, will she be able to love another?

Cody Steves wants marriage and family, but he loves being a Texas Ranger. At any time, he could ride into a job and not come out alive. How could any decent man marry, knowing he could leave a widow and orphans behind? But the beautiful Juliana Duke captures him in a way no other has.

When he learns of a secret plot to take over the Duke Ranch, Cody must risk everything to save Juliana. Little does he know, the outcome will be nothing like he's planned.

Streams of Courage by Sandra Merville Hart

In a world turned upside down by war and betrayal...will his role as a spy bring them closer...or tear their future apart?

The war that Julia Dodd prayed to avoid is now reality, and with it, her world has been turned on its head. Her fellow citizens, who stood with her in their support of the union, have crossed firmly to the side of the south. And her mother, lost in her grief over the loss of her husband and children, can think of nothing but protecting Julia's brother's inheritance. She insists that her daughter seek a wealthier husband than Ashburn Mitchell.

Ash knows what his fellow citizens think of him when he refuses to fight for the Confederacy. Shouldering the accusation of being a coward and refusing to hide behind his limp, Ash remains in Vicksburg to support his family as a saddler while his two best friends join the fight. Struggling to increase his business so he can marry the woman he loves, Ash becomes a spy in support of the Union. He can't fight for the South but won't raise a musket against them.

As tragedy instigates Ash to risk greater danger to speed the end of the war, Julia can only pray it won't cost them everything. She's already lost her father and two siblings. Must she lose the man she loves too?

www.ingramcontent.com/pod-product-compliance
Lightning Source LLC
Chambersburg PA
CBHW070606170726
48291CB00003B/718